Laura pressed harder on the accelerator. She hit an ice patch and felt a little skid that made her stomach lurch. But she kept a tight, white-knuckle grip on the wheel until the car seemed to right itself. Then she signaled.

In the side mirror, she noticed the BMW speed up.

"Son of a bitch," she muttered, pressing harder on the gas. The pedal was almost against the car floor. She was running out of road ahead.

The engine roared as she turned the wheel and swerved in front of the pursuing BMW. The snow hurtled toward her windshield almost faster than the wipers could brush it away. It felt like the tires were gliding on ice—toward oncoming traffic in the other lane. Laura was certain she'd smash into an SUV heading her way. Squinting at the headlights, she rode out the skid and moved back in her lane. All the while, her heart felt like it was about to explode in her chest.

Laura glanced at the rearview mirror again. The BMW was closing up the small gap between them.

It was the same car she'd seen at the gun store in Monroe, the same car she'd seen by Martha's townhouse on Lopez Island. Laura was almost certain now . . . Was she slated to die in some "accident" on Stevens Pass?

The fire that swept through Eric Vetter's cabin last month and killed him—that had been an *accident*, too.

These people were experts . . .

Books by Kevin O'Brien

ONLY SON

THE NEXT TO DIE

MAKE THEM CRY

WATCH THEM DIE

LEFT FOR DEAD

THE LAST VICTIM

KILLING SPREE

ONE LAST SCREAM

FINAL BREATH

VICIOUS

DISTURBED

TERRIFIED

UNSPEAKABLE

TELL ME YOU'RE SORRY

NO ONE NEEDS TO KNOW

YOU'LL MISS ME WHEN I'M GONE

HIDE YOUR FEAR

THEY WON'T BE HURT

Published by Kensington Publishing Corporation

KEVIN O'BRIEN

THEY WON'T BE HURT

PINNACLE BOOKS
Kensington Publishing Corp.
www.kensingtonbooks.com

PINNACLE BOOKS are published by

Kensington Publishing Corp.
119 West 40th Street
New York, NY 10018

All Kensington titles, imprints, and distributed lines are available at special quantity discounts for bulk purchases for sales promotions, premiums, fund-raising, educational, or institutional use. Special book excerpts or customized printings can also be created to fit specific needs. For details, write or phone the office of the Kensington sales manager: Kensington Publishing Corp., 119 West 40th Street, New York, NY 10018, attn: Sales Department; phone 1-800-221-2647.

This book is a work of fiction. Names, characters, businesses, organizations, places, events, and incidents either are the product of the author's imagination or are used fictitiously. Any resemblance to actual persons, living or dead, events, or locales is entirely coincidental.

ISBN-13: 978-0-7860-3885-5
ISBN-10: 0-7860-3885-3

First Pinnacle printing: August 2018

10 9 8 7 6 5 4 3 2 1

Printed in the United States of America

First electronic edition: August 2018

ISBN-13: 978-0-7860-3886-2
ISBN-10: 0-7860-3886-1

This book is for the wonderful and talented
Jennie Shortridge
and the talented and wonderful
Laurie Frankel

ACKNOWLEDGMENTS

My gifted editor and friend, John Scognamiglio, is once again at the top of my thank-you list, and right up there with him is everyone at Kensington Publishing Corporation. I'm so lucky to be working with such a terrific group of pros.

Another great big thank-you goes to Meg Ruley, Christina Hogrebe, and the brilliant team at Jane Rotrosen Agency. You guys are wonderful.

Thanks also to the cool dudes in my Writers Group: David Massengill, Garth Stein, Colin McArthur, and John Flick. And speaking of writers, I'm so grateful to my fellow Seattle 7 Writers for all their support, especially the core members: Garth, Jennie and Laurie (again), Dave Boling, and Suzanne Selfors—and a special shout-out to Erica Bauermeister and Carol Cassella, who have my long overdue thanks. Erica was a tremendous help, providing some terrific ideas I used in my previous thriller, *Hide Your Fear*, and Dr. Cassella helped me with some medical questions in *Tell Me You're Sorry*. About time I got around to acknowledging those contributions!

I'd also like to thank the following individuals and groups for their support, encouragement and friendship: Dan Annear and Chuck Rank, Jeff Ayers, Ben Bauermeister, Pam Binder and the Pacific Northwest Writers Association, A Book for All Seasons, The Book Stall, Amanda Books, Marlys Bourm, Terry and Judine Brooks, George Camper and Shane White, Barbara and John Cegielski, Barbara and Jim Church, Anna Cottle and Mary Alice Kier, Tommy Dreiling, Paul Dwoskin, the folks at Elliott Bay Book Company, Bridget Foley and Stephen Susco, Matt Gani, Cate Goethals and Tom Goodwin, Bob and Dana Gold, my friends at Hudson News, Cathy Johnson, Ed and Sue Kelly, Elizabeth Kinsella, David Korabik, Stafford Lombard, Paul Mariz, Roberta Miner, Dan Monda, Jim Munchel, Meghan O'Neill, the wonderful people at ReaderLink Distribution Services, Eva Marie Saint, John Saul and Mike Sack, John Simmons, Roseann Stella, Dan Stutesman, George and Sheila Stydahar, and Mark Von Borstel.

Finally, thanks so much to my family.

CHAPTER ONE

"Huh, someone left the gate open," Jae observed from the passenger seat.

Wes Banyan had already lowered the driver's window to punch in the six-digit code on the little box at the start of the driveway. The frigid night air drifted into his rented Ford Fiesta. After two days and nights of driving in and out of the Singletons' compound, Wes now knew the front gate's code by heart. The property was surrounded by a tall fence with barbed-wire trim along the top. Jae referred to the house—nestled on a huge wooded lot overlooking Lopez Sound—as the "family cabin." After hearing her call it that for the last few days, Wes had been expecting a cottage with a pot-bellied stove, maybe some bunk beds in a spare room and an outhouse in back. Instead, it was a freaking six-bedroom mansion.

That was just like her. Jae Singleton was full of surprises, not all of them good.

Wes was determined to break up with her tonight.

And if he was going to do it, he needed to do it now, before he dropped her off at the house.

They'd met at a frat party three weeks ago. They were both freshmen at the University of Washington. Wes had seen her around Alder Hall and been immediately attracted to her. Jae was a gorgeous blonde with big green eyes and a lithe body. She smelled nice, too. She actually asked him out, which left Wes a bit stunned, because he knew he was hardly anybody's idea of a stud. Pale and skinny, he shaved only twice a week. A friend of his sister's once deemed him "geeky cute." He figured that was a fairly accurate compliment, and about the best he could hope for—at least until he started shaving more often. Girls who looked like Jae Singleton didn't usually date geeks.

Wes had friended Jae on Facebook, and he noticed she posted something on her timeline about their upcoming dinner date:

> Going out to dinner at The RAM tomorrow night with a cute guy named Wes. We're just getting to know each other. He's super-smart, funny and really nice. He probably doesn't know yet that I adore flowers. Flowers, flowers, flowers!

"Gee, you think she expects you to bring her flowers?" his roommate, Steve, asked him. "I mean, could she be any more obvious? You should post something on there saying you like blowjobs. Blowjobs, blowjobs, blowjobs."

Steve also mentioned that he knew a girl who posted stuff on Facebook about her dates to make an ex-boyfriend jealous: "She might be using you, man. I mean, just saying . . ."

Wes tried not to pay too much attention to his roommate, a chubby, sarcastic know-it-all whose chances of getting a girl—any girl—were in the vicinity of zero. Steve seemed to assume the two of them were in the same boat, just a couple of losers. He also wrongly assumed that Wes was only out to get laid. In truth, Wes was still a virgin, and the impending date with Jae left him breathless and scared. Here was this beautiful young woman who made him feel so important. He didn't want to screw it up.

Wes brought Jae mini carnations when he came to her dorm room for their date the following night. Over dinner, she seemed interested in everything he said. And at the end of the evening, when he walked her to her door, she gave him a slightly wet kiss on the mouth.

It was one of the best nights of his life.

On their second date, Jae told him about the guy she'd recently broken up with: a junior in a fraternity, Carson Something—one of those last-name-first-name guys. Wes pictured a cocky, rich party boy, the type who smoked cigars and hit golf balls at the range after class—sometimes in his plaid bathrobe, because that was just the way Carson rolled. He probably had one of those perfect five-o'clock shadows if he went a day without shaving.

From the way Jae talked, it was pretty obvious she still liked him. But it was too late for Wes. He'd already fallen for her. *Smitten,* his grandmother might have said. It didn't matter that his roommate was right about her Facebook posts, which went on and on about how she'd never been out with a guy who was so nice and considerate, *"so much nicer than you-know-who!"* she wrote. If Jae was trying to convince Carson that she was in love with someone else, Wes didn't mind being that someone else.

On date number three, they'd made out furiously, and she'd even let him feel her up. She didn't pull away or anything—so he must have been doing it right. The whole experience was pretty intoxicating for him.

Then, like an idiot, he told Steve about it.

"Some over-the-bra action, big whoop," Steve replied. "That's all you're probably going to get, considering who her old man is."

Steve acted as if Wes was an absolute moron for not knowing that Jae's father was Scott Singleton, the former Seahawks linebacker. Wes had to go online to find out more about him. After discovering God, Scott had become a self-ordained minister and started his own religious sect: the Church of the True Divine Light. Handsome and youthful-looking, he wanted to outlaw all abortions, advocated conversion therapy for gays (including electric shock, ice baths, and verbal admonishment—anything as long as it got the job done), and he firmly believed that a wife should be subservient to her husband. When a fellow NFL player was suspended for beating his girlfriend, Scott caused a brief uproar by telling the press: "Sometimes there are reasons for these things between couples—and it's not always bad."

Headquartered near Spokane, the Church of the True Divine Light had over 480,000 followers across the country. Scott Singleton had gotten rich in the religion business, and he had a lot of political pull.

Jae had told Wes that her father was in public relations. Small wonder she'd lied about her old man—especially at progressive University of Washington, where Scott Singleton might as well have been a card-carrying neo-Nazi.

Wes didn't much agree with anything Scott Singleton and his church stood for. But Jae wasn't shoving her father's beliefs down his throat. So he decided not to hold it against her.

Besides, she'd invited him to spend Thanksgiving weekend with her at her family's cabin on Lopez Island. "I'm a good cook, you'll see," she told him.

Wes couldn't afford to fly home to the Chicago area, and he'd figured he'd be stuck in the near-empty dorm for the holiday. But Jae had thrown him a lifeline. Hell, she was offering him a dream come true: four nights alone with her in a cabin in the woods. He got butterflies in his stomach just thinking about it. He wondered why she wasn't spending Thanksgiving with her family, but decided it really didn't matter. Why even bring it up?

It wasn't until after Wes had rented the car for their trip that Jae told him "some family" would be at the cabin, too. And it wasn't until they were on the ferry to Lopez that Jae found out the *entire* family was coming—her mom, dad, and all four siblings. None of the kids—apparently, that included Jae—wanted to double up, so there wouldn't be any room for Wes at the island house. At the last minute, he had to book himself a single queen room at the Lopez Islander Resort for the next four nights. It would take a huge bite out of his savings.

Wes realized it would have been cheaper for him to have flown home and celebrated Thanksgiving with his own family in Winnetka.

And he would have had a hell of a better time, too.

He spent the first two days of the extended weekend running errands for Jae's mother, a beautiful but bossy platinum-haired woman in her late forties. His room-mate, Steve, would have called her a MILF. The care-taker's minivan was in the shop, so all chauffeuring duties fell upon Wes. A cook, a maid, and a woman who served the dinner had to be shuttled around on Thanksgiving Day, from the ferry to the "cabin" to the hotel. The three women had rooms just down the hall from him at the Islander. He was staying with the help. The irony wasn't lost on him.

Wes was also in charge of picking up Scott Single-ton on Thanksgiving afternoon. Scott arrived by sea-plane and talked on his phone the whole time Wes was driving him to the compound. He appeared a bit older in person, and had silver streaks in his curly brown hair. But he was still ruggedly good-looking. He just wasn't too friendly.

"Do me a favor and get my bag for me, will you, Brad?" he said distractedly when Wes pulled up to the house.

Wes was in good company. Singleton couldn't get the name of their caretaker right either. Apparently, the guy was new. He was a handsome, nervous-looking, wiry guy in his early twenties. He lived in a small apart-ment above the three-car garage, which was separate from the house. He must have been hiding in there most of the time while Wes was busting his ass for the Singletons. The caretaker's name was Joe. But at the beginning of the meal, when Singleton called the help into the dining room for a solemn Thanksgiving prayer, he twice referred to the guy as "Jim"—and Mrs. Singleton corrected him both times.

Wes actually felt sorry for Joe—and for the three other servants. They looked so downtrodden, standing there in meek silence while Singleton prayed at the head of the big table, elegantly set with flickering candles and a cornucopia centerpiece.

Wes sat between Jae and her sixteen-year-old sister, Willow, who had a raging cold. She kept coughing and blowing her nose throughout dinner. Wes was convinced he'd be deathly ill before the week was out. The youngest kid, eleven-year-old Connor, was nice to him. But the older brother was a jerk. And the oldest sister ignored him. He didn't much like the family.

After a couple of days, he wasn't sure he much liked Jae either.

She was nasty to her sisters and constantly arguing with her mother. Plus, she'd barely paid any attention to him throughout the trip.

The two of them had just come back from a party at the house of one of her "island friends." It was a snotty, cliquish group. Jae kept disappearing, leaving him to stand there alone with his beer. At one point, she told him she might go back to Seattle on Monday with one of her friends. Would he mind terribly?

Yes, he minded. It broke his heart. It proved he wasn't really important to her after all.

But Wes said it was fine with him. He said he might just leave tomorrow morning and save a couple of hundred dollars on the hotel room cost. Maybe he could get some money back for taking the rental car back early.

Jae barely even blinked. It was as if she didn't care that he was leaving early, or that he'd spent a small fortune on this trip and had an utterly miserable time.

That was the moment Wes decided he had to break up with her. And he had to do it tonight—before he dropped her off at the family compound. If he waited until they got back to school, he'd chicken out or talk himself out of it. He was tired of feeling like a chump. What had he been thinking? He'd known from the start she was out of his league. If he broke up with her tonight, he would return to the dorm tomorrow with a clean slate.

Driving her back to the compound, his stomach was in knots. He didn't want a confrontation. He just wanted to end things with her.

The only radio station the car picked up on the island played nonstop Christmas music. Slightly drunk, Jae sang along with each selection. When "Simply Having a Wonderful Christmastime" came on, Wes reached over and switched off the radio because he absolutely loathed the song—and because he couldn't stall any longer on having *the talk* with her.

"Hey, why'd you do that?" she asked. "I love that song!"

Figures, Wes thought. But he didn't say anything. He just tightened his grip on the steering wheel, sighed, and shook his head.

"What's wrong with you tonight anyway?" she asked. "I mean, would it have killed you to be nice to my friends? All you did at the party was sulk."

"That's because I didn't know anyone—and nobody would talk to me." He took his eyes off the road for a moment to glance at her. "You introduced me to—like—a total of three people, and then you disappeared. You left me there all alone. I felt like an idiot . . ."

"Well, I'm sorry, but they're my friends, and I haven't seen most of them since the summer! And you were being a grouch. What was I supposed to do, stick by your side and hold your hand the entire night?"

"It might have been nice if you'd held my hand there just once," he murmured.

Jae sighed and then looked out the car window. "You know, maybe it's a good thing you're leaving tomorrow."

"Probably," he said, "because this isn't working out, none of it is."

Wes kept waiting for her to say something, but she didn't. He wondered if that was it. Were they broken up? Or did he actually have to say the words?

Up ahead, he spotted the side road that led to the Singleton compound. He slowed down and took the turn. The dark road snaked up a wooded hill. Branching off the narrow two-lane road were driveways and winding lanes that led to other houses and cabins. Through the trees, Wes spotted a few lights in the distance, but very few. Most everyone was asleep at this hour. He'd made this trip several times now but was still uncertain about a couple turns. He usually had someone in the car giving him directions. He was already worried about getting lost after he dropped Jae off tonight.

The silence in the car made him even more nervous.

The woods grew so dense that Wes couldn't see much beyond the car's headlights. Last night, he'd almost hit a deer. Now he imagined some guy in a hockey mask brandishing an ax, springing out of the darkness into the illuminated path.

Wes shuddered.

"What's wrong with you?" Jae asked.

"Nothing. I'm just cold, that's all," he murmured.

"You need to turn right at the Tall Pines sign," she muttered.

Nodding, Wes followed the gravel road to the right. He knew the compound was around one of the curves coming up. He kept following the road, and then he spotted the big house. A couple of the lights were on upstairs. He slowed down and pressed the switch on the armrest to lower his window.

That was when Jae noticed someone had left the front gate open.

He turned into the driveway. The older brother's Fiat was parked in front of the house, so Wes pulled up beside the garage. The windows above the garage were dark. Wes figured the caretaker was asleep.

"That's weird," Jae said. "All the curtains are closed on the first floor . . ."

"What's so weird about it?" Wes asked.

"We never close the curtains," Jae said. "There's no reason to out here in the woods." Frowning, she glanced back toward the open gate.

Wes followed her gaze. Then he turned toward the house again. He could see light peeking through the slits between the curtains. Maybe someone had left a few lights on for her downstairs and decided to leave the gate open, too.

Was that really so unusual?

Jae seemed to shrug it off. She turned toward him and sighed. "Well, I guess I won't see you until I get back on Monday . . ."

Wes cleared his throat. "Well, actually, I thought—"

"I'll miss a couple of classes, but who cares?" she interrupted.

She didn't seem to understand that he wanted to break up.

"You know, I think it works out better that you're leaving tomorrow," Jae continued. She flicked her blond hair and then rolled her eyes. "My mother has been riding her broomstick all weekend. You must think she's awful. She totally screwed up my plans for us this weekend. It was supposed to be just you and me here . . ."

Wes squirmed a bit in the driver's seat. He had a hard time believing that. For starters, didn't the caretaker live there year-round? And second, if they were alone in that big house in the middle of the woods, it would have been pretty damn scary—especially at night, like now.

He thought he saw a curtain move in one of the first-floor windows.

"Do you think someone's waiting up for you?" he asked.

"At this hour?" she said. "I doubt it."

Wes couldn't help thinking something was wrong. Then again, the house, its surroundings—and even Jae—seemed strange to him. She'd been concerned about the gate and the curtains just a minute ago, but not anymore. Of course, she was still a little drunk, so her judgment might be off.

Jae smiled and touched his shoulder. "Tell you what. I'll make you a sandwich for the ride home tomorrow."

"Oh, you don't have to," he said. "In fact, listen, I really think we—"

"Nonsense," she interrupted. "There's all that turkey left. And you have a mini-fridge in your room at the Islander. You can keep it fresh for tomorrow. Come on in with me while I make the sandwich."

"No, really, I think—"

"Okay, then you stay put. I'll be back in just a couple of minutes . . ."

She opened the passenger door.

"Jae, wait—"

But she jumped out of the car and shut the door.

"Shit," Wes muttered under his breath.

He watched her weaving slightly as she headed to the front door. She seemed to take forever to find the keys in her purse.

Wes kept the headlights on, figuring that might help Jae in her search. Besides that, everything about this place gave him the creeps right now. He just wanted to get out of there.

He lowered the window a crack and then glanced back over his shoulder at the open gate again. He heard a noise and swiveled around in time to see Jae duck inside the house. He realized it was just the sound of her unlocking and opening the front door.

Wes let out a little laugh. "Quit creeping yourself out," he said under his breath. Still, he reached for the armrest and pressed the lock for the car doors.

Slumping back in the driver's seat, he glanced at his wristwatch: 1:46 A.M. He couldn't believe he had to wait around here while she made him a lousy sandwich. He had no intention of eating it. When she'd invited him to spend this "intimate weekend" with her at "the cabin," Jae had said something about showing him what a great cook she was. Outside of opening a bag of Fritos and a couple of Diet Cokes, he hadn't seen her perform any tasks in the kitchen so far. Maybe this turkey sandwich was supposed to prove something to him.

Wes listened to the car engine idling. Past it, he thought he heard a scream.

He sat up straight.

The shrill, aborted wail seemed to have come from inside the house. He was almost certain it was Jae.

He switched off the engine and listened. There wasn't another sound. He kept staring at the house, waiting for one of the curtains to move again. But everything was so still. Even the tree branches weren't moving.

He glanced up toward the windows above the garage—still dark. Obviously, the caretaker hadn't heard it. But without a doubt, there had been a scream.

Maybe one of the other kids had played a joke on her and surprised her or something.

Biting his lip, Wes took out his phone and speed-dialed her number. It rang twice and then went to her voicemail: *"Hi! It's Jae,"* the familiar, perky record-ing said. *"I can't pick up right now. So you know what to do!"*

Wes grimaced. He didn't want to hear that voice-mail recording right now. He wanted to hear her. He wanted Jae to tell him everything was fine and she'd be out with his sandwich in a minute.

Instead, he waited for the beep. "Hi, it's me," he said in a slightly shaky voice. "Are you okay? I heard a scream. I'm worried. Call me—or come out and tell me everything's okay just as soon as you can. All right?"

He clicked off and anxiously stared at the front door.

He thought about calling the police, but what if nothing was wrong? They'd come out here and wake up the entire family—all for nothing.

Well, that's one way to make sure she'll never want to see me again, he thought. He let out a nervous chuckle.

But then he thought he saw something, and the fee-ble smile disappeared from his face. It looked like someone had just ducked behind a big tree at the edge of the driveway. Wes stared at the tree for a few mo-ments, but nothing moved. He told himself it was just his imagination playing tricks on him.

The car lights automatically shut off.

Wes had forgotten that he'd switched off the engine. He quickly turned the key in the ignition and started the car again. The headlights came on once more.

Just go, he thought. *Drive away. Something isn't right. Something happened in that house. And if you're mistaken, it doesn't matter that you've driven off. You're breaking up with her anyway. Once you get to the main road, you can call her again and explain that you got tired of waiting. Just go, for God's sake. Go . . .*

Wes's trembling hand hovered over the gearshift.

He heard a door slam, and he glanced toward the front of the house again.

There was no one by the front door. But at the side of the house, he saw someone dart between the trees—heading toward the driveway. It wasn't his imagination this time. It was a man, walking at a brisk, determined, robot-like clip.

Panic-stricken, Wes couldn't move. He watched the shadowy figure coming closer and closer to the driveway. It didn't look like Mr. Singleton or Jae's older brother. He disappeared behind some shrubs for a few seconds.

Wes went to start the car, but realized the engine was already running.

The man emerged from behind the bushes and zeroed in on the car. He held a gun in his hand.

"Oh, Jesus," Wes whispered, his heart stopping.

The man raised his gun.

Wes heard a shot ring out. From the windshield bits of glass sprayed him in the face. *God, this isn't happening,* he thought.

He reached for the door handle, but a second shot punctured the glass again, and Wes knew he'd been hit. It felt like someone had slammed a hammer into his upper chest. He saw the dashboard dotted with his own blood.

The front of his jacket was wet.

The man moved even closer to the car.

Moaning, Wes started to black out.

Two more shots echoed in the still night—and then nothing.

CHAPTER TWO

Sunday, November 26—9:29 P.M.
Friday Harbor, San Juan Island, Washington

On the way to his car at the far end of the parking lot, Jason Eichhorn felt a strange kind of elation. He knew it was wrong. The swarthy twenty-nine-year-old was a stringer for *The Seattle Times*, covering a horrible multiple murder. But he'd just had dinner at The Rumor Mill with two guys from CNN, a correspondent from *Time,* an older, Pulitzer Prize–winning reporter from the AP, and a smart, sexy redheaded correspondent from NBC News—some pretty impressive company. They were tapping his expertise about the local haunts and the ferry system.

Reporters from all over the country had descended upon the island, where the county sheriff's office was located. It was the same way on Lopez Island—and in Anacortes on the mainland. Jason's dinner companions had invited him to come back to Friday Harbor Suites with them and have a drink at the bar. But he wanted to return to his room at the far-less-expensive Orca Inn so he could phone his wife, Debra, at home in Bellingham. He couldn't wait to tell her about how he'd been hanging out with these big shots. Plus, he missed her. Deb had taken time off work for Thanksgiving weekend, and they were supposed to have spent the entire Saturday together. But then the newspaper suddenly needed Jason to cover a big story.

Really big.

Scott Singleton and his entire family had been brutally murdered at their Lopez Island vacation home.

There was one survivor, a college student who had been dating one of the Singleton daughters. He'd been shot three times and was now in critical condition at Island Hospital in Anacortes. The *Times* had sent another stringer there, waiting for the kid to get out of intensive care. Police investigators were hoping that once he was conscious, Jae Singleton's boyfriend might give them a description of the shooter.

The Singletons' caretaker, a young man who lived on the premises, apparently slept through the whole thing. He found the bodies early Saturday morning: first, the wounded, unconscious college student, lying beside his car in the driveway; and then the seven dead inside the house.

Jae Singleton seemed to have returned home and surprised her killer—or killers. The other victims were in their pajamas, bound and gagged, and stabbed repeatedly. Jae's body—along with her father's—had been discovered on the first floor. Jae appeared to have been attacked and stabbed in the front hallway, but collapsed and died in the living room. Scott Singleton was found facedown on the sofa in his study. He'd been beaten savagely before someone slit his throat. The others were found in various rooms on the second floor.

The senseless, violent murders had people across the country locking their doors and windows. The veteran reporter from the Associated Press said he hadn't seen anything quite like it since he was a young intern at the *Chicago Sun-Times* in the summer of 1966, when some creep murdered eight student nurses in their townhouse/dorm quarters. "I guess maybe the Tate-LaBianca murders in sixty-nine brought about the same kind of national panic, too," he said, amending his own statement. "This isn't just a local thing on these islands. Hell, even people in Maine are scared. It's the same gut-sickening terror all over. No one feels safe."

"I'll bet gun sales go up again," said the woman from NBC.

While a jazz quartet played onstage and a waitress took away their dinner plates, one of the CNN guys passed around his phone. Another reporter friend had sent him photos from inside the Singletons' house. Jason looked at only one of the pictures—of the oldest daughter, twenty-two-year-old brown-haired Mandy, in a bloodstained pink gingham camisole and shorts. With her hands tied behind her, she lay on her side at the foot of an unmade bed. Crimson splotches marred the baby blue bedspread. Her eyes were open with a frozen, stunned stare. Jason couldn't make himself look at any of the other pictures.

Little by little, more details began to emerge about the caretaker, twenty-five-year-old Joseph Mulroney. Mrs. Singleton had hired him to look after the Lopez

Island grounds in September. Mulroney couldn't explain how he'd managed to sleep through everything—including the gunshots right below his bedroom window. There was no evidence of a break-in at the gated grounds. Mulroney had been covered with blood when the police and paramedics arrived. He claimed to have been trying to revive eleven-year-old Connor Singleton, who had shown signs of life just minutes earlier. This was contradicted in an initial report from the coroner, who set the boy's time of death at around one in the morning—along with the other family members. The most damning evidence of all came when investigators looked into Mulroney's background. They discovered he'd been released from a state-run psychiatric facility earlier in the year.

Though Mulroney looked like a prime suspect, the AP reporter had mentioned over dinner that Willy Garretson, the young caretaker at the house Roman Polanski and Sharon Tate had rented, had been the police's first suspect in her murder. He, too, had slept through the night—while the five victims were viciously slain within shouting distance of his separate quarters on the grounds.

Joseph Mulroney was a thin, handsome, timid-looking guy. "Like Bundy," mentioned the man from *Time*, "a real charmer, the boy-next-door type."

"The angel-faced killer," the woman from NBC added. "That's what they'll end up calling him."

Mulroney was cooperating with the San Juan County Police, and he'd even agreed to take a lie-detector test for them. He hadn't been charged with anything yet. They'd moved him from his apartment at the Singletons' Lopez Island compound to Friday Harbor on San Juan Island so he'd be near the sheriff's office. In fact, they'd put him up at the Orca Inn—at the other end of the hall from Jason. He'd spotted Mulroney a couple of times at a distance. A cop was stationed in the corridor, keeping guard. It was still up for grabs whether the guard was protecting Mulroney from the public or the other way around.

As the impromptu dinner party at The Rumor Mill broke up, a couple of the reporters offered to switch lodgings with Jason. They were jealous he was so close to all the action, right there practically in the command center. The Orca Inn was also close to the restaurant and the ferry. Jason could have easily walked the few blocks to The Rumor Mill, but it was chilly out and he'd been feeling lazy, so he'd driven.

Now he was the last of their group to leave the parking lot. He and the other journalists had closed the restaurant. As Jason headed to his car, somebody shut off the lighted sign above the entrance. The town had been all abuzz when he'd pulled into the crowded lot three hours ago. Now it seemed asleep. A brisk wind off the San Juan Channel cut through him, and Jason shivered. He reached into his pocket for his car key.

That was when a man stepped out of the shadows near the Dumpster at the side of the restaurant. "Hey, excuse me," he said.

Startled, Jason halted in his tracks. He couldn't quite see the man's face. The stranger wore a dark rain slicker and a knit hat. He looked like a fisherman.

"I'm totally lost," the man said. "Is the ferry terminal somewhere around here?"

Jason smiled and nodded. "You're only a couple of blocks away. The terminal is on Front Street. This is First Street right here, and all you have to do is—"

"How about if you drive us there?" the man interrupted, his tone suddenly changing. He pulled a gun out of his pocket. "Okay, asshole?"

With the car key in his hand, Jason gaped at him. He couldn't move—or say anything. He saw the man's face now. He was about thirty-five, with a heavy blond beard stubble and cold, pitiless eyes. "Don't even think about pressing the car alarm," he growled.

Jason quickly shook his head. "I won't, I promise." He swallowed hard. Then with a shaky hand, he pressed the button on the key fob device to unlock the car doors. The headlights flashed on his Hyundai Sonata.

"Hey, c'mon, kiddo," the man called.

It took Jason a moment to realize the guy was talking to someone else. A second man emerged from behind the Dumpster. He wore a dark Windbreaker that must not have been too warm, because he was rubbing his arms and shivering as he trotted toward the car.

"We've got our ride," the first man said, shoving the gun back inside his coat pocket. He glared at Jason again. It was obvious he still had the gun pointed at him from inside his jacket pocket. "Get behind the wheel. Try anything, and I'll blow your goddamn head off."

Jason just nodded. But he still couldn't move. He glanced at the other man, now stepping into the light.

Seeing him this close, Jason gasped.

The guy was in his mid-twenties—with dark hair

and a thin build. He looked a little frightened. The woman correspondent from NBC News was right.

He had the face of an angel.

"Your attention please. We are now arriving at our destination. All passengers must disembark. Please take a few moments to make sure you have all your personal belongings . . ."

With his window open a crack, Jason listened to the announcement over the public-address system. He watched the other Anacortes-bound passengers returning to their vehicles on the ferry's car deck. Cold, sweaty, and scared, he'd been sitting at the wheel of his car, strapped in his seat belt for the last ninety minutes.

The gunman in the front passenger seat had long ago confiscated Jason's phone and wallet and tucked them into his coat pocket. The man had removed his knit cap and used it to conceal the gun in his hand. He'd taken his eyes off Jason for only a few fleeting moments at a time.

To Jason, it seemed like they'd been in the car forever. When the boat had pulled away from the dock at Friday Harbor, most passengers had climbed out of their vehicles and gone up to the main cabin. But Jason and his two passengers had remained inside the Sonata on the car deck.

He'd found out the gunman's name. Joseph Mulroney had let it slip early on. "I'm scared, Vic," he'd said. He was in the backseat, wearing Jason's Mariners baseball hat, which he must have found on the floor.

"Oh, fine," Vic muttered. "Stupid. Why don't you give him my Social Security number while you're at it? Would you chill? I'm sure the cops haven't caught on. They probably think you're still in your room at the Orca Inn, flogging your dolphin to the adult channel . . ."

But Joseph Mulroney couldn't calm down. He kept whimpering and anxiously peering out the windows. It was like having a scared puppy in the backseat. At one point, about ten minutes after the ferry had left San Juan Island, he had a meltdown.

"I want to go back," Mulroney cried. "Please, let's go back to the hotel, Vic. Please . . ." He started screaming. "I can't stand this!" He repeatedly hit the armrest with his fist. Vic finally dug into his pocket and gave him a couple of pills. He coaxed him into swallowing them without water.

With Vic so distracted, Jason probably could have jumped out of the car and made a run for it, but he was too frightened, too caught up in Mulroney's frenzied panic attack. Jason hadn't realized until it was over that he'd just missed an opportunity to escape. By then, Mulroney had calmed down. Halfway across the channel, he was curled up on the backseat, dozing.

"Look at him," Vic whispered, glancing over his shoulder at his friend. "Just like a little kid, a regular Boy Scout. You'd never guess he was capable of chopping that nice, God-fearing family into so many bloody pieces."

Shuddering, Jason wondered about the relationship between the two men. Mulroney came across as a tortured soul, vulnerable and volatile, a scared boy. Vic seemed like the smarter of the two, more ruthless. At the same time, he was terribly immature. Using an expression like "flog your dolphin" for masturbating was just what Jason might have expected from a crude, stunted adolescent who enjoyed pulling the wings off flies.

At the Rumor Mill dinner, someone had mentioned that the police were trying to locate a friend of Mulroney's, a fellow former resident of Western Washington Psychiatric Institute. Apparently, he'd escaped.

Jason was pretty certain he'd found him.

He remembered Truman Capote's *In Cold Blood*, and the two killers of the Clutter family, Perry Smith and Richard Hickock. Hickock was the cold, calculating one who had planned the robbery. Smith was the sensitive hard-luck case who fascinated Capote, the one who went berserk and started the killing.

The Singletons had also been burglarized: Purses and wallets had been emptied, and laptops and smartphones were missing. A maid who had served the Singletons their Thanksgiving dinner said they owned a silver tea service, candlesticks, and silverware. The killer—or killers—must have made off with those as well. Jason imagined Vic planning the burglary, only to have his "Boy Scout" friend go crazy in the middle of it and kill everyone in the house.

He didn't dare ask Vic what had actually happened, and it made him ashamed. Some reporter he turned out to be. He was supposed to be curious and ask questions. But Jason figured his chances of surviving the night were better if he didn't know anything.

"You're a reporter, aren't you?" Vic had asked about

fifteen minutes ago. The ferry had just passed Lopez Island, the scene of the crime.

"Why do you ask that?" Jason replied. For some reason, he imagined answering "yes" might increase his chances of getting killed.

"Because it's off-season on the islands, and every stinking hotel is full—and what they're full of is reporters. Besides, I heard you talking to your pals in the parking lot." He leaned against the armrest on the door and laughed. "Boy, if they could see you now, huh? You're out-scooping them all. I'll bet you're already thinking about what a great story this will make, an exclusive. The rest of them will be begging to interview you . . ."

Jason stared past the ferry deck railing—at the black horizon and the choppy gray water. He shook his head. "Right now, I just want to get out of this alive."

"Were they talking about me in the restaurant?" Vic asked. "Were you guys jawing about the caretaker's friend, seen around town on Lopez for the last couple of weeks? Do they have a description of me?" He ran a hand over his blondish marine-recruit buzz cut. "Are they on the lookout for a handsome dude with shaggy blond hair?"

Jason figured Vic must have cut his hair himself within the last day or two.

"How much do the cops know about me?" Vic pressed.

"I honestly have no idea," Jason murmured. "We'd heard something about the police searching for an acquaintance of his." He nodded toward the backseat. "'A person of interest,' they said. None of us had a name or any details."

"But now you have a name, don't you, smart guy?" he whispered.

Jason said nothing. He couldn't look at him. He felt sick to his stomach.

Vic chuckled again.

"I have to go to the bathroom," Jason told him. "I mean it, I really need to pee."

"Sorry." Vic shook his head. "But go ahead and piss in your pants if you want."

"Please," Jason said under his breath.

"Nope, no bathroom breaks for the driver. Too much can happen during a short trip to the toilet. At the Orca Inn, there's a cop standing guard in the hallway, and he'll back me on that statement—especially after the county sheriff reams him a new butthole for losing their number one suspect." He slapped Jason's shoulder with the back of his hand. "I sat in that lobby for two hours. I figured no one would notice me with all you reporters coming and going. If the cops were on the lookout, they didn't have their eyes peeled for a guy with a buzz cut and glasses. I just sat and waited for that stupid guard to take a bathroom break. Sure enough, around nine o'clock, I saw him duck into the privy off the lobby. I had Joe out a side door of the hotel within two minutes. I left the TV on in his room. If we're lucky, they won't figure out until tomorrow morning that our boy is gone. By then, we'll be far, far away."

And I'll be dead, Jason thought. He clutched the steering wheel tighter to keep his hands from shaking too much. An awful dread was eating away at his gut. The car was cold, but he couldn't stop sweating.

As the ferry approached the Anacortes dock Jason half-expected to see the terminal area aglow with police lights. He hoped for it and dreaded it at the same time. He had a feeling Vic wouldn't give up easily. They'd probably take him hostage or something.

Beyond the deck railing, he didn't see any swirling red and white police lights at the terminal. It looked quiet. The next ferry run wouldn't be until morning, so no cars were waiting.

Jason suddenly realized that as far as the two of them were concerned, he was excess baggage now. They'd needed him to get them here to Anacortes, and after that, he was expendable. The smart thing for them to do was to kill him and hide his body. It might be a couple of days before anyone would find him. Vic and Joe could be halfway across the country by then. If they let him live, no matter what he promised, all three of them knew that, by dawn, the police and the press would have Vic's name and an updated description of him; they'd have a description of the getaway car, too—and even the license plate number.

Jason listened to the chatter and laughing as people headed back to their vehicles. Someone sang a slightly sour rendition of "Jingle Bell Rock." Headlights flashed as passengers pressed their key fobs to unlock their cars. All the doors opening and shutting made a clamor that echoed throughout the deck.

Once they were off this ferry, Jason knew he was as good as dead.

Someone in the lane on their right climbed into his SUV and slammed the door shut.

Joseph Mulroney woke up with a start. "What? What's going on?" he asked.

Jason watched him in the rearview mirror. He looked disoriented and unnerved. The baseball cap was askew on his head.

"Relax, kiddo," Vic said. "We're pulling into Anacortes. A few minutes from now, we'll be on the open road . . ."

In the next lane, between them and the ferry railing, a forty-something brunette climbed into the passenger side of a VW Bug. She accidentally tapped her door against Jason's door. Jason turned and gaped at her.

"Sorry," she said distractedly, shutting her door. Then a man ducked into the VW's driver's seat. The woman glanced across at Jason. They were so close—if their windows had been open they could have reached out and shook hands.

Vic was distracted, still trying to calm his anxious friend in the backseat: "For Christ's sake, just go back to sleep. Everything's fine . . ."

His hands still taut on the wheel, Jason locked eyes with the woman. He silently mouthed the words *Help me*.

She half-smiled and squinted at him.

He moved his lips again: *Help me*. He wanted to scream it.

"What the fuck do you think you're doing?" Vic hissed. "Look at me."

Obedient, Jason turned to face him.

"Don't look back at her," he whispered. Then he seemed to force a smile. "Don't even think about it, smart guy."

Jason noticed the tip of the gun barrel protruding beneath the knit cap draped over Vic's hand. It was pointed at him. He flinched at the sound of several car engines starting.

"Vic, she's still looking at us," Mulroney said under his breath. "What are we going to do? What if she recognizes me?"

"Smart guy here better pray she doesn't." He frowned at Jason. "We won't need you or your car very much longer, pal. We're so close to a clean getaway. And by tomorrow morning, you'll have quite a story to tell your newspaper. Do you really want to fuck things up for all three of us—at this point?"

Jason wondered if they actually planned to let him go. He wanted to believe it but couldn't.

"Start the car," Vic said.

Keeping his head down, Jason turned the key in the ignition. He didn't look up until he heard the rumble of the cars rolling over the ferry ramp. His car was near the front of the boat. The lane started moving. Jason shifted into drive. The ferry worker waved him forward. For a fleeting moment, he thought about pushing hard on the accelerator and slamming into the car in front of him. Maybe the gun would fly out of Vic's hand—and onto the floor. Then he could leap from the driver's seat and run like hell.

But he was too scared.

Besides, how many people around here—in addition to himself—would get shot if he tried something like that?

Vic smiled and nodded at the ferry worker as they cruised past him onto the ramp.

Traffic moved at a slow crawl through the terminal area. No one in the car said anything. But Jason could hear Mulroney whimpering in the backseat. The procession of vehicles started to dissipate as they drove through town on Highway 20.

Jason realized his last chance of possibly getting help from someone had been on the ferry—and he'd blown it. They'd probably get rid of him once there weren't so many other cars around. Up ahead, Jason knew, was a long, sparsely lit road that led to the Swinomish Reservation. Jason wondered if his passenger in the front seat knew about it. They could dump his body in a ditch somewhere along that road, and it might be days before someone found him.

Jason thought of his wife—and his parents, and home. Tears stung his eyes.

"I was supposed to call my wife tonight," he said in a shaky voice. He quickly wiped the tears away and fixed his gaze on the long, straight two-lane highway ahead. There were still two cars in front of them and several more behind. "You switched off my phone when you took it away. Debra's probably been trying to get ahold of me for the last couple of hours. If you'd let me talk to her, I promise I won't give you away . . ."

Vic leaned back and said nothing. Mulroney had stopped whining. Maybe he'd fallen asleep again. Jason couldn't see him in the rearview mirror anymore.

"Please, let me call my wife," he whispered.

He wanted to hear her voice one last time.

"So—your old lady's home alone," Vic said. "What's your neighbor's name?"

Jason glanced at him. "Um, Belcher—Stan and Elaina Belcher. Why?"

"Debra's probably too busy fucking Stan Belcher to give a crap where you are right now." He let out a loud cackle.

You slime, Jason thought. He shifted restlessly in the driver's seat and tried to swallow his anger. "The way I figure," he said steadily, "if my wife isn't worried about me, there's no reason I can't keep driving you guys for the next day or two. I can take you wherever you want to go. The cops won't be looking for three men. I can get gas and groceries and food for you—no questions asked. I could even check into a hotel for you. There wouldn't be any trail, because no one's looking for me. You'd be safe . . ."

"It makes sense, Vic," Mulroney said.

Jason realized the young man was awake. Biting his lip, he waited for Vic's response. If they kept him on, it would buy him more time.

Just ahead, he saw a sign for the turnoff to the Swinomish Reservation.

"Gee, that's a terrific idea," Vic finally said, dead-pan. "As if you wouldn't squeal to the first gas station attendant or hotel clerk you met. Give me a break. It would be just like with that bitch in the VW next to us on the ferry. Nice try, smart guy. No. In a very short time, your services will no longer be needed."

Biting his lip, Jason passed the access road to the

reservation. He drove in silence for a few more minutes.

"There's a Shell station coming up on the right," Vic announced. "We're gonna make a little stop."

Jason checked the dashboard. He had nearly a full tank. Then he looked up. In the distance ahead, he spotted the lighted yellow Shell sign at an intersection.

"What's your PIN code?" Vic asked.

Jason hesitated, and then sighed, "Seventeen, twenty-two, oh-nine." Now that they knew how to get his money, there was no reason to keep him alive.

His stomach in knots, Jason signaled and then pulled into the gas station. They seemed to be the only customers there at this hour of the night. He saw the ATM sign in the window of the small convenience store.

Tossing Jason's wallet in the back, Vic repeated the PIN code for Mulroney. "Got that, kiddo? You need to get us some traveling money."

"I can't go in there," Mulroney said. "What if he recognizes me?"

"That's a chance we'll have to take. Keep the baseball cap on. Get as much cash as they allow, and then do it again. Whatever you get, we need to make it last. And button up. It's cold out there. C'mon, get cracking . . ."

With a nervous sigh, Mulroney climbed out of the car. Adjusting the Mariners cap on his head, he ducked into the store.

Jason watched the chubby, olive-skinned clerk behind the counter glance up from his magazine as Mulroney made a beeline to the ATM. While he waited for the money, Mulroney snuck a look at the clerk and then checked over his shoulder at the security camera in the store.

"As long as we're here, could I please use the bathroom?" Jason asked. He figured maybe he could write a message for help on the restroom mirror in soap—along with his license plate number. He'd seen someone do that in a movie once. "Please? I really have to go," he added.

Vic shook his head, "Nope. Like I said, if you can't hold it in, pee in your pants. I don't care."

The clerk peered out at them—then at Mulroney at the cash machine. Jason wondered if Vic's young friend was right. Had the clerk recognized him? Was it possible the police were already looking for the fugitives?

But the clerk started reading his magazine again. He only briefly looked up when Mulroney finished at the ATM and hurried out of the store.

Mulroney opened the back door and jumped inside the idling car. "I got four hundred dollars," he said, out of breath. "The machine only distributed two hundred at a time, max. I put the card in twice." With a shaky hand, he gave the money and the card to Vic.

"Good boy." Vic shoved the money in his coat pocket and then he nodded at Jason. "All right, get back on the road—same direction as before."

Jason took one last look at the clerk, still intent on his magazine. Then he reluctantly started out of the gas station. Without having to stop, he pulled back onto Highway 20. There were no oncoming cars. The ferry traffic had moved on, and now it was as if Jason and his two passengers had the long, lonely roadway to themselves. He didn't say anything. He heard the wheels humming on the pavement.

"Hey, listen, thanks very much for all this," Mulroney said, leaning close to him. "I'm really sorry we've inconvenienced you. But I promise we'll pay you back somehow . . ."

Vic snickered, "Yeah, we sure will."

"I mean it," Mulroney said, sitting back.

"I know you do," Vic said. "That's what makes you so sweet." He slapped Jason's shoulder and pointed to a road coming up on the left. "Turn there . . ."

Jason felt his stomach lurch again. Signaling, he slowed down and made the turn. It was part of his job to know the area. The road led to a chemical plant and a lumber mill—and nowhere else. He could smell the acrid odor churning from both facilities. The side road was unlit, and the smooth pavement soon became a gravel road. Along the left shoulder was a gully. Jason listened to the pebbles ricocheting against the underside of the car. On the right, he could see the silhouette of the chemical plant and its smokestacks against the night sky. There were a few lights on in one building, but he imagined the place was deserted at this hour.

"Where are we going?" he finally asked—though he already knew why they'd turned down this dark, dead-end road. He tried his damnedest not to cry. He didn't want Vic to see his tears.

"I think my pal is right," Vic said, unfastening his seat belt. He kept the gun pointed at him. "It's time we started treating you better—I mean, considering that you've loaned us money, and driven us all this way, and treated us to your enchanting company. I wasn't very nice earlier. I figure—if you want a quiet spot to take a piss, you've got that coming. No one will see you out here. Keep going just a little farther down this road. You'll have lots of privacy . . ."

Jason knew his body would end up in that gully—amid the overgrown weeds.

He couldn't stop shaking. He thought he might throw up, but held it back. Yet he couldn't stop the tears from streaming down his face. "Please, no," he whispered.

If Vic heard him, he didn't react at all.

They'd passed the chemical plant and now approached the mill yard on their right. Individual stacks of wood, each about the size of a trailer, lined the other side of a tall fence that bordered the lot. Up ahead was the entrance to the mill. But the gate was closed. The road widened to what must have been a turnabout for trucks. Two crude dirt paths branched off the cul de sac.

Jason realized this was his last chance.

Taking a deep breath, he pushed his foot down hard on the accelerator and jerked the wheel to the left. The engine roared and tires screeched as the car spun out of control. Plumes of gravel and dirt engulfed them.

Vic was thrown against the dashboard, but he still had the gun in his hand. "You son of a bitch!"

Jason reached for his door handle, ready to jump out of the car. Then, all at once, he felt something slam against the side of his head. It must have been the gun butt. He heard a crack. The pain was awful, and he cried out. But—somehow—he managed to open the car door. The vehicle was still moving as he jumped out and tumbled onto the hard, cold gravel. In his panic, he barely felt the impact. He just kept moving. His survival depended on it. Bleeding and sore, he tried to crawl down past some bushes by the road. He couldn't see anything beyond that. He hoped to lose them in the shadowy overgrowth.

But Jason couldn't get to his feet. He kept stumbling. His head was spinning, and he couldn't see anything. It wasn't just the darkness. The blow to his head had done something to his vision.

He heard the car skid to a stop. The engine was still idling. The door clicked open, and then there were footsteps.

"You prick," Vic muttered. "You're just where I want you . . ."

He was coming closer. Jason could hear the gravel crunch under each step.

Breathless, he frantically scurried deeper into the bushes. But the ground seemed to give out beneath his feet, and he fell into the ditch. It knocked the wind out of him. He tried to get up.

He was on his knees when Vic descended on him.

"Vic, don't!" Mulroney cried.

Jason's vision seemed to right itself. He could see Vic standing over him—and the gun aimed at his face.

He heard a click.

"Fuck," Vic growled.

Another click. The gun was jammed.

"Goddamn piece of shit," Vic grunted. He changed his grip on the weapon and used the butt end to strike Jason in the head again—and again.

Jason went down after the second blow. He flopped into a slimy, freezing puddle of water at the bottom of the gulch.

He thought he was dead.

Vic must have thought so, too.

Jason didn't know how long he'd been lying near the bottom of the ditch.

He remembered hearing Mulroney anxiously ask his friend what had just happened. Vic had muttered a reply that had led to an argument. But Jason hadn't been able to make out the words—until Vic had bellowed: "Just get in the goddamn car!"

Then Jason had heard the Sonata's doors shut and the car peeling away.

Was that five minutes ago—or an hour? Jason wasn't sure.

He just knew his head was throbbing. Blood covered half his face, and his whole body ached. His hands were raw—with bits of gravel embedded in his palms and fingertips. He must have hurt his arm, too. Every time he moved it a certain way, the pain was excruciating. He crawled out of the ditch, and then tried to get to his feet, but his ankle gave out and he almost fell.

On his hands and knees, Jason crawled to the driveway. His vision still wasn't right. Things kept going in and out of focus.

He realized that somewhere along the line he must have pissed in his pants, because he didn't have to pee anymore. He was wet, cold, and smelly from falling into that dirty puddle, so it didn't make much difference—except to his dignity.

He glanced over at the mill. Maybe it had a night watchman. Jason screamed for help. If there was a response, he couldn't hear it. He finally managed to stand up and started hobbling toward Highway 20. But pain shot up from his ankle through his leg with every step. He was dizzy and disoriented. He thought he saw some headlights in the distance. Jason wondered if they were even real, because he kept seeing spots. Still, he trudged on in that direction, stumbling several times. The highway seemed so far away.

He wondered if this would be his fate: to have survived being car-jacked by two killers—only to collapse and die before being rescued. He didn't think he'd make it. And if he ever reached the highway, how long would it take before someone stopped for him?

Blindly, he pressed on until the gravel under his shoes turned to smooth pavement. He couldn't stop shivering from the cold. Nausea and dizziness overwhelmed him. He finally braced himself against a signpost and vomited. He remembered as a kid feeling better after he threw up. Not this time. He felt even worse.

Jason spotted a pair of headlights coming down the road. He staggered toward the yellow dividing line and started to wave his arms—even though the right one still hurt like hell. His head began to spin again. Before he knew what was happening, he collapsed on the pavement.

He looked up and saw the light getting brighter and brighter. He remembered what people who have had near-death experiences sometimes said about seeing a bright light.

He wasn't sure if the car would stop—or if a car was even there at all.

Jason thought maybe he was already dying.

CHAPTER THREE

Monday, November 27—8:38 A.M.
Leavenworth, Washington

From the front porch, Laura Gretchell watched her neighbor's SUV head off down the long driveway. Calling Patti Bellini her "neighbor" was kind of a stretch, because Patti lived a half mile away. But the addresses were spread far apart on this rural road, and the Bellinis were indeed on the next lot down.

Laura and her husband, Sean, lived on a vine-yard/winery they'd bought four months ago with his inheritance. They'd named the wine brand after Sean's late father: Gerard's Cove. Until this past spring, the only thing Laura had known about managing a winery was what she'd picked up from *Falcon Crest* reruns.

Their three children seemed to have adjusted well to the move from Seattle. Sophie, sixteen, and Liam, twelve, had just caught the buses to their respective new schools about an hour ago. They'd inherited Laura's brown hair and skinny frame. James, four, took after his father, with sandy-colored hair and a sturdy body. James was in preschool with Patti's son, Leo. Laura and Patti took turns driving the boys back and forth.

Laura waved good-bye to James and then stepped back inside her three-story farmhouse. Built in the 1930s, the house looked like something from an Edward Hopper painting. With its brick fireplace and coved archways, the living room had that WPA-era feel. The dining room had a built-in hutch and the original art deco overhead light fixture. But the kitchen must have been updated about twenty years ago with black appliances, pale green marble countertops, and cherrywood cabinets. Laura thought it looked "ugly as sin," as her grandmother used to say. Unfortunately, all those black appliances still worked without a glitch. So it would be a while before Laura could remodel. One good feature about their "nineties kitchen" was the open-concept layout that incorporated the eating area and the family room, which had a big-screen TV, a second fireplace, and a sliding glass door that looked out at the vineyard.

The landscape was kind of desolate right now, but that was normal this time of year in Central Washington. It was off-season. Their wine-tasting room, in a little Ralph-Lauren-type rustic cottage near the main road, was closed until February.

Laura was very much alone there.

Her husband had decided this was the perfect time for a research trip to some French and Italian wineries. Laura had wanted to go with him and have her mother come stay with the kids, but Sean had shot down the idea. He'd said the trip was all business: cheap hotels, a tight schedule, and lots of driving. He'd be gone two weeks.

Laura wasn't quite convinced he was going to have a terrible time, driving around the French and Italian countryside, touring wineries, sampling wines—with bread and cheese, no doubt. Hell, it would have been like a second honeymoon for them. She really didn't understand why she couldn't have accompanied him. But she wasn't about to beg him to take her. It put a slight strain on things before he left.

This was Sean's first extended trip since they'd moved here. Laura was still not used to the house—especially now with him gone. He was usually home during the day—in his study up on the third floor—and in season, people worked in the vineyard all day. Now the place seemed deserted and scary. The closest police and fire stations were fifteen minutes away, near downtown Leavenworth. Sean had insisted on keeping a gun in their bedroom closet and a fire extinguisher on every floor.

As Laura locked the front door, it occurred to her that with Patti driving to town right now, there wasn't another soul within a mile—except maybe the occasional car that sped by on Rural Route 17.

She headed into the family room, picked up the remote, and unmuted the television. The set had been on for about an hour now—the *Today* show.

Since the move, she'd become one of those people who walk into a room and automatically turn on the TV. She'd never been that way in Seattle. It wasn't like she was any less busy now. She simply felt lonelier. The vineyard and the winery had been more Sean's dream than hers. He'd been talking about it and setting money aside ever since she'd first met him twenty years ago. All that time, he'd been with Weyerhaeuser, toiling away at a marketing job he didn't like very much. Now he was doing what he wanted.

Except for having to say good-bye to some close friends, moving here had proved no great sacrifice for her. In fact, she'd grown a bit tired of Seattle. It had become too crowded, and traffic was a nightmare. They'd lived near downtown on Capitol Hill, where everyone was plugged into their smartphones, ignoring each other, not looking where they were going or driving. A stroll down a crowded sidewalk wasn't just lonely—it was frustratingly futuristic and even dangerous. Sean, who was pretty conservative, often complained about the aggressive panhandlers hitting him up for money outside the local supermarket and the smell of stink-weed on every corner. Laura was more liberal in her politics, but she had to admit she was pretty tired of it, too.

Maybe things were the same in most cities. Either way, as far as Laura was concerned, the idea of moving to a vineyard in Central Washington didn't seem too bad.

She wasn't totally cut off from civilization. Seattle was a scenic, three-hour drive away. Plus, the Bavarian-style village of Leavenworth was a popular vacation destination, full of cute hotels and resorts. A few of their friends had already been there to visit them.

The move didn't put much of a crimp in Laura's career either—if she could call it a "career." She'd been a part-time substitute teacher in Seattle. She used to be a full-time teacher, and she'd loved it. But then something happened not too long after Sean and she had gotten married—and a couple of years before Sophie was born. "The Incident," she and Sean called it.

It was one of those things that had been building and building. Her big problem student in the third grade had been Donald Clapp, a husky little jerk who was always disrupting the class and picking on this one poor undersized kid named Joey Spiers. Little Joey was an easy target. His clothes were always dirty, and he had some learning disabilities. He never fought back or complained or cried. Maybe Laura was a bit overprotective of Joey. But the sweet, sad boy seemed to have enough woes that he didn't need Donald's constant abuse. Laura had repeatedly sent Donald to the principal's office and even had him suspended once.

Donald's father maintained she was persecuting his son for absolutely no reason. Mr. Clapp proved to be an even bigger problem than his kid. He was a short, pale man with milky blue eyes, a thin mustache, and a macho swagger. It seemed like the scowl on his face was a permanent affliction. He showed up at the school one day and stood outside her classroom window, staring in at her like a gargoyle. After a couple of minutes, Laura called the principal, Tom Freeman, on her cell phone. The police eventually showed up and escorted Mr. Clapp off the property.

"The Incident" happened a week later—on a Tuesday morning. She'd sent Donald to Tom Freeman's office yet again the previous day. On Tuesday morning, Laura was relieved to notice Donald was absent. She'd just finished taking attendance when Mr. Clapp came charging into the classroom. Laura didn't even see the switchblade in his hand. It all happened so fast, she barely remembered anything beyond the children in her class shrieking and crying. Clapp slashed at her face—three times. Tom Freeman had spotted Clapp earlier running down the school corridor and followed him into the classroom. Tom tackled him to the floor—before Clapp had gotten a fourth slash in.

At the hospital, Sean never left her side. At first, Laura thought Mr. Clapp had blinded her, because one of the cuts was just above her left eyebrow, and her eye had filled with blood. The doctors said it was a miracle no facial nerves or muscles were severed. She had several plastic surgery operations. The scars were hard to miss for the first year. Every time Laura looked at herself in the mirror, she couldn't help thinking of the creep who had done this to her. She felt like a walking billboard of his handiwork. It was as if she would be stuck having Mr. Clapp in her life forever.

Clapp got ten years for assault. But during his fourth year in prison, he died of cancer. Laura never found out what happened to Donald. And she lost track of Joey as well.

Even with Sean's support and several months on a psychiatrist's couch, Laura had a tough time walking into a classroom again. After a while, she managed okay, but couldn't make herself teach full-time. She was reluctant to become too involved or familiar with any of the kids. It felt safer to be a substitute. She could come in, do her job, and leave.

The scars weren't so noticeable now. Sometimes if she didn't get enough sleep or she was extra stressed about something, the mark on her forehead and the two long lines on her left cheek seemed more prominent. But she was almost used to them. In fact, in the last few years, it always surprised her when she caught someone staring. It didn't really bother her much.

She was still a bit wary of strangers. And sometimes, small confrontations made her sick to her stomach—like whenever someone snuck in front of her in line at the supermarket checkout. Standing up for herself, Laura was always worried some stranger would go crazy on her. That was another reason why she hadn't minded moving away from the big city.

She'd recently submitted her résumé to the Leavenworth schools. She didn't anticipate an overwhelming demand for substitute teachers here. But maybe it would get her out of the house once in a while, which would be welcome—especially during this off-season at the winery.

As she washed the breakfast dishes, Laura listened to the news reports on TV. She occasionally peeked over toward the family room to look at the screen.

"I know Scott and his family of angels are all in heaven right now," said the woman in front of a cluster of microphones. Like Laura, the woman was in her early forties. She had straight, flaxen, shoulder-length hair that she wore in pigtails. It was a slightly bizarre "little girl" look she might have pulled off if not for her careworn face and a heavy application of mascara. She wore a white blouse with a sailor collar.

"Sherry Singleton and I were close friends," she went on, her voice quavering. "Sherry was the sweetest, gentlest person—and a loving mother. I'm going to miss her laugh, and I'll miss swapping recipes with her . . ."

Laura got tired of craning her neck to look at the television. With her hands still wet, she finally stepped back from the sink and watched as the woman on TV dissolved into tears. Her name was Marilee Cronin. Standing beside her was her husband, Lawrence, a quiet, slender, fifty-something man with glasses and slicked-back copper-colored hair. He wore a shiny blue suit. He put an arm around his wife to comfort her. The two of them had been all over the news since Saturday. Along with the late Scott Singleton, they were the head ministers of the Church of the True Divine Light.

Marilee seemed to pull herself together for a minute. "The people who are bent on destroying our church are the ones ultimately responsible for this," she declared. "They're as guilty as the deranged lunatic who committed these heinous murders. The haters may have killed Scott and his family, but they'll never destroy what Scott stood for, lived for, and died for . . ."

"Oh, brother," Laura muttered, returning to her dishes.

Marilee had been making a lot of speeches on news shows in the last two days, most of them preachy, politically charged eulogies that made Scott Singleton out to be a martyr. Their church had recently been criticized by certain ex-members who claimed brainwashing and extortion-like tactics were employed to maintain the church membership. Ex-members of the True Divine Light were harassed. Some people who disagreed with Scott Singleton's politics felt the church's tax exemptions with the IRS should be revoked.

Laura had never liked Scott Singleton or what he'd stood for. But she certainly didn't think he and his family deserved to die.

She'd first heard about the murders on the car radio while driving back from the Wenatchee airport Saturday afternoon. She'd just dropped off Sean for the first leg of his trip to Europe. The details on the radio had been a bit sketchy at the time. Singleton, his wife, and their five children had been slain in their Lopez Island summer home late Friday night. The children's ages ranged from eleven to twenty-two.

Despite what Marilee said, there was no initial indication that the brutal murders were politically or religiously motivated. It appeared to be the random, violent act of a madman, who was still out there someplace.

The news had been unnerving for Laura and the kids. Although Lopez Island was more than four hours away—and that included a ferry ride—somehow it didn't seem to matter. The murders might as well have occurred just down the block. Of course, it didn't help that Sean had just left for two weeks, and none of the employees would be around for a while. Laura figured their home by the vineyard was probably even more isolated than the Singletons' Lopez Island house. Liam had slept with his baseball bat at his bedside the last two nights. Sophie admitted she'd barely slept at all. As for Laura, she'd been very tempted to move the gun from the closet to her nightstand drawer. But she was more afraid of the gun than she was of a possible intruder, so the weapon stayed in the closet.

Little by little, details began to emerge about the murders. Apparently, Joseph Mulroney, the caretaker at the Singletons' compound, became a principal suspect. He'd been cooperating with the San Juan County Police—right up until last night, when he'd disappeared.

Laura had heard about it on the radio when she'd woken up this morning. And they were talking about it now on TV. Laura turned off the water at the sink, dried her hands, and moved toward the family room.

"Twenty-nine-year-old Jason Eichhorn, a reporter with *The Seattle Times,* is at Island Hospital in Anacortes this morning—in satisfactory condition," the reporter said into his handheld microphone. The thirtyish, red-haired guy-next-door-type wore a blue rain slicker and stood in front of the Anacortes ferry terminal. An incoming vessel loomed in the background. "Though he has a broken arm and a sprained ankle, along with nineteen stitches in his head, Eichhorn says he feels lucky to be alive after a harrowing two-hour ordeal at the hands of two dangerous fugitives . . ."

Onto the screen came a grainy photo of a bruised, haggard-looking young man in a hospital bed. It looked like some reporter friend of his might have snuck in and taken the shot on the sly with a cheap phone. Eichhorn's arm was in a sling, and a bandage covered the top of his head like a turban. He gave a thumbs-up sign with his good hand. He seemed to put on a brave smile for the camera, but it wasn't very convincing. "I figured for sure I was dead," he said in a shaky voice-over, which was so muffled they put subtitles along the bottom of the still photo.

Laura realized the TV station was rerunning the same report they'd run an hour ago. Apparently, there were no updates on the whereabouts of Joseph Mulroney and his friend. The station showed the men's mug shots again. She found Mulroney oddly cute with a vulnerable, boyish quality. His shaggy-haired, thirtysomething accomplice, Victor Moles, looked arrogant and stupid. There was something about his half-closed eyes that made him seem cold and cruel—and very dangerous.

They explained on television that according to the *Seattle Times* reporter-hostage, Moles had recently changed his appearance. So someone had come up with a composite photo of Moles with a buzz cut and another with the buzz cut and glasses. The slightly altered—almost cartoonish—versions of Moles were so disturbing to look at that Laura felt the hairs stand up on the back of her neck.

She glanced over at the window above the kitchen sink, almost expecting to see that creepy, waxy-looking version of Moles lurking outside her house—those cruel, half-closed eyes staring in at her.

On TV, the news reporter explained how the police had been trying to track down Victor Moles since he'd escaped from the same state-run mental hospital where Mulroney had been confined. Mulroney had been released in March. But his cohort got out five months later by slitting a guard's throat with a piece of broken glass. The guard survived, but an extensive manhunt was ongoing. Authorities had questioned Mulroney about his friend in early August, but Mulroney had claimed to know nothing. Until last night, the police had been following a lead that Moles had fled to Northern California.

"The two suspects drove away in a red 2014 Hyundai Sonata," explained the reporter. "The Washington State license plate number is WJO820 . . ." The number was displayed across the bottom of the screen.

"An employee at a Denny's in Everett believes the two suspects stopped by the twenty-four-hour restaurant late last night," the reporter continued in voice-over as a shot of the restaurant was shown. "Manager Roseann Stella said a man fitting Moles's description entered the establishment at around midnight and ordered two hamburgers to go. She said another man was waiting for him inside a red car, parked in the lot."

Laura nervously wrung the dishtowel in her hands. Everett put the escaped killers about two hours away from the winery. But then they might not have headed east. They could have continued south toward Seattle or Portland.

With a sigh, Laura grabbed the remote from the kitchen counter-bar and switched channels. It was another newscast—and more about the Singleton murders. They had a diagram of the Lopez Island house, showing each room. A silhouetted image marked each spot where a body had been found.

"And this I don't need to see," Laura murmured, quickly changing the channel again. She settled on Turner Classic Movies. They were showing *Raintree County*. In Civil War garb, Montgomery Clift was wooing Eva Marie Saint. Laura had seen the movie before. It was one of those big, lengthy spectacles—perfect to distract her most of the morning while she cleaned up and tried to keep her mind off the Singleton murders.

After a few minutes mesmerized in front of the TV, Laura tore herself away. She moved the bar stools and started sweeping up under the counter-bar. James always left on the floor a considerable sampling of whatever cereal he'd eaten for breakfast. This morning it was Cap'n Crunch—along with a penny, an animal cracker, and several macaroni noodles from yesterday's lunch. Laura was bent over, maneuvering the mess into a dustpan, when the doorbell rang.

Startled, she quickly straightened up. The broom slipped out of her hand and hit the parquet floor. She didn't move for a few seconds. *Relax*, she thought. *It's probably just Patti, on her way back from dropping off the boys*.

The bell rang again—and then again.

She headed into the front hallway. "Alright already," she muttered.

Then the person started banging on the door.

Laura stopped in her tracks. She knew Patti wouldn't do that, unless it was an emergency.

She warily checked the peephole. With the slight distortion from the curved glass, she could see it was a man—with dark hair and wearing an army fatigue jacket. He took a step back on the porch, and Laura recognized him as the vineyard's only ex-employee, Dane Lorenz. He was a short, wiry man with wavy dark brown hair and a goatee. He'd made a good first impression, but after only a month at the job, it was clear everyone loathed him. He was also surly and lazy, and had a drinking problem. Sean had given Dane several warnings before finally firing him two weeks ago.

Laura had no idea what he was doing here now. But she felt a confrontation coming.

He stepped up to the door and pounded on it again. "Hello?" he yelled. He looked like he had no intention of going away.

Laura thought about setting the chain lock and opening the door a crack to find out what he wanted. But she realized that would just tick him off. Besides, those chain locks were never much protection. One good kick could probably break it.

Biting her lip, she reluctantly opened the door.

Dane put a hand up on the doorway frame and gave her a cocky grin. "Well, well, it's the lady of the house . . ."

Laura held onto the doorknob and nodded at him. "Hi, Dane, what can I do for you?"

"Is he in?"

"Yes, but he's on a conference call right now," she lied. "It could be a couple of hours. What is it you wanted? Maybe I can help."

"I didn't get my last paycheck in the mail yet," he said, glaring at her.

"Hmm, they all went out last week. Maybe there was a delay because of the holiday. I'll be sure to—"

"And he should know that I'm filing for unemployment," he interrupted.

"I'll be sure to tell him, Dane," she said, nodding again. "Sean will get back to you later today—or tomorrow at the latest. And next time, you don't have to drive out and make a special trip. You can just email or phone . . ." She took a step back so she could close the door. "Now, if there's nothing else—"

"Hey, don't be so quick to brush me off," he said.

Laura glanced down and saw he had his foot in the doorway.

When Sean had fired the son of a bitch, it had occurred to her that they probably hadn't seen the last of Dane. He seemed like one of those insidious disgruntled ex-employees, one who wasn't past returning to his old workplace with an assault weapon to shoot everyone. She couldn't help wondering if he was hiding something inside his baggy army fatigue jacket right now.

Laura worked up a polite smile. "I'm sorry. I don't mean to rush you out of here, but—"

"Rush me out?" he laughed. "You haven't even invited me in."

"As I started to say . . ." Laura let the polite smile fade. "You caught me at a bad time, Dane. I really need to go. Is there anything else?"

"I left my other jacket in the employee break room. I want to pick it up."

Laura nodded. "Well, now isn't a good time. We'll be sure to send it to you." She started to close the door again.

His hand went up against it. He gave her a sly smile. "He's not really home, is he?"

"What?" she asked—though she'd heard him.

"You're all alone here . . ."

Though her stomach was in knots, she glared at him— her best teacher's glare. "No, my husband is really home,

Dane. He's busy—and so am I. Once again, I'll be sure to tell him you were here. Now, would you please go?"

He defiantly stared back at her and said nothing for a moment. Finally he shook his head. "I'm coming back," he grumbled. Then he turned and stepped off the front porch.

Laura remained in the doorway. She watched him spit on the ground on his way to his old pickup truck. He jumped inside and slammed the door. After starting up the truck, he gunned the engine, peeled around, and then sped down the driveway.

Laura was shaking as she shut the door. She locked it and fixed the chain in place.

She hurried back into the kitchen, snatched her phone off the counter, and speed-dialed Sean. Of course he was in Europe and couldn't do much. But at least he could call Dane, pretend to be home, and tell him to back off.

While the phone rang on the other end, Laura grabbed the TV remote and muted the movie.

Sean didn't pick up. Laura got the generic message that the customer she was trying to reach was unavailable right now. His phone must have been turned off—or maybe he was out of a calling zone.

Laura waited for the beep: "Hi, hon, can you call me when you get a chance?" she asked. She could hear the edginess in her own voice. "It—it's no emergency or anything, but give me a call, okay? Love you." She clicked off.

On her phone, Laura brought up her recent emails and checked the trip itinerary Sean had sent her. It showed he was staying at the Econo Lodge in Paris tonight. She didn't even know they had Econo Lodges in Europe. He had a phone number for the place. Laura did the math. Paris was nine hours ahead, so it was around 6:15 in the evening there. He could be at the hotel. Maybe he was recharging his phone.

She dialed the number for the hotel. The operator answered: *"Grand Hôtel du Palais Royal. Puis-je vous aider?"*

Laura understood just enough French to know *Grand Hôtel du Palais Royal* was a far cry from the Econo Lodge. There must have been some sort of mix-up. *"Uh, avez-vous . . ."* Her French was pretty pathetic. She gave up and hoped the woman understood English. "Could you connect me with Sean Gretchell's room, please?"

"Sean Gretchell," the woman repeated. It sounded nice in her French accent. A few seconds passed. "Mr. and Mrs. Gretchell will be checking in the day after to-morrow. Would you like to leave them a message for when they arrive on Wednesday?"

"Mr. and Mrs.?" Laura repeated, baffled. "Mrs. Gretchell isn't on this trip with him. I should know be-cause I . . ."

But then she fell silent.

"Pardon?" the operator said.

"Are you sure the reservation is for Mr. *and Mrs.* Gretchell?" Laura asked.

"Oui," the woman answered. "Would you like to leave them a message?"

"Ah, no, thank you—*merci,*" she murmured. Then she clicked off.

Laura didn't want to believe it. She went online and googled *Grand Hôtel du Palais Royal.* It was no bargain-basement inn. There was nothing "Econo" about it. Located in the heart of Paris, it looked fancy, romantic, and pricey as hell. She googled *Econo Lodge Paris*, and got nothing. It didn't even exist. Sean had made it up.

She remembered how she'd asked Sean if she could come with him on this trip, and he'd pooh-poohed the idea because the excursion was all business. "Cheap hotels and a tight schedule" was how he'd described the trip.

It didn't make any sense. It was just so unlike Sean to be carrying on with another woman. He was completely devoted to her and the kids. He was a very handsome guy: blue eyes, chiseled features, and athletic. He'd always had women—and men—interested in him, and yet Sean seemed totally oblivious to it. He'd never given Laura cause to worry.

In fact, after "the Incident," her facial scars didn't change the way Sean looked at her and made love to her. He made her feel as if she were still beautiful and desirable. If it hadn't been for him, she never would have survived that whole ordeal. Sean was the reason the scars didn't bother her so much anymore. As far as she knew, he'd never had eyes for anyone else.

Laura figured there had to be some sort of explanation to account for this other *Mrs. Gretchell,* who, starting Wednesday, would be spending three nights with Sean in an expensive hotel in the middle of Paris. Hell, she was probably already with him in some other French wine city.

Laura grabbed the remote again and turned the volume back up on *Raintree County*. There was a Civil War battle going on.

Sitting down on the sofa, Laura pulled up Sean's trip itinerary on her phone once more. He definitely had the date and the hotel name wrong for the Paris leg of his trip. How much of the itinerary was a lie? Was this woman touring all over Europe with him?

Past the noise from the television, she thought she heard someone on the front porch. Had Dane come back?

She put down the phone and got to her feet. Hurrying to the front hallway, she could hear someone rattling the doorknob, trying to get in.

Laura froze. She didn't know what to do.

The person on the other side of the door stopped tugging at the knob. For a moment, nothing happened. Then the brass flap to the mail slot in the door flipped up.

Laura saw a set of eyes peering in at her through the opening. She screamed and ran back toward the family room to grab her phone. But just as she reached the sofa, she saw a second man on the other side of the sliding glass door. He wore baggy cargo pants, a dark Windbreaker, and a knit hat. He glared at her and started tugging at the door handle.

She could clearly see his face—and the dull, cruel eyes. She'd seen that face on TV less than an hour ago. It didn't seem possible.

Panic-stricken, she stood there and watched him struggle with the lock.

Laura grabbed her phone from the sofa. She remembered the gun in the bedroom closet upstairs. She swiveled around and headed toward the front of the house.

In the hallway, she stumbled and dropped the phone. It slid across the floor. She hadn't dialed 9-1-1 yet. Laura left the phone on the floor and raced up the stairs. She and Sean had an old landline on the nightstand in their bedroom.

She staggered up the last couple of steps to the second floor and ran down the hallway to the master bedroom. Shutting the door behind her, she locked it and then snatched the phone off her nightstand. She dialed 9-1-1.

Breathless, she listened.

Nothing.

Laura anxiously tapped on the phone cradle. There was no dial tone. The line was dead. She realized they must have cut the outside phone wire.

Just then, she heard glass shattering downstairs. Someone had broken a window—maybe the window in the kitchen door.

Ducking into the closet, Laura frantically searched through Sean's sweaters on the upper shelf. She got on her tiptoes. The gun was somewhere behind one of the neat stacks. Sweaters toppled down from the shelf. One landed on her face, and she brushed it aside. She was crying by the time she finally found the revolver.

She had no idea how to fire the weapon. Though no expert himself, Sean had tried to teach her how to use it, but she hadn't wanted to even touch the damn thing. Now she wished she'd paid more attention to him.

She heard whispering downstairs. It wasn't the TV.

Desperate, she glanced out the bedroom window,

hoping to find a way to climb outside and escape. She saw a car parked in the driveway, and her heart leapt. For a second, she thought someone had just driven up and might rescue her. But then she realized it was the same car they'd described on TV—the red Hyundai the two killers had stolen.

She heard the rumble of them running up the stairs. The footsteps got louder. One of them tugged at the doorknob. Laura watched it twitch back and forth. They started pounding on the door. She thought they'd break it down.

Fumbling with the gun's safety, Laura fired a warning shot. She winced and saw a little explosion of plaster in the wall by the doorway frame. The feel of the gun going off in her hand scared the hell out of her.

It must have frightened them, too, because the banging suddenly stopped. She heard murmuring.

"I've got a gun!" Laura called out nervously. *Like they don't already know that*, she thought. Laura hated the way she sounded like a terrified little girl. She took a deep breath. "I've called the police!" she warned, more control in her voice this time. "They'll be here any minute now. My purse is downstairs—on the kitchen counter. There's money in it. Take what you want and leave!"

"We have your phone, Laura," one of the men called back to her. His voice was ironically gentle.

They know my name, she thought.

"And we've cut the phone line," he continued. "We know the police aren't coming. It's useless to pretend. Now, open up. We promise we won't hurt you . . ."

"That's not the only cell phone I have!" she yelled,

moving toward the window again. She wondered if they'd believe her lie. "I mean it! The police are on their way! Just leave, okay? I don't want to hurt anyone either. Now, get back . . ."

She remembered the phone in the wine-tasting house. It must have been an overseer's cottage at one time. In the back part of the shop, by the restroom, was a big closet with a black rotary-dial phone on the wall, and it still worked. Laura could see the cottage from her window, and the phone wire was still intact. At least, she was pretty sure it was a phone wire.

She heard one of them whispering again. A floorboard squeaked.

Laura leaned closer to the window. Shortly after moving in, she'd checked possible escape routes from the second and third floors—in case of a fire. But it had always been from a window in one of the kids' bedrooms—never from here. Now she realized she might be able to climb out the window onto the front porch roof and then scuttle down the drainpipe. There were a lot of places on the property where she could hide after calling the police.

Trying not to make any noise, she carefully opened the window. Cold air drifted into the room.

She could still hear them murmuring to each other in the hallway. It sounded like a hushed argument. "I don't give a shit!" one of them finally bellowed.

There was a click, and another click. Then a shot rang out.

Laura spun around in time to see the lock blasted off the bedroom door.

In a panic, she fired the gun again, completely missing both men as they charged into the room. The bigger one—with the cruel eyes—barreled in first.

The younger man grabbed his friend's arm. "No, Vic, please, don't! We don't want to hurt her!"

Her back against the wall, Laura tried to fire the gun again.

But the big man lunged at her and threw her onto the floor. The gun flew out of her hand.

"Don't hurt her!" the younger man cried. "We need her!"

Bent over her, the man had his fist clenched. And yet he hesitated.

For a moment, Laura thought he might not hit her.

"Bitch," he grunted.

She saw his fist whooshing toward her face. There was a loud crack and, with it, an awful pain.

Then Laura saw nothing.

CHAPTER FOUR

Monday—10:17 A.M.

When Laura came to, she was on the floor. The young man hovered over her and gently dabbed a cold washcloth to her lower lip. She noticed blood on the cloth.

She lay there for a moment, afraid to move. She recognized him as the Singletons' caretaker. She remembered his name from the TV news: Joseph Mulroney.

Laura figured she'd been unconscious a few minutes, long enough for the other one to have gone through her and Sean's dresser drawers. He'd made a mess of it, too. Clothes were strewn on the floor. A few drawers had even been completely yanked out of the dressers and emptied.

Her attacker—the older, huskier one, Victor Something—had taken off his jacket and stocking cap. He had pale skin, a buzz cut, and a pug face. With his manic, twitchy manner, he seemed hopped up on something. He rifled through her jewelry drawer.

"Are these real pearls?" he asked, holding up a necklace that had belonged to Sean's late mother.

Stupefied, Laura gazed at him.

The younger man turned toward his friend. "We're not stealing anything," he said. "I told you that three times already."

The man frowned at him and put the necklace back in the drawer.

Joseph Mulroney handed her the damp washcloth. "I'm really sorry about all this," he whispered. "You weren't supposed to get hurt. That's the last thing I wanted."

Laura just stared at him.

"The gun I took away from you," his friend, Victor, said. "Is it the only one in the house?"

Laura figured if he wasn't looking for valuables to steal, then maybe he'd been searching for another gun. "It's the only one," she finally answered.

"You lied earlier about having an extra phone. Why should we believe you now?"

Glaring back at him, Laura sat up and leaned back against the wall. "Because it's the truth, and I know if you found another gun in the house I'd be in real trouble, wouldn't I?"

"Bet your ass, lady."

"Don't talk to her like that," Joseph murmured.

Laura couldn't figure out what was going on with these two. Just minutes ago, she'd thought they were about to kill her. Now, the younger one acted like he really cared about her—and the other one, Victor, probably could have shot her dead right there without giving it a second thought.

He pulled the revolver out from where he had tucked

it in the back of his pants—under his shirttail. "So where are the bullets for this thing?"

"In the closet—on the upper shelf, where the sweaters are," she replied.

He headed for the closet.

"Are you okay?" Joseph whispered, still hovering over her. "Did he hurt you bad?"

"I'll live," Laura said. "I hope."

At that, she heard Victor chuckle, "Yeah, we'll see. Hey, there's a full box of bullets here, some nice sweaters, too." He emerged from the closet and set the box on her dresser. "Now we're cooking with gas. So—how soon before your husband comes home?"

Laura hesitated.

"Look at her," he said. "She's trying to think of the best answer. Should she tell the truth or should she lie? I tell you, I don't fucking trust her . . ."

Joe straightened up and faced him. "She just told you where the bullets were, and she wasn't lying about that. I need her . . ." He pulled Victor toward the doorway and whispered something to him.

"My husband's away on a business trip," Laura spoke up. "He's not coming back for another two weeks. But I'm expecting a call from him soon, and if I don't pick up, he might get worried. Also—you should know, I have a neighbor who'll be bringing home my youngest child from preschool in about three hours. My other two children are coming home at around four o'clock."

Both men turned to stare at her. She had their attention now.

"You're free to take the car. If you tie me up, you'll have a good three-hour start to wherever you're going. You could be in Montana or Oregon by the time anyone got to me. The car is parked in the garage. It even has a full tank of gas. The keys are in my purse downstairs."

"Did you hear that, Vic?" Joe asked.

His friend nodded and hurried out of the bedroom.

Laura listened to him running down the stairs.

Joe turned to her. "We don't want your car," he said. "But we need to take it out of the garage so we can park ours in there. The cops are looking for that car. I know it's not likely, but someone might spot it from the road. We can't take any chances."

Holding the washcloth to her mouth, Laura studied him. She wondered why he was telling her all this. It sounded as if he and his friend planned to stay for a while. It was too frightening to imagine what they might want. The thought of them being anywhere near her children made her physically ill.

She heard the front door slam. Then there was the sound of a car starting up.

Joe reached down toward her, and she automatically recoiled.

"I was just trying to help you up," he said. "You don't have to be afraid of me."

"I'm fine here—for now," she said.

Joe sighed. "You don't recognize me, do you?"

"Yes, I recognize both of you," she said steadily. "I saw both you and your friend on the news. I know the police are looking for you. Listen, I—I'm willing to go to my bank and withdraw money to help you get away . . ."

Standing over her, Joe frowned. He didn't seem convinced.

Laura wondered what she'd have to say to persuade them to leave before the kids came home. "You—you can take me with you," she said in a shaky voice. "I'd be a help to you . . ."

She figured even if they ended up killing her and dumping her body somewhere, at least her children would be safe.

"You're going to help us," he said, "but not like that."

"What do you mean?" she asked warily.

"I'll explain later," he answered. "Right now, my friend and I are pretty hungry . . ."

She stared at him.

"We've been driving around for hours," he went on. "Since last night, we've been getting by on some old peanuts and snack chips Vic had in his backpack. We could really use a decent breakfast."

"You want me to—fix you breakfast?" she asked.

"Would you mind?" He held out his hand to her again.

But Laura didn't take it. She gazed at him for another moment and then stood up on her own.

Joe's friend, Vic, came swaggering in by the kitchen door with his backpack.

For Laura, it was just one more ominous indication that the two men intended to stay a while. She stood at the counter with a pair of scissors, cutting open a new package of bacon for their breakfast.

Before she knew what was happening, Vic threw aside the backpack and charged toward her. "Goddamn it!" he bellowed, grabbing her wrists and shaking the scissors out of her hand. They fell to the floor, one blade just missing her foot. He pushed her aside and turned to his partner. "What the hell is wrong with you, letting her handle scissors? You don't even have your gun out! You're barely watching her! Use your head, stupid!"

Stunned, Laura caught her breath and backed against the counter. She watched him stomp over toward the sink, open the lower cabinet door, and yank out the plastic garbage pail. Refuse spilled onto the floor as he tugged the nearly full trash bag out of the container. He tossed it aside, scattering more debris onto the floor. Without a word, Vic quickly collected the cutlery from the butcher-block knife holder on the counter. He pitched the knives into the pail. Laura winced at the sound of them clinking and clanking inside the receptacle.

But Vic didn't stop there. He went through the drawers—pulling some of them all the way out and dumping them onto the floor with a loud crash. He hurled more knives and utensils into the garbage receptacle—the pizza cutter, a potato peeler, cheese knives, serving forks, anything with a sharp edge or sharp end. By the time he was done, Vic seemed out of breath. He hauled the pail toward the kitchen door. "Watch her!" he barked to his friend, and then he headed outside.

Laura turned and glanced out the window over the

sink. She saw Vic lug the pail to the garage's side door. He opened it and ducked inside.

Turning again, she gazed down at the horrible mess he'd left on her kitchen floor.

"I'm really sorry," Joe whispered.

She numbly gazed at him. Was he actually apologizing for his friend trashing her kitchen? Right now, that was the least of her worries. Yet Joe seemed sincere.

At the same time, he still had the gun in his hand, and it was pointed at her.

Laura started picking up things from the floor, shaking off the coffee grounds and crumbs, and then setting them on the counter. Garbage was strewn all over the place. The utensils would need to be cleaned in the dishwasher or scrubbed in the sink.

Joe was supposed to be guarding her, but he'd become distracted by a young Elizabeth Taylor in *Raintree County*. With the gun still in his hand, he stood in the middle of the family room staring at the TV.

But he snapped to attention when Vic came through the kitchen door again.

"What are you watching that for?" Vic barked. "Turn to the news, CNN or whatever."

At the sink, Laura glanced over her shoulder at Joe. He grabbed the TV remote and started surfing through the channels.

Vic strutted into the kitchen. "Where the hell's our breakfast?"

"You want me to cook for you with utensils that

have been on the floor—along with about two days' worth of garbage?" She rinsed off the spatula.

"So what's stopping you from making the coffee?"

Laura dried her hands and pulled the package of ground Starbucks beans out of the cupboard.

"What's this?" Vic asked. From the counter he'd picked up a six-inch, yellow plastic cylinder with an orange cap.

"It's an EpiPen," Laura replied, moving to the Mr. Coffee machine on the counter. Four of the EpiPens had spilled from a drawer that Vic had yanked out of the cabinet. "It's medicine for my older son," she explained. "He has allergies. Could you please put that down?"

But Vic was reading the directions on the side of the tube. "What's he allergic to?"

"Nuts—and peanut oil," she said. "We have to be very careful about what he eats." Laura didn't want to tell him any more. Why let him know about her family's vulnerabilities? He seemed fascinated by the syringe.

She got the coffee started. "If you want bacon with your breakfast, you'll have to go back to the garage and get a knife or scissors to open the package."

He finally put down the EpiPen and pulled something from his pants pocket. Laura didn't quite get a look at it, but then, Vic flicked his wrist and a knife blade sprung out of the handle.

Laura saw the switchblade and gasped. She immediately thought of Mr. Clapp.

Dazed, she watched Vic, in one quick motion, slit open the package of bacon with his switchblade. He pushed the blade back into its handle, and then tucked the weapon into his pocket again.

Kicking aside garbage and several items on the floor, he made his way to the refrigerator. "Hey, kiddo, how do you like your eggs?" he called to his friend.

"We're having eggs?" Joe asked. He'd put his gun away and now sat on the sofa with the remote in his hand. "Could I have them scrambled, please? But not too runny, okay? I don't like them runny. Thank you!"

He sounded like a kid, giving his friend's mom a breakfast order after spending the night at their house.

Vic handed her the carton of eggs. "You heard him. And I want mine fried."

Laura wordlessly took the carton of eggs from him and set it on the counter. She went back to frying up the bacon. The smell of the sizzling meat began to fill the kitchen.

Vic pulled a carton of orange juice from the refrigerator and guzzled from it. He raised the carton and called to his friend, "Hey, how about some OJ?"

"No, thanks! Hey, you don't happen to have Hawaiian Punch, do you?"

Vic laughed. He started rummaging through the bread box on the counter.

Laura couldn't believe he was serious. She sighed. "The closest thing I have to fruit punch is grape juice."

"That sounds good. I'll have a grape juice, please."

"Hey, think fast!" Vic said, tossing a muffin toward his friend in the family room. Joe missed it, and the muffin hit a heavy lamp on the end table—almost knocking it over. Crumbs exploded and rained down onto the rug.

Joe scooped what was left of the muffin off the floor. "I got it!" he announced. "It's okay, five-second rule . . ." He started to eat the half-muffin.

It was all Laura could do to keep from taking the hot frying pan and slamming Vic in the face with it. Instead, she poured a glass of grape juice and took it to Joe. He thanked her. She got down on her knees and started collecting the muffin crumbs.

"Oh, I'm sorry," Joe said. "Let me help you—"

"Never mind," she muttered, frowning. "I've got it."

With his mouth full, the glass of juice in one hand and the muffin in the other, Joe gazed at her sheepishly.

Laura went back to fixing their breakfast. She set out a Starbucks mug for Vic's coffee, because she'd be damned if she let him drink out of the *World's Best Mom* mug Liam had given her—or any of the other mugs that had sentimental value for her or her family.

Coffee in hand, Vic wandered back toward the family room. Apparently, there was nothing on the national news about them at the moment. So Vic kept busy looking through the bookcases and cabinets. He was probably searching for more sharp objects—or maybe something of value. Every time he took a DVD or a CD from the bookshelf to look at it, he'd just let it drop on the floor and move on to the next one.

While Vic was distracted in the family room, Laura slipped the EpiPens back inside a drawer. She figured: *out of sight, out of mind.* Each pen had a needle beneath the orange cap, and she didn't want Vic confiscating them. If Liam had an attack, he could die without an EpiPen handy.

The pens couldn't really be used as a weapon. The needle might stun Vic—and the medication might make him sick. But she couldn't hope to disable or cripple him with an EpiPen. She was better off bashing him in the face with the frying pan.

She wondered, if she were somehow able to put Vic out of commission, could Joe be persuaded to give up? She couldn't be sure. Vic appeared to be calling all the shots, and Joe seemed so gentle and harmless. But obviously, he had some issues. He kept apologizing to her, but at the same time, he kept letting his friend terrorize and torment her. It was as if he thought by saying "I'm sorry" it would make everything all right—no matter how horrible. She imagined Joe apologizing to Mrs. Singleton just moments before his friend stabbed her to death.

While she cooked their bacon and eggs, Laura wished she had something she could slip into their food or drinks to knock them out. Sean had a prescription for sleeping pills, but he'd taken the pills with him to Europe.

She didn't want to think about Sean in Europe right now. Why did he need sleeping pills when he had his girlfriend with him? How was he going to feel when he got the call in Paris that she was dead?

She glanced over at the digital clock on the microwave: 10:46. Would these two still be here when Patti brought James back from preschool at 2:30?

The volume went up on the TV. "Investigators have obtained this surveillance video from a North Seattle 7-Eleven," the news anchor was saying. "It shows a man police believe is the Singleton murder suspect,

Victor Moles, confronting a clerk as he walks out of the store without paying for a twelve-pack of beer . . ."

Laura stepped back from the stove to look at the TV—and the grainy footage of two men just inside the doorway to the 7-Eleven. The scruffy, blond-haired man with a case of beer under his arm certainly looked like Vic. The skinny, young clerk with a dark complexion came around the counter to stop him, and Vic shoved him. The clerk backed off, and Vic kicked over a display sign before stomping out of the store.

Laura glanced over at Vic, who had the remote in his hand. He was grinning at the TV.

Joe had fallen asleep on the sofa.

"The clerk contacted the Seattle Police immediately after the altercation," the newscaster explained in voice-over while they once again showed Vic shoving the man, this time in slow motion. "The incident occurred at one-forty-two on Saturday morning. Investigators are concerned because, if the man in this video is indeed Victor Moles, that puts one of the two fugitives nearly a hundred miles away from Lopez Island when the Singleton family was slain."

On TV, they showed a mug shot of Vic—and another one of Joe. "Moles—along with Joseph Mulroney, the caretaker at the Singletons' vacation home—has been positively identified by *Seattle Times* reporter Jason Eichhorn, who was abducted late last night—"

"So where's my breakfast?" Vic asked her. He turned down the volume.

Laura returned to the stove and fixed his plate.

"Keep Sleeping Beauty's grub warm," he said, moseying up to the counter-bar and sitting on one of the bar stools. "And get me some more coffee."

While she poured the coffee with a slightly shaky hand, Laura considered throwing it in his face—then maybe bashing him over the head with the glass pot. The coffee was hot, but not exactly scalding.

She knew she'd only end up getting herself killed. Then again, wasn't that going to happen anyway? She couldn't be sure.

Vic took a pill out of his shirt pocket. He popped it in his mouth and then slurped some coffee to wash it down. Laura figured it was an upper, which would explain his twitchy, edgy manner. When she set the plate of food in front of him, he ate like a pig. He spilled some runny egg yolk on the counter, then mopped it up with his toast and inhaled it.

She turned away and busied herself at the counter, covering Joe's plate with some aluminum foil. On the news, they were rehashing the details about the fugitives' escape from Lopez Island. She wondered if the man in the 7-Eleven surveillance video had really been Vic.

Moving over to the sink, Laura started washing the utensils that had been on the floor. Steam rose up and started to fog the window in front of her.

While she washed a soup ladle, Laura saw something outside and gasped.

Immediately, she glanced over her shoulder to make sure Vic hadn't heard her—or noticed what she'd just seen. He was still stuffing his face and looking at the TV. With the water running in the sink and the TV on, he obviously hadn't heard her—or the pickup truck that had just pulled up to the garage.

True to his word, Dane was back.

She could see him through the window, just above where the steam fogged the glass. He'd climbed out of his pickup. Still wearing the army camouflage fatigue jacket, he poked around the side entrance to the garage. She and Sean had transformed the studio apartment over the garage into a break room for the workers in the vineyard. It had a bathroom, kitchenette, a big closet, a table and chairs, and even a cot if someone wasn't feeling well. Dane had claimed earlier this morning that he'd left his jacket in there. Was that really what he was after?

Laura peered over her shoulder at Vic again. From where he sat, he probably couldn't see out the window—or at least, he couldn't see they had a visitor.

Outside, Dane looked in the general direction of the house, but he didn't seem to notice her. He ducked inside the garage. The doorway into the garage was just to the right of the stairs up to the break room. She wondered if Dane was right now noticing the red Hyundai Sonata they'd been talking about on the news all morning. Or maybe he'd gone directly upstairs to look for his jacket. She couldn't remember whether or not they'd locked the break room door at the top of the steps. She imagined Dane coming back down and knocking on the kitchen door to demand the key.

Laura peeked back at Vic again, and then she started to write in the steam on the window. With her finger, she spelled out the words deliberately and carefully, because she was writing backwards: DANE – CALL 911.

"Hey," Vic grunted.

She swiveled around and tried to block his view of the window.

"You should've cooked more bacon," he said. He nodded toward the other plate on the counter. "Give me some of his."

Laura fetched Joe's plate, pulled back the foil, and set it in front of Vic. "Help yourself," she muttered. Then she moved back toward the window. Her message had faded a bit as more steam rose up from the sink. She prayed Dane would see it.

He came out the garage's side door with a jacket over his arm—and a boom box in his grasp. Sean had left it in the break room so the employees could listen to the radio in there. It wasn't worth much, but Dane was stealing it anyway, the son of a bitch.

He looked toward the house as he closed the garage's side door. He seemed to catch sight of her in the window.

He suddenly froze.

Laura stared back at him and gave a little nod. Could he read the message on the window? She wondered if he'd do anything. He was trespassing and stealing from them, and here she was—hoping he'd call the police for her. Of all the people who might have been able to help her, it had to be this creep who showed up.

"Shit!" Vic bellowed.

With one stroke, Laura quickly wiped the message off the window. Then she turned around.

Vic was standing now. He must have caught sight of Dane outside. Enraged, he grabbed his plate and hurled it at her. The plate missed her and smashed against the cupboard. Food and shards of pottery ricocheted off the cupboard door and scattered all over the floor.

Laura recoiled against the counter.

On the sofa, Joe woke up with a start.

"Who the fuck is that?" Vic snapped, pointing toward the window.

"It—it's just one of the workers from the vineyard," Laura explained. "He said he might come by to get his coat. I forgot—"

"He's seen the car," Vic said. "And you, you just stood there at the window, watching him, not a peep out of you. I'll bet you thought you had a good thing going." He took the switchblade out of his pocket again. "Well, watch this . . ."

He headed out the kitchen door.

"No!" Laura screamed. She turned to Joe, who sat up on the sofa and scratched his head. "Please," she gasped, "you have to stop him . . ."

But Joe seemed too out of it to do anything. He just squinted at her.

Laura ran to the kitchen door in time to see Vic approaching Dane.

He had the unopened switchblade hidden behind his back. "Hey, you, what do you think you're doing?"

"Take it easy, pal," Dane said, waving him away. He didn't seem at all intimidated. "I'm just picking up some things that belong to me. So back off . . ."

Vic kept coming at him.

Dane sneered at him and shook his head. "Oh, we got a tough guy, huh? Listen, douche bag, I don't—"

He didn't get a chance to finish.

Vic sucker-punched him, a sudden powerful, straight-on slam to his nose.

At the kitchen door, Laura winced.

Blood streamed from Dane's nostrils, dripping down his chin and onto the front of his jacket. He looked stunned. The coat and the boom box fell to the ground.

Vic hit him again, another forceful blow against the side of his head. It knocked Dane off balance.

"Stop it!" Laura shrieked. She turned and yelled into the house, "Joe, for God's sake, do something! He's going to kill him . . ."

By the time Joe came up behind her to see what was happening, his friend had gone berserk. He started pummeling Dane. He held him up by the front of his fatigue jacket and repeatedly punched him in the face. When Vic finally released him, Dane crumpled to the ground. Just moments before, he'd been so tough, so arrogant. But now he was curled up on the driveway crying and whimpering. Gravel and dirt flew into the air as Vic kicked him again and again.

Laura kept screaming for him to stop. Joe hurried past her and ran outside.

But Vic pushed him away. Joe stumbled back and fell down on his backside. "C'mon, Vic, please . . ."

With a flick of the wrist, Vic opened the switchblade. Then he grabbed Dane by his hair and snapped his head back.

His face covered with blood and tears, Dane looked dazed, utterly helpless.

"No, wait! Don't!" Laura yelled.

Horrified, she watched Vic slit Dane's throat.

From Dane's neck, a geyser of blood spurted across the driveway.

A hand over her mouth, Laura turned back into the house. She didn't know where she was going. She just needed to get away. She stumbled in the family room—over something Vic had dropped on the floor. All at once, she toppled over. She landed on the floor and tried to get a breath.

She must have been in shock, because the next thing she knew, Joe was hovering over her.

"This wasn't supposed to happen!" he whispered. "It's just—with Vic, you can't get him mad. He's like a crazy man. I couldn't have stopped him. No one could have. Are you okay? I'm so sorry, I really am . . ."

Laura numbly stared at him.

Once again, Joe was apologizing to her—as if it were just one more little thing that couldn't be helped.

CHAPTER FIVE

Monday—11:20 A.M.

"Forty-two bucks and some change," Vic grunted, pocketing some bills. Then he slapped Dane's wallet and keys on the kitchen counter. His face and clothes were splattered with blood. "It was hardly worth getting my knife wet."

He lumbered over to the kitchen sink, turned on the water, and slurped from the faucet.

Laura was still sitting on the floor—with Joe standing over her. She was trembling. On the window just above Vic's head, she could see the faint remnants of her message: DANE – CALL 911. But Vic hadn't noticed it yet.

He rinsed off his switchblade and dried it with a paper towel. "Well, maybe we can use the son of a bitch's credit cards for a day or two. That piece-of-shit pickup of his doesn't look like it would even get us as far as Spokane. I noticed a spot behind the garage. I'll park it there." Vic nodded at her. "Do you know if he told anyone he was coming here?"

Laura shook her head. She felt sick to her stomach.

"You better pray he didn't," Vic said. "Meanwhile, get off your ass. You're gonna help me bury him in the vineyard."

Her eyes widening, she shook her head at him again.

"No, Vic, please," Joe interceded. "Don't make her. If you—if you could cover him up and drag his body out to the vineyard, I'll bury him tonight. Okay? Just get him out of sight for now. Can't you see she's sick? Don't make her do it. We've put her through enough already. And we're going to need her help, Vic. That's why we're here, remember? Please . . ."

Vic sighed and then frowned at her. "You got some tarp—and rope?"

Laura nodded. "In the shed on the other side of the garage."

"What size is your husband?"

She stared back at him. She didn't understand the question.

"His jacket size," Vic said. "Small, medium, large, or what?"

"Large," she answered.

He turned and headed down the hallway toward the front of the house. After a few moments, Laura heard hangers rattling. Then Vic returned to pass through the kitchen. He was wearing Sean's fall-weight, tan bomber jacket. Vic had taken it from the front hall closet. "It's cold as a witch's tit out there," he muttered, heading out the door.

Laura cringed at the sight of him in her husband's jacket. Though still shaky, she managed to get to her feet and make her way toward the kitchen. On the green marble counter, she saw Dane's empty wallet and his keys—with a rabbit's foot on the key ring. Blood smeared the countertop—and part of the rabbit's foot.

Unsteadily, Laura moved to the sink. "My head," she murmured. "I need an aspirin. I thought I noticed the bottle on the floor. Do you see it, Joe?"

"Um, no, at least not yet," he replied, standing behind her.

Laura figured he was looking down. She took the sponge and wiped away what was left of her 911 message on the window.

But then she saw Vic dragging Dane's limp corpse toward the vineyard, leaving behind a large puddle of blood. Steam drifted from the slash across Dane's throat. Laura felt her stomach turn.

Suddenly, she lurched forward and threw up in the sink.

She braced a hand on the countertop and turned on the cold water to rinse the wretched mess down the disposal. Her throat burned. She thought she was going to vomit again, but it passed. She kept her eyes closed so she wouldn't catch another glimpse of what Vic was doing outside. After a moment, she sipped from the faucet, turned off the water, and stepped away from the sink. She shuddered.

Joe grimaced at her. "Maybe you should get yourself cleaned up and lay down a while, huh?"

Laura realized some vomit had caught in her hair and spilled down the front of her sweater.

He reached out to her. "C'mon, Mrs. Gretchell, let me help you upstairs . . ."

Laura didn't pull away this time. Joe walked her up the stairs and into her bedroom. Amid all the clothes

Vic had dumped from her dresser drawers, she found a clean dark blue pullover on the floor.

"I'm really sorry for the mess in here," Joe said, standing in the bedroom doorway. "Vic gets kind of carried away . . ."

She let out a sad, dazed laugh. "That's the understatement of the year. And there you go, apologizing for him again."

"What do you mean?" he asked.

"I mean, we just watched him kill an unarmed, defenseless, beaten man," Laura said. She had a hand on her throat. "And to you, well, that's just your old pal Vic getting carried away again. How many people have you seen him kill?"

"That man's the first," Joe said. "Was he a friend of yours? I'm sorry—"

"Why do you keep apologizing for him?" Laura yelled.

Joe didn't answer.

She picked up one of the drawers Vic had left on the floor and tried to slide it back into the dresser. But her hands were shaking too much, and she gave up. "Maybe you should get in touch with the Singletons' next of kin," she muttered, setting the drawer on her bed. "Then you can apologize to them, too. You can tell them how sorry you are for what your friend did to that entire family . . ."

Joe shook his head. "Vic didn't kill the Singletons. He wasn't even on Lopez. He was in Seattle when it happened."

Laura stared at him. Maybe that man in the convenience store surveillance video really was Vic. "So are you saying *you* killed them?" she asked.

"No! I was asleep!" Joe yelled. "I don't know why I didn't wake up, but I swear, I didn't hear anything!" He slammed his fist against the doorway frame. Tears welled in his eyes. "God, why doesn't anybody believe me?"

He leaned against the wall, covered his face, and sobbed for a few moments. "Seeing all that blood just a few minutes ago, it—it took me back to Saturday morning, waking up and finding them dead in that house, the whole family, all the blood . . ."

A part of Laura wanted to reach out and comfort him. But she couldn't. "If you're innocent and Vic's innocent, why did you run away?"

Joe wiped his nose with his sleeve. "Vic said the police and everybody else had already made up their minds that I killed the Singletons. The cops, they put me up at a hotel on San Juan Island, and I was trying to do as much as I could to help them, answering their questions and all. I didn't ask Vic to come. He just showed up. He said I had to get out of there and go on the lam. He said it was my only chance of avoiding the electric chair."

"They don't have the death penalty in Washington State," Laura said.

Joe seemed stumped for a moment, and then he just shrugged.

"Earlier, when you were talking to Vic, you mentioned that you two came here because you needed my help. What did you mean?"

He glanced down at the carpet. "I can't say right now."

"But you didn't just come here randomly," she pressed. "You chose this house—or you chose me—for some reason. You knew who I was before you even came here. Am I right?"

Joe nodded. "I saw an article in the newspaper a few months ago about you and your husband buying this winery. I figured it—well, I figured this would be a good place to hide for a while, since it seemed kind of remote and all. I figured you might help us . . ."

"How? I mean, exactly what do you want me to do?"

He looked at her and winced. "You know, you still have throw-up in your hair."

Laura frowned at him and then retreated into the bathroom.

"Keep the door open a crack, will you?" she heard Joe ask. "I promise I won't look in or anything. It's just that Vic will go through the roof if I let you lock yourself in there."

Laura left the door ajar. She caught her reflection in the medicine-chest mirror. In addition to having vomit on her hair and down the front of her, she was a sickly ashen color. Her lip was slightly swollen from Vic slugging her a couple of hours ago. She smelled awful, too. She draped the clean pullover on the shower curtain rod, and then carefully took off her sweater. Leaning over the sink, she ran some soap and hot water through the strands of hair that had been splattered. "So—you're not going to say how you want me to help you," she called. "Am I supposed to guess?"

"Vic thought I shouldn't ask you to do anything for us—not until the kids come home."

Laura stopped rinsing off her hair.

She realized they were going to use her children as pawns. They planned to make the kids hostages in order to get her cooperation for something. For the last couple of hours, she'd been hoping to persuade the two of them to leave before her kids came home. And all the while, they'd just been biding their time, waiting for the first child to come through the front door.

Laura shut off the water. The handle squeaked. In her bra and jeans, she backed away from the sink and sat down on the side of the tub. Water from her wet hair dripped down her shoulder, arm, and stomach. She started to cry.

"You okay in there?" Joe called.

She reached over and pulled a tissue from the dispenser on top of the toilet tank. She blew her nose, and then took a deep breath. "So you're going to hurt my children if I don't cooperate with you, is that it?"

There was silence for a moment. "Vic promised me no one will get hurt."

"Do you still believe that—after what just happened?"

Once again, there was a long pause. "He's trying to help me."

"For God's sake, what is wrong with you?" Laura asked, getting to her feet. She glanced toward the opening in the doorway, and then started to wash the soiled sweater in the sink. "If you're truly innocent, Joe, don't you see how you're only getting yourself deeper and deeper into trouble thanks to Vic? Before he sprung you from that hotel on San Juan Island, you were just a 'person of interest.' That's what they were calling you on the news. But now you're the prime suspect and a fugitive . . ."

She glanced over toward the doorway again. She could see his shadow moving around in the next room. It looked like he might be picking up some of the strewn clothes. Laura hoped she was getting through to him.

"Vic beat up that man and stole his car, didn't he?" she asked, but she didn't wait for an answer. "You didn't lay a finger on that reporter, I'll bet. But because of Vic, you're an accessory to a robbery and maybe even kidnapping and assault. And now he just murdered a man . . ."

"Did you know him?" Joe asked once again—from the bedroom. "Was he a friend of yours?"

"He worked for my husband, but he wasn't really a friend." Laura stood over the sink and let the sweater soak. "But that's not the point, Joe. The point is that Vic has made things a hell of a lot worse for you. It wasn't your idea to run from the police and steal a car, was it?"

"No," she heard Joe murmur.

"So why are you letting him ruin any chance you have of clearing your name?"

"You don't understand. Vic's my only friend. He's always looked out for me, ever since we first got to know each other in this—this *hospital*. See, I was there because I'd messed up a guy, and then I tried to hurt myself. This hospital, it had a lot of disturbed, violent criminals locked up there . . ."

Disturbed, violent criminals like Vic? Laura wanted

to ask. She knew Joe was talking about the psychiatric facility they'd mentioned on the news. But she hadn't heard anything on the broadcasts about *why* Joe and Vic had been locked up in the institution.

"What do you mean you 'messed up' a guy?" Laura asked, glancing at the crack in the doorway. "Are you saying you beat him up?"

"Yeah, really bad," Joe admitted. "I put him in the hospital. It's a long story. The short version is that his name was Larry, and he was a coworker at this packing and shipping job I had. It was a really nice job, too. I mean I got to pack stuff to send to people—you know, presents and all that? Anyway, Larry, he'd been razzing me for weeks and weeks, and I finally lost it. I went kind of nuts, and started hitting him. Afterward, when I realized what I'd done, I put both my fists through a window and cut them up pretty bad."

"What did Vic do that landed him in this—place?" she asked.

"According to Vic, he threw something through a huge picture window at some big shot's house."

Laura hung the damp sweater on the shower curtain rod and then dried her hands. Vic's story sounded like a lie. It didn't make sense that they'd put him in a state-run psychiatric facility for merely smashing a window. She put on the clean pullover. "It's kind of strange that you both ended up in that place for breaking windows," she said. "Are you sure that's all he did?"

"Well, Vic said it was kind of a conspiracy, because he and this rich guy's daughter had a thing going on, and the guy had it out for him. Anyway, in the country club—that's what we called the hospital, 'the country club'—Vic looked out for me. A lot of guys there would have made my life miserable if it weren't for Vic. He was like my protector. After I was released, I wrote to him and we kept in touch. A few months later, Mrs. Singleton hired me to look after their Lopez Island house while no one was there—y'know, kind of a house-sitter for the off-season. Anyway, while I was there alone, Vic suddenly showed up. Turned out he escaped from the country club."

"They mentioned that on the news," Laura said. "They said he almost killed a guard. He slashed the man's throat with a piece of glass . . ."

"That guard was a real bastard," Joe pointed out. "I'll bet they didn't mention that on the news. Anyway, Vic said he was worried about me being on the outside and on my own and all. So he kept coming around to the island house. Vic even got me to stop taking the medication the doctors at the hospital prescribed. He said I didn't need any prescriptions as long as the two of us stuck together . . ."

Laura sat down on the edge of the tub again. She had a ponytail barrette in her hand from the medicine chest. "I think your doctors know better than Vic about what you need," she said.

"That's where you're wrong," Joe argued. She could hear him shuffling around in the bedroom. "As Vic pointed out, where was my old doctor when the police had me locked in that hotel room? Vic's the one who came to help me. He didn't have to get involved. He could have gone anywhere and just disappeared, but he took a real chance and got himself into a lot of trouble coming to rescue me."

"Rescue you?" Laura repeated. With the barrette, she clipped her hair back. "Is that what Vic told you? Joe, you're in a hell of a lot of trouble thanks to him. You'd have been better off if you'd stayed in that hotel room. It sounds to me like Vic needs you a lot more than you need him. He was a fugitive alone, but now he's forced you to go on the run with him. He hasn't helped you, he's hurt you. And I'm worried he's"—her voice started to crack—"I'm worried he's going to hurt my children. Joe, I'm begging you." She got to her feet and glanced over at the door. "You need to stop him. I promise I'll help you. You just need to . . ."

She choked on the next word.

In the crack of the doorway, between the hinges, she saw an eye peering in at her. It was Vic, she could tell.

Laura pulled the door open. Vic didn't move from the doorway. He glared at her.

Joe was sitting at the end of the bed with his head down in defeat.

Laura didn't know when Vic had come in. But he'd obviously heard enough.

She stared back at him defiantly. "You know every word I've said is absolutely true," she whispered.

His response was sudden.

Laura didn't even have time to recoil.

Vic hit her in the face so hard that he knocked her unconscious.

CHAPTER SIX

Laura woke up with a horrible headache and a sore jaw. She was in the bathtub. There wasn't any water in it—except for what dripped down from her wet sweater hanging on the shower curtain rod above her. She was clothed. Her hands, feet, and legs had been bound with some of Sean's neckties. One of Sean's belts pinched her arms to her sides so that she couldn't reach forward and untie her feet.

In her lap was a frozen bag of peas. It took her a moment to figure out that Joe must have held it to her chin for a while to keep the swelling down.

She could hear the TV blaring downstairs—some show with a lot of yelling and screaming. There must have been something wrong with the TV reception, because the sound kept cutting in and out.

Moving her shoulders back and forth, Laura tried to loosen the belt's grip on her arms. She tugged at the wrist restraints and wiggled her feet to loosen the ties around her ankles. The bag of peas slid off her lap and became wedged between her hip and the side of the tub. With every movement, her head ached even more. The noise from the TV downstairs wasn't helping either. People were chanting, *"Jer-ry,* Jer-*ry,* Jer-*ry . . ."*

She finally realized one of the men downstairs was watching *The Jerry Springer Show.* The sound going in and out was obviously the participants' profanities getting bleeped out. Next to watching the evangelical channel, this was Laura's idea of torture-by-TV—especially with the volume cranked up so high.

Not being a Springer fan, she had no idea what time his show aired, which was unfortunate. She wanted to know how long she'd been unconscious, and she was worried about what would happen when Patti dropped off James at 2:30.

Laura kept struggling with the tie-restraints. She figured if her head didn't explode by the time she freed herself, maybe she could escape out the bedroom window. They certainly wouldn't hear her past all that shouting on TV.

She tugged and pulled at the ties around her wrists until her skin burned. Some of the ties were among Sean's favorites. Well, too bad. He could cry on his girlfriend's shoulder about it. Laura still didn't want to think that was true about this other *Mrs. Gretchell.* She wondered if Sean had tried to call her back yet. She was pretty sure Vic had switched off her phone when he'd confiscated it. If Sean couldn't get through, he might call someone and have them come check on her. She'd told him it was "no emergency or anything," but she'd been pretty adamant that he call her back.

All her struggling with the restraints wasn't in vain. The ties around her wrists finally loosened and she

managed to free one hand. But her arms were still con-
strained. She awkwardly pulled at the belt until she
could reach for the buckle. She finally grabbed it, took
a deep breath, and then unfastened it. The belt slid
down and the buckle clinked against the inside of the
tub. At last, she could move her arms. She bent forward to untie the restraints around her ankles.

All at once, the TV went silent.

Laura froze. She heard someone running up the
stairs.

She frantically pulled at the ties around her ankles.

The footsteps in the second-floor hallway got closer.

Joe rushed into the bathroom. Vic was behind him.

"An SUV is coming up the driveway!" Joe said, out
of breath. He stooped down and started tugging at the
ties around her ankles.

"Is it two-thirty?" Laura asked anxiously.

"A quarter to three," Vic said.

"Oh, God, it's my neighbor, Patti, with my son," she
said. She kept thinking about what had happened to the
last person who had come near the house.

Joe struggled to unfasten the ties. Some of the knots
had only gotten tighter from all her wiggling. Neither
one of the men seemed to notice that she'd nearly lib-
erated herself from the makeshift restraints.

Laura looked up at Vic. "Please, don't hurt anyone.
I'll make up some excuse to my neighbor so that she'll
take James for the rest of the afternoon. I'll send them
away. There's no reason to bring my child into this.
He's just a toddler. Please . . ."

Vic smirked. Reaching into his pocket, he pulled out
the switchblade and flicked it open.

Laura automatically shrunk back.

"I think I'd like to meet your kid." He pushed Joe aside and, in one motion, he cut the ties around Laura's ankles. He turned and pointed the knife at her. "This neighbor of yours, you've got sixty seconds to get rid of her, or I will. Now, hurry up . . ."

Joe helped her out of the tub. Laura's head throbbed as she stood up. She felt nauseous and wobbly on her feet, but she managed to make her way through the bedroom to the hallway. Vic started down the stairs in front of her. "C'mon, move it," he hissed.

It wasn't Vic's command that made her pick up the pace, but rather the sound of the SUV's door opening and shutting. Joe hovered behind her. She rushed to the front door.

But as she reached for the doorknob, Vic grabbed her arm. "Don't try anything cute," he whispered. "We're listening. And remember, the kid stays. Leave the door open a bit, so we can hear you . . ."

He stationed himself on one side of the door. He still had the switchblade in his hand.

Laura opened the door and stepped outside. She still felt a little woozy. But the cold air was bracing. With an unsteady hand, she half-closed the door behind her.

She wanted to scream at Patti to drive away as fast as she could. But her neighbor had already switched off the engine, climbed outside, and come around the front of the SUV. She was in her mid-thirties and pretty, with dimples and wavy, shoulder-length red hair. She opened the back door to help James out of his toddler seat. She glanced over her shoulder at Laura. "I decided to treat the boys to Mickey-Dee's, and I was so worried about them spilling in the car . . ."

She handed James a McDonald's bag, and he ran toward Laura.

She stepped down from the porch to meet him. She took the bag from James and then grabbed his hand.

Patti murmured something to her son, Leo, who was still in the back. Then she turned to face Laura. "And after all my fretting about the boys making a mess, look what I just did when I turned into your driveway. Am I a klutz or am I a klutz?" She showed Laura the chocolate milkshake stain down the front of her beige fisherman's knit sweater. "Do you mind if I come in and get cleaned up?"

Laura glanced back at the house—and then at her friend. She didn't dare try to tell Patti what was happening. Vic was watching her every move. One look of alarm on Patti's face, and Vic would probably slit Patti's throat—and her little boy's. Then there would be three bodies in her orchard.

"Laura, can't I come in?" Patti asked.

She shook her head. "Ah, now's not a good time . . ."

Patti laughed. "Are you serious? You're not really going to make me drive home like this, are you?"

"I'm sorry," Laura said, shaking her head again.

Patti squinted at her. "What's happened? Laura, are you okay?"

"I don't know what you mean," she answered, holding James closer to her side. He started to squirm.

"I mean, well, you look kind of beat up." Patti stepped toward her. "What's going on?"

Laura realized that from where Patti stood, she might

be able to spot Dane's car, parked behind the garage. She knew Vic was watching them now, maybe thinking the same thing. "Nothing's going on, Patti," she said. "I was napping, that's all."

"Well, can't I come in and clean off? I promise I won't stick around. I'll be in and out—"

"No," Laura interrupted. "I'm sorry."

Patti's eyes narrowed, and then she looked past Laura's shoulder toward the front door. "Something's wrong, I can tell . . ."

The McDonald's bag rustled as Laura clutched James even tighter. She cleared her throat. "The only thing wrong is that I don't appreciate you giving my child junk food in the middle of the afternoon," Laura said evenly. "And now you want to come in and mess up my clean house. I don't see why you can't wait until you get home to clean up."

She hated seeing the hurt, baffled look on her friend's face.

"You're kidding, right?" Patti whispered.

"I'm very serious . . . and very disappointed," she answered. She stroked the top of James's blond head.

Patti stared at her for another moment. "Unbelievable," she muttered. Retreating to her SUV, she shut the back door. "From now on, you can drive your own kid to preschool." She marched around to the driver's side of the vehicle, ducked into the front seat, and slammed the door.

Laura listened to the engine start up, and then watched the SUV turn around and head down the driveway toward the road. For James's sake, she had to keep from breaking down and crying.

She was glad her friend was safe, but couldn't help feeling that there went her last chance for help.

She got down on her knees and hugged James. She kissed his cheek and then held him at arm's length. "Honey, we have company," she said.

"You have three missed messages," said the mechanical voice on the line. *"First message sent Monday, ten-oh-six a.m. . . . ."*

Holding the smartphone to her ear, Laura was perched on the edge of the sofa. Vic sat beside her, and this close, she couldn't help noticing his BO. In front of them, *SpongeBob SquarePants* was on the muted TV. It had kept James entertained for the last half hour. He and Joe now sat at the kitchen counter with a pad of cheap drawing paper and James's crayon box.

Laura had told James that the two strangers in their house were friends of his father's, and they'd be staying a while. "A *very short* while," she added—with a scowl at Joe and Vic. James was intuitive enough to avoid Vic. But he instantly warmed up to Joe. It was strange to see them coloring together like a couple of friends. Laura couldn't help wondering how Joe had gotten along with the Singleton children.

At least James wasn't scared or traumatized by the two men—not yet. For that, Laura was grateful. Vic kept the knife in his pocket and the gun tucked in his pants under his shirttail. He'd just confirmed something Laura had suspected: She had two missed calls from Sean and another from her daughter.

Laura listened to the first message:

"Hey, babe. What's going on? You sounded strange on the message. It's around seven o'clock here. Call me back as soon as you get this. I was going to head out and grab some dinner, but I'll wait until I hear back from you. So—call me. Love you."

Laura wondered if this was putting a crimp in dinner plans with his girlfriend. At the same time, he sounded genuinely concerned. And the familiar "Love you" at the end of the message made her heartsick for him.

"Message two," said the disembodied voice on the other end of the line, *"sent Monday, twelve fifty-seven p.m. . . ."*

"Hey, it's me again." Sean said. "The home phone is going straight to voice mail, and you're not picking up your cell. So I'm really starting to worry. Call me, okay?"

"Message three, sent Monday, one-fifty-five p.m."

"Hi, Mom," Sophie said on the recording—past a lot of chatter in the background. She was probably in a crowded corridor between classes. "Dad texted me during English Lit. He's worried something happened to you, because you're not picking up your phone. And obviously you aren't getting your texts, because I just texted you and didn't hear back. Anyway, Dad's freaking out. So call him back, okay? Text me when you get this so I don't start to freak out, too."

There were also four text messages: three from Sean, and another from Sophie.

Vic wanted her to text back Sean and assure him everything was fine. Laura carefully composed a message:

Dear Sean,

Sorry I couldn't get to the phone. Everything ok
here. Mr. Clapp came by to work on front yard
and must have cut a phone wire. Might see your
dad soon, will give him your love . . . miss you!

Laura

She was about to hit the send button when Vic
snatched the phone out of her hand. "Wait just a goddamn minute," he muttered. "'Dear Sean,'" he read
aloud. "You must think you're clever as hell. I read
your last couple of texts to him, and you never pulled
this 'Dear Sean' shit. No one puts that at the beginning
of a text, and no one writes their name at the end. And
who's this Clapp guy? That's some sort of code, isn't
it?"

"He's our yardman," Laura lied. "He sometimes
trims back the trees. I thought I'd give an explanation
for why the house phone's not working."

"You expect me to swallow that crock of crap?
Don't make me slap the shit out of you in front of your
kid." Vic handed the phone back to her. "Rewrite it.
Leave out the 'Dear Sean,' and the bullshit about his
old man and this Clapp dude."

Laura took the phone and stared at it for a moment.

"Do what I'm telling you," he said. "Y'know, it'll
take me about two seconds and no effort at all to snap
your kid's neck like an old, dry twig."

"I'm thinking!" she hissed. It occurred to her that it
was a stupid idea to plant all those distress signals in

the text to Sean. Even if he called the police, what would happen if they showed up at the house? Vic wasn't about to give himself up. It could turn into a hostage situation—or even worse.

She typed up a new text to put Sean's mind at ease:

Hey you,

Crisis averted. Sorry to worry you. Home phone will get repaired tomorrow. It's a long story. Running around like crazy here. We'll talk later. Get some sleep. Sending lots of love . . .

XXX

She handed the phone back to Vic. Reading the message, he grunted in what seemed to be a tone of approval and sent the text. He handed the phone back to her. "Okay, now a message for the girl," he said.

With a sigh, Laura composed a quick text:

Everything fine here. Got a hold of dad. Thanks. C U soon! XX

"Hey, Mom!" James called from the kitchen. "Come see our pictures! Joe's drawing a picture of a man . . ."

"In a minute, sweetie," she called over her shoulder. She surrendered the phone to Vic again. He glanced at her message and sent it. Then there was a beep, signifying an incoming text.

Laura tried to see who it was from, but Vic pulled the phone close to his face so she couldn't get a look.

He smirked. "Your husband's going to bed. It's almost midnight there. He'll call you when he wakes up in seven hours."

He typed something and sent it.

"What did you just say to him?" she asked.

"I sent him a couple of X's like you did in your short text yesterday."

Laura just stared at him. There was something so incredibly creepy about him sending a text that Sean assumed was from her. She imagined Vic continuing to do that—even after killing her and the kids.

He switched off the phone and shoved it in one of the pockets of his cargo pants. "So much for family talk. Now why don't you go keep your brat quiet for a while?"

He picked up the TV remote and switched to one of the news stations.

On her way to the kitchen counter-bar to check on James, Laura tidied up some of the mess Vic had made in the family room. She put away the CDs and DVDs he'd taken off the shelf and dropped on the floor. She still had a lot to clean up in the kitchen but ignored that for now.

"Look-it, Mom," her little boy said, showing her his drawing: a rectangle with four sticks attached to the bottom of the box. He'd colored the inside of the rectangle brown. "Can you guess what it is? Can you guess?"

"Well, does it say 'bow-wow'?" she asked. "Or do you tell it to 'giddy-up'?"

"Woof!"

"It's a wolf," she said.

"It isn't a woof!" James declared. "It says, 'woof'!"

"Oh, it's a dog, of course," Laura said. She stole a look at Joe's crayon drawing. It was a very detailed sketch of a thin-faced, sinister-looking man in his mid-forties, all in one color—purple. Joe was actually a pretty talented artist. "That's really good," she commented. "Who's it supposed to be?"

Joe slid the drawing down the counter so it was in front of her. "This is the third time I've tried to draw him. The other two sketches are in Vic's backpack. They're from memory. A couple of weeks ago, this man came to the Singletons' house on Lopez. I'd never seen him before. He was wearing one of those shiny, expensive-looking jogging suits. It was black. And he smoked a cigar. He met with Mr. Singleton outside. No one else was home. I guess they didn't know I was there. My apartment's over the garage, right by the driveway, where they were talking. They got into this big argument—"

"Joe, look, I drew a napple tree," James interrupted. "See the red napples?"

"Cool," Joe said. "Now your doggie's in the park. Maybe you can draw some more trees." He looked up at Laura. "Where was I?"

"In your apartment, watching Scott Singleton and the man argue," Laura said. "Did you hear what the argument was about?"

He shook his head. "But at one point, this guy . . ." Joe tapped at his drawing with his finger, "he threatened Mr. Singleton. I heard him. He said, 'You and your whole'"—Joe hesitated, looked at the back of James's head, and then mouthed the word *fucking*—

"'family are going down. We'll destroy you.' Well, Mr. Singleton got really angry, and he pushed the guy up against his car. I thought he was going to beat him up. But he just held the guy by the front of his jogging suit, then plucked the cigar out of his mouth and flicked it down the driveway. He muttered something to the guy, but I couldn't hear. Once Mr. Singleton let go of him, the man got into his car and drove away. The weird thing about it was the guy didn't seem very scared. Me, I would have been petrified."

"Did you tell the police about this?" Laura asked.

"Not right away. Like I said, it happened two weeks ago. I didn't think about it until I was stuck alone in that hotel room on San Juan Island. I told the police on Sunday morning, but I'm not sure they believed me. Plus, I guess I wasn't very helpful. I couldn't even tell them what kind of car the guy drove. I just remember it was black. Anyway, I've been drawing pictures of him ever since, trying to get his face down . . ."

Joe climbed off the stool and tiptoed into the family room. Vic's backpack was on the opposite end of the sofa from where Vic was now dozing. Joe searched through it and finally took some folded papers from the bag.

Vic stirred. "You watching them?" he grumbled.

Joe nodded. "I think she'll help us. Listen, Vic, I really don't think we'll need to—well . . ." He lowered his voice and bent down close to his friend.

"Look-it, Mom," James said, showing Laura his drawing again.

"That's terrific, sweetie," Laura said. All the while,

she kept peeking over at Vic and Joe in quiet conference.

"Hey, Joe, look-it!" James yelled, holding up his drawing.

Vic waved his friend away. "Keep that little bastard quiet," he grumbled. He stuck a throw pillow behind his neck and tipped his head back.

Laura shushed James and patted him on the shoulder. She glared at Joe as he returned to the counter-bar. She kept thinking he could put a stop to this right now, while his buddy was napping. All he had to do was hit him over the head with something and knock him out. But he wouldn't.

Joe must have read her mind, because he said nothing. He avoided eye contact with her as he unfolded his other two sketches and set them on the counter.

One drawing, in blue pen, was almost cartoonlike. There was a passing resemblance to the man in the crayon sketch, but the face was broader. Joe had written some statistics next to the drawing:

6 ft. tall
About 180 lbs.
Dark brown hair
Age 40-50
Lined face, dark complexion, tan?

The other drawing was a pencil rendering with a lot of detail and careful shading. Joe must have spent hours working on it. The man's thin face was wizened in this portrait and had a passing resemblance to a younger

Clint Eastwood. He appeared angry in the sketch. Beneath the artwork, Joe had scribbled the word "Zared."

"What's Zared?" Laura asked.

"That's the man's name," Joe answered.

"Did you tell the police?"

Joe nodded. "They said Mr. Singleton didn't have any 'known associates' by that name."

"But you heard Mr. Singleton call him Zared . . ."

"Well, not exactly," Joe replied, scratching his chin. "At least, I can't tell you when Mr. Singleton actually said the man's name. But I know the man's name is Zared."

Laura wasn't sure how reliable Joe's story was. She looked at the three sketches again. "And you think this Zared person is the one who"—she hesitated and lowered her voice—"*K-I-L-L-E-D* the Singletons?"

"Well, he threatened Mr. Singleton and the family, and he sure seemed to mean it."

"But you have no idea why," Laura said.

"No, but there's a waitress, Martha, at the Last Sunset Café on Lopez, and last month, she told me that a lot of strange things had been going on at the Singletons' summerhouse."

"Like what?"

"She wouldn't say, but Martha's one of those people who seem to know a lot about a lot of stuff going on around town. I'll bet she might have a pretty good idea who Zared is, too. But it's not like I can go back to Lopez Island and ask her, not now."

Laura stroked James's back. She stared at Joe. "So—you want me to go to Lopez and talk to this waitress, is that it?"

He nodded. "Show her the sketches. She might recognize him. Maybe she has an idea of why the Singletons were—you know, *K-I-L-L-E-D*."

"And while I run this errand for you, you and Vic will be holding my children hostage," she whispered. "Is that how it's supposed to work?"

"I promise," Joe said. "They won't be hurt."

Laura resolutely shook her head. "I'm not leaving my children alone with you—and *him*." She shot a look toward Vic, still napping on the sofa. "Besides, if this waitress really knows something, wouldn't she have gone to the police by now?"

"But maybe not. Anyway, I think it's worth a try."

"Joe, there are other ways we can contact her. We could fax one of your sketches to her at the restaurant—or scan it and send it to her in an email. We could do it all from my husband's office upstairs . . ."

"The police can trace a fax or an email," Joe argued. "Then they'd figure out we're here. But if you drove to Lopez Island and went to the café, how is anyone to know who you are? You can say you're a reporter or something. The island is crawling with them. No one would connect you to Vic and me. You'd just be asking Martha about the Singletons and the man in these drawings."

Laura kept shaking her head. "I can't leave my kids here with you. Don't ask me . . ."

"I told you she wouldn't cooperate," Vic called to them from the family-room sofa.

Laura flinched. She wondered how long he'd been awake—and listening.

With a grunt, he pulled himself off the couch and

lumbered toward the counter-bar. "She doesn't give a shit about you, buddy," he muttered, slapping Joe's shoulder with the back of his hand. "I told you it was a stupid idea."

"You said a swear!" James declared.

Laura put her hand on her son's back again.

Vic trudged into the kitchen and opened the refrigerator. He took out the carton of orange juice and guzzled from it. He left the refrigerator door open. "The thing is, lady, you have no choice." He set the carton on the counter. "If you don't cooperate, you and your little tribe are dead. Then we'll take your car, your money, and your jewelry, and we'll be in a whole other part of the country by the time someone walks in here and finds your rotting corpses."

Laura stepped around the counter-bar, brushed past him, and shut the refrigerator door. She took a glass from the cupboard and poured some juice in it. "Say I go on this errand for you, what kind of guarantee do I have that you're not going to hurt anyone?"

"You have *my* guarantee," Joe piped up.

But Laura was looking at Vic, and she didn't take her eyes off him. "I want to hear it from you."

He slowly pushed the glass of orange juice toward the edge of the sink, still full of utensils. Then, with a self-satisfied grin, he let the tumbler drop. The glass broke. "I like it from the carton," he murmured. "It's fresher that way."

Her little boy looked up from his drawing. For the first time, James seemed to comprehend what was happening. He looked frightened. His lower lip quivered.

"If you're not going to give me any guarantee," Laura said, "once I'm on the road, what's to keep me from going to the police?"

"If so much as one cop comes around here, you can kiss your family good-bye." Vic moved over to the counter-bar again. He put his finger close to James's head and mimicked firing a gun. "This one will be the first to go, I promise you."

James started crying.

"Vic, you're scaring him," Joe murmured.

Laura felt her stomach lurch. She hurried around the counter-bar and scooped up James in her arms and held him close to her. He hitched his legs around her waist. "There now, sweetie," she whispered into his ear. "It's okay . . . it's okay . . ."

She glared at Vic—and then at Joe. "What if this Martha person can't identify the man in your sketch?" she asked, trying to keep her voice steady. "What if I can't get her to tell me anything?"

"Well, then," Vic said. "If I were you, I wouldn't bother coming home."

CHAPTER SEVEN

Monday—3:29 P.M.
Leavenworth

If, last year, someone had told Sophie Gretchell that the class heartthrob would be driving her home from school, she'd have said they were crazy.

Sophie reminded herself of that now—as she and her boyfriend, Matt, pulled out of the high school parking lot in his old beat-up Toyota Corolla. It was probably too soon to call Matt her "boyfriend." It had been only three weeks since their first date, and the relationship hadn't gotten too heavy or hot yet. Matt was still trying to win her over. Maybe that was why he went for her. Sophie was just about the only girl in their junior class who didn't foam at the mouth at the sight of him. Matt probably regarded her as a challenge. Then again, the joke could be entirely on her. What if all this was just an elaborate punk-you for the bookish new girl in class? Maybe he was waiting until she fell crazy in love with him, and then he'd unceremoniously dump her. She didn't really believe that, but it seemed possible considering her history.

Sophie hadn't been even remotely popular at her high school in Seattle. She considered herself sort of an ugly duckling with her unmanageable curly brown hair and her skinny, shapeless build. Plus, she was taller than nearly half the boys in her class. *"A beanpole,"* is how someone described her in an online *Rate Your Classmates* post some sadistic A-lister had concocted. Other descriptions of her in the post included: *Pirates Dream = Sunken Chest, Two Peas on a Breadboard,* and *Who?*

Next to Sophie's name, another classmate had written: "Perfect Candidate for a Makeover," and Sophie took that to heart. She went to Macy's cosmetic counter for an honest-to-God makeover, and the result had her resembling a Kiss band member. Then there was the hair-straightener that left her hair limp and greasy-looking. There was the expensive fake tan in a bottle that turned her face tangerine, and a padded bra that prompted snotty Denise Berry to post on Instagram: "Falsie Alert on Gretchell! Could those things look more fake? Did she really think we'd believe she suddenly grew boobs during one three-day weekend?" Finally there was the cheerleading tryout that was a disaster. No matter how many times Sophie tried to reinvent herself, she didn't click with any clique.

Still, she had her books and one good friend since fourth grade, Barb Riddle, to keep her company. It really didn't matter that she wasn't winning any popularity contests or dating anyone. But then in the middle of sophomore year, Barb moved to Boulder.

So when Sophie's parents announced they'd bought a winery in Leavenworth, she thought, *Fine with me.*

When she saw how isolated they'd be at the winery, Sophie decided to volunteer for different after-school activities—mostly tutoring kids and reading to toddlers at the public library. She'd given up trying to be popular. She just wanted to keep busy. She'd also given up on trying to tame her curly hair and slouching so that she didn't tower over half the boys in her class. Besides, now that she was a junior, most of the boys were starting to catch up or they were taller than she was. Sophie actually started feeling better about herself, but not so confident that she didn't still have some doubts.

Sometimes she thought Matt—along with the rest of her new classmates—would soon catch on that she was nothing special, and then he'd drop her. Maybe that was why she kept him slightly at bay. She didn't want to get hurt. She also refused to let her sudden popularity go to her head.

Still, Matt was handsome, with wavy black hair and green eyes. He was the alternate quarterback on the varsity team. And for a jock, he was surprisingly considerate and sensitive.

All in all, Sophie was pretty content sitting in the passenger seat of Matt Brunelle's banged-up Corolla. A piece of duct tape kept the glove compartment from flopping open. A *Go, Cascade Kodiaks!* sticker decorated the back bumper. And Coldplay was on the radio.

Once he dropped her off, Matt would have to turn around and head back to the school.

"You really don't have to drive me all the way home," Sophie said, watching the raindrops accumulate on the windshield. "You can let me off at the bus stop. I mean, either way, I'll still make out with you a little when you drop me off."

Eyes on the road, Matt chuckled, "Just a little, huh?"

That was as far as they'd gone—some heavy making out and a little petting. Sophie was still a virgin— and not especially eager to change her status, at least, not until she was sure Matt was serious about her.

Then again, maybe that was why he was driving her home from school—to show just how serious he was.

"I mean it, Matt," she said. "Last time you took me all the way home, you were late getting back for football practice and Coach Martinson chewed you out in front of the whole team."

Matt glanced at his wristwatch. "I've got plenty of time. Besides, I want to make sure you're safe."

"I'll be fine. I sincerely doubt the Singleton killers are hanging around Leavenworth."

The murders on Lopez Island were all anyone had talked about at school that day. It seemed practically everybody in her class knew someone who lived on Lopez or they claimed they were friends with someone who knew one of the Singleton kids. Sophie had hardly slept a wink since Saturday, when she'd heard about the gruesome murders. And now, the suspected killers had escaped—and they were believed to be somewhere in Washington State.

So of course, practically everyone in school assumed the killers were somewhere around Leavenworth.

The city, tucked near the Cascade foothills, was a popular tourist destination because the center of town intentionally resembled a quaint old village in the Bavarian Alps. Even the Starbucks and McDonald's had a *Ye Olde* look to their storefronts. There were a ton of touristy shops, restaurants, and a couple of beer gardens. A Christmas store was open all year around. The hotels and inns looked like chalets. The town had a big festival when the Christmas lights were lit each year, and Sophie had to admit, it looked pretty gorgeous at night.

Leavenworth seemed like the last place on earth two fugitive killers would hide out. And yet, despite her brave façade, Sophie was on edge. And she wasn't the only one. Her dad had texted her around lunchtime today, worried that something might have happened to her mom—who wasn't answering her phone. He hadn't said anything about the Singleton murders, but Sophie was pretty sure he'd been thinking about them.

It turned out her mom was okay, of course.

Still, everyone was a little jumpy.

"That bus drops you off at least half a mile from your driveway," Matt said. "And it's cold and rainy and getting dark out. I'll feel better taking you home."

"You're sweet, Matt," she said. "Thank you. But you shouldn't worry. Like I say, I don't think those two psychos are anywhere around here." She figured if she kept saying it out loud, she'd actually start to believe it. "They're probably out of the state by now."

Switching on his windshield wipers, Matt cracked a smile. "You can't be too sure. I mean, for all we know, they might have gotten yodeler hats, strapped on some lederhosen, and are hiding in plain sight in the center of town this very minute."

Sophie didn't quite hear him because she'd just noticed her brother, Liam, standing alone at the bus stop near the town center. He was skinny and pale with wavy brown hair that had at least three cowlicks at any given time. He looked slightly pathetic in his blue jacket that was one size too big. Sophie figured he must have missed his school bus. No surprise there. He was a bit spacey at times, in his own little world.

At his school in Seattle, Liam had been King of the Sixth Grade Nerds. At least, that was how Sophie thought of him. He'd had an entourage of geeky friends over at the house practically every weekend. He was a movie nut, and he kept a stack of film magazines by his bedside. He was quite skilled with video equipment and would go on and on ad nauseum about the way scenes were shot in *Star Wars* or *Lord of the Rings*. He'd read somewhere about a group of teenagers who remade *Raiders of the Lost Ark* shot for shot. So Liam had talked his nerd buddies into doing the same thing for *Psycho*. Though half his crew hadn't even heard of the movie, Liam had figured there would be a minimum of sets and stunts. So he made them watch the Hitchcock film at least ten times. They'd started filming, but he had to abandon the project when they moved to the winery. So, unlike Sophie, Liam really regretted leaving Seattle.

"Could we pick up my brother?" she asked Matt. "Would you mind? He's right there at the bus stop."

Matt slowed down and signaled. "But this means we can't make out in the car when I drop you off!" he groaned.

She laughed. "Oh, c'mon, like we were really going

to park in front of my house at four o'clock in the afternoon and tongue-wrestle—with my mom home, no less."

"I was kidding, Sophie," he said, pulling over to the bus stop.

"Thanks," she said, putting her hand on his arm for a moment. Then she lowered her window and called to her brother: "Hey, little boy, would you like a ride? I have candy in the car . . ."

Liam frowned at her. "That's so creepy!"

She nodded at the back door. "Get in, dopey."

Liam climbed into the backseat. "Thanks, you guys!" he said, shutting the door.

Matt pulled back into traffic. He shot a glance in the rearview mirror. "Hey, dude."

"Hey," Liam said. "Don't you have football practice or something?"

He chuckled. "You sound just like your sister."

Sophie half turned in the passenger seat. "What happened? Did you miss the school bus?"

"Yeah," Liam answered, opening his backpack. He took out his Sony camcorder and checked it. "This eighth grader almost beat me up."

Matt laughed. "Listen to how laid-back he sounds about it!"

Sophie wasn't surprised. Liam could sometimes let things just roll right off him. "What happened exactly?"

Her brother aimed the camcorder out the car window and looked through the lens. "Well, this guy, George Shayner, he came after me. I thought for sure he might've broken my camera, but he didn't." Liam put the camera down in his lap for a moment. "Anyway, he was mad because I asked his girlfriend, Kristin Farrow, if she'd be Janet Leigh in my *Psycho* remake. I told her she didn't have to be naked for when she got stabbed in the shower, and she could shoot the whole scene in a bathing suit. But for the opening scene, I'd need her to look like she was in her underwear, but she could do that in a bathing suit, too, like a two-piece . . ."

Sophie shook her head and sighed. "God, the poor little girl probably didn't have a clue what you were talking about. You probably traumatized her. That's the kind of thing they'd send you to the school psychiatrist for."

Matt was grinning as he took the turn onto Rural Route 17. "What did she say?"

"She said I was mentally defective and I should get the hell away from her." Liam checked his camera again. "Then later, after school let out, and I was walking to the bus, I saw Kristin with this guy George Shayner by the side door, and I waved at her. She whispered something to him, and all of a sudden he came charging toward me. He grabbed my backpack and threw it aside. I really thought he might have broken my camera . . ."

"You're lucky he didn't break your neck," Sophie said.

"I tried explaining to him that it was a real compliment, because Kristin is blond and pretty like Janet Leigh. But he wasn't really listening. He pushed me a couple of times and called me a 'little perv' and stuff like that. But he really didn't hurt me. Y'know, I don't think he or Kristin has ever seen the movie. It was all just kind of a misunderstanding. Anyway, so I got detained and missed the school bus . . ."

"*'So I got detained.'*" Matt chuckled again. "God, I love this kid . . ."

Sophie rolled her eyes. Her little brother was so sweet and unassuming. He didn't have any grudges against the girl or her boyfriend. And it hardly occurred to him that he might have had the crap beaten out of him. All he cared about was his movie project and his Sony Handycam camcorder, which he'd bought with the money he'd earned mowing lawns all last summer.

For the rest of the way home, Liam shot the scenery along Rural Route 17—or maybe he was recording the movement of the raindrops on the car window, Sophie wasn't sure. He didn't put his camcorder back in its case until Matt slowed down to turn into their driveway.

They passed the wine-tasting cottage. "Liam, do me a favor and get out first," Sophie said. "I'll be in after you in just a minute or two, okay?"

"Why? So you guys can get all lovey-dovey?"

"Don't be annoying. We just gave you a ride home."

"Sorry," he muttered.

When they pulled up in front of the house, Liam grabbed his backpack and opened the door. "Thanks, Matt!"

"Take it easy, dude!"

Liam ducked out of the car and shut the door. Matt kept the engine on. The windshield wipers squeaked. He put one hand on the top of Sophie's seatback and smiled at her. "What do you say I blow off practice and the two of us just drive around for the rest of the afternoon?"

"Don't tempt me," Sophie said.

He moved in close to kiss her, but then hesitated. Something had caught his attention outside her window.

Sophie followed his gaze and looked over toward the house.

Her mother stood on the front porch with James in her arms. She sort of blocked Liam's way to the front door, which was only a quarter of the way open. She stared at the two of them in the car.

Matt straightened up and put both hands on the wheel. "What's the deal with your mom?"

"I don't know," Sophie murmured. She gave him a quick kiss on the cheek. "Thanks for the ride. I'll call you later, okay?" She opened the door and climbed out.

"Bye, Matt!" her mother called—with a halfhearted wave.

Shutting the car door, Sophie headed toward the front porch. "What's going on?"

Her mother gave her a tense look and then waved at Matt again. "Bye, Matt!" she said, louder this time.

Her mother didn't move until the Corolla turned around and started down the long driveway.

Sophie stood there in the drizzle. She noticed her mother's chin was bruised. "Mom?"

Her mother put a hand on Liam's shoulder and then looked at her. "Don't be afraid," she said.

The door behind her mother yawned open. Sophie saw a stranger on the other side of it.

Suddenly, she couldn't move.

"Just do what they tell you," her mother said.

Sophie stared at the man. She'd seen his face on the news this morning—and again, online several times during the school day. His last name was Moles, and he was one of the men wanted for slaying the Singleton family.

She glanced over toward the far end of the driveway. She could see Matt's Corolla in the distance, turning onto the rural road. The car disappeared behind some trees.

Sophie felt as if she couldn't breathe.

She turned toward her mother and her brothers. Behind them in the doorway there were now two men, two strangers in their house. But they weren't strangers. She knew exactly who they were.

The one named Moles had a gun.

He smiled at her and licked his lips.

CHAPTER EIGHT

Monday—3:56 P.M.

"Well, well, Matt just texted," Victor Moles said with a smug grin on his face. He had Sophie's phone in one hand and his gun in the other. He was reading all her recent texts. "Lucky Matt will call you later tonight. And there's a couple of small X's here. Isn't that sweet?"

Sophie had been terrified the two men would tie them up—the same way they'd bound and gagged most of the Singleton family before murdering them.

Victor Moles seemed to be the one in charge. The gray-and-blue striped V-neck sweater he wore looked oddly familiar. With his gun drawn, he'd herded everyone into the living room and had them squeeze in together on the sofa. Then he'd made her and Liam surrender their phones and backpacks. He'd checked out Liam's camcorder to make sure it didn't have a Wi-Fi feature.

"Can I have that back when you're through looking at it, please?" her brother had politely asked. Sophie couldn't believe his nerve. He was sitting on the other end of the sofa. Their mom was sandwiched between them with James squirming on her lap.

The one named Joe talked his friend into letting Liam keep his camcorder.

But the two men held onto the phones. Sophie noticed Vic seemed to relish peering at her text conversations. She just wanted to scream. It was such an invasion of privacy. He may as well have gone through her bedroom drawers or read her diary. If she weren't so scared, she would have been furious.

"I'm answering him, 'K' with a couple of little X's," Vic said, working his thumbs over Sophie's phone screen. "But, between you and me, honey, when lover boy calls tonight, you might not be picking up the phone."

Vic kept leering at her. It made Sophie's skin crawl. But she sat there quietly, obediently.

Now that he had his camcorder in his lap, Liam kept quiet as well. But Sophie half-expected him to try to escape or do something he'd seen in some stupid action movie—only to get himself and the rest of them killed.

"Are either of you two expecting any visitors tonight—or during the day tomorrow?" Vic asked, pocketing their phones.

Both she and Liam timidly shook their heads.

"Expecting any calls?" He winked at her. "I mean, besides lucky Matt?"

Sophie frowned. She and Liam both shook their heads at him again.

Vic finally stopped smirking at her and turned to her mother. "So—what's for dinner?"

"I have no idea," she said, holding James closer.

"Well, get in the kitchen and start thinking about it," he said. Then he turned to his friend beside him. "You watch her and the little brat—and keep the chitchat to a minimum. Princess and Junior are going to give me a tour of the rest of the house, starting upstairs with their bedrooms . . ."

Sophie automatically recoiled. She grabbed hold of her mother's arm. She figured their bedrooms would be where he'd tie each of them up.

Her mother shook her head at Vic. "I'm not leaving you alone with my kids."

He let out an exasperated sigh. "Shut up and get dinner started. Joe, tell her not to get her panties in a bunch."

"Vic just needs to make sure there aren't any other phones or laptops in the house," Joe explained. "I promise, no one will be hurt."

Her mother didn't budge from the sofa. She gave him a wary look.

"I swear to you," Joe said. "I mean, how could I expect you to help us tomorrow if we harmed any of your kids?"

Sophie wondered how her mother was supposed to help the two men.

Vic lumbered over to the bottom of the stairs. With a hand on the newel post, he turned to them. "C'mon, you two, move it. Off your butts . . ."

"You don't have to be rude, Vic," Joe murmured.

Sophie let out a dazed little laugh. *Yes, if you're going to kill us, at least be polite about it,* she thought. Obviously, this Joe person was a little off. His manner was so gentle and passive. He didn't seem to want to harm anyone, and yet the police were after him for slaying an entire family.

Liam stood up first—followed by her mother and James.

With uncertainty, Sophie got to her feet and moved to the stairway. She was shaking, and her stomach was in knots. She hesitated a moment at the bottom of the steps, while her mom carried James toward the kitchen. Joe was behind them. Sophie couldn't help feeling this was the last time she'd ever see her mother.

Vic sighed impatiently. "C'mon, get going . . ."

He made her and Liam lead the way upstairs. In the hallway, she passed her parents' bedroom. The door was open. The place was in a shambles. Sophie wondered if her bedroom was in the same condition.

"Do your folks keep a gun in the house?" Vic asked, trailing behind them.

"No," Liam answered.

Vic swatted him on the back of his head. "Lying little shit—"

Sophie spun around and pulled her brother to one side. "He's not lying. He just doesn't know about it . . ."

This, of course, was a total lie. They both knew about the gun in their parents' bedroom closet. After seeing the mess in the master bedroom, she figured Vic or Joe must have already found it. Vic was probably just testing them. "My dad has a gun on the shelf in their bedroom closet, behind his sweaters," she said. "You'll find a box of bullets there, too."

"Really? Dad has a gun?" Liam asked, rubbing the back of his head. He was quite the little actor.

Vic seemed satisfied.

Vic's friend, Joe, wasn't lying. Vic wanted a tour of the bedrooms—along with their dad's study on the third floor. Unlike their parents' bedroom, the other rooms hadn't been touched. So, starting with Liam's bedroom, she and her brother were forced to empty the desk and dresser drawers, clear off the shelves, and go through the closet—just to show the son of a bitch there were no extra phones, hidden weapons, or sharp objects. It was exhausting, and they created an absolute mess. Liam's bed and the floor were covered with piles of clothes, shoes, hangers, and all sorts of junk from his desk and his shelves.

Vic emptied Liam's wastebasket and dumped in it an eclectic assortment of things he deemed contraband: Liam's iPad, a souvenir mini baseball bat her brother had bought at a Mariners game, an old letter opener, a sturdy but completely fake replica of Thor's hammer, a flashlight, a pair of scissors, and a drawing compass.

Most of the time Vic half-sat on Liam's desk with the gun in his hand, barking orders at them, making wisecracks about Liam's things, and occasionally leering at her.

Sophie quietly became angrier and angrier. At least she was a little less frightened. What Vic was making them do didn't mesh at all with the news accounts of the Singleton murders. She hadn't seen anything on TV or read anything online about the rooms in the Lopez Island house being torn apart. It didn't seem like the same situation at all.

From what they'd said earlier, it was obvious the

two fugitives had made some kind of deal with her mother. They were forcing her to do something for them tomorrow, some errand. And in the meantime, they planned to stay here the night.

Was there a chance she and her family would survive this? Or would this deal her mother had made with the two murderers merely delay the inevitable?

Every now and then, she heard James downstairs letting out a shriek. That wasn't unusual. He got wound up and loud sometimes in the late afternoon. Sophie was relieved to hear most of his screams followed by giggles. Her mother must have been distracting him.

But if her mom had seen the look on Vic's face after each shriek, she certainly would have tried harder to keep James quiet.

Sophie shuddered. She couldn't help thinking that if Vic started shooting, her baby brother would be the first to die.

James let out a screech and then laughed. "You moved first, Joe!"

He and Joe sat on the family room floor, playing "chicken" with a couple of James's toy trucks. It was obvious Joe was losing on purpose, pulling his truck to one side long before it might have collided with James's truck. "Oh, rats!" Joe said. "You won again. I want a rematch . . ."

From the kitchen, Laura kept an eye on them as she tried to get dinner started and the utensils put away. But it was hard to keep her mind on food when her two older children were upstairs alone with Vic. Any minute now, she expected to hear a scream or a thud or maybe even a gunshot. Her nerves felt as if they were scraped raw.

She kept thinking about Dane's corpse lying out in the vineyard right now. She wasn't sure whether or not she should tell Sophie and Liam what had happened. They needed to know just how dangerous Vic was. But they'd already figured out these two men were the fugitive suspects in the Singleton murders. They were already terrified. She didn't want to panic them even more.

She found a package of ground Italian chicken sausage in the freezer, and pulled a jar of Newman's Own spaghetti sauce from the cupboard. She'd make penne. She started cooking the sausage, while from another cupboard she took out a recently opened bottle of red wine to add to the sauce later.

It suddenly occurred to her that her kitchen and pantry were overstocked with an assortment of wines. Starting with dinner, all she had to do was keep refilling Vic's glass, and by ten o'clock, he'd be passed out or, at the very least, "slow on the draw." She might be able to wrestle the gun from him.

Then again, Vic was probably a violent, abusive drunk. If he started drinking, how long would she and her kids be at risk until he finally lost consciousness?

She glanced over at Joe sitting on the floor with her son. She was pretty sure he'd surrender once Vic was put out of commission.

She heard a thump from above. It made her flinch. Laura had to tell herself that someone had merely dropped something on the floor, nothing more.

She took a deep breath and moved into the family room. Grabbing the remote control, she switched on the TV to an episode of *Sid the Science Kid* she'd DVR'd earlier. "Jamie, look what's on now," she said. "It's your favorite show. Why don't you sit and watch Sid while I talk to Joe?"

James's shoulders slumped and his face bunched up. "I want Joe to watch Sid with me!"

"Well, I really need to talk with Joe—just for a little while. He'll come watch TV with you in a few minutes, okay?"

Her son didn't answer. He was already mesmerized by the show.

She moved over to the counter-bar, and Joe joined her. "Vic said we shouldn't be talking," he murmured. Still, he sat down on one of the bar stools.

"I just wanted to say, James likes you," she whispered. "You're really good with him."

He half-smiled and shrugged. "Well, I like kids."

"I'm not sure Vic does," Laura said. "I don't trust him around my children, Joe. In fact, I have to admit, I'm terrified that he's alone upstairs with Sophie and Liam right now. I saw what he did to that man this afternoon. I can't help thinking . . ." She shook her head. "To-morrow, you want me to drive to Lopez Island to talk to this waitress, Martha, about this Zared person . . ."

Laura nervously drummed her fingers on the counter-top. She wasn't sure if either one of those people even existed.

"That's at least six or seven hours I'd be gone. I'm sorry, but I couldn't leave my children alone with Vic that long. Hell, I'd be a wreck leaving them alone with him for seven *minutes*."

"But your kids won't be alone with him. I'll be here."

"No offense, Joe, but you were here this afternoon when he slit that man's throat. You didn't want that man to die, and you wanted to stop it, but you couldn't."

"I swear, I won't let him hurt any of your kids, Mrs. Gretchell."

There was something about the way he said her name that sounded eerily familiar.

"You can trust me to make sure nothing bad happens," he said.

"That's the other thing, Joe," she said, wincing a bit. "As much as I want to believe you're innocent, the fact is you're wanted by the police for murdering seven people, some of them just kids. There's no mother in her right mind who would feel safe leaving her children with either of you. I'm sorry."

He gave her a wounded look. "But you just said I was good with James . . ."

"Yes, while I'm here, watching you. But I'm not about to drive off and leave you alone with him—or any of my kids. I'm sorry." She put her hand on his arm. "Joe, I want to help you, but not this way. I can't. Don't ask me to leave my kids here with you and Vic. If you're really innocent, you'd—"

"I am innocent!" He jerked his arm away. "I thought you of all people would believe me."

"What do you mean me *of all people*?"

"I told you, I was asleep when they were killed!" he

went on. "I don't know how it happened! I don't know how anybody got through that front gate. Maybe someone snuck in when the two older kids got back from dinner. They were all fine when I fell asleep. I didn't kill anybody. I couldn't have. Earlier on Friday night, I was in my room—"

"You mean the apartment above the garage?" she asked.

Joe sighed and gave a nod. He seemed to calm down a bit. "I was watching TV when Mr. Singleton called and asked me to come to his study . . ." Joe stopped and took a deep breath.

Laura recalled the news accounts. Scott Singleton's body was discovered in his study. He'd been beaten savagely—*tortured*, according to some news accounts. And his throat had been slashed. "What time did he call you?" she asked.

"Around ten-thirty," Joe answered. "I remember, because Mr. Singleton said to come to the side door. His study had its own entrance. He said he didn't want me to wake up anybody. Everyone was home by then except the college girl, Jae. A couple of the kids were in bed. I was really nervous because this was my first time meeting Mr. Singleton and I wasn't sure exactly why he was calling me to his study at that hour. I thought maybe I was in trouble."

"Wait a minute." Laura frowned at him. "You hadn't met him?"

He shook his head. "No, it was Mrs. Singleton who had hired me. Earlier in the summer, I had this job with a landscaping crew. We were working in the yard of this superrich family, and Mrs. Singleton came over to their house to play tennis. I was one of four guys there that morning, and I was trimming the hedges around the tennis court. I won a coin toss. It was light work. But mostly, the other guys wanted the job because, well, for older ladies, Mrs. Singleton and her friend—the lady who owned the house—they weren't bad to look at in their tennis outfits and all. I think Mrs. Singleton stopped and talked to me for like maybe two minutes—mostly about gardening. And based on that, my boss, Mr. Neff, told me the next day that somebody wanted to interview me for this groundskeeper job . . ."

Above them on the second floor, Laura could hear movement, but nothing sudden or loud.

The savory smell of the sausage cooking started to fill the kitchen. She excused herself and went to stir the meat and reset the burner to low. All the while, she wondered if these people hiring Joe knew he'd spent time in an institution. She wanted to ask if it had come up in the interview, but thought better of it. They must have known. They had to have conducted a background check on him. Maybe Sherry Singleton was a true Christian in the sense that she wanted to give this unfortunate young man a second chance. Maybe she hoped to convert him or something.

Laura poured Joe a glass of water, brought it to him, and sat back down next to him. "Go on," she said. "You were about to interview for the groundskeeper job."

"Thanks." He sipped his water. "So—I went in for the interview, and I guess it went well, because I met Mrs. Singleton again, and I got hired to look after their house on Lopez. That was back in late September. Like

I told you earlier, it was mostly a summer place for them. So it was just me there most of the time. It was really kind of an easy job. I just had to keep the grounds looking nice and check inside the house every few days. Whenever somebody wanted to stay over, Mrs. Singleton called me in advance. Some cleaning woman would come by, and I'd help pull all the white sheets off the furniture so it would be ready for occupancy. That's how Mrs. Singleton would put it, 'Could you help get the house ready for occupancy, Joe?' It was almost always Mrs. Singleton who spent the night there. She was usually alone. A few times she brought a couple of the kids with her. The older kids sometimes came there unannounced with friends. But Mr. Singleton, he was never there . . ."

Laura squinted at him. "But you told me earlier that you saw him in the driveway, talking to that Zared person . . ."

He nodded—a few more times than necessary. "Oh, yeah, but he—well, he just sort of showed up that afternoon. No one called ahead or anything. I noticed the car come in, and I looked out the window, and I saw him go into the house. I recognized him—from TV and from photographs in the house. I figured I should go down and introduce myself, and I was about to do that when this other guy showed up . . ."

"Zared," she said.

Joe nodded again. "That's right. They had the argument in the driveway—like I told you about. Mr. Singleton didn't stick around very long after the other man drove off. So I never got a chance to introduce myself to him. The first time I actually saw him face-to-face was Thanksgiving night. He had me and the kitchen help come into the dining room, and he said a prayer over Thanksgiving dinner. He kept getting my name wrong. I was worried he didn't like me very much. So—just as I said, when I knocked on the outside door to his study for this meeting, I was pretty nervous."

Laura studied him while he talked. She could tell he was omitting something. She wasn't getting the entire story. From years of teaching, she'd learned how to detect when a kid was lying—or not giving her a completely accurate explanation about something. They never quite looked at her, or they fidgeted, or their speech patterns gave them away. Joe was unconsciously giving out all those telltale signs. He might not have been lying per se, but he seemed to be holding back something he didn't want her to know about.

"Did you tell all this to the police?" she asked.

He nodded nervously.

"Exactly the way you told me?"

Joe nodded again and took another sip of water.

No wonder the police didn't believe you, she thought.

"What's wrong?"

"Nothing," she sighed. "So—what happened when you talked to Scott Singleton that night?"

Joe shrugged. "Well, he invited me into the study and gave me a dark beer, something imported. I sat down on the sofa and he—he sat across from me with his beer. He told me I was doing a good job on the grounds and that he was glad to finally meet me and all. He was really friendly. After about twenty minutes, his cell phone rang and he said he needed to take the call. He said it wouldn't be long, and when he was done, he'd walk over to my apartment so we could finish our conversation."

"For twenty minutes, he talked about the good job you were doing on the grounds?"

Joe nodded.

"And he wanted to finish up that conversation later?" Laura gave him a sidelong glance. "Joe, I can't imagine a conversation like that taking any more than five minutes—maybe ten at the most."

"Well, we talked about other stuff, too," Joe said, restlessly shifting around on the bar stool. "He asked me about my religion, and I asked him about football. Like I say, he was really friendly." Joe made a face. "I think I smell something burning. Is whatever's on the stove okay?"

Laura went to check on the sausage. It was fine. She drained the fat from the pan and added the wine and the Newman's Own. "So—go on, I'm listening," she said, standing over the stove. "It was about eleven o'clock. Mr. Singleton was supposed to come by your apartment above the garage and talk some more about—*stuff.*"

Joe let out a sigh. "Well, when we were in his study, before his cell phone rang, Mr. Singleton had started talking about my insurance. He said it was important, and he wanted to talk some more about that."

Laura glanced over her shoulder at him. "You mean he wanted to discuss your employee health benefits?"

"That's what I thought at first," Joe replied. "But he said this was my *spiritual coverage.* He said he wanted to talk about the *insurance for my soul* and my future and all."

"I see," Laura said. She left the sauce to simmer and glanced at James in the family room. He was wrapped up in his show, not listening to them at all. She walked over to the counter-bar so that she was face-to-face with Joe.

"So—I went back to the apartment and started to clean up a little," Joe said. "I didn't want Mr. Singleton thinking I was this major slob. Actually, the place wasn't that messy, but I wanted to leave a good impression, y'know? Only Mr. Singleton didn't show up, and after a while, I fell asleep on the sofa." He gulped down some water and stared down at the countertop. "I must have been really tired, because I didn't wake up until early the next morning. I was still in my clothes and still on the couch. I was shivering, because it was cold in my place and I didn't have a blanket over me or anything. I remember getting up and going to the bathroom, and then looking at the clock. It was just after six. I glanced out the window to see if it was raining or snowing, and that's when I saw the extra car parked in the driveway with the driver's door open. And the kid was lying there on the gravel, and I could see the blood . . ."

Joe took another sip of water. "I ran downstairs. I didn't put on a jacket or anything. I'd fallen asleep with my shoes on. That's how tired I must have been. Anyway, I checked on the kid, and he was still breathing, but he was unconscious. I knew he was Jae's boyfriend because he'd been at dinner on Thursday night. I wanted to cover him with a blanket or something, but there was nothing inside the car. Then I noticed the windshield and the windows were cracked and had bullet holes. I don't know how I slept through those gunshots, I really don't. Anyway, I remember thinking I should have brought my phone so I could call the police or an ambulance. I ran to the house and pounded on the front door. But no one answered."

"Didn't you have keys to the house?" Laura asked.

"Yeah, and I had them on me when I went to meet Mr. Singleton. But I must have dug them out of my pocket when I was getting sleepy, because the police found my keys in the apartment—on the end table by the sofa. One of the cops who questioned me really homed in on that: *'You took your keys out of your pocket to nap, but you didn't kick off your shoes.'* He thought it was strange or suspicious or something. But I really didn't need to have my keys on me—as long as I was home and not going anywhere, right?"

"Makes sense to me," Laura said.

"Anyway, I couldn't get in their front door. So I tried the side door to Mr. Singleton's study. It was unlocked . . ." Joe winced. "I found him dead on the sofa. He'd been stripped down to his underwear, and his hands and feet were tied. He was beaten up really bad. His throat was slashed. There was blood all over the carpet—and on the glass-top coffee table and on the magazines on top of it . . ."

He cleared his throat. "There was a—a landline phone on Mr. Singleton's desk, and the police asked me a few times about that—why I didn't pick it up and call nine-one-one. But I guess I just freaked out. I started screaming—mostly for Mrs. Singleton. I thought she and the kids might still be asleep upstairs. I ran toward the front of the house to go up there, and that's when I saw the blood on the floor in the front hallway. It was on the wall, too. It sort of made a trail into the living room, and I found Jae in there on the carpet. She had on a tan coat, but most of it was cut up and stained with blood . . ." He touched his left cheek. "And there was a big slash here on her face. Her eyes were still open, and she had this sort of tired, dazed expression on her face. I could see she was dead. I didn't touch her at all. The police asked why I didn't call nine-one-one then. But I still didn't know about the others upstairs. I guess my thinking was muddled. I remember just wanting to find someone else there who was alive—and conscious. I figured maybe somebody broke in and killed Mr. Singleton. And poor Jae and her boyfriend just came in at the wrong time. I thought the rest of the family might still be okay, sleeping upstairs. Pretty stupid, I know. But I'd slept through everything, and I figured maybe they had, too."

Laura just stared at him and slowly shook her head. She wasn't sure how she would have reacted. Though she'd questioned some of what he'd told her earlier, this part of the story seemed tragically real.

"Anyway, I ran up the stairs, and I saw Mrs. Singleton there in the second-floor hallway, lying against the wall. I didn't see her face, because her back was to me. Her feet were tied around the ankles and her hands were tied behind her . . ."

Almost the same way you and Vic tied me up earlier, Laura thought, but she didn't say anything.

"She had on this long silky pink nightgown," he continued. "Only I thought it was pink with dark red flowers—until I noticed the material was torn and the red blooms were actually blood. I looked down the corridor, and all the bedroom doors were open. One of them had blood smeared on it. That's when I figured they were all dead. I raced downstairs and called the police from the kitchen phone."

"It sounds like you didn't touch anyone," Laura murmured. "But the news reports said you were covered with blood."

He nodded. "The lady on nine-one-one wanted me to stay on the line, but I told her there was a kid lying outside in the cold and he was still alive. So I hung up. Before I went outside, I just needed to double-check upstairs. I thought maybe one of the kids was spared. Willow and Connor were the youngest, and they'd spent a couple of weekends at the house with their mother. I especially liked Connor. He was a good kid. He'd just turned eleven in October. He was the baby of the family . . ."

Laura couldn't help glancing over at James, sitting on the floor and watching TV.

"I saw a couple of the others, and when I got to Connor's room, I found him in his pajamas, lying face-down beside the bed. His little hands and feet were tied up, I don't know, I . . ." Joe let out a heavy sigh, and tears came to his eyes. "I just had to put him back on his bed. I felt like he belonged there, y'know? I know it's crazy. Anyway, when I started to pick him up, he let out a moan or something. One of the cops told me later that dead bodies can do that sometimes. But I thought he might still be alive, so I tried mouth to mouth and pumping on his chest. By the time I finally realized he was dead, I was pretty much covered in blood. And then I remembered the poor guy lying out in the driveway, shot and freezing. So I pulled the quilt over Connor and hurried downstairs. I got a coat out of the front closet, ran outside, and used the coat to cover up the guy from the neck down. He was still breathing, still unconscious. But I talked to him and said things like, 'Hang in there, guy,' and 'Help's on the way.' Finally, the police and the ambulance showed up."

He wiped the tears from his face and then looked at her. "Anyway, that's what happened. Do you believe me?"

Laura hesitated. Her eyes wrestled with his, and then she nodded. "I believe you, Joe."

He smiled gratefully. "I knew you would. I told Vic in the car on the way here, I told him, 'Mrs. Gretchell's going to believe me. She'll know I'm innocent. She'll help us.'"

Laura stared at him.

The smile faded from his face. "You don't remember me, do you?"

Laura had no idea what he was talking about. She shook her head.

"My grandmother legally adopted me and changed my last name," he said. "I used to be Joey Spiers. You were my teacher in third grade."

"My God, Joey," she whispered. Of course she remembered him—the poor, abused little kid with the dirty clothes, the boy she tried so hard to protect.

He nodded. "You looked out for me. You saved my life, Mrs. Gretchell. I told Vic, we need to see my old teacher. She saved my life once before. She'll do it again."

CHAPTER NINE

Monday—5:33 P.M.

In Joe's face, Laura could now see the pitiful, timid little boy from years ago. She remembered the way he took Donald Clapp's constant abuse without crying or complaint—as if it were something he just had to accept in life. Now she understood why he couldn't stand up to Vic. He was still the same kid inside.

Joe said she'd saved him, but she couldn't have done a very good job of it if he'd ended up in an insane asylum and was now on the run for murdering a family of seven.

"You do remember me," he said, smiling. He planted his elbows on the counter-bar and folded his arms.

She tried to smile back. "I used to wonder what happened to you, Joe. The last I'd heard was—seventeen years ago. I was told you'd moved in with your grandmother in Tacoma."

"That's right, thanks in part to you. She got custody of me and—"

"Joe! Come look!" James called from the living room. "Joe? Come here!"

"In a minute, honey," Laura said. "Joe and I are talking . . ."

Joe climbed off the bar stool. "It's okay. I'm keeping you from your work. Vic will get ornery if he doesn't eat dinner soon. We'll talk later. You're going to help me now, aren't you?"

Laura hesitated.

"Joe, come look-it!" James called.

"I know you will," he said. Then he turned and joined James in front of the TV.

Laura opened the box of dry pasta and put a big pot of water on the stove to boil. She could hear shuffling upstairs. She glanced at the stove clock. Sophie and Liam had been up there with Vic for an hour and a half.

She looked over at Joe and James, sitting on the floor together, the light from the TV flickering across their faces in the dimly lit room. James's toy trucks were still in front of them.

"Joe? Is it all right if I go upstairs and check on my kids?" she asked.

He nodded, but didn't quite take his eyes off the television. "You can tell Vic what's for dinner. He'll want to know."

Laura headed toward the front of the house. As she approached the stairs, she gazed at the front door. If she quietly slipped out right now, what would happen? Could she make it to the wine-tasting cottage and call the police from that old rotary phone, and then get back before either Joe or Vic realized she wasn't in the house? Probably not. The trip would take at least five minutes, maybe ten. And she hadn't forgotten what Vic had said about shooting her and her children the moment he spotted a cop on the premises.

She couldn't risk it. But if Liam or Sophie could quietly walk out that door and just keep walking, they might be able to save themselves. At the same time, she didn't want either one of them taking any unnecessary chances.

Laura hurried upstairs. In the hallway, she found the linen closet door open. The closet had practically been emptied out. Towels, linen, toilet paper rolls, Kleenex boxes, medical items, and toiletries all lay on the floor in a heap against the wall. She stepped over the mess and continued down the hallway. She saw Liam's bedroom had been ransacked, too. And now her children were being forced to tear apart Sophie's room. The place looked as if it had been turned upside down. Shelves and bookcases had been cleared, and there was a mountain of books and junk on the floor. Piles of clothes covered each twin bed. Vic sat on the cushioned window seat with his legs stretched across it and his feet up. He held the gun in one hand and had Sophie's Magic 8 Ball in the other. It seemed to fascinate him.

With his camcorder, Liam was recording him on the sly. Laura had a feeling Vic knew about it and was secretly delighted—or at least, amused.

With a haggard look on her face, Sophie was emptying the contents of a dresser drawer onto her bed.

"Are you guys okay?" Laura asked guardedly.

"Oh, we're in the pink here," Vic answered, shaking the 8 Ball. "Aren't we, kids?"

Liam and Sophie stopped to stare at her. From the miserable looks on their faces, they might as well have been a couple of POWs peering at her through a barbed-wire fence. Sophie seemed to be holding back tears. Neither of them said a word. It was almost as if they'd been forbidden to talk.

"What's for dinner?" Vic asked.

"We're having pasta and meat sauce," Laura replied.

"Yum," Vic murmured. "Sounds like you and Joe were chatting up a storm downstairs. I thought I told you to keep the conversation to a minimum."

"If you have a problem with that, maybe you should take it up with Joe. He was doing most of the talking."

Vic smirked. "About old times, *Mrs. Gretchell*?"

"Among other things."

"Hey, did you kids know that your mom and Joe go way back to when he was in third grade? She was his teacher. Your mom helped shape the mind of a famous mass murderer. How about that?"

Sophie wiped her eyes and blinked at her. "Is he serious?"

"Really?" Liam asked. He had the camera on a strap on his shoulder, and he let it drop to his side.

"*Suspected* mass murderer," Laura said. "Dinner's in twenty minutes." She looked at Sophie and Liam again and tried to give them a reassuring smile, but she knew it was in vain. Reluctantly, she turned away and started down the hall.

"We'll be done here soon!" Vic called cheerfully.

Seeing Vic bully her children left Laura enraged and frustrated. She wanted to slap that snarky expression off his face. She paused by the mounds of sheets and towels by the linen closet. Among all the different medications dumped on the floor, she wished there were some kind of poison or sleeping pills or even laxatives—anything she could slip into Vic's dinner tonight that would incapacitate him. And if he had to suffer a bit in the process, that was fine by her.

But there was nothing amid the pile of things. She thought again about getting him drunk on wine—and the risks involved to her and her kids.

Downstairs, she found Joe and James still watching TV together. She kept glancing back at them while she fixed dinner.

It was strange to think that when she'd last seen Joe, he was only four years older than James. He'd been a quiet kid with a cute face. He had dimples when he smiled, but that was rare. His long, shaggy brown hair was always dirty. Nothing he wore seemed to fit, and most of the time, his clothes were filthy. On a couple of occasions, he showed up for school in a ratty pajama top instead of a shirt. She knew Joey was the only child of a single mother, and it became more and more apparent his mother didn't give a damn. Laura sent a tactfully worded note home with Joey, letting her know that some of the other children were complaining about his hygiene. And this was third grade, when most kids didn't notice things like that—especially the boys. But Donald Clapp had noticed. He'd started teasing and bullying Joey. Laura did her damnedest to stifle him before the other kids joined in the harassment.

Ms. Spiers didn't respond to her note. But the following day, Joey came to school in clean clothes. He wore the same clothes for the rest of the week—until they stank. And then he wore them again, still unwashed, part of the next week.

Ms. Spiers pulled a no-show at the parent-teacher conference. Laura tried to imagine how awful Joey's life at home was.

Each time one of her students had a birthday, they got a little present from Laura. She'd ask them to stay after class and give them a card with a little trinket inside. Sean's father was an amateur carpenter and had a woodshop in his garage. He made these wooden cutouts that she painted. It was probably politically incorrect, but the boys got stars and the girls received daisy-shaped cutouts. The birthday student's photo was in the center. Laura mass-produced them each month. The kids with birthdays during vacations and weekends all got their little birthday keepsake the day before the break. When Laura gave Joey Spiers his star, he seemed absolutely awestruck by the gesture. It broke her heart that he seemed so grateful for so little.

She became very protective of him. From the window of the teachers' lunchroom, she'd watch Joey on the playground. She lost track of how many times she ran out there to discipline Donald—for throwing pebbles at Joey, for tripping him, for pushing him off the monkey bars. The monkey bars incident was one of the times she sent Donald to the principal, Tom Freeman.

It was also the only time she saw Joey cry. He'd had the wind knocked out of him when he'd hit the ground. Otherwise, he never complained about the abuse. He didn't even seem to have enough sense to avoid Donald. He just took it.

Donald was disruptive in class in general, but often he'd blurt out something derogatory about Joey—that he was stupid, that he was a pig, or that he "smelled like a steaming pile of dog shit." The "dog shit" re-mark netted Donald a lot of laughs and another trip to Tom Freeman's office. When Donald hurled these in-sults at him in class, Joey would always look a bit sur-prised or confused. Sometimes, Laura could see that he was hurt and didn't want to show it.

She talked to the principal about getting in touch with Joey's mother. The woman needed to know that her son was being bullied. Laura wondered if she was one of those mothers who slept all morning and made her child wake, dress, and feed himself before school. Maybe that explained it. Joey often came to school sick, too.

Laura never heard from Ms. Spiers. But Donald's father showed up to defend his obnoxious kid. And to emphasize his contempt for her, Mr. Clapp planted himself outside her classroom window that one morn-ing so he could glare through the glass at her.

A few days after that incident, Laura spotted Donald in the school cafeteria, picking on Joey again. He swiped Joey's brownie and upturned his lunch tray, spilling a bowl of chili all down the front of Joey's shirt. The tray-tipping was obviously deliberate.

Laura sent Donald to Tom Freeman's office once again. She came across a shirt for Joey in the lost and found. Then she took him into the private lavatory off the teachers' lounge so he could wash up and change. But he didn't seem to know what to do. He just stood there by the sink—with chili splattered down the front of him and a worried expression on his face.

"Joey, honey, you need to take off that shirt," she told him, standing in the bathroom doorway. She had the lost-and-found shirt draped over her arm. "C'mon, it's okay . . ."

He unbuttoned his shirt and pulled it off.

Laura gasped.

His slight shoulders, back, and chest were bruised and covered with at least a dozen reddish welts that looked like burn marks. And he was so emaciated, she could see his rib cage.

Laura took a deep breath and tried to conceal her shock. But tears came to her eyes. She bent down and took the soiled shirt from him. Then she gently touched one of the welts that looked new. It was on his upper chest. "Joey, what happened here? Did you get burned?"

He winced a little but didn't say anything.

"You know, I think I'll have the school nurse take a look at you," she said. "Maybe she can put something on these marks to make them heal faster. Do they hurt?"

He nodded.

"Did you get burned?"

He nodded again. "Mommy's cigarettes," he murmured, "because I was bad."

Laura stopped to take a few more deep breaths. "Well, let's get you fixed up, honey. I promise it won't hurt." Her voice began to shake. "I promise no one will hurt you again . . ."

She had Joey wait in the teachers' restroom while she ran down the hall to the principal's office. She pulled Tom Freeman away from disciplining Donald so that he could see what Ms. Spiers was doing to her little boy. After one look at Joey, Tom immediately contacted the Department of Children and Family Services.

The following day, Joey wasn't in school. Laura learned that he was temporarily staying with his grandmother in Tacoma while Children and Family Services investigated the extent of his mother's abuse. Donald Clapp was absent that day as well.

But Mr. Clapp showed up—quite unexpectedly.

While Laura was recuperating in the hospital, she got updates—usually over the phone, but sometimes in person from Tom Freeman. The school principal didn't sugarcoat things for her. Mr. Clapp's attorney maintained that she'd unduly persecuted his client's son. And Donald claimed she gave Joey preferential treatment over all the other children in the class. Meanwhile, a court-appointed lawyer for Joey's mother asserted that—without another adult present—Laura had made Joey partially disrobe and then she inappropriately touched him. Tom said that although the charges were ridiculous, an official investigation was pending. So—while still in her hospital bed, Laura was interviewed for ninety minutes by two brisk women from the Board of Education.

Laura didn't admit to them—or anyone besides Sean—that she wondered if there wasn't a grain of truth in what Mr. Clapp's attorney had said. She loathed Donald, and it was mostly for the way he picked on poor Joey. It was true: She felt very protective of that little boy, and she wanted to help him.

Her concern for Joey kept her mind off her own troubles while she recuperated in the hospital. Her injuries kept her out of the lawyers' offices and the courtroom, but while still recovering, she signed four different affidavits—one against Mr. Clapp and three against Ms. Spiers.

In the end, Laura was cleared of all accusations. Mr. Clapp ended up in prison. After he died there, his wife moved with her kids to Eugene and remarried.

Joey's grandmother was awarded custody of him. His worthless mother served very little time in jail and spent several months in a state-run rehab facility. She was allowed supervised visits with her son twice a year. Laura had a feeling the woman didn't bother showing up for any of them.

Laura had often wondered what had happened to Joey. Now she knew. And now he expected her to help him again.

From the kitchen, she glanced over at Joe and James, still mesmerized by the kids' show on TV. It wasn't lost on her that the last time she'd tried to help Joe, she'd wound up with thirty-eight stitches in her face.

The wastebasket taken from Liam's bedroom was now full, almost overflowing. Beside it were more items Vic had deemed as contraband from the other rooms, closets, and bathrooms. It was an eclectic assortment: two flashlights, the baby-monitor set from the linen closet, a can of aerosol hair spray, various medications, a nail file, the modem to their dad's desktop computer, another letter opener, an ancient pay-as-you-go phone, three pairs of scissors, an old wooden ruler with a sharp metal edge, a set of knitting needles, Sophie's laptop, and several other items.

He also kept her father's checkbook, an iPod Classic, and all the money he'd uncovered—including loose change. He even took Liam's Homer Simpson piggy bank.

He stopped in her parents' bedroom and stole a pearl necklace from her mother's jewelry drawer. It had belonged to Sophie's grandmother and was supposed to go to Sophie when she got older. Vic slipped it into the pocket of his cargo pants.

Sophie's hatred for the guy was surpassed only by her fear of him. She didn't like it when her own brother poked around her bedroom. And here was this murderer, making her clear off every shelf and empty every drawer for his inspection.

As she unloaded her desk drawers, Sophie worried Vic would want to read her diaries. She wanted to be a writer when she graduated from college. Early on, she'd figured it would be smart to keep a record of everything she was going through—so that, some day, she could use it in one of her books. The three maroon notebooks held two years' worth of private reflections, embarrassing moments, heartaches, and fantasies. She kept the diaries buried in the bottom of her desk drawer—under a pile of school assignments and short stories she'd written. The journals looked pretty inconspicuous amid all the other things she'd already dumped on the floor.

"What are those?" Vic asked, nodding at the books. He was standing beside the window near her dresser.

"Notebooks for school," she lied.

Liam was by her bathroom door, subtly recording the two of them.

Vic seemed to buy her explanation. Then he looked out the window—for the fourth or fifth time. There was a tree outside it, blocking the view of the vineyard. "You could climb out onto that branch and then right down the tree." He smirked at her. "Or maybe you and your boyfriend, Lucky Matt, already know that."

Sophie gave him an icy stare.

He turned to Liam. "Cut that camera shit out and make yourself useful. Come with me . . ."

Biting his lip, Liam lowered the camera.

Vic led him into the hallway. "Hey, Joe!" Sophie heard him call. "I'm sending the kid down to show you where they keep the hammer and nails. I need to nail shut a window in the girl's room. I want you with him when he gets them. Then send him back up to me!"

Sophie heard Joe yell something back at him, but she couldn't make out the words.

With Vic out of the room, she moved toward Liam's wastebasket—full of items Vic feared they might use to defend themselves. She eyed the knitting needles on top of the heap. She was just about to reach for them when Vic stepped back into the room.

Sophie picked up a couple of sweaters from the floor instead. She heard Liam running down the stairs.

Now that they were alone in the bedroom, Vic gave her that lecherous look again. Sophie did her best to ignore him. She picked up some more clothes from the piles on the floor and returned them to her dresser drawers.

"If you need to use the bathroom, honey, do it now," he said, sitting on the edge of the twin bed she usually slept in. "But leave the door open a crack."

Even if her life had depended on it, Sophie couldn't have peed with him right outside her half-open bathroom door. But she welcomed any chance to get out from under his filthy gaze for a couple of minutes. She ducked into the old-fashioned pink-and-white tiled bathroom and splashed some water on her face.

She left the faucet running and crept over to the small frosted-glass window above the hamper. The window seat's picture window didn't open, and he'd just announced his plan to nail shut the only other window in her bedroom. But he hadn't bothered to check this window yet—maybe because it was small. Still, Sophie figured she could squeeze through it if she wanted to. The window was above a garden trellis outside. She wasn't sure if she could lower herself from the ledge to the trellis—or if she'd have to jump.

With one knee on the hamper, Sophie reached up and raised the window. It squeaked, and she coughed to cover up the noise. She got the window open high enough to poke her head out. She couldn't lower herself to the trellis from here. She'd have to jump, and the trellis looked pretty rickety. She might crash through it and kill herself.

Feeling defeated, she pulled her head back in and quietly closed the window. She heard Vic moving something around in the bedroom. "Well, you sure have a pretty collection of panties here," he called to her. "I can imagine you in them . . ."

Sophie shut off the faucet. She saw her apprehensive reflection in the mirror.

"So—are you a virgin?"

Sophie didn't answer. She thought about the Singleton murders again. She'd seen photos of the family. A couple of the girls were a little older than her, and very pretty. But according to the news reports, no one had been raped or molested.

Was it something they'd kept from the press?

"Did you hear me?" Vic called. "I asked if you're a virgin."

She hesitated. "That—that isn't any of your business."

"Maybe I'll just have to find out for myself later."

Sophie said nothing. She stayed in the bathroom—and wondered what was taking Liam so long.

It was too quiet up there.

Laura stood at the bottom of the stairs and anxiously listened. She couldn't stand the idea of her daughter up in her bedroom alone with that murderer. She'd seen the way he'd looked at her earlier.

It had only been a minute or two since Liam had come downstairs—and then he and Joe had headed down to the basement. Only a minute or two, and she was going crazy. How could Joe expect her to drive off tomorrow and leave her children alone with him and Vic for hours?

She hurried back through the kitchen and then to the top of the basement stairs. She saw Joe and Liam coming up the steps. Joe had the hammer in his hand, and Liam carried an old Welch's jelly jar full of various nails.

"What took you so long?" she whispered to her son. "Hurry up, honey. I don't like your sister being alone up there with him."

"We weren't sure what size nails he needed, so we got these," Liam explained, showing her the jar. Joe handed him the hammer, and Liam made a beeline for the front hall.

Laura heard him running up the stairs a moment later. She turned to Joe. "Listen, if I go to Lopez Island tomorrow, you'll have to agree to at least one condition. The most important thing is that I'm able to phone here at least every couple of hours and talk to my children—so they can assure me they're fine."

Joe hesitated. "Well, I'll have to clear that with Vic."

She gave him her best teacher's stare. "Well, you'll have to make him understand. I won't go unless you agree to that . . ."

Sophie stayed in the bathroom until she heard Liam return. Even though she hadn't used it, she flushed the toilet and then washed her hands. She emerged from the bathroom in time to see Vic nailing shut the bedroom window.

She and Liam quietly watched him finish the job.

Then he made the two of them lug his collection of confiscated materials and plunder downstairs.

Sophie found Joe sitting on the floor in the family room with James. They were playing with James's toy trucks and watching *Sid the Science Kid* on TV. It was a bit bewildering to see her baby brother hanging all over this accused murderer. Her mom didn't seem to mind. She was in the kitchen fixing dinner.

"Hey, kiddo," Vic said to his friend. "Do me a favor and help Junior here haul this crap out to the garage, will ya? Somebody else can look after the brat."

Joe quickly got to his feet. He seemed almost as scared of Vic as they were. He collected Liam's loaded trash can from Sophie and nodded politely at her.

Vic opened the basement door, glanced down the stairs, and then shut the door. "Remind me after dinner to nail this door shut," he said to Joe.

Sitting down on the family room floor, Sophie took over keeping James amused. Her baby brother was clearly unhappy to see Joe step outside. "Joe!" he yelled. He even started to cry a little—until she distracted him with the trucks.

But then Vic grabbed the remote and stepped between them and the TV. He changed channels from *Sid the Science Kid* to the evening news, and James became all pouty again.

The Singleton murders were still the top story on the local news. The newscaster said a man "tentatively identified as Victor Moles, a person of interest in the Singleton murder case," had been recorded by a security camera as he'd stolen some beer and confronted a clerk in a Seattle convenience store at the time of the Lopez Island killings.

This was a revelation for Sophie, who had assumed Vic had murdered the whole family. It seemed that he now had an air-tight alibi.

The news show also had an update on Wes Banyan, the University of Washington freshman who had been dating Jae Singleton. He was still in critical condition, but stable. He wasn't yet able to identify or describe the man who had shot him in the Singletons' driveway. It was unclear from the newscast whether or not Banyan had been shown mug shots of Vic and Joe.

Sophie couldn't help wondering if Joe had been telling the truth earlier when he'd said they were innocent.

The next spot on the news showed Marilee Cronin, one of Scott Singleton's partners in his church. "Scott had the courage to say what we're all thinking," she said at some press conference while flashbulbs popped. She wore a red blouse with a huge bow at the neck. Her fake-looking flaxen hair was swept all to one side and fastened in a strange-looking single pigtail. "Well, Scott may have been murdered for speaking his mind against the degenerates who hope to undermine our moral values. He may have had his throat slashed for speaking *our* mind, but his voice will not be silenced . . ."

Sophie had lately seen enough of this woman on TV to hate her. She turned away from the screen and tried to keep James entertained.

Liam returned with Joe. He gave the young man a wide berth. He was obviously a little more cautious around him than their baby brother was.

"Do you need any help in the kitchen, Mrs. Gretchell?" Joe asked.

"Joe, get in here," Vic commanded. He plopped down in Sophie's dad's lounge chair.

Joe meekly returned to the family room.

"Sit down," Vic said, nodding at the sofa. He

scowled at James—and then at Sophie. "Does that kid have to be in here?"

She wordlessly grabbed James by the hand and led him to the kitchen counter-bar, where Liam sat, filming the two men on his camcorder.

"Don't hang out with them," she heard Vic rebuke his friend. "What are you trying to do, *bond* with them or something?"

Sophie helped James climb up on the bar stool beside Liam. "You know, I think you're really pushing your luck photographing that creep," she murmured to her brother. "Do me a favor and keep James occupied while I help Mom, okay?"

"Hey, they've got pay-per-view here," Vic announced. He cranked up the volume on the TV.

Staring at him, Sophie realized the gray-and-blue striped sweater Vic wore actually belonged to her father. That was why it had looked so familiar earlier. He must have stolen it out of the closet. So there he sat in her dad's chair, wearing her dad's sweater, while her mom slaved away, fixing his dinner. For a second, Sophie imagined him as her father, and the thought made her stomach turn.

She stepped into the kitchen and started to set out the plates and napkins.

Standing at the stove, her mother looked like the scared, abused wife. It broke Sophie's heart to see her so shaky and on edge. It scared her, too. Everyone in the family always turned to her mom during a crisis. And here she was, on the brink of falling apart. The

scars on her face were more noticeable, which sometimes happened when she was extremely stressed. An
ugly reddish bruise had formed on her chin from where
Vic must have hit her earlier in the day.

"What happened there?" she whispered to her mom,
nodding at her chin. "Did he do that to you?"

"It's nothing," her mom murmured. "What happened upstairs?"

"You saw," she said under her breath. "It's going to
take a week to clean up that mess—if we're all still
alive."

Her mother pulled a bottle of red wine from the cabinet. "Did he—try anything?"

Sophie just shook her head. She was too embarrassed to go into it now. "He stole Grandma's pearl
necklace from your drawer."

Her mother sighed and returned to the stove. She
stirred the boiling pasta.

With the TV volume so loud, Sophie figured it was
safe to keep talking with her mother. "Did you just
hear that on the news about Vic? He was in Seattle at
the time of the—"

Her mother nodded. "Yes, I know."

"Do you think it's possible they haven't really killed
anyone?"

"I'm not sure about Joe," her mom said under her
breath. "But Vic is dangerous. I know he's a killer. Don't
do anything to get him angry. Please, honey. Tell Liam,
too. He'd kill you without giving it a second thought.
Believe me. I know what I'm talking about . . ."

* * *

Vic had chosen a Steven Seagal movie from the pay-per-view lineup. He'd pumped up the volume so loud that it was oppressive. On the screen, some man had just gotten stabbed in the eye, and the blade was shown coming out the back of his head.

Vic let out a cheer.

Sophie sat at the kitchen counter-bar with James, trying to distract him and making sure more of his dinner went into his mouth than onto the floor. For the last twenty minutes, she'd been listening to the screaming, explosions, and nonstop cursing from the TV. James had given up pointing out when someone "said a swear." Sophie sat between her little brother and the TV so that he couldn't see the movie's gratuitous nudity and violent sequences.

She glanced over at Vic, still in her father's recliner. Liam had set a TV table at his side. He'd also set up one for Joe, still seated on the sofa. Joe didn't seem to enjoy the movie as much as his buddy. Liam had given them place mats, forks, and napkins, and then he'd retreated to the counter-bar to sit with her and James. He'd resumed recording the two uninvited houseguests every few minutes.

"Hey, kid—Lee-ham," Vic called, mispronouncing Liam's name. "Come look at this. I want you to eat in here with us. Why are you in the kitchen with the women anyway? Are you a fairy or something?"

Liam grimaced, but didn't say anything—nor did he move.

Their mom set two small bowls of salad on the counter in front of Liam. "Could you take these to them?" she whispered. "And go ahead and sit with them if it makes the bastard happy. This is about the only time I'd let you watch a movie like that. You might as well take advantage."

"I already saw it a while back at Kyle's house," he whispered. "It's a sucky movie, Mom." He shuffled into the family room with the salads.

A few moments later, Sophie heard a crash. She and James almost jumped off their stools.

"I don't eat that goddamn rabbit food!" Vic growled.

Sophie could see the broken bowl and a trail of lettuce, croutons, and cherry tomatoes on the rug in the family room.

"Vic, please," Joe murmured. "C'mon . . ."

James looked frightened, on the verge of crying. Sophie stroked him on the back. "It's okay, Jamie," she whispered. "Never mind him. He's just a big jerk."

"I'm allergic to rabbit food," Vic announced with a laugh, "just like you're allergic to peanuts, Lee-ham. Your mama told me about that, kid. One peanut and you're dead, right?" He called toward the kitchen. "Are there any peanuts in the spaghetti sauce tonight, Mama? Better not be!"

Sophie kept stroking James's back to calm him. What Vic said didn't even make any sense. He was just being obnoxious for the sake of being obnoxious.

Liam ignored him as he picked up the mess. Joe got up to help him.

"Leave it for one of the women!" Vic grumbled. "Sit down—both of you. You're blocking the goddamn movie. You're a better door than a window."

Sophie didn't want her mother to have to clean up after him, so she climbed off the stool, grabbed some paper towels, and hurried into the family room. She was careful not to block his precious view of the TV as she picked up the salad, which was now just rubbish.

Her mom came in with the dinner plates of pasta and bread. Joe muttered a polite "Thank you," while Vic immediately started stuffing his face.

Sophie noticed Liam recording him again.

Her mom returned to the kitchen and then brought them each a glass of red wine. She served Joe first and then set a glass on Vic's TV table.

"What the hell is this?" he asked, glaring at her.

"It's a very good cabernet," she answered.

"So good that maybe I'll have another glass? And then a few more glasses, right? And maybe I'll get so drunk, I'll pass out. Is that what you're trying to do?"

"Of course not, I just thought—"

Before she could finish, Vic swatted the wineglass off the table. It flew across the room and with a loud pop, shattered against the wall.

At the kitchen counter-bar, James let out a startled scream.

Liam captured it all on his camcorder.

A splotch of red wine bled down the family room wall. Shards of glass were everywhere. On her hands and knees, Sophie could see a few pieces in the rug, catching the light. She tried not to move for fear of cutting herself.

"Get us sodas!" Vic shouted over James's crying. "And keep that kid quiet! I'm trying to watch a movie here!"

Snatching up Joe's wineglass, her mother hurried back to the kitchen.

Sophie got to her feet and threaded around the shards of glass. She was worried about James. If he didn't quiet down, Vic was bound to go after him—maybe even hurt him. She stood James up on the bar stool and wrapped her arms around him. She gently pushed his face into the crook of her shoulder to muffle his sobs.

"Hey, that's enough!" Vic yelled at Liam. "Cut that shit out!"

Sophie turned in time to see her brother setting the camcorder in his lap.

"Give that to me," Vic said.

Sophie had a feeling the minute Vic got ahold of the camera he'd smash it to pieces. She stood there frozen and held James close to her.

Liam hesitated.

"Gimme!" Vic bellowed. He held his hand out.

Liam stared at him. Then he gazed down at his camcorder. He had a forlorn look on his face—as if he knew what would happen to his prized camera once he surrendered it. He took a deep breath and then hurled the camcorder toward the big wine splotch on the wall. With a loud bang, the camera smashed into pieces and left a gouge in the plaster.

Then Liam went back to staring defiantly at Vic.

"You little shit!" Vic sprang to his feet, tipping over the TV table. The plate—along with the pasta and meat sauce—landed on the rug. He reached back and pulled his gun out from under his shirttail.

Joe jumped up from the sofa and stepped in front of Liam. "No, Vic, wait—"

"God, no, please!" Sophie heard her mother scream.

Vic yelled at his friend: "Move!"

Joe shook his head. "Vic, you're tired. You were driving all last night, and you practically haven't had any sleep since yesterday morning. You don't want to do this. Mrs. Gretchell is going to help me tomorrow. She's doing us a favor. We promised her. No one's going to get hurt."

"Get him out of my sight," Vic hissed.

Joe didn't move.

Over near the counter-bar, Sophie held onto her baby brother. She watched in horror as Vic turned the gun toward the two of them.

"You heard me, Joe," he said. "Get that kid out of here. Get them all out of my sight or I'll execute the whole fucking family right now."

Sophie had no doubt he meant every word.

CHAPTER TEN

Monday—6:09 P.M.

"C'mon, c'mon, please, hurry up," he whispered.

Joe herded them into Sophie's room. Laura had taken James from Sophie and carried him upstairs. She'd gotten him to stop crying. But he looked terrified. His whole body was trembling. In Sophie's room, like in the hallway, Laura and the kids had to step over or weave around the piles of things that had been pulled off shelves and yanked out of closets.

Once they were inside Sophie's bedroom, James let out a few frail cries. Laura found an uncluttered spot on one of the twin beds and sat down with him. She rocked him in her lap.

Sophie and Liam followed her into the bedroom. "Oh, my God," Sophie whispered to her brother. "I couldn't believe it when you threw your camera. That took guts, it really did . . ."

But Liam didn't seem excited about it at all. His face had turned pale, and he was visibly shaking. He brushed past his sister, ducked into her bathroom, and shut the door. A few moments later, Laura could hear him throwing up and coughing.

"You guys need to keep quiet," Joe whispered. He stood in the bedroom doorway. He looked almost as sickly as Liam. "I don't know how long you'll have to stay in here, but please, just—just keep still. I've seen Vic get this way before, and you don't want to make him any madder . . ."

Laura couldn't help thinking that she'd already seen Vic *this way* at least two other times—today.

Sophie knocked on the bathroom door and asked her brother if he was okay.

Laura shushed her. "Sophie, honey, leave him alone."

"Please, just keep it down," Joe said. "Stay in here, and don't come out unless I say it's okay. I'll be out here in the hall." He shut the door.

Sophie leaned against the dresser and covered her face with her hands for a few moments. Then with a sigh, she started to pick up some of her clothes and put them away in her closet.

In their silence, Laura could still hear the TV blaring downstairs.

She kept rocking James and smoothing back his hair. "Liam, honey," she called softly. "Are you all right in there?"

"Yeah!" he answered, his voice a bit strained and muffled. "Just give me a few minutes, okay?"

"I still can't believe he broke his camera like that, his precious camera," Sophie whispered. She put some clothes in her dresser. She glanced toward the bathroom. "I think he's crying in there," she said, barely even whispering.

But Laura understood her. She understood what each one of her children was going through right now. They were terrified. And there was nothing she could say to calm them, nothing that wouldn't be a lie.

There was one little piece of encouragement she could hold onto. Downstairs, she'd just seen Joe stand up to his friend. When Vic had pulled out his gun, Joe had stepped between him and Liam—and he'd talked his buddy out of killing them. If Joe hadn't done that, Liam very well might have been lying out in the vineyard beside Dane tonight.

"Listen, honey," Laura said quietly to her daughter. "Tomorrow, they want me to go to Lopez Island and run this errand for them . . ."

Sophie stopped putting clothes away and stared at her.

"I don't want to leave you kids alone here with them, but I don't have a choice. While I'm gone, you have to be careful not to antagonize Vic. You saw it tonight. You can't get him mad . . ."

"What are you talking about? I didn't do anything!" Sophie hissed.

"I know you didn't—"

"He's the one who started throwing glasses and plates around and breaking everything. Not only is he a pig, but he's bat-shit crazy on top of it. No one was provoking him, Mom."

"I know, I saw, I was there," she whispered. "I'm just saying—avoid him as much as you can tomorrow . . ."

"You might as well tell me to avoid a snake."

"And be nice to Joe. Making friends with him is our best chance for survival. At this point, I'm pretty sure he won't let anything bad happen to . . ." She pointed to James, who had his face against her shoulder. Laura could feel his drool or tears dampening her pullover.

"Was he really a student of yours?" Sophie asked.

Laura nodded. "Third grade. He had a pretty tough, messed-up childhood."

"Why am I not surprised?"

"I'll tell you about it sometime," Laura said.

Sophie smiled a little. "Hey, downstairs—with the wine earlier, was he right? Were you trying to get him drunk?"

Laura shrugged. "I thought it was worth a shot. I guess he's not as stupid as he looks."

Sophie put a few more things away. "So—Joe thinks there's someone on Lopez who can help prove he's innocent, and he wants you to find them, is that it?"

"Pretty much."

"So after you leave here tomorrow, you're going to the police, aren't you?"

Laura sighed. "Vic promised me that if he sees one policeman or police car here, he's going to . . ." She mouthed the words *kill everyone*. "And I don't think that's an idle threat."

"Well, what if Joe's wrong?" Sophie whispered. "What if he's crazy—and he really killed those people? I mean, wasn't he in an institution? That's what they said on the news. Plus, just looking at him, I can tell, there's something a little off . . ."

Laura nodded. "I know."

"While you're out there, are you at least going to call Dad? Maybe he'll know what to do."

"Honey, what's he going to do? He's in Europe."

Sophie got down on her knees and collected a few things at the foot of the bed. "Yeah, but Dad always seems to know . . ." Her voice trailed off.

Laura couldn't see her face. "Well, your dad hasn't had the displeasure of meeting Vic, so I don't think he's in a position to make a terrific judgment call on . . ."

Sophie stood up, empty-handed. Shaking her head, she put a finger to her own lips.

"What?" Laura asked.

She hurried to her desk and hunted around for something amid the mess on the desktop. She finally found a legal pad and a pen. Laura rocked James some more. She watched Sophie write on the legal pad. Her daughter brought the pad over to her, and Laura read it:

THE BABY MONITOR IS ON & UNDER THE BED. HE'S LISTENING TO US NOW.

James let out a little moan as Laura set him on the bed. She got down on the floor, and Sophie lifted the bedspread for her. She could see the baby monitor there in the darkness, amid a few dust bunnies. The green light was on. It was just her luck that this was one of the rare times the batteries worked in the damn thing. They'd last used the baby monitor months ago in Seattle, when James had had a cough and a fever. Since then, she'd kept the monitor set in the linen closet. She realized Vic must have found it, and planted the device under Sophie's bed earlier today. He obviously had the receiver half of the set and was listening to their every word right now.

She felt a wave of dread wash over her. What had they been talking about? What had Vic heard and how damaging was it?

They hadn't mentioned any brilliant escape plans. She'd merely told Sophie to avoid Vic and be friendly to Joe. Sophie had compared Vic to a snake, and she'd said something about Vic not being as stupid as he looked.

As much as hearing that might make him fly off the handle, Laura couldn't help laughing a little. She sat back down on the edge of the bed and giggled some more. Yet she had tears in her eyes.

"What's so funny?" Sophie whispered.

Laura shook her head. "I'm just punchy."

"So are we just going to leave it on?" Sophie asked under her breath.

Laura nodded. "Let's," she said quietly. "We might be able to use it to our advantage—somehow. For now, just be careful of what you say."

Sophie shuddered and rubbed her arms. "I feel like he's in the room with us."

"Why's everyone whispering?" James asked—in a loud whisper. He crawled off the bed and started picking through a pile of books on the floor.

Laura managed a smile, "We're whispering because it's just about your bedtime." She got to her feet and started to clear off the top of the bed. "C'mon, honey. Why don't you lie down here and see if you can fall asleep?"

She glanced over at the bathroom door and wondered about Liam. Sophie must have seen her and read her mind, because she knocked on the door. "Are you okay in there?"

"I'm fine. I'll be out in a minute, okay?"

"Well, crack open the window, will you? I don't want your barf smell wafting into my bedroom."

Sophie returned to the bed and picked up the legal pad. With a sigh, she tore off the top sheet and slid it under the bathroom door.

"We'll buy you a new camcorder, honey," Laura called to him. "I promise."

Standing amid the pile of books on the floor, James pouted at her. "Is that man going to yell at us again?"

Laura shook her head. "Not tonight, I hope." She patted the bed. "C'mon, lie down."

"But I want George," he murmured.

George was his stuffed tiger. George was the name of every favorite stuffed animal he had. Even if the stuffed animal was a famous Disney movie character, James redubbed it George. He also gave the name to his short-lived goldfish and a turtle that lasted a month before it escaped and died behind the radiator in his bedroom in Seattle.

"George is on vacation tonight." Laura pulled back the bedspread and gave the pillow a pat. "C'mon, sweetie. You can rough it and sleep in your underwear tonight. I don't think you're going to like anything from Sophie's books, but I can tell you a story—"

Laura stopped talking. She realized the TV downstairs had been turned off.

Sophie noticed, too. She stopped putting her clothes away.

They could hear Vic coming up the stairs.

Laura reached for James and steered him to the bed.

"But I don't wanna—"

She shushed him. "You've got to be real quiet, honey," she whispered.

She had a feeling Vic had heard enough on the baby monitor earlier to send him over the edge.

Liam opened the bathroom door. He still looked pale. He must have heard the footsteps, too, because he didn't say anything. The piece of paper from the legal pad was in his shaky hand.

They stood and listened to Vic and Joe murmuring in the hallway. Laura couldn't make out the words. She couldn't quite tell from Vic's tone if he was angry or not. She sat down on the bed so that she could shield James in case Vic barged in and started shooting. She wanted to tell Sophie and Liam to get away from the door and take cover, but for a moment, she couldn't talk.

She saw the doorknob move back and forth. There was no lock on Sophie's door.

"No, Vic, please," she heard Joe whisper.

Laura glanced around the room for something she could use to defend her kids and herself. But Vic had already turned the place upside down and cleared out any possible weapons.

The door squeaked and seemed to bend in—as if someone heavy was leaning against the other side.

"Come on out," Vic called.

No one in the room moved.

"Come on out," he repeated, more firmly. "Don't keep me waiting."

Laura wondered why he didn't just open the door. If he was going to come in and start shooting, he would have done that by now.

She stood up and moved toward the door.

Liam ran in front of her. "No, Mom," he whispered.

She gently pushed her son aside and moved around him. With her hand a bit unsteady, she reached for the doorknob and tried to turn it. But it didn't move. She tugged and jerked at the knob, but it still didn't budge.

"C'mon out," Vic growled. "I want to talk to you!"

"The door's stuck," Laura called. "The knob won't turn. Try it on your side."

She didn't hear any movement on the other side of the door. "Give it a good pull!" Vic said.

Laura tried, and Liam even attempted to help her. "It's impossible," she said loudly. "The doorknob's stuck!"

She heard Vic chuckle. "And it's going to stay stuck the rest of the night. We'll let you out in the morning."

"What?" Laura yanked at the doorknob, but to no avail. She couldn't figure out how he'd locked them in. "Wait a minute! My children haven't had any dinner. Joe?"

"Joe's not going to help you," Vic replied. Then he murmured, "Come on, kiddo." From the floorboards squeaking, it sounded like they were moving down the hall—toward the stairs.

"Wait!" Laura yelled, twisting and pulling at the doorknob. She finally gave up.

Then she heard the TV downstairs blaring again.

CHAPTER ELEVEN

Monday—10:11 P.M.

For dinner they all shared a package of Gummi Bears and a pack of Rolos from Sophie's desk drawer. The Rolos tasted fine, but had a chalky film on the chocolate shell, and Sophie confessed she didn't know exactly how old the pack was, but it had made the trip from Seattle. No one complained.

James finally drifted off to sleep around seven-fifteen—without his stuffed tiger, George. He was briefly awoken by some hammering downstairs. Sophie thought Vic might be nailing shut another window, but then Laura remembered he'd said something earlier about blocking their access to the basement. The pounding lasted only two or three minutes, and then James drifted back to sleep after that.

They were careful about what they said aloud. Laura had a whispered argument with Liam, who was hell-bent on trying to escape out Sophie's bathroom window. He was convinced he could make the jump onto the trellis—and then to the ground. Laura thought it was way too risky. The trellis roof was too weak to withstand his body weight—especially if he leapt onto it. He was liable to crash through the thing and break his neck. The noise would certainly alert Vic, and an escape attempt tonight would probably put Vic over the edge. Liam might not have Joe to step between him and Vic the next time. So Laura wouldn't allow it. When Liam had excused himself to use the bathroom about an hour ago, she'd given him a "Don't Even Think About Trying It" look.

Sophie stayed busy cleaning up. But Liam was going a bit stir-crazy without his smartphone or a computer or the TV. They had Sophie's clock radio, but there were only two stations that came in clearly: one country and one easy listening. Liam liked neither. And they couldn't even have a decent conversation because they knew Vic was listening in.

At least they each had a place to sleep. James was all set. Laura had insisted Sophie take her own bed. She would sleep on the window seat, where she now sat with one of Sophie's books in her lap. Sophie had an old sleeping bag in her closet—left over from sixth grade. It had pink, white, and purple tulips on it. Liam said he'd sleep in the bag, but he pointed out that if Vic changed his mind and decided to kill them all in their sleep, he'd die of embarrassment when the police found him in that thing.

"But you'll already be dead, stupid," Sophie pointed out.

She'd finished straightening up the room, and now sat on her bed, reading one of her books. "And God, would you stop pacing around? You're driving me crazy!"

"I can't help it. I'm bored!"

"Well, why don't you take one of your famous ninety-minute showers? I'd like to know what you do in there for so long. In fact, wait a minute. On second thought, I really don't want to know."

"Oh, screw you!"

"Hey," Laura gently interrupted. She frowned at Liam. "Language. And we're stuck here until morning, so try to get along. If you two start bickering, I'm really going to lose it."

Sophie looked over the top of her book at her. "Honestly, Mom, I don't think there's another person under eighty who uses the word *bicker*."

Laura ignored her. "You know, none of us may have a chance to shower tomorrow. If neither one of you wants to take a shower, I could sure use one. I could use a change of clothes, too. Sophie, you don't happen to have a pullover or a . . ."

Laura trailed off. She heard someone coming up the stairs.

Sophie put her book down.

They all watched the door and waited.

The door creaked and then seemed to bow inward again. Laura wondered what Vic was doing to make the knob stick. She also wondered what he wanted at this hour. They hadn't been making much noise at all.

The door opened. Vic was alone. He carried a crowbar in his hand. All Laura could think was that he was going to beat one of them to death with it.

He pointed to her and then crooked his finger. "Come with me, Teach," he muttered. "Your old man called and left a message. You need to call him back."

Laura got to her feet. She warily stepped out to the hallway with him.

Liam took a step toward them. "Mom?"

Vic shut the door—practically in his face. He took the crowbar and wedged it into the doorframe—near the doorknob. He gave it a little shake to make sure it was snug in there. Laura realized the taut pressure against the door immobilized the latch and kept the knob from turning. It was very resourceful. She'd been right earlier: He wasn't as stupid as he looked.

He led her down the hall to her bedroom. She reached for the light, but he swatted her arm away. "You can talk to him in the dark," he said. "Sit on the bed . . ."

Stumbling over some clothes on the floor, Laura made her way to the bed and sat on the edge. Vic plopped down beside her—so that their legs were touching, almost pressed together. This close, she smelled his breath and his body odor. He took her phone out of the pocket of his cargo pants and handed it to her. "Okay, you can listen to his message."

Laura pressed the code to play back her messages.

"You have one new message at ten-oh-seven p.m.," the automated voice announced.

"Hey, babe," Sean said. "I'm bummed I've missed you. Damn. Well, I hope you're just in the shower or something, and you can call me right back. It's a little after ten your time. I don't want to head out until I've talked with you. I miss you. I miss your voice. Okay, call me. Love you."

The beep sounded to signify the end of the recording.

Hearing his voice, Laura wanted to cry. But she refused to break down in front of Vic—or rather, *beside* Vic. His shoulder, arm, and hip—the entire side of his body—were pressed against her.

"So call him back, and let him know everything's fine," Vic said. "I'll be listening. I want to hear everything you say to each other. If you give any indication there's trouble here, believe me, there will be. Now, go ahead, dial the number."

She speed-dialed Sean's number. It rang only once, and he picked up. "Hey, babe, I'm so glad to see your name on the screen . . ."

"Hey, you," she managed to say. "How's Europe? Where are you now? I think your itinerary said you were in Paris."

"Actually, I'm in Burgundy right now. I'll be in Paris tomorrow night. Never mind that itinerary. I screwed up on it. I miss you. I miss the kids. Are they still up?"

Vic's head was practically against hers as he listened in. "Ah, Sophie's on her phone talking to Matt," she said. "And Liam's taking a shower. So—I'm afraid you're out of luck if you want to talk to either of them."

"Liam needs to figure out some other place to have his Liam-on-Liam action sessions. He's using up all the hot water."

"Yeah, I know," Laura murmured.

"So what happened to the phone yesterday—or rather, today? I guess it's still your today there."

"I'm not sure what happened, but it's still out. I called

the utility company, and they said it might not get fixed until tomorrow afternoon. They didn't say what the problem was. Anyway, how's everything there?"

"Fine," he said. "Actually, no, I miss you, and—well, you sound like you're upset with me. I can always tell—even when you're trying to cover it up. What's wrong?"

Laura could smell Vic's breath. She wished she could turn her head away from him. "Nothing's wrong. I'm just bushed. It's been a long day. The phone line going kaput was one of many little disasters today, nothing really worth going into here."

"You know, I thought about you all day yesterday," he said. "It was your first day completely alone there, wasn't it? Was it a little scary?"

"No, it was fine."

"Well, when you called and left me that message, you seemed a little shook up about something. What happened?"

"Nothing, really, I can't even remember. But everything's fine now."

"Oh, God, you *are* upset with me, aren't you? I can tell. Is it because I didn't want you along for this trip? Laura, honey, it's work, and it's been pretty tedious so far. Yesterday, I drove four hours to some vineyard in Alsace to listen to this gentleman farmer who looked like Gérard Depardieu talk about mildew and mealy-bugs for ninety minutes. His English was even more terrible than my French, and I could hardly understand him. I spent the whole time nodding and fake-smiling at him until my face hurt. Believe me, babe, you're not missing a thing."

"Okay, so you've convinced me," Laura said weakly. "Sorry you're not having a better time, and really, I'm sorry if I sound a little grumpy."

She couldn't help wondering how much of what he'd just said was true. Or had he spent all of yesterday with the other Mrs. Gretchell? Maybe he wasn't meeting this woman until tomorrow night, when they were supposed to check into the Grand Royal Palace Hotel together—or whatever the hell the name of the place was. Sean talked about reading the tone of her voice. Well, she could tell from his tone that he wasn't being completely honest with her.

Vic's knee nudged against hers, and he sighed impatiently. He twirled his finger in front of her as a sign to wrap up the conversation.

"Listen, I need to take a load out of the dryer before it starts to wrinkle," she said. "That's why I missed you earlier. I was down in the basement. We'll talk more tomorrow night. I promise it won't be so rushed—and I'll be in a better mood."

"Well, don't forget that package is arriving tomorrow between three and five, and you have to sign for it."

"Oh, that completely slipped my mind," she murmured. He'd sent her a text about it yesterday. "Well, if I'm not here, one of the kids will sign for it."

There was silence on the other end of the line. "Um, two questions," he said finally. "Where do you have to go? And why aren't the kids in school tomorrow?"

"Oh, of course," she said. "I'm sorry, I wasn't thinking. Of course I'll be here."

"You have to be, because you're the only one who can sign for it, and it's very important."

"Okay, I promise," she said. "Honey, I really need to go. I'm sorry. We'll talk tomorrow, okay?"

He didn't say anything for a moment. "I love you," he murmured at last.

"I love you, too," she said. "G'night—or rather, good morning."

She clicked off. Once again, she wanted to cry— and she might have, too, if she were sitting alone in the darkened wreck of a bedroom. But she wasn't alone, and now Vic's body seemed to press harder against hers. She could smell his breath again.

Laura handed him the phone and quickly got to her feet.

"Joe told me you're making some demands about this trip tomorrow," he said. "You want to call in every couple of hours or some such bullshit like that."

"Yes, I'll need to make sure my kids are okay."

"Well, that's just peachy with me, because we'd planned on something like that all along. This morning, we bought you a cheap, prepaid phone at Walmart to use on the trip tomorrow. We want a progress report from you every two to three hours."

Laura squinted at him. "Really? So you were planning on that? Joe didn't say anything."

"Well, you know Joe," he said. Laura could see him smiling in the dark. "I mean, you can tell just looking at him, *there's something a little off* . . ."

That was almost an exact quote of what Sophie had said in the bedroom earlier. Did Vic want her to know he was eavesdropping on them? Or was he just amusing himself?

"Where is Joe?" she asked.

"He nodded off on the sofa downstairs," Vic said.

"Do you think I could get some cookies, crackers, or fruit to bring back to the bedroom?" she asked. "My children haven't had any dinner. And they'll fall asleep faster on a full stomach."

Vic shook his head. "Nope, bad kids go to bed without their supper. You tried to get me drunk. Junior smashed his camera, and the Princess has been shooting me superior, dirty looks since she first set eyes on me this afternoon." He got to his feet and shoved the phone in his pocket. "You'll all just have to go to bed hungry."

He nodded toward the hallway, and Laura took that as a cue. She stepped over a pile of clothes and headed back down the corridor.

"I know what you're thinking," he said. "If your buddy Joe was here, he'd give you and the kiddies something to eat, maybe even cake and ice cream . . ." Vic tugged at the crowbar and pulled out the flat end from between the door and its frame. "It's true," he continued, "Joe's very fond of you and your brood. I'll bet you think that's lucky, because he'll protect you from me, the big, bad bogeyman. Well, let me clue you in on something. He was real fond of Sherry Singleton, too—and her tribe."

Vic opened the door for her. "Joe liked all of them— right up until he hacked them to pieces."

Laura scowled at him, but couldn't quite look him in the eye. She stepped into the bedroom, and the door slammed shut behind her.

*   *   *

Joe was awake.

From the window seat in Sophie's bedroom, Laura watched him outside. She was half-sitting up, huddled under the blanket and bathrobe that served as her bed-covering. Joe had come around from the back of the house. He carried a shovel. Laura realized he must have just buried Dane in the vineyard. She could see Joe's breath in the moonlight. Leaning on the shovel, he gazed up the driveway toward the road in the distance. After a minute, he hung his head and his shoulders began to shake. She realized he was crying.

"Mom?" Sophie whispered.

Laura glanced over at her daughter, sitting up in bed.

"Can't you sleep?" Sophie asked. "Do you want the bed? Because it doesn't matter to me . . ."

Laura shook her head. "I'm fine, but thanks, sweetie. What time is it?"

Sophie glanced at her clock radio on the nightstand. "Ten minutes to two."

Laura looked out the window again and saw Joe head toward the back of the house. Maybe he hadn't finished digging Dane's grave yet. Maybe he'd just been taking a break.

She listened to Liam's snoring. He was in the sleeping bag at the foot of James's bed. She'd been worried about Liam because there were no EpiPens in Sophie's room. But she didn't want to ask Vic for one. He would have said no anyway.

Pulling back her bed-covering, Laura got to her feet. She nodded at Sophie and then pointed to the bathroom. "Why don't you try to go back to sleep?" she said—for Vic's benefit, in case he was awake and listening in. She crept to the bathroom, switched on the light, and waited in the doorway.

Sophie climbed out of bed and joined her. She closed the bathroom door.

Laura had borrowed one of the oversized T-shirts Sophie usually slept in. This one was old with a wash-faded photo of the band New Direction on the front. Sophie wore a nightshirt that had "Property of Cascade Kodiaks" across her chest. Sitting down on the edge of the tub, Sophie yawned. She smoothed her curly hair back from her face, which was dabbed with acne medication. "How long will you be gone tomorrow?" she asked quietly.

Laura lowered the toilet lid and sat down. "Most of the day, I'm sure. You'll be in charge of things here while I'm gone. I'm counting on you, honey."

"I think Vic is the one who'll be in charge of things," Sophie murmured. She rubbed her arms. "What do you think your chances are of actually tracking down this person who's supposed to prove Joe didn't kill anybody?"

Laura had been awake this whole time, wondering the same thing. For all she knew, Joe could have invented this Zared person that he'd sketched. The name even sounded fanciful, like a comic book super-villain. As a kid, Joe used to concoct elaborate excuses for why he'd forgotten his homework or come to school on a cold November morning without a jacket—and he always seemed to believe his own stories. Laura wondered if this waitress, Martha, even existed. Maybe she was a figment of Joe's imagination, too.

She looked at her daughter and sighed. "I'd say my chances of making any headway at all are between ten and twenty percent."

"Mom, this whole thing doesn't make sense," Sophie whispered. "I mean, even if you find this person and she has a perfect alibi for Joe, he and that . . . that *reptile* are still guilty of beating up that guy in Anacortes and stealing his car. They're also guilty of kidnapping and breaking and entering or whatever you'd call this home-invasion situation . . ."

"It's even worse than that," Laura whispered. "Vic killed someone. One of the workers unexpectedly came by this morning. Remember Dane?"

Gaping at her, Sophie nodded.

"Vic killed him."

"How?"

Laura hesitated. "Vic slit his throat. He has a switchblade on him—in addition to the gun."

"Where was this?"

"It happened behind the house—by the garage. I saw the whole thing. Vic washed away the blood on the driveway. Dane's pickup is parked behind the garage, and Joe's burying his body in the vineyard right now."

Sophie covered her mouth. "My God . . ."

"I'm sorry, honey. But I think you ought to know what you're up against tomorrow."

Sophie didn't say anything for a moment. Finally

she shook her head. "Don't you see, Mom? That's just what I'm saying. Even if neither one of them had anything to do with the Singleton killings, they're still guilty as hell of all this other stuff—including murder now. So what's the point of sending you to Lopez Island on this wild-goose chase tomorrow?"

Laura sighed. "Technically, Vic's the one who did the beating, the stealing, and the killing. Joe was an accessory, but there are special circumstances with him. To his credit, he tried to stop Vic from killing Dane this morning. Besides that, like you said, Joe's a little off. Despite Vic's claims, I think there's a good chance Joe didn't kill the Singletons. And if that's true, then maybe the authorities will go easy on him for everything else."

"I don't know, Mom," Sophie muttered.

"Okay, so it's a long shot," Laura admitted. "But if I'm able to find someone who can prove Joe's innocence in the Singleton case, then I think he'll be on our side. He'll do everything he can to get Vic to leave us alone and go. I really believe he'll help us—if we help him."

With a hopeless look, Sophie stared down at the bathroom's pink rug and stuck her big toe under the edge of it. Her long, skinny arms were crossed in front of her. "And you say the chances of that happening are between ten and twenty percent. So—are those our chances of survival, twenty percent at the most?"

"It's why I wanted to talk to you, honey," Laura said. "So much of what happens here tomorrow will depend on you. If this Lopez Island connection doesn't pan out, I'll go to the police. Vic wants me to call with a progress report every couple of hours. I'll stall them. I'll give him some story about getting another lead and needing another hour. They've agreed to let me talk to you when I check in. If I'm going to call the police, I'll let you know by telling you, *'Say a prayer everything works out all right . . .'"*

"'Say a prayer,'" Sophie repeated.

Laura nodded. "Then you'll know I'm calling the police as soon as I hang up with you. The police will probably take about ten minutes to get here—at least. So you'll have to watch your time and create a diversion of some sort. Because if Vic sees one cop—"

"He'll start shooting us, I know, you told me," Sophie said with a nervous edge.

"Or he could use one of you as a hostage."

Sophie rubbed her forehead. She looked as though she might start to cry.

"Honey, I'm sorry, but you've got to listen to this. You need to be prepared. Now, Vic and Joe seem to favor the family room and the back part of the house. So—if you're downstairs, create a diversion somewhere there in the back part of the house—"

"Like what? What am I supposed to do?"

"I don't know. Maybe faint, break something, or start an argument with Liam, anything that will distract them. I'll tell the police to come in from the front. So if you're downstairs, do what you can to keep Vic and Joe in the family room—away from the front windows."

"And what if we're upstairs here, locked in my room?"

"Try and let me know, and I'll alert the police you're on the second floor. If you're downstairs, try and corral your brothers into the kitchen, and I'll tell the police you'll be there."

Sophie stared at her for a moment, "Is that it?" she asked. "Is that our plan?"

"Well, if you or Liam can somehow get out of the house, I don't think they've cut the phone line from the cottage. Remember the old black phone on the wall in that closet? It still works. If something should happen to me, and you need to call the police, you might be able to do it from there. The key to the cottage is under the square flowerpot around back . . ."

Sophie nodded. "I remember," she said, but she still seemed uncertain. "But what do you think is going to happen to you?"

"I don't know, honey. Nothing is certain right now." She reached over and took Sophie's hand. "When I call in tomorrow with my progress report, and you and I talk, I'm sure Vic will be listening in. He may not want you to let on if something's wrong on this end."

"What do you mean?"

"Well, he—he may tie you guys up or something. Or maybe he won't want me knowing that one of you is hurt. But I'll want to know, Sophie. You'll need to tell me in code if something critical has happened. You can let me know by saying . . ." she hesitated.

"I'll tell you I'm *'nervous,'*" Sophie suggested. "And if everything's okay, I'll say I'm *'tired.'*"

"*'Nervous'* is bad, and *'tired'* means everything's okay," Laura said, nodding.

"And *'saying a prayer'* means you're calling the police," Sophie whispered. She started to tremble, and tears came to her eyes. "Mom, I'm scared . . ."

Laura got up and sat down beside her on the edge of the tub. She put her arms around her.

"I think he's going to kill us," Sophie sobbed into her shoulder. Her voice was muffled. "I really do. I don't know if I can do anything to stop him. I'm so afraid . . ."

Laura shushed her. "You've been so good today, so strong," she whispered, rocking her in her arms. "I'm so proud of you, sweetie. You need to know that. You just have to keep being strong. Tomorrow's going to be a big challenge, but we're going to pull through this. You're a smart, resourceful young woman. I know you'll do your best . . ."

It was all Laura could do to keep from bursting into tears, too. Her heart ached, and she was filled with a sickening dread.

She felt as if she were sending her daughter into a horrific battle tomorrow.

And the chances for survival were less than twenty percent.

CHAPTER TWELVE

Tuesday, November 28—7:03 A.M.

On the local morning news, there was a story about a woman in Salem, Oregon, who claimed to have seen two men who fit the descriptions of Joseph Mulroney and Victor Moles. The witness said that on Monday night, she'd seen both men in a Costco parking lot. They climbed into a red Hyundai Sonata and drove off.

This amused Vic to no end.

It probably helped account for his good mood this morning. He was almost finished with his breakfast, and so far—miracle of miracles—he'd made it through the meal without breaking any plates or glassware.

He and Joe ate in front of the TV again. They'd raided the master bedroom closet once more. Vic was wearing another one of Sean's sweaters, and Joe had on one of his shirts, which was too big on his skinny frame. With the remote in one hand and a fork in the other, Vic stuffed his face and flipped through the various news programs for updates. It was frustrating for

Laura because she was in the kitchen, catching only snippets.

Jae Singleton's boyfriend was still in an Anacortes hospital's intensive care unit and still unable to identify the man who had shot him.

But in North Seattle, after being shown several mug shots, the 7-Eleven clerk had positively identified Victor Moles as his assailant on the night of the Singleton murders. That certainly had to be another reason Vic seemed so pleased with himself this morning.

One news program pointed out that several Lopez Island merchants had seen Vic in town in different stores and restaurants. But that revelation didn't seem to bother Vic.

The police and press had dug up some background information on the two fugitives—with the focus on Joe, now the only suspect they could place at the Singleton home at the time of the murders. The news reported that Joseph Spiers was his birth name, and his birth certificate showed *father unknown.* His abusive mother had died in a car accident six years ago, and his grandmother had passed away last year. When the TV reporter started delving into how Joe met Vic in a state-run psychiatric institute, Vic changed the channel.

Laura had thought he'd be interested in seeing the news reports about himself. But then she realized Vic probably didn't want anyone hearing about his criminal background. Maybe Joe didn't even know the extent of it. He'd been pretty vague about why Vic had ended up in that institution.

Vic settled on a news program that showed Marilee Cronin giving yet another weepy speech about the virtues of the late Scott Singleton and the Church of the True Divine Light. "God, this bitch gives me a pain," he announced. But he kept watching.

Laura did her best to ignore him—as did Sophie and Liam, sitting with James at the counter-bar. Sophie kept James occupied and eating his breakfast.

When Vic had stomped into Sophie's bedroom an hour ago, demanding that Laura fix them breakfast, he'd wanted the kids to stay locked in the room. But Laura had pointed out that her children had been deprived of dinner the night before, and she'd insisted on making their breakfast before she left.

Liam was ravenous. But both Laura and Sophie were too nervous to eat much. They could only pick at the eggs, bacon, and toast. However, Laura filled up on coffee. She'd slept only about an hour or two last night. And she needed to stay alert today for a three-hour drive over a mountain pass to Anacortes—and then a ferry ride to Lopez Island.

She looked haggard and pale. Her scars were showing, but some makeup had helped conceal the bruise on her chin. She wore a black sweater and jeans.

She'd texted her neighbor, Patti. It was Laura's day to drive the boys to preschool, but she said James was staying home today. So Patti would have to take her own son to school. It was a curt message, meant to discourage her neighbor from swinging by or calling.

Sophie had sent a text to Matt, explaining she was sick and wouldn't be in school today, but she would talk to him later tonight.

Both text messages had been supervised and approved by Vic, of course.

Laura had instructed Sophie to step outside and wave away both school buses when they pulled up near the end of the driveway at seven-thirty and seven-forty respectively. She also told her about the special delivery from Sean expected between three and five that afternoon. Someone was supposed to sign for it. Laura was worried it might be a case of wine, which would require an adult's signature. "You'll just have to tell them to come back later," Laura had advised her daughter.

Once again, all these instructions had been Vic-approved.

He wanted Laura to leave the house by seven-fifteen at the latest. She had to be on the ferry that left Anacortes for Lopez at 10:35. After breakfast, Vic turned down the TV volume and used Laura's phone to check road conditions on Stevens Pass.

"'Patches of snow and ice on the roadway,'" he said. "Snow tires are recommended." He swaggered over to the kitchen and handed Laura the pay-as-you-go phone. "I want you to call this number and ask if Martha's working today."

While he read off the number, Laura—with an unsteady hand—entered the digits on the small phone. It rang twice before a woman answered. "Last Sunset Café," she said loudly—over a lot of chatter and clanging in the background. The phone reception was a bit choppy.

"Hello, is Martha working today?" Laura asked.

"'Til three," the woman said. "If you want to talk to her, now's not a good time. We're awfully busy . . ."

"No, that's okay, thank you," Laura said, clicking off. She was surprised and relieved that there really was a Martha. The waitress wasn't just a figment of Joe's imagination. Maybe this fool's errand wasn't completely futile.

She turned to Vic—and Joe, who now stood behind his friend. "Martha's there until three," she said. She started to hand the phone back to Vic.

But he shook his head. "That's yours. It's all charged up. Get your coat. I don't want any long good-byes." He handed her Joe's sketches of the man he called Zared.

All morning long, Laura's stomach had been in knots. Now the knots just got tighter. Suddenly, she could hardly get a breath. She turned to Vic. "I need to talk with you first—in private," she managed to say. She headed into the front hall, and he followed.

"Well, make it snappy," Vic grunted. "And I don't want any long last-minute trips to the can."

"Listen . . ." She swallowed hard. "You—you expressed your concern last night and again this morning about me possibly going to the police while I'm gone. Well, if you want to make sure I don't do that—if you want insurance, you can always accompany me to Lopez. You saw on the news. In all the photos they have of you, your hair's long. And the police sketches don't do you justice. No one will recognize you. And if you're worried they will, you can just stay in the car. Meanwhile, Joe can stay here and look after my kids . . ."

Vic smiled. "I'm flattered you want me along for the ride, Teach. But no, you're on your own. As for wondering if you'll go to the cops, well, I have three insurance policies right here."

He grabbed her purse off the table in the hallway

and handed it to her. He'd already looked through it twice this morning. "Get your coat," he said.

Laura's hands were still shaking as she loaded the phone and Joe's drawings into the purse. "Joe, can I talk to you?" she called, her voice cracking.

He came into the hallway. Liam and Sophie were behind him. Sophie carried James, who was squirming in her arms.

Laura gazed at Joe while she took her peacoat out of the closet and put it on. "Joe, I looked after you once, remember?" she said. "I'm counting on you to look after my children."

He nodded, but he looked a little frightened—as if he didn't feel up to the task.

Sophie and Liam broke past Joe and ran to her. Sophie was crying.

Laura hugged and kissed them as if it were the last time. "It's going to be okay," she whispered. "I'll see you tonight . . ."

She couldn't help thinking it was a lie.

Vic opened the front door. "Okay, enough of this shit, c'mon, get going . . ."

James started shrieking as Laura pulled away from them.

Vic grabbed her arm and led her outside. The morning air was chilly and harsh. It felt like it might snow. She started to glance back at her children, but Vic shut the front door and continued to drag her toward the car. "C'mon, get your keys out," he muttered. "I'm freezing my ass off here . . ."

She looked back toward the house.

Vic impatiently grabbed her purse and dug out her

keys. He chuckled at the thin plastic trinket attached to her key ring. About half the size of a credit card, it was a replica of a Washington State license plate that spelled out MOM. It had been a gift from Liam last year. With the device on her fob, Vic unlocked the car. Then he handed her purse and keys back to her.

The Toyota Sienna's windshield and windows were slightly fogged from the morning frost. Climbing behind the wheel, Laura shut the car door. She started the engine and the heater, then rolled down the window. She wiped the tears from her face and glared up at Vic. "If you hurt one of my kids, I swear, I'm going to hunt you down."

He just snickered.

Laura raised the window and headed down the driveway. Her hands tight on the wheel, she began to cry again.

She was still sobbing when she made the turn for downtown Leavenworth several minutes later. She spotted a police car parked on the shoulder of the road near the intersection. Biting her lip, she cruised past it and kept going.

Laura glanced at the squad car in her rearview mirror. It hadn't moved.

She couldn't help feeling as if she'd just made the worst mistake of her life.

CHAPTER THIRTEEN

Tuesday—8:24 A.M.

Sophie washed the breakfast dishes. She kept glancing over toward the family room at Vic—in her father's chair. She'd expected him to start leering at her again the way he had yesterday—now that her mom wasn't around. But to her relief, he didn't seem too interested in her this morning.

He didn't seem interested in what was on TV either. He kept flipping through the channels, and every few minutes he got up and went to the front of the house. Once, he even walked outside. A couple of times, he muted the TV and told everyone to shut up. Then he peered out the windows and went to the front of the house again.

Sophie realized he was worried that her mom might have gone to the police. A part of her enjoyed seeing the son of a bitch so anxious and unsure. Unfortunately, every time he got up to look out a window he reached for the gun he kept concealed under his shirttail.

Joe wasn't quite as restless. He'd offered to help her with the dishes, but Vic had barked at him that it was women's work, and he'd insisted his friend watch TV with him.

Liam sat with James at the breakfast table, keeping him entertained with a couple of James's board games: Robot Turtles and Raccoon Rumpus. Sophie and Liam had warned their little brother that if he had to talk, he needed to whisper. James had agreed. But he'd already twice violated the agreement by calling to Joe to come play with them. It was kind of pathetic to see the look on Joe's face as he sat there on the sofa at Vic's demand. "I'm sorry, I can't," he said, both times. And he really did seem sorry, too.

Sophie wondered how this guy was supposed to protect them from his friend. Even if her mother found this person to prove Joe's innocence, Joe would never get Vic to leave unless Vic wanted to leave.

In the past hour, both Liam and James had taken bathroom breaks. Each time, Vic sent Joe to stand guard in the front hallway outside the powder-room door while they did their business. Joe was just his errand boy, totally under his thumb.

Sophie pitied him, but at the same time, she didn't like him much. She didn't have the soft spot her mother had for him. After all, the police wanted the guy for murder. And even if he was innocent, he was still hanging around with this total creep who was most definitely a murderer. Sophie wasn't depending on Joe to come to their rescue. But her mother had told her to be nice to him, so she tried to be as pleasant as possible under the circumstances. Still, it was an effort.

After nearly an hour of channel surfing, Vic had finally settled on some World War II submarine movie starring

Cary Grant. They'd been watching the movie for about ten minutes when he shot up from the chair again. He muted the movie and tossed the remote on the seat cushion. Then he reached for his gun and started toward the front of the house. "Joe, close the curtains in here," he said. "I don't want to hear a peep from anybody."

It was no false alarm this time. Sophie heard a car coming up the driveway.

"Everybody, be quiet!" Joe whispered. He pulled the drapes shut across the sliding glass door. The family room turned dark.

Sophie followed Vic toward the front of the house. "It might be the delivery guy," she whispered. "He could be early. For God's sake, don't—"

"Shut up!" Vic hissed. With his gun drawn, he waited on one side of the door.

Sophie stopped in the hall, just past the kitchen doorway. Out the living room window, she saw an SUV pull to a stop in front of the house. She heard a door open and shut, and then watched their neighbor, Patti Bellini, step around from the driver's side. She wore a ski jacket, and her curly red hair was blowing in the wind. She stopped and opened the SUV's back door. "Honey, what is it?" she asked, her voice slightly muffled.

Sophie felt someone come up behind her, and she realized it was Joe. She turned to him. "That's our neighbor and her little boy . . ."

Vic kept glancing back at them—and then at the living room wall. It took Sophie a moment to figure out he was looking at a mirror above the couch. He could see everything Mrs. Bellini was doing. "I'm going to fucking kill her," he whispered.

"She's got her kid in the car, Vic," Joe said under his breath. "Just wait. She might go away . . ."

Sophie could hear Mrs. Bellini again. "No, I'll just be a minute, honey," she said to her son. Then she closed the car door and approached the house. Sophie couldn't see her anymore, but then she heard the knocking.

"Laura!" their neighbor called. "Laura, it's me! I got your text! Can we declare a truce?" She knocked again and rang the doorbell.

Sophie heard her footsteps on the front porch. Then she saw Mrs. Bellini at the window, peeking into the living room. "Laura? I can drive James today, and I promise I won't feed him a thing! He can starve first! Laura? Too soon to joke about it?"

Sophie didn't move. She heard Joe behind her, whimpering.

Mrs. Bellini knocked on the door again, and then Sophie saw the doorknob turning.

Vic was shaking his head. He had the gun ready.

The door opened. "Laura?" Mrs. Bellini called. "You couldn't have left yet . . ."

Sophie rushed to the door and blocked the way. "Hi, Mrs. Bellini," she said, out of breath.

Their neighbor took a step back on the porch. "I'm sorry, Sophie. I hope I didn't scare you . . ."

Sophie tried not to look at Vic, standing right beside her. She stepped onto the porch, and half-closed the door behind her. "That's okay," she said, shivering from the sudden cold. "Ah, if you're looking for my mom, she isn't here."

Mrs. Bellini stared at her. "What happened?"

Sophie hesitated. She didn't have a good lie handy.

Any minute now, she expected Vic to yank the door open and start shooting.

"Honey, why aren't you in school?"

"Food poisoning," Sophie heard herself say. "We—we had fish for dinner last night, and Mom thinks something must have been wrong with it, because all of us were sick most of the night. Mom went to the drugstore to pick up something the doctor recommended."

"Oh, you poor kids," Mrs. Bellini said. "Is there anything I can do?"

"No, but thank you," Sophie said.

"Ginger ale sometimes helps—and Saltines. How are you fixed for those?"

Sophie nodded a few times. "We're fixed fine, thanks, Mrs. Bellini."

"Well, tell your mom I came by to say I'm sorry. We had a little bit of a squabble yesterday. It's not worth going into. And have her call me if you guys need anything." She backed away. "You get inside the house now—before you catch a cold on top of everything else."

"My mom will call you later tonight, okay?" Sophie said. Then she ducked back inside, closed the door and slumped against it.

Vic was still waiting there with his gun ready.

Sophie listened to the retreating footsteps. The SUV's door opened and shut. A moment later, she heard the vehicle heading down the driveway. Their neighbor had no idea how close she'd come to getting killed. Sophie's heart was still racing.

She glanced at Vic and shuddered.

He actually looked disappointed.

CHAPTER FOURTEEN

Tuesday – 11:43 A.M.
Lopez Island, Washington

The Last Sunset Café was one of those places that seemed to be hiding from the world. A rambler-style structure from the fifties just outside the center of town, it had a big parking lot that was about a third-full with about a dozen other cars besides Laura's. There was a recycling and donation station in the far corner of the lot.

At first, Laura wasn't sure she had the right place, but then she spotted the LAST SUNSET CAFÉ neon sign in the front window, alongside a lighted sign for Rainier Beer.

Between home and here, in the last four-plus hours, she'd counted a total of seven police cars. Two of those squad cars had been parked in the ferry terminal at Anacortes. Laura had figured the police were there hoping to catch Joe and Vic returning to the scene of the crime. Parked in the ferry lane, she'd been so tempted to climb out of her car, walk over to the cops, and tell them everything. Instead, she'd pulled out the pay-as-you-go phone and called her cell number.

Laura wondered if Vic would renege on their deal and not let her talk to her children. Well, then she'd have to go to the cops. She merely needed one little push in that direction. All she had to do was get out of her car and wave at them.

Vic answered after three rings. "What?"

She could hear the TV blaring in the background. "I'm in Anacortes," she explained, "in line for the ferry to Lopez Island."

"Well, why the hell are you calling now? You haven't even gotten to Lopez yet."

"It's been three hours," Laura said. "That was the agreement. I was to call in every two or three hours."

"Well, call us again after you've talked to the wait-ress—"

"Wait! I want to talk with Sophie. That was part of the agreement, too."

She heard him grunt. There was some muffled con-versation, and then Sophie got on the line: "Mom?"

"Honey, how are you?"

"We're all fine. We're *tired*, but fine.

"Mrs. Bellini stopped by. She wanted to take James to preschool. But I managed to send her away. The de-livery guy hasn't come yet. Now we're just sitting here watching TV, first some Cary Grant submarine movie, which was okay. And now it's *Singing in the Rain*, which is great, but he keeps switching channels, driving everybody crazy. I swear, he must have ADD or some-thing . . ."

"Gimme!" Laura heard Vic bellow in the background.

All Laura could think was that Sophie was pushing her luck with him.

"The deal was you could check in with her," Vic had growled into the phone. "I didn't say she could tell you her whole goddamn life story. Call back after you've talked to the waitress."

Then he'd hung up.

That had been over an hour ago. During the ferry ride to Lopez and the drive to the restaurant, Laura kept reminding herself the kids were okay. *Tired* meant they were okay.

She climbed out of the car, buttoned up her pea jacket, and headed into the Last Sunset Café. The place was a bit dilapidated—with mounted fish on the knotty-pine paneled walls. All the fake plants were covered with a layer of grease and dust. The seats in the booths and the stools at the counter were covered in a lime-green vinyl—with dark green tape covering the tears. The specials were scribbled on an eraser-board by the counter-bar. The meatloaf sandwich and fries for $5.99 got top billing. Laura noticed a small framed sign by the cashier's station:

Our credit manager is HELEN WAITE.
If you want credit, go to Helen Waite!

The place was half full with about thirty customers. Laura didn't see a jukebox, but "Cherish" by The Association played over some speakers and competed with the clanking of silverware and the subdued chatter.

"Sit anywhere you like!" a waitress with a tray of dirty dishes called to her. She wore an archaic-looking brown and beige uniform.

"I'd like to sit in Martha's section," Laura asked.

"Pick a table and I'll send her over!" the waitress replied. Then she ducked into the kitchen.

Laura sat down at a two-top by the window—with a view of the parking lot. It was a wood-top table with about ten layers of dark, shiny varnish.

Someone slapped a paper menu on it—along with some tinny-looking flatware, a napkin, and a glass of water.

Laura glanced up at the skinny, forty-something waitress. She had a weak chin and a pink streak in her limp blondish hair, which was pulled back in a pony-tail. Laura noticed a tattoo of Winnie-the-Pooh on the woman's arm as she handed her a menu. The name tag on her uniform read MARTHA.

"For lunch, I recommend the chicken pot pie," she said. "We're also still serving breakfast. And if you're going that route, I recommend the pecan waffle." She nodded at a lanky fifty-something man at a neighboring table. He wore a black V-neck that showed a tuft of black chest hair. The hair on his head was gray-black and thin-ning, and he had a Kirk Douglas cleft in his chin. "This gentleman just ordered it, and he's very happy."

The man must have overheard, because he nodded and smiled at them.

"Are you Martha?" Laura asked.

The waitress glanced at her own name tag and then looked at Laura as if she were an idiot. "Actually, no, I stole her identity—and have now assumed her glamorous lifestyle."

Laura noticed the man at the other table chuckled.

"I'm just pulling your leg, hon," Martha said. "Why do you ask?"

Laura hesitated. The cleft-chinned man still seemed to be listening. "I—I heard from a friend that you were the best waitress here."

"Well, thanks," she smiled. "So what can I get you to drink?"

"Diet Coke, please."

"Be right back with that," she said, heading toward the kitchen.

Laura opened her purse and took out Joe's sketches of Zared. She laid them over the place mat. Then she glanced at the menu.

When Martha returned with her Diet Coke and a straw, she set the glass down over to one side. She didn't seem to pay any attention to the sketches.

"I guess it's kind of callous to ask," Laura said, "but are you doing a lot more business since the Singleton murders? I mean, I'm sure the island must be full of reporters . . ."

"Are you kidding me?" Martha said. "Like locusts, they've taken over. There's a whole flock of his ministers and followers here, too, not to mention detectives. You should have been in here during the breakfast rush. It was insane."

"My friend told me that you might know a few things about the Singletons that the police and the press don't know," Laura said.

The waitress smiled, but narrowed her eyes at her. "Who told you that?"

Laura noticed Mr. Pecan Waffle was looking at them again.

"This friend of mine," she repeated quietly. "He indicated you had some unique insight into the case." She pointed to Joe's sketches. "He also thought you might recognize the man in these drawings . . ."

Martha glanced at the sketches for less than two seconds. She shook her head. "Never seen him before. I don't know what your friend is talking about. The Singletons didn't come in here too often, and when they did, they didn't share much with me—especially all that money they had. Not to speak ill of the dead, but they were lousy tippers. Have you decided on what you're having?"

Laura glanced at the menu again. "Ah, just a bowl of the chicken noodle soup, please."

Martha grabbed her menu. "You got it."

As the waitress retreated to the kitchen, Laura noticed Mr. Pecan Waffle smiling at her again. She turned away and stared down at Joe's drawings. She'd had a feeling this trip was going to be a big bust.

With a sigh, she started to collect the sketches.

"Did you draw those?"

Laura looked up. It was Mr. Pecan Waffle. He'd gotten up from his table and was standing next to her.

"No, a friend of mine drew them," she replied.

He stared at the drawings. "I don't mean to pry, but from a distance, I thought I recognized one of these guys. Do you mind?"

"Actually, they're all supposed to be the same guy," Laura explained. "My friend's an amateur artist."

"Who's it supposed to be?"

"That's what I'm trying to find out. It's probably just a wild-goose chase."

The man picked up one of the drawings and squinted at it. "I'm here visiting family," he said. "Thought I'd get a little peace and quiet. Talk about bad timing. What—are you a reporter?"

She nodded. "Freelance. So—does he look familiar to you?"

He handed the drawing back to her. "I'm afraid not, now that I've gotten a good look at these. Sorry I can't be any help. But good luck." He wandered back to his table—and his waffle.

Laura started to collect the sketches again. But then she saw Martha coming her way with the bowl of soup and some crackers. Laura left the most detailed sketch on the table. Martha set the bowl and crackers down next to it. "There you go. Let me know if you want more crackers."

Laura pointed to the sketch. "I'm sorry, but are you sure this man doesn't look familiar to you? He might have been a customer . . ."

Martha frowned. "I already told you that I didn't recognize him. Showing that to me again isn't going to change things. Just the soup today?"

Laura wanted to ask if she knew Joseph Mulroney, but Mr. Pecan Waffle seemed to be eavesdropping. "Yes, just the soup," she said. "Thanks."

Martha scribbled out a check, tore it off her pad, and set it on the table. "Enjoy!"

Laura watched her walk away. She figured she could catch her again before heading out, and then she would ask about Joe. She took a sip of the soup and scalded her tongue.

The place filled up while Laura waited for her soup to cool off. Mr. Pecan Waffle had stopped staring at her, and become interested in something on his smartphone. Laura ate her soup. When she spotted Martha at the cash register, she quickly left three dollars on the table, grabbed her coat and purse, and then hurried to the register with her check.

"How was the soup?" the waitress asked as she took the check—along with the twenty Laura handed her.

"Great," Laura said. "Listen, my friend said that Joseph Mulroney used to come in here to eat sometimes. I was wondering if you ever waited on him or—"

"I'm sorry," Martha said, plopping some bills and change into Laura's hand. She glanced around. "As you can see, lots of people come in here every day. And I'm really not that good with faces. Now, we're getting kind of busy here. Have a nice day."

She turned away and ducked into the kitchen.

Defeated, Laura stepped outside, buttoned up her jacket, and wandered back toward the car. She'd desperately wanted Joe's story to have some basis in fact. She hated to think it was possible he'd murdered anyone. She had no choice now but to go to the police—and risk endangering her children. She imagined Vic using one of them as a hostage. Knowing Vic, he'd probably kill the other two children just to let the police know he meant business.

Laura started trembling. Tears stung her eyes.

When she got to her car, she reached into her purse for the pay-as-you-go phone. She wondered if Vic could have rigged the phone so he'd somehow know if she dialed 9-1-1 on it. Laura didn't have much technical knowhow, but the possibility didn't seem so farfetched to her.

"Hey!" someone yelled.

Laura looked up to see Martha with a sweater over her shoulders. She hurried toward her, waving a check. "Hey, that wasn't a twenty you gave me!" she shouted. "Did you think I wouldn't notice?"

Baffled, Laura wiped her eyes and stared at her. She'd given the woman a twenty and received the correct change.

Martha met up with her at the car. "Get out your purse. People are watching," she whispered. "C'mon . . ."

Laura still didn't understand. She raised her purse slightly. It was already open.

"Listen, I couldn't talk earlier, because the place is crawling with cops, reporters, and Divine Light disciples," Martha said. "They're probably watching us now. You don't know who's who. I heard you tell that guy you're a reporter. If you want a scoop on the Singletons, how much would it be worth to you?"

Laura blinked. "How much do you want?"

"Well, I have some stories," Martha said. "And the first one is a bargain at five hundred dollars. But I want you to keep my name out of it." She handed the meal check to Laura. An address was scribbled on the back. "That's my place. I'll be there after three-thirty . . ."

Laura shook her head. "I can't wait around that long. Besides, how do I know you're on the level?"

Martha glanced back at the restaurant for a second and turned to her. "You go up to Western Washington University in Bellingham and track down a sophomore named Doran Wiley. You ask him about the Singletons and Eric Vetter. After talking to him, you'll know I'm on the level. By the way, that little tip will cost you forty dollars. Consider it a down payment against the five hundred."

Laura hesitated. "Wait. What about the man in the sketches?"

"It's like I told you. I don't recognize him."

"But something strange was going on with the Singletons? Something that would explain why they were killed?"

Martha smiled. "Like I said, you talk to Doran and ask him about the Singletons and Eric Vetter. There's a ferry leaving here in an hour. You can go up to Bellingham and be back to Anacortes in time for the four-thirty ferry returning here. Swing by my place at five-thirty, and bring the money."

"Were you—*on the level* about not knowing Joe Mulroney?" Laura pressed.

"No, too many people were around who might want information like that for free." She took another anxious look over her shoulder at the café. "But you're paying, so I'll tell you the truth. Yeah, he used to come in a lot for breakfast, always ordered the ham and cheese scram. I thought he was a real sweet guy." She held out her hand, waiting for her forty-dollar down payment.

"What about the other one, his friend, Victor Moles?" Laura asked. "Was he ever in the restaurant?"

Martha frowned. "The son of a bitch stiffed me once, so I never waited on him again. Did you see him in that Seven-Eleven video on the news? That's just like him, a total sleaze. Hey, y'know, the police are keeping this quiet, but I overheard them talking in the restaurant. This Moles character might have been shoving around that puny, little convenience store clerk at the time of the murders, but his prints were all over the Singleton house." She held out her hand again. "That one you got for free, but I still want my deposit."

Laura took two twenty-dollar bills from her purse. "So you think Victor Moles is still a suspect?"

Martha plucked the money out of her hand. "I'm just telling you what I overheard."

"What about Joe Mulroney?" Laura asked. "Do you think Joe actually killed the Singletons?"

Martha stashed the bills in her apron, "Like I told you, he seemed like a nice, sweet kid," she said. "But yeah, I think he's guilty as sin."

Then she turned and hurried back into the café.

Vic abruptly answered the phone: "What's going on?"

"Let me talk to Joe," Laura said, matching his curtness.

She sat in her car—in the parking lot of The Last Sunset Cafe. The lot was starting to fill up with other restaurant customers.

"I'll tell Joe whatever you have to say," Vic said.

"Well, at least let him listen in—like you listened in to my conversations with my daughter this morning and my husband last night. This concerns him."

Laura figured if Joe was in on some more of the conversations, maybe he wouldn't be so quick to let Vic make all his decisions for him.

Vic grumbled something under his breath. Then Joe came on the phone: "Hello? Mrs. Gretchell?"

"Hello, Joe," she said. "I talked with Martha—"

"Were you really there?" Vic interrupted. "They have a sign by the cash register. What does it say?"

Laura thought for a moment. "Something about 'going to hell and wait.'"

"Okay, go ahead," he grunted.

"I talked to Martha," Laura continued, "and unfortunately, she couldn't identify the man in your sketches. But she said that, yes, something—fishy was going on under the Singletons' roof, something that might explain why the family was killed. She wouldn't say what though. She's charging me five hundred dollars for the information. I'm supposed to meet her later this afternoon with the money. In the meantime, she told me to talk to someone named Doran Wiley at Western Washington University. Does that name ring a bell?"

There was silence on the other end.

"Joe?"

"Um, yeah, he—he was the caretaker there before me," he finally answered.

"Did you ever meet him?"

"No. But what—what would he know? I can't imagine he'd have any real useful information for you."

Laura could tell she'd hit a nerve. She remembered Joe telling her last night about Scott and Sherry Singleton, and she knew she hadn't gotten the whole story. Maybe she'd get the whole story from Doran Wiley.

"Martha said I'm supposed to ask this Doran person about someone named Eric Vetter," Laura explained. "Do you know who that is?"

"Eric Vetter?" Joe said. "No, I've never heard of him."

"Well, obviously Doran Wiley has heard of him—or he knew him. Maybe that's the 'real useful information' he has." Laura wondered why neither one of them had been mentioned in any of the news stories. Certainly the police would have interviewed the former caretaker, just as procedure. Joe had replaced him only two months prior to the murders. Had he been fired? For all she knew, this Doran Wiley could be a suspect the police were keeping under wraps.

She'd been half-watching the restaurant, but her car windows were starting to fog. "Joe?" she asked, swiping the condensation off the driver's window.

"Yeah?" he asked.

"So—it looks like I'll have to catch a ferry back to Anacortes and drive to Bellingham to track down this Doran person. Then I'm supposed to come back here to Lopez Island to meet with Martha again—so she can sell me this information on the Singletons. Is that all right with you?"

"Well, okay, I guess," Joe said. "Don't you think so, Vic?"

"Fine," he muttered.

"Now, here's the bad news," Laura said. "And it's bad for all of us. I checked the ferry schedule. I won't be able to get back to Lopez until five-twenty. The next ferry off the island has me getting into Anacortes at seven-fifty tonight. Then it's three hours on the road—

that is, if Stevens Pass is still open. It was starting to snow pretty heavily when I drove through there a little while ago. So—I won't be home until eleven o'clock tonight at the earliest."

She loathed the idea of leaving her children with Vic that long.

"Did I hear her right?" Sophie yelled in the background. "She's not coming back until eleven tonight?"

"Shut your hole!" Vic barked. "Nobody's talking to you."

"Joe?" Laura said. "Can I trust you to make sure my children are safe until then?"

"Hey," Vic chimed in. "You know, I'm listening in here."

"Yes, I'm well aware of that," Laura said. "Joe?"

"I promise, no one will be hurt," he said.

She waited a moment, listening for a reaction from Vic. But there was nothing.

"Okay, then," she said. "I'll call back in a couple of hours after I talk with this Doran person. Can I talk to my daughter now?"

"Sure," Joe said. "Drive safe, and thanks."

Laura heard Vic snicker in the background. Then there was some muttering, and finally Sophie got on the line: "Mom, is it true? You're not coming back until eleven?"

"I'm afraid so, honey. You're just going to have to hang on. How are you?"

"I'm *tired*," Sophie replied with an edge in her voice. "We're all tired."

"I know, honey. I'm depending on you. Take care of

your brothers. Be patient with Joe. And as for Vic, just don't antagonize him."

"Yeah," Vic chuckled. "There's no telling what he'll do."

Laura had forgotten for a moment that he was listening in.

"Hi, Mom!" she heard Liam call.

James let out a squeal: "Mommy!"

It broke her heart to hear their voices. It was like they were crying out to her from a prison cell in some faraway country. And she couldn't help wondering if she'd ever see them again.

"All right, enough of the chitchat," Vic grunted.

Then Laura heard a click, and the line went dead.

CHAPTER FIFTEEN

Tuesday—12:24 P.M.

Sophie was tired, nervous, scared, and angry. She couldn't believe her mother wasn't coming home until eleven tonight. She didn't think she could endure ten and a half more hours of this. And once her mother arrived home, if they all were still alive, then what? Vic wasn't about to go quietly.

Vic had told her to fix their lunch—like she was his slave or something. So she was making grilled cheese sandwiches and Progresso Tomato Basil soup. That was one of her standard "Mom's Not Home and I Have to Cook" meals.

This morning, she'd been so relieved that Vic had seemingly lost interest in her—no more of his creepy leering and flirting. And yet, there had been this tiny part of her that was disappointed. She hated herself for having that perverse little shred of regret. The guy couldn't have been more repugnant. Was she drawn to the danger? Or was she just desperate for attention?

Then about an hour ago, James had started to get

restless, and Liam couldn't keep him still and quiet. Every little noise James made—every whine—seemed to grate on Vic's nerves. Sophie had thought he might, at any minute, jump out of that easy chair and wring James's little neck. She'd asked if the boys could be allowed to go play in the backyard, where Vic could see them through the sliding glass door. He'd quickly agreed, and she'd opened the drapes to the glass door. Her two brothers had put on their jackets and gone outside to toss around James's Nerf football. Joe had joined them.

And Sophie found herself alone with Vic again.

He slid right back into his flirting and smirking. He licked his lips or rubbed his chest whenever he spoke to her. Ensconced in her father's chair, he kept scratching at his crotch. He invited her to sit and watch TV with him. Sophie opted to Windex the kitchen counters and appliance surfaces instead. But that didn't stop him from talking to her.

She couldn't completely ignore him, because she didn't want to make him angry. So mostly she stayed busy cleaning, and every once in a while, she'd look at him and nod or shrug or shake her head.

He said he'd watched some porn movie on pay-per-view last night, and it still had him all "cranked up."

That comment Sophie ignored.

"Have you ever watched an X-rated movie?" he asked.

She tried ignoring him again.

"Well, have you? Don't be embarrassed . . ."

Sophie could feel herself blushing. She stopped

cleaning the oven door to glare at him. "Yes, I watched part of one with some friends once. I found it boring—and gross."

She really wished he'd just shut up and watch TV. This wasn't flirting. This was harassment, and she found it repulsive and unsettling.

"Well, maybe you just weren't watching it with the right person," Vic said. He nodded toward the sofa. "Come sit and watch one with me. I'll pull the drapes closed. They won't see us . . ."

"I don't think so, but thanks anyway," she muttered.

"That's not a request," he said, getting to his feet. "I'm not asking. I'm telling you . . ."

Sophie froze.

He moved over to the sliding glass door and started to pull the drapes shut.

Outside, Liam stopped to stare at them. The Nerf football sailed in the air right past him.

That was when her mother had phoned, thank God.

Sophie had called to Joe and her brothers to come inside. She'd noticed the look of disappointment on Vic's face as he'd taken the phone out of his pants pocket.

And now she would have to endure ten and a half more hours of him.

Standing at the stove, Sophie wondered how they'd survive until her mother came back tonight. Vic was too crazy and volatile. He was sure to hurt someone before the day was over. It actually seemed less risky to try escaping now than to wait it out until eleven o'clock tonight.

She had a plan, and needed to let her brother in on it.

Liam was sitting at the breakfast table, playing the Sneaky Snacky Squirrel card game with James and Joe. Vic was wrapped up in a *Jeopardy!* rerun on the Game Show Network. To Sophie's utter amazement, he sat there and muttered the answers before the contestants did. "What is the Magna Carta, you idiot," he'd grumble. "What is the Sea of Japan . . ." Sophie hadn't realized just how smart he really was—and that made him even more dangerous.

"Liam, could you come help me in here?" she called.

"Ah, shucks, just when I was winning," he said, deadpan. "Carry on without me, guys." He forfeited his cards and came around the counter-bar.

"Could you get the plates and bowls, please?" she asked, pointing to the cupboard.

"Not that I'm complaining, but you called me away from the game just to do that?"

"I think I know a way for us to get out of here," she said under her breath. "Listen up, because we might not have another chance to talk—"

"But Mom said—"

"I know, but she's not coming home for ten more hours, and we could all be dead by then," she whispered. "Just listen. After lunch, I'm going to ask to take a shower, and I'll insist that Joe stand guard outside the bathroom . . ."

She glanced over at Joe, still playing cards with James. Vic was still mesmerized by *Jeopardy!*—"What is the Blarney Stone, moron . . ."

"I think Vic will want to take over guard duty," Sophie quietly explained. "He's been flirting with me, and the chance to stand outside the bathroom where I'm showering might be too much for him to resist . . ."

Liam set the plates and bowls on the counter. "Aren't you kind of overestimating just how hot you are?"

She shot him a look over her shoulder as she stirred the soup. "Just shut up and listen. If Vic leaves you and James alone—even for only a minute—grab James and get out. If you can make it to the cottage, call the police from the phone in the closet there. You know where Dad keeps the key to the cottage?"

Liam's eyes widened and he nodded attentively.

"Get the soupspoons and napkins, will you?" she asked at a normal volume.

"While I'm calling the cops, what are you going to do?" Liam whispered.

"I can see the cottage from my bathroom window. Once I know you guys are there, I'll climb out and make the jump."

"But Mom said—"

"I know, it's risky and dangerous. But we really don't have much of a—"

"Hey, what's all the chatter about?" Vic yelled from her father's chair.

"Nothing!" Sophie said. "We're out of potato chips. Do you want Fritos with your sandwich and soup?"

"Yeah, pile 'em on," he said. Then he turned his attention to the TV again. "What is Sodom and Gomorrah . . ."

"You heard him," she whispered to her brother. "Pile some Fritos on the scumbag's plate. And listen. If the trellis breaks when I make the jump—and it probably will—then, they'll come after me. But don't let that distract you. You and James lay low in the cottage. If you see a car coming down the road, and think you can flag it down, go for it. I'll try to make my way to the warehouse in the far corner of the vineyard."

With a spatula, she took the sandwiches off the griddle. "You got all that?"

"Yeah, but this is totally what Mom told us not to do. If Vic doesn't end up killing you, Mom will." He dumped some Fritos onto Vic's plate. "Joe, you want some Fritos?" he called.

"Yeah, thanks!"

Liam shook some Fritos from the bag onto Joe's plate. "What if Vic doesn't go upstairs?" he whispered. "What if he isn't all that interested in standing outside the bathroom while you're in there naked? What are we supposed to do?"

"Then nothing happens. You and James stay where you are, and at least I get a shower out of the deal."

Both Liam and her mother had taken showers in her bathroom last night, but she hadn't—and she kind of regretted not grabbing the chance when she'd had it.

Sophie poured the soup into the two bowls. "Lunch is ready!" she announced.

While Vic and Joe ate in front of *Jeopardy!*, she made the same lunch for her brothers and herself. She and the boys ate at the counter-bar. Vic made it through lunch without throwing his plate or any glassware, thank God. He pretty much left them alone, except for razzing Liam a bit. "Hey, Junior, are you eating Fritos?" he asked. "Aren't they made with peanut oil or some shit like that? I don't want to see you go into shock, man. You've got to watch yourself . . ."

Liam ignored him, and Vic finally went back to his game show.

"Who is Jack Kerouac . . ."

After lunch, Liam and Joe offered to help with the dishes, but Sophie thought it was more important for them to keep James occupied and quiet. So they returned to the breakfast table with James and resumed their squirrel card game. Sophie collected the plates and bowls and stacked them by the sink. She glanced over at Vic and cleared her throat. "Before I use up all the hot water washing the dishes, I'd like to take a shower," she announced from the kitchen. "Is that okay with you?"

Without looking away from the TV, Vic shook his head.

"Why not?" Sophie asked. Then she realized the Game Show Network was having back-to-back *Jeopardy!*, and Vic didn't want to tear himself away.

"In twenty minutes, when this show is over, you can take a shower or a bubble bath or whatever the hell you want to do." Vic was still staring at the TV screen. "Then I'll be free to guard the bathroom door."

"I'd rather have Joe guard the door," she said. "That's his job for you, isn't it?"

"I don't mind, Vic," Joe said.

Sophie waited. She hoped Vic didn't decide to use the crowbar on her bedroom door again.

Vic looked her up and down. He smiled. "Go ahead, Princess. Get yourself clean and pretty." Then he glanced over toward his friend at the breakfast table. "Joe, you can have the honors. If she tries to lock the door, kick it down." He turned his attention to the TV again.

Joe got up from the squirrel card game to follow Sophie upstairs. She gave a furtive look at her two brothers and felt her insides tighten up. Was this plan of hers a huge mistake?

"Liam, if that package arrives while I'm in the shower, you'll have to sign for it," she said. "If they need an adult's signature, you'll just have to send them away."

Her brother nodded. He looked scared.

She turned to Vic. "If that happens, try not to freak out and shoot the delivery guy, okay?"

He chuckled. "I'll try my best, sweet tits."

She turned away and headed for the stairs—with Joe trailing behind her. "Your friend's a disgusting pig," she whispered.

"You shouldn't egg him on like that," Joe replied under his breath.

Upstairs, in her bedroom, Sophie selected a change of clothes from her dresser and closet. "If my mother's able to help you, how are you going to get Vic to leave without hurting anybody?"

Joe stood by her bedroom door. "Vic's already agreed to it. He promised me. I'll make sure no one gets hurt."

With the clean clothes draped over her arm, Sophie stared at him. "I really wished I believed you," she said. Then she turned and headed into the bathroom.

"Please, don't shut the door all the way," she heard him call. "On my honor, I'll stay right here."

Sophie left the bathroom door open a sliver. Pulling back the shower curtain, she turned the shower on full blast and accidentally doused her shirtsleeve. She hoped the humming pipes and spraying water would drown out the sound of her opening the window. She moved over to the small, frosted-glass window and slowly pushed it up. It squeaked a bit, but she kept pushing until it was completely open. She glanced over her shoulder at the door—to make sure it was just how she'd left it. No one was trying to peek in.

With one knee on the hamper, she boosted herself up and peered outside—at the driveway and the wine-tasting cottage. She shuddered from the chilly November breeze that started to sweep into the bathroom. Any minute, she expected to see Liam and James running away from the house. She checked the drop to the trellis roof below. She figured if she climbed out the window and lowered herself until she was clinging to the ledge, it would only be a six- or seven-foot jump from there. She prayed the rickety-looking roof wouldn't cave in on her.

There was still no sign of her brothers outside.

Moving away from the window, Sophie went to listen at the door. She figured she'd soon hear Vic and Joe having a whispered conversation in her bedroom. She'd been so certain Vic would come upstairs to take Joe's place.

But it was quiet in the bedroom. She wondered if Liam had been right. Maybe she'd overestimated her own allure. Maybe Vic was more interested in *Jeopardy!* than in peeking in on her naked.

Rubbing her arms from the cold, Sophie crept back

to the window and looked outside again. She could see her breath and started to tremble. But she stayed by the window and waited for Liam and James to appear down there.

Joe sat down on the floor and leaned against the frame of Sophie's bedroom doorway. He listened to the shower roaring in the bathroom.

He felt awkward and slightly unnerved to be in a teenage girl's bedroom. That was why he couldn't really go past the threshold. It reminded him too much of early Saturday morning, when he'd staggered into Willow Singleton's bedroom. Like Sophie, she was sixteen.

When he'd talked with Mrs. Gretchell last night about the Singletons, he'd mentioned that he'd gone into two other bedrooms besides Connor's. But he hadn't gone into any details. After phoning the police, he'd first gone up to Dean's bedroom. He'd been the oldest son. Joe found him sprawled facedown on his bedroom floor—clad only in a pair of gray briefs with white trim. His hands and feet had been tied, and blood stained the beige carpet on either side of him—like angel's wings. Someone had thrown a blanket over his head. Except for the unmade bed and a tipped-over desk chair, nothing in the room had been disturbed. There had been no signs of a struggle.

Willow's room was across the hall. When Joe peered in, he was relieved not to see her corpse. Had she escaped somehow?

Like Sophie, Willow had her own bathroom. The door was open just enough that Joe could tell the light was on. He passed through her bedroom—cheerleader's pompoms were wedged behind one corner of the mirror over Willow's dresser; the sheets lay in a tangle on her canopy bed.

The bathroom door creaked as he pushed it open a few more inches. He noticed blood on the green and white tiled floor. He opened the door even farther and saw Willow, clad in panties and a T-shirt, curled up on the floor under the sink. The T-shirt was ripped in places and soaked with blood. Her feet had been tied together. Her arms were on either side of the sink's pedestal—with the wrists tied together. Her blond head was awkwardly tilted and pressed against the pedestal's base.

After seeing Willow, Joe knew what he'd find in the other bedrooms. But he went into Connor's room anyway.

The images of the dead were burned in his brain.

Now he listened to the shower and gazed at Sophie's bathroom door—slightly ajar. He felt a bit sick. He closed his eyes and hoped it would pass.

He heard someone screaming downstairs. It sounded like little James.

Joe stood up.

There were footsteps on the stairs. Then he saw Vic come around the corner toward him. "You look half-asleep on the job, kiddo," he said loudly—over the wailing. "I'll take over . . ."

Her ear to the door, Sophie heard them arguing in her bedroom. But she couldn't make out what they were saying. She thought she heard screaming, too.

She moved over to the vent and listened. The screams were coming from downstairs.

Her heart racing, she moved back to the window and looked out at the landscape below. She didn't see her brothers down there. She knew Vic had come upstairs. He'd left them alone in the family room at least a minute or two ago. She wondered if Liam had lost his nerve. Why was James shrieking?

Something had gone wrong. And any minute now, she expected Vic to burst into the bathroom—only to find her fully dressed and the window open.

Sophie quickly closed the window and shucked off her outer clothes. In her bra and panties, she grabbed her bathrobe off the hook on the back of the bathroom door. The door moved slightly, and the hinges squeaked. She threw on the bathrobe and put her head under the shower to wet her hair. Then she turned off the water and pulled a towel off the rack.

She could clearly hear them talking in her bedroom now: "Vic, I know you. I know what you're up to. Listen, she's a nice girl . . ."

She could also clearly hear James downstairs shrieking—like he was hurt or terrified.

Sophie opened the bathroom door. "What's going on? What did you do to my little brother?"

Vic frowned at her. "Relax. I just tied him up. I tied them both up."

She started to move past him, but he pushed her back into the bathroom. He stepped in after her.

"Vic, don't," Joe said. "Please . . ."

Sophie shrunk away from him.

"Shit," he muttered, glaring at her. "It's as cold as a

polar bear's prick in here. Did you have the window open? You sneaky little bitch, you were trying to escape . . ."

"I—I opened the window to let the steam out," she said.

All at once, he yanked open the front of her robe. "Do you always shower in your bra and panties?"

Recoiling, Sophie pulled at the front of her robe to cover herself up. "Only when there's a pervert in the house," she shot back.

He slapped her. It was so sudden and hard that she fell back against the hamper and landed on the bathroom floor.

"I'm gonna nail that goddamn window shut," Vic announced. Then he turned, brushed past Joe, and stomped out of the bedroom.

Momentarily stunned, Sophie remained on the floor with her back against the hamper. She touched her sore cheek. Her ear was ringing, but she could still hear James's screams from downstairs.

Joe came to the bathroom doorway. "Were you really trying to escape?" He actually looked disillusioned with her.

Frowning, Sophie got to her feet. She pushed back her wet hair and then tied the sash of her robe. "My mother practically saved your life when you were a kid. Right now, she's out there somewhere trying to help you again. And this is how you repay her?"

Joe winced. He opened his mouth to speak, but didn't say anything.

Sophie hurried past him, out the bedroom and down the

stairs. Joe followed her. As she approached the kitchen, she heard her baby brother's cries getting louder. It was a heartbreaking sound.

She stopped dead at the kitchen entrance. James was standing by the oven. His wrists were tied to the oven door handle with a couple of dish towels. He kept screaming and struggling to get free.

Liam was curled up on the kitchen floor—by the cabinet under the sink. Some bottles of cleanser and laundry detergent were scattered on the floor. The cabinet door was open, and it looked as if Liam had gotten stuck reaching for something under the sink. It took Sophie a moment to realize Vic must have tied his hands to the drainpipe.

"Oh, God, no!" she heard Joe cry—over her baby brother's shrieks of protest.

Sophie ran to Liam first, and got down on her knees. "What did he—"

"He used the cord from the waffle iron," Liam muttered. His face was all flushed. "He's got it tight as hell. You better get to Jamie first before he has a total meltdown . . ."

She turned toward her baby brother, and saw Joe hovering over him, trying to unfasten the knots in the dish towels. James had tears running down his face. He stomped on the floor.

"It's okay, buddy," Joe was saying. He had tears in his eyes, too. "I'll get you untied. Just give me another minute . . ."

Before Sophie could go help him, Joe had untied James. But her baby brother suddenly didn't want anything to do with his new friend. He cried out to Sophie and ran into her arms.

She caught a glimpse of Joe, looking hurt and ashamed.

"C'mon, we have to help Liam," she told James. She looked under the sink at the cord tangled around the pipe and his wrists. "God, how did he do this?" she muttered.

"He was kneeling on my back the whole time he tied my hands together," Liam muttered. "You were right, damn it. He—he really wanted to be up there while you were in the shower . . ."

Sophie shushed him, and blindly reached into the cabinet and started tugging at the cord. James had one hand on her back and with the other he patted Liam on the leg. "Sophie will get you out . . ."

"Can I help?" she heard Joe ask.

"No," Liam said curtly.

Sophie heard the kitchen door slam. She glanced up in time to see Vic swagger by with the hammer and some nails. She realized he must have stashed them in the garage with the other "contraband" items he'd confiscated earlier. It looked like he wasn't about to waste any time before nailing shut that bathroom window.

Leaning against the oven, Joe still had the dish towels in his hand. He shook his head at his friend. "God, Vic, why did you do it?"

"You gave me the idea for under the sink," he said, heading for the front hallway. "Remember Willow?"

Joe hung his head down.

Sophie heard Vic lumbering up the stairs. She wasn't

sure what he and Joe had been talking about. But she knew one of the Singleton kids was named Willow.

With James hanging on her, she reached under the sink again and pulled at a knot in the cord around Liam's wrists.

"I think you're getting it," Liam moaned. "It—it feels looser . . ."

As Sophie struggled with the restraints, she heard hammering above them.

She caught a glimpse of Joe, still standing by the oven. He looked like he was about to cry.

"What was he talking about?" she asked. "Who's Willow?"

Joe shrugged. He wouldn't look at her. "It's just something bad I saw," he murmured. "That's all . . ."

CHAPTER SIXTEEN

Tuesday—3:19 P.M.
Bellingham, Washington

On the Western Washington University campus, Laura finally found a student walking alone who wasn't wearing ear-buds or engrossed in a smartphone. From the car window, she asked the skinny young man if there was a way to find out where a particular student lived—and maybe get his class schedule. The young man gave her directions to the Campus Services Building on Bill McDonald Parkway.

The young woman with dreadlocks who manned the desk at Campus Services was probably a student, working there part-time. She looked miserable as she tore herself away from her laptop to assist Laura. She didn't seem a bit interested in the story Laura had concocted about how she was Doran Wiley's aunt, here for a surprise visit. The girl just nodded tiredly as she consulted the computer on the other side of the counter. "He's in Mathes Hall . . ." She slapped two pieces of paper on the counter in front of Laura. One had a map of the campus and the other was a temporary parking permit for Laura's dashboard. The girl circled Mathes Hall on the map and scribbled down Doran's room number.

"Thank you," Laura said. "Is it possible to get his class schedule for today? I don't want to have to—"

The young woman started shaking her head and went back to her laptop. "We don't release class schedules as a matter of policy. If it's an emergency, you need to go to the administration office."

Doran Wiley's roommate didn't have Doran's class schedule either. Their dorm room was on the seventh floor. It smelled like dirty gym socks. One side of the small room had ski posters on the wall. Ski equipment was stashed by a steamer trunk in the corner. On the wall next to the other bed was a Beastie Boys poster— along with mini-posters of half-naked, buxom young models Laura didn't recognize. The place was kind of a mess—as was Doran's roommate. Laura figured she must have woken him from a nap when she'd knocked on the door. His red hair was unkempt, and he wore a ratty-looking flannel shirt, cargo shorts, and black socks. "Doran was just here like a little while ago," the roommate said. "He was going to grab a late lunch at the Commons."

"The Commons," Laura repeated. "Where is that?"

"The Viking Commons—it's like just next door. You go out the front door and hang a right."

"Thank you," Laura said. "This is going to sound strange, but I haven't seen Doran since he was a little boy. Could you tell me what he looks like?"

The roommate nodded toward the corkboard above the desk on the Beastie Boys side of the room. "Well, step on up and visit the shrine . . ."

Laura moved over to the desk and saw about twenty different photos tacked to the corkboard. The first one to catch her eye was an eight by ten portrait of a tan, handsome young man with a confident, dimpled smile and dark hair that had a sexy, messy bed-head look. She couldn't tell if it was a high-school graduation portrait or a model's head shot. The same handsome guy was in all the other—smaller—photos. In some, he was shirtless; in others, he had a girl hanging on him; in others, he wore football gear. There were several selfies, too. Laura thought it was a little weird that so many of the photos displayed above his desk were of him alone. Doran Wiley didn't seem to mind himself one bit.

"Well, that gives me a pretty good idea of what he looks like, thanks," she said.

"Yeah, check out the Commons. He's probably there with his harem."

The roommate was right. The Viking Commons was just next door. The huge cafeteria had a wall of windows that offered a sweeping view over the treetops of Bellingham Bay. A mix of savory food smells—mostly chili—immediately hit Laura. The place wasn't too crowded at this off-hour. There was no one at the salad bar, and only a handful of people stood in line at the food counter. It didn't take long to spot Doran Wiley at one of the long tables in front of the windows. He didn't exactly have a harem with him—just two girls who were sort of flashy-looking and another guy, a chubby character who resembled Jonah Hill. As Laura approached them, she could see they'd been snacking on nachos and sodas. They had their smartphones out. Doran wore a black knit cap that seemed a bit affected and a black T-shirt.

"Hi, I'm sorry to interrupt you guys," she said.

Only the Jonah Hill clone looked up from his phone at her.

"You're Doran, aren't you?" she said to his friend. "Doran Wiley?"

He finally glanced at her. He had brown eyes, and was indeed very good looking. But he seemed too well aware of it. He half-smiled at her—as if mildly amused.

"I was wondering if I could talk with you for a couple of minutes," Laura said.

One of the girls flanking Doran giggled.

"Cougar alert!" his friend muttered. This remark got some more giggles from the group.

"And you are?" Doran said, sitting back in the chrome and black plastic chair.

The Jonah Hill lookalike leaned across the table and whispered something that sent one of the girls into a sniggering fit.

"You don't know me, but I—well, my name's Laura, and I'm a freelance reporter. I'd really appreciate it if I could talk to you in private—for just a few moments."

Though still smiling, Doran looked as if he were already bored with her. He glanced at his phone again. "What about?"

Laura sighed. "I'd like to talk about your stint as caretaker for Scott and Sherry Singleton. And I'd also like to ask you about Eric Vetter."

Doran looked up from his phone. His smile had disappeared. He got to his feet and darted around the table. Grabbing Laura's arm, he pulled her over toward a table-bussing station and the trash and recycling receptacles. "Who told you that I knew Eric Vetter?" he growled under his breath. "Where'd you hear that?"

Laura wrestled her arm away. She was dumbfounded at the way he'd suddenly lost his cool. Glancing over at his friends, she could tell they were equally surprised.

"I didn't know him. I never even met the guy," Doran continued. "Or if I did, I don't remember. As for the Singletons, I already talked to the police and a reporter from the *Seattle Times*. I worked at the Lopez Island home for three months over the summer, and they were there only a few weekends. I haven't been on Lopez since I left the job in August."

Laura studied him and glanced once again at his posse. From the manner in which he'd so quickly whisked her away, she had a feeling his friends knew nothing about his job with the Singletons. For someone so vain, she'd have thought he would relish his peripheral role in this huge news story and all the attention it would bring.

"I'm sorry if I said something to embarrass you in front of your friends."

He scowled. "I'm not embarrassed . . ."

"Good, because someone told me you might know a few secrets about the Singletons, things the police don't know."

"Well, that's bullshit. Who the hell told you that?"

"A source," Laura said. "I won't divulge my sources.

You need to know that if you decide to share some things—"

"I'm not sharing anything with you, lady," he interrupted. "And I already told the cops everything I know."

Laura opened her purse and reached inside for Joe's sketches.

"Earlier, you said you were freelance, right?" he asked.

Nodding, Laura showed him Joe's most-refined, detailed rendering. "Does this look like anyone you know? Maybe somebody you saw at the summerhouse?"

He frowned at the picture, and impatiently shook his head.

"Please, give it a good look. Does the name Zared sound familiar?"

"No, it doesn't," he said. "Getting back to you— freelance, that means you're not working for any particular news agency or newspaper, right? You're just chasing down a story you hope to sell to some news place. Am I right?"

"That's right," she said, still holding up the drawing. "Are you sure the man in this sketch isn't even remotely familiar? I mean, is there a chance it's Eric Vetter?"

"Get that fucking thing out of my face," he whispered.

Laura took a step back.

"Freelance! Shit, you're not even a real reporter. Why the hell should I talk to you, bitch? Fuck off."

He turned and started back toward his friends.

She watched him sit down with them. He popped a nacho in his mouth and muttered something that made them laugh.

"Ha, *Scarface*. You're awful, Doran!" one of the girls said. She went back to looking at her smartphone.

Laura felt a momentary pang of anger and hurt—and for just a second, she was forced to think about Mr. Clapp again. But it was just a brief distraction. She saw the smartphone in that stupid girl's hand, and Laura wished she had her phone with her right now. Then she could look up Eric Vetter and find out who he was—and why the mention of his name seemed to unnerve this cocky young creep.

There was something about the caretaker job that Joe hadn't told her. And Doran Wiley didn't want her to know about it either.

Laura glanced at her watch: 3:50. What the hell had happened to the time? There was no way she would make it to Anacortes for the 4:30 ferry to Lopez, not even if she drove eighty miles an hour the whole way. The next ferry wasn't until six.

She took the ferry schedule out of her purse, studied it, and did the math. If she still hoped to get home by eleven, she'd have only twenty minutes to go meet Martha and then catch the 7:10 ferry off Lopez. She hoped Martha lived close to the ferry terminal.

Once again, she missed her regular phone with its MapQuest and Google applications.

Laura headed toward the exit, but stopped to talk to a young woman near the salad bar: "Excuse me, but I don't know the campus very well. Is there a cyber café or a place where I can get access to a computer?"

The girl told her that Wilson Library was practically right behind the commons, and they had computers there.

Laura thanked her. Before heading out of the cafeteria, she glanced back toward Doran Wiley and his entourage. They were talking and laughing and looking at their phones. None of them seemed to know she was still there.

But not far from the table-bussing station, she noticed a young blond man sitting alone at a long table. He had a slightly pretty, Aryan-looking face with full, pouty lips. And he knew she was there. He stared directly at her.

She hadn't noticed him in the cafeteria earlier. She remembered Martha saying that Singleton's disciples were around everywhere and she had to be careful about what she said out loud. But that had been back on the island.

He was still staring.

Laura turned away and hurried out of the cafeteria.

CHAPTER SEVENTEEN

Tuesday—3:56 P.M.
Leavenworth

"Yeah, what's going on?" Vic asked, sounding groggy.

The volume went mute on the TV.

The last time Joe had checked on him, Vic had been dozing in the easy chair in front of *The Jerry Springer Show*. Vic had already herded the kids upstairs, and used the crowbar on the door again to keep them holed up in Sophie's bedroom. He'd also sent Joe into the living room to watch for the delivery person. Vic was especially concerned about that, maybe even a little paranoid. He seemed convinced the delivery person was part of some kind of ambush. It really didn't make sense, because Mr. Gretchell had been the one who wanted Mrs. Gretchell to sign for a package this afternoon—and the guy was in Europe with no idea what was happening. Still, Vic was jumpy as hell about the whole thing. Sophie hadn't been too far off when she'd advised Vic not to freak out and kill the delivery person.

Joe had been instructed to alert Vic when the UPS or FedEx truck arrived. Then he was supposed to round up the kids and send Sophie downstairs to sign for the package. Joe would remain upstairs with the boys while Vic kept watch just inside the front door.

Vic had given him Sophie's smartphone so he could play games on it and not be bored to smithereens sitting there alone on the living room sofa by the front window. Joe knew it was wrong, but after a while, he'd gotten tired of playing games on the phone. So he'd started looking over Sophie's photos—of her, her family, and her boyfriend. Everyone looked so happy and nice in the pictures. Joe even read some of the texts between Sophie and the boyfriend. There had been nothing too intimate or earth-shattering about their correspondence. But some of their chatter was cute—even funny at times. Joe wondered if this was what it was like for normal people with families, partners, or good friends.

He'd just switched back to the solitaire game when he'd heard Mrs. Gretchell's phone ringing.

He listened to Vic's grunt in response to whatever Mrs. Gretchell was telling him. Then Vic wandered through the living room. Glancing Joe's way, he took the phone from his face for a moment. "She met with the other caretaker, the one before you, and she came up with a big fat nothing," he said. "But she wants to speak with you after she talks to the brats. I'll bring the phone back down. Stay put and keep your eyes peeled . . ."

Vic started up the stairs. "We're still waiting on that special delivery from your old man," he said into the phone. "The kiddies are having themselves a time-out in the bedroom right now, because they were being a pain in the ass . . ."

Joe heard Vic's footsteps above—and his murmuring. He couldn't quite make out the words.

". . . because the little bitch tried to climb out the bathroom window!" he exclaimed. That part, Joe heard.

The bedroom door creaked as Vic dislodged the crowbar. Joe listened to more muttering. Then Sophie's voice came through pretty clear for a moment: "We're all fine, Mom, just *tired*—really, really tired . . ."

Vic must have been feeling magnanimous, because Liam and then James briefly talked to their mother. But once again, Joe couldn't discern what they were saying.

After a couple of minutes, he heard the bedroom door creaking again—and James's muffled crying. It was heartbreaking. Vic came down the stairs and handed him the phone. "She wants to talk with you . . ."

Vic stood there by the newel post watching as Joe spoke into the phone. "Hello, Mrs. Gretchell?"

"Hi, Joe," she said. "Listen, I met with Doran Wiley and didn't have much luck. But I could tell he was covering something up—something about working for the Singletons. I seemed to hit a nerve when I mentioned Eric Vetter. Are you sure you don't know who that is?"

"No, I swear," Joe murmured.

"Well, do you know of any reason why Doran Wiley wouldn't want to talk about his caretaker job for the Singletons?"

"No," Joe answered. But in truth, there were some things about his time at the Singletons' compound he didn't want to discuss himself—some things that disgusted him.

"Well, your friend Martha seemed to think Doran could tell me something. But it's his hostile reaction to my questions and what he wouldn't say that seem important to me. I'm here in front of the university library, and I'm going to do a little research. Then I'm headed back to the island. In the meantime, once again, I'm counting on you to look after my kids."

"I will, I swear," he said.

"So—what happened earlier with Vic and my kids?"

Vic grabbed the phone out of his hand. "I already told you what happened," he barked. "Call back when you've actually got something to report."

He clicked off and then headed into the bathroom.

Joe took a look out the window. He didn't see anyone in the driveway. He glanced at the bathroom door and then slowly crept up the stairs. He knocked on the doorframe of Sophie's bedroom. He didn't want to tap on the door and possibly dislodge the crowbar—even though it was wedged in there pretty damn tight.

He was still holding her smartphone. "Sophie?" he called quietly.

"What?" she said.

"I'm sorry about what happened with Vic earlier," he whispered. "You shouldn't make him mad, I've told you that. The way he gets, he even scares me sometimes. But—well, he's been a good friend to me. I wish you'd just try a little harder to get along with him."

"Yeah, well, your loyal friend has slugged my mother, slapped me, and last night he came close to shooting my brother. Plus, he has us locked in here now. So you'll pardon me if I have a hard time accepting your apology for that creep. Listen, if you're not going to let us out of here or help us, I wish you'd just leave us alone."

Joe was about to say *I'm sorry*, but thought better of it. He retreated down the hall and then down the steps.

He glanced out the front window, and again, he didn't see anything.

In the downstairs bathroom, the toilet flushed.

Joe sat down on the sofa just as Vic emerged from the bathroom. "If you want to make things easier for yourself," his friend said, "you'll stop being so chummy-chummy with those brats." He headed into the family room, and a moment later, the TV volume went up again.

Joe didn't want to think about what his friend meant by that statement. He wondered if Vic had heard him talking with Sophie upstairs.

Vic always seemed to know what was going on— even back when they'd been in the *country club* together. Vic had been the one who had come up with that name for the place. *Psychiatric facility* just sounded so awful. Joe remembered feeling utterly terrified his first few days there. He'd seen enough prison movies to know what to expect, even though, technically, the place wasn't a jail. Still, there were bars on the windows, locks on the doors, and guards in the corridors—along with everything else they had in prisons: an exercise yard, a cafeteria, a library, communal showers, and an occupational-therapy room. They also had predators who targeted newbies like Joe.

It didn't matter how much Joe tried to keep to himself and blend into the scenery. This scrawny, hairy guy with a goatee who called himself Spider seemed to home in on him. After Donald Clapp, and Larry, the coworker he'd put in the hospital, and others like them, Joe should have been used to getting picked on. Spider wasn't really any worse than the others. He made fun of Joe, tripped and shoved him, and stole food off his tray during meals. In the showers, Spider tried to grab his butt or get him in a headlock. And then he'd accuse Joe of checking him out, which was absolutely ridiculous. But the craziest part about it was that Joe could have beaten the crap out of Spider if he wanted to. Joe was just afraid. The last time he'd lost his head and beaten up a guy, it had been Larry; and as a direct result of that, he'd ended up in this psychiatric facility. So when Spider picked on him, Joe just took it.

He wasn't exactly sure how or when he met Vic, but the two of them started hanging out together. Having Vic around seemed to discourage Spider from bothering him. He was Spider-repellent. Unfortunately, Vic wasn't around all the time. Spider grabbed every opportunity when Joe was alone to harass him and push him around. "Hey, are you Victor Moles's bitch?" he taunted him in the exercise yard on a Good Friday. Spider pushed him so hard that Joe slammed into a brick wall and cut his forehead. "Are you guys a couple now? Is he giving it to you, Joe-Joe?"

This happened in the presence of several other inmate-patients—or *club members*, as Vic called them. Joe never told Vic what had happened or how he'd gotten the cut on his forehead. Vic already disliked Spider intensely, and

Joe didn't want to cause an incident. But apparently someone else informed Vic about the exercise-yard altercation.

On Easter Sunday, in the shower room, without warning, Vic went crazy. He attacked Spider and started beating him savagely. He ended up breaking Spider's jaw and biting off his ear.

Vic was transferred to another floor with the ultra-crazies, and he stayed there until around Memorial Day. Spider spent almost the same stretch of time in the infirmary. And when he was released, he never bothered Joe again, never even got near him.

No one bothered Joe at all.

Vic became his best friend and protector. Despite what Spider had said, there was nothing sexual about their relationship. Still, Joe's psychiatrist, Dr. Halstead, warned him that Vic was a lot more dangerous than Spider. He said Vic was a manipulative sociopath. When Joe told this to Vic, he almost expected his friend to go berserk. But Vic merely made a face like he'd tasted something sour, and he said, "That shrink of yours, he doesn't have your best interests in mind."

He encouraged Joe to lie to his psychiatrist, lies that would get him an early release. And Vic was right. Joe got out of there and became an outpatient. They had him on medication, which took care of a lot of his problems. He stayed in a halfway house and got a good job working for a landscaper. He wrote to Vic at the country club, saved his money, and was actually pretty happy.

He was just out of the halfway house and renting a

room in someone's basement when the Singletons' caretaking job landed in his lap.

Less than a week before he started working for the Singletons, the police showed up at the house where Joe had rented the basement room. He was horrified to learn that his friend had slashed a guard's throat with a broken Coke bottle and escaped from the country club. The guard, a weasel named Gary Warren, had survived. Joe remembered Warren had always been nasty toward him. Warren had seen Spider picking on him countless times and hadn't done a thing to stop it. Joe knew he should feel bad about what had happened to Gary Warren, but he didn't.

And he knew he should have notified the police when Vic called him just a day later, but he didn't.

The police checked in with him again a few days after that. Joe lied and said he still hadn't heard from his friend. He figured he owed Vic at least that much. The police said they were following a lead that Vic had gone to New Mexico.

If only he had.

In his next conversation with Vic, Joe made the mistake of telling him about his wonderful new job on Lopez Island and the nice—famous—people who had hired him. When he mentioned he was alone there most of the time, his friend seemed to take it as an invitation to swing on by whenever he wanted.

Vic's visits to the Singletons' summer home were unnerving. Joe was never sure when he'd show up. Sometimes he'd surprise him by howling like a wolf outside the compound fence. Vic always thought that was a funny way to announce himself. Mostly, he'd call saying he was on the ferry or already somewhere in town waiting to be picked up. Once on the premises, Vic made himself at home. He treated the Singleton compound like his personal kingdom. Joe was always worried sick someone in town would catch on that Vic was paying him these visits. The police were still looking for him. Both of them could get arrested. But Vic didn't care. He was so reckless, always pushing his luck, "borrowing" things from the house, eating their food, watching their TV, using their toilets, and even wearing some of Scott Singleton's clothes. He sometimes went to town on a Vespa that belonged to one of the Singleton kids.

Joe was always cleaning up after him, covering his tracks. He was never sure when Mrs. Singleton might pull one of her surprise visits. He didn't even want to think what would happen if she ever showed up and discovered Vic settled in her beautiful house.

The first weekend in October, Mrs. Singleton arrived unannounced with her sixteen-year-old daughter, Willow. Joe got a call from Vic just minutes after they'd driven up to the house. When he phoned Vic back, he was still out of breath from helping Mrs. and Miss Singleton with their overnight bags. Vic said he was on the island, at the Last Sunset Café, and he needed to be picked up.

Joe begged him to go away. But Vic wouldn't hang up—even as Mrs. Singleton buzzed Joe from the house intercom. Vic kept saying he wanted to meet Mrs. Singleton. He'd seen photos, and thought she was kind of hot for an older lady. What was the teenage daughter like? Was she doable?

"Vic, she's just a kid," Joe said. "And I'm telling you again, you can't come here. I like this job, and you're going to ruin it for me. Please, go away . . ."

Vic wasn't happy he had to head back to the mainland.

Joe spent most of the afternoon running errands for Mrs. Singleton. He was exhausted by the time he went to bed. But he couldn't fall asleep right away—especially when he noticed a light go on in the master bedroom in the house across the way. He saw Mrs. Singleton in the elegantly appointed room—all beige and white with splashes of lavender here and there. He kept expecting her to close the drapes, but she didn't. He figured she must have forgotten he was right there, just across the driveway turnaround. Joe sat up in bed, and watched her start undressing. He always thought Mrs. Singleton was attractive. Blond, with a creamy complexion, she had one of those taut, gym-toned bodies. Joe had first noticed the day he'd met her, when he'd seen her play tennis at her friend's house.

Dumbfounded, he sat and watched as Mrs. Singleton pulled her sweater over her head. She had her hair in a ponytail. Wandering over to the window in her bra and slacks, she unfastened the band from the back of her head and shook out her hair. Then she reached back and unfastened her bra.

Joe watched her take it off. "Wow," he murmured, staring at her small, shapely breasts. He slid his hand under the covers. He couldn't believe his luck. He figured, any minute now, it would run out. She'd pull the curtains shut, or maybe she'd somehow spot him in his darkened bedroom across the way, gawking at her and playing with himself. Then she'd be horrified. He kept thinking that Mrs. Singleton had been so nice to him, she'd trusted him, and she was there for a pleasant, wholesome weekend with her young daughter. On top of all that, her husband was an important minister, which meant she was very devout and religious.

But he couldn't stop staring. She wiggled out of her pants, and then stepped out of her panties. The way she slid them down her long legs was so graceful—and erotic. Joe could see every inch of her as she hung up her clothes, pulled a nightgown from the dresser, and then even took a phone call. Mrs. Singleton stood there naked by the window, casually chatting on the phone. Joe could even hear the faint murmuring.

She talked on the phone for at least five minutes. Joe couldn't hold back. Even after he'd come, he didn't stop watching her. He waited until she ducked into the bathroom. Then he got up and cleaned himself off.

When he returned to bed, he saw that she'd switched off the lights in the master bedroom.

The next day, Joe ran more errands for her and Willow. All the while, he couldn't look either one of them in the eyes. And all the while, he prayed he'd get another show that night.

He kept checking the master bedroom window as he got ready for bed. It was early, and he wasn't a bit sleepy. But he didn't want to risk missing her. At ten o'clock, he saw the light go on in there, and he spotted

Mrs. Singleton in her sweater and jeans. She came over to the window, and then closed the curtain.

"Shit," Joe murmured.

He wondered if she'd somehow figured out that he'd been watching her the night before. He tried to sleep but couldn't.

The intercom buzzed at five minutes to eleven. Joe scurried out of bed and snatched up the phone: "Hello?"

"Joe, could you—oh, damn it—could you come over here right now?" she said. "I—I've got this emergency. Please, hurry . . ."

He threw on his jeans and a T-shirt, tied up his sneakers, grabbed his keys, and ran down the stairs. He stepped outside and saw Mrs. Singleton already waiting across the way with the front door open. She wore a floor-length, pink satiny bathrobe. Her hair was down around her shoulders. She looked frazzled and angry.

"What's the matter?" he asked. "What happened?"

She shushed him. "For God's sake, don't wake Willow!"

He felt stupid for talking so loud.

"C'mon, hurry," she whispered. She closed the door behind him and rushed up the stairs. "I can't get the water to turn off! It won't stop. It's in the master bath. I hope you know what to do . . ."

Joe hoped he knew what to do, too. He didn't know much about plumbing. But he followed her up the stairs and down the hallway to the master bedroom, where he'd seen her undress the night before. He could hear water rushing.

He headed into the bathroom, which was white and gray tiled with ultramodern-looking fixtures. Water poured from a waterfall spout into the Jacuzzi tub. Joe quickly bent over the side and gave the spigot a turn. But it just kept turning and turning—and the water just kept flowing.

"Can you fix it?" she asked, standing over him. Her voice was shrill. "You can fix it, can't you?"

"I'm not sure," he said, feeling panicked.

"Well, you know plumbing, don't you? I mean, why would you have taken a job like this if you don't know anything about plumbing? My God . . ."

Joe tried pressing in on the spigot and turning—and then pulling at it and turning. Neither technique did any good. The water kept streaming out of the strange-looking spout. Baffled, he scratched his head.

"Well? Can't you get it to stop?"

"I'm trying . . ." He remembered some guy giving him a quick orientation tour of the place back in late August. He'd shown Joe the main shutoff valves in the utility room by the kitchen.

"What good are you?" she snapped. "What are we paying you for?"

"Let me—let me try this . . ." Joe said. She was making him so nervous. He hurried over to the double-sink vanity and opened the cabinet doors. He found some pipes with valves in the corner closest to the walk-in shower.

"How's that going to help?" she went on. "Stupid! Do you have any idea at all what you're doing? My God, how am I going to explain to my husband why I hired you?"

Joe was shaking. He wanted to tell her to stop yelling at him. He reached into the cabinet and twisted the valve. He reminded himself: *righty tight-y, lefty-loose-y.*

"If you can't do a simple . . ." she trailed off. "Well, I'll just have to call a plumber, and at this hour, getting him to come all the way out here, it's going to cost an arm and . . ."

The water went off with a surrendering squeak.

Joe let out a sigh.

After all the gushing water and her screaming, the sudden silence was lovely.

Neither of them said anything for a few moments.

Sheepishly, he glanced up at Mrs. Singleton. She was shaking now, too. The front of her robe had come loose, and he could almost see her breasts. "I'm so sorry, Joe," she whispered. She had tears in her eyes. "I didn't mean to talk to you like that. My husband usually picks whoever looks after the grounds here. This is the first time I've done the hiring, and I thought . . ." She shook her head. "I had no right to speak to you that way. Please, forgive me . . ."

Joe closed the cabinet and straightened up. "Then I'm not fired?" he asked timidly.

"Oh, no," she said, shaking her head. "You must think I'm horrible . . ."

"It—it's probably just a washer that needs replacing . . ."

"Will you ever forgive me, Joe?" she asked, stepping closer to him. She put her hand on the side of his face. "How could I be so mean to such a sweet, handsome man? Say you don't hate me . . ."

He opened his mouth, but he couldn't talk. He was getting aroused, and he was terrified she'd notice.

But she took hold of his hand and slowly brought it up to the front of her robe.

Joe let her slide his trembling hand inside the robe to cup her soft breast. He let her lean in and kiss him on the lips.

And when she began to rub the front of his jeans, he didn't pull away.

They had sex on her bathroom rug that night.

The next day, he went online and looked up the brand of bathroom hardware the Singletons had in their master bath. He figured out how to change the spigot. All he needed were some water pump pliers. But he couldn't find any in the utility room, so he used a wrench. It turned out the spigot was just loose—a lot of fuss for nothing.

Mrs. Singleton was alone for her next surprise visit to the summerhouse. They made love in the kitchen, the living room, and the master bedroom. It was strange being in the bed she usually shared with her husband. Afterward, Joe used the bathroom, where they'd had their first encounter. He went looking for a Band-Aid to replace one on his arm that was coming undone. He never found any Band-Aids. But he found a pair of water pump pliers in one of the cabinet drawers.

He never asked Mrs. Singleton about it.

Of course, he had to tell Vic about his secret affair with the mistress of the house. His friend claimed to be happy for him, but he was annoyed by the possibility that Mrs. Singleton might be dropping by more frequently. "Tell her to let you know ahead of time when she's coming," he insisted. "Tell her you want to know so you can look forward to her visit. Anticipation and all that shit . . ."

Joe told her. So during Vic's visits, at least they got advance warning when Mrs. Singleton was on the way.

Whenever she brought along one or two of the kids for the night or a weekend, she was more discreet about where she and Joe made love, but not very. Joe never had much say in it. Mrs. Singleton called all the shots. While her children played or slept in the house, she and Joe had sex in the woods, in his quarters above the garage, in her car, in the boathouse, and even in Mr. Singleton's study—on his leather sofa. Joe remembered that time especially, because while they were doing it, he could hear the kids down the hall, laughing at some TV show.

She was almost as reckless as Vic.

It was a small island, and everyone knew everyone else's business. He'd been worried about Vic before, and now he was worried people would somehow figure out what was going on with Mrs. Singleton and him.

Joe had become friendly with Martha at the Last Sunset Café. But she was kind of a gossip. She indicated that Scott and Sherry Singleton had gone through several caretakers. He remembered her talking under her breath to him at the counter while he had his usual Cheese and Ham Scram: "There's already been a lot of stuff on the news about that so-called church of theirs. But I think something truly weird is going on at that house. Mark my words—sooner or later, I'll wager sooner—there'll be a big scandal."

"What are you talking about?" Joe asked, though he wasn't sure he wanted to hear the answer.

"I'm just saying," she replied. "Somebody's doing something they oughtn't."

Later, as Martha gave him his check, she asked: "Not that I miss him, but I haven't seen that friend of yours in a while—Nick or Rick or whatever his name is. Are you still hanging around with him?"

"Ah, no," Joe lied. "I was never really that friendly with him."

"Good, because I think he was bad news."

Joe realized, in many ways, she was right. While he'd needed Vic at the country club, in the outside world his pal was a major burden and not worth all the trouble he caused.

Joe's favorite times at the compound were when he was there alone. He remembered an afternoon, during one of Mrs. Singleton's visits, when she'd had to attend some party on the island. She'd left the youngest, Connor, in Joe's care. He and the boy had gone into town for ice cream and then had walked on the beach. That had been a good afternoon.

But for the most part, he'd grown tired of both Vic and Mrs. Singleton. He was grateful to both of them for everything they'd done for him. But he couldn't keep up the balancing act—with these two people coming and going. He hated deceiving Mrs. Singleton about Vic's too-frequent visits. Mrs. Singleton and Vic were such risk-takers, and yet Joe had a feeling he was the one who would end up screwed.

Vic was getting more and more resentful of the Singletons, whose use of their own home cramped his style and sent him into hiding. He also seemed jealous of the hold they had over Joe—especially Mrs. Singleton.

As Thanksgiving approached, Joe was instructed to get the house and grounds ready for the whole Singleton family—right down to the special-order cornucopia centerpiece he was supposed to pick up at Lopez Village Market. Although he'd glimpsed Scott Singleton having an argument with a man in the driveway two weeks before, this would be Joe's first time actually meeting the man—the man whose wife he was screwing.

So he dreaded the Thanksgiving weekend with the Singleton family. It didn't help that Vic showed up on the previous Tuesday and vowed to stay so he could talk to Scott Singleton about working at the compound alongside Joe. It was a ridiculous idea. He was a fugitive from justice, a criminal. No one was going to hire him. He'd been getting by on some money he'd "borrowed" from an acquaintance after escaping from the country club. Joe had been worried that his friend would start stealing things from the Singleton house to hock for extra cash. But so far, he hadn't noticed anything missing.

He finally persuaded Vic to leave Wednesday morning—just a few hours before the first wave of family members were due in. But Vic hinted he might be back to have a "serious talk" with Singleton.

Joe was expected to do a lot of driving back and forth that weekend, but the minivan died on him in the driveway on Wednesday afternoon. The garage had to tow it and didn't have a loaner, so Jae Singleton's boyfriend had to run all the errands. Joe kept remembering that night in the master bathroom and what Mrs. Singleton had said about how her husband and some friend had hired all the previous caretakers before him. He remembered her asking him when she was freaking out over the plumbing mishap, "What good are you? What are we paying you for?" Now, with the minivan out of commission, he imagined Mr. Singleton asking him the same question.

Singleton didn't say much to him at all on Thanksgiving Day. He called him into the dining room with the kitchen help for the dinner prayer, and he got his name wrong. That was as close as they came to talking. But on Friday night Singleton buzzed him on the intercom and said he wanted to see him in his study.

Joe was convinced Singleton knew all about his shenanigans with Mrs. Singleton. Or maybe he'd heard from someone in town that his new caretaker had a friend who had pretty much made the Singletons' second home his second home. As Joe got ready for the meeting, he remembered the last time he'd been in the study for more than just a minute or two: It was when he and Mrs. Singleton had had sex on the leather sofa. Also Vic used that study quite often. Joe wondered if maybe Mr. Singleton had noticed something was broken or missing.

Joe walked into the study with a tight knot in his stomach. Nodding toward the leather sofa, Singleton told him to sit down. He poured him some fancy imported dark beer and talked about the good work he was doing. Joe kept waiting for him to lower the boom.

But instead, Mr. Singleton started asking about his spirituality and saying he needed *insurance for the soul*. Joe wasn't sure what the hell that meant. But Mr. Singleton's phone rang, and he said he'd swing by Joe's apartment in a few minutes to finish their conversation.

Joe remembered walking back to his quarters over the garage.

The next thing he knew, it was early morning but still dark out. He saw the extra car parked near the garage and Jae Singleton's boyfriend lying in a pool of blood on the driveway.

The police questioned him for hours and hours. They put him up at a hotel on San Juan Island. He wasn't under arrest, just a "person of interest." Joe was truthful about almost everything he told the police. But he didn't tell them about the affair with Mrs. Singleton. He also lied about Vic, and claimed he hadn't seen him since they'd been in the psychiatric institute together. It was a stupid lie, and Joe knew it. Several townspeople must have spotted Vic from the times he'd eaten out, gone for a beer run, or come and gone on the ferry. Joe also figured the police would find Vic's fingerprints all over the Singleton house.

Joe had been ready to come clean and tell the police everything. But then Vic snuck into his hotel room and practically forced him to flee. Joe felt sort of helpless around him. He couldn't stop his friend from getting him into deeper and deeper trouble. Mrs. Gretchell was right about that. Joe remembered being terrified when Vic had hijacked a ride from that man and later practically killed him. In fact, until he'd seen the news yesterday morning, Joe had thought the poor guy was dead.

Now he could hear the TV blaring in the family room. It sounded like a soccer match or something. He wished he were back on that beach with Connor Singleton.

Hell, he'd settle for being back in that hotel room on San Juan Island. Then maybe he'd have another chance to straighten things out with the police.

He shifted restlessly on the living-room sofa, and took another look out the window. Was Sophie right? Would Vic lose it and end up killing some poor, innocent delivery guy? Joe felt sick with dread. He couldn't control Vic, and he knew something horrible was going to happen in this house—maybe to one of those kids upstairs.

Vic would be the one to do it, and, of course, Joe would blame himself.

CHAPTER EIGHTEEN

The Google logo came up on the computer screen. In the search box Laura typed *Eric Vetter*.

Western Washington University's Wilson Library had four "guest" computers in the Reserve area. All Laura had to do was show the young man behind the circulation desk her photo ID and promise to give up her spot after an hour if someone was waiting. But there was only one other person using the computers: a young, stocky East Indian man who snacked on Good & Plenty while he jotted notes in a spiral notebook.

Laura had just checked MapQuest.com for Martha's address, and she was in luck. The directions were pretty simple, and she was 1.5 minutes from the ferry terminal. Laura could still make it home by eleven tonight if she didn't linger too long at Martha's house.

Maybe Martha could explain why Doran Wiley had gone kind of crazy at the mention of the name Eric Vetter. Laura remembered Doran's exact words: *"Who told you that I knew Eric Vetter? I didn't know him. I never even met the guy."* It struck her as odd that he seemed to be talking about Vetter in the past tense.

Now that she saw the first Google search result, she understood why. It was a *Seattle Times* article from October 23. The headline read:

Divine Light "Minister" Eric Vetter, 51, Dies in Fire

The photo of Vetter showed a handsome, though wizened, square-jawed man with short grayish hair. He looked very sporty.

He had perished when a blaze swept through his weekend cabin in the woods outside La Conner. The article quoted a press release from the Church of the True Divine Light:

Among his many duties for the ministry, Eric Vetter was dedicated to providing scholarships and assistance to young men and women who help spread the word of the church on college campuses and surrounding communities.

The article explained that these college students were called the Messengers. Vetter often took different Messengers and Messenger candidates on weekend excursions in the woods, often four at a time. Sometimes they stayed at his cabin in La Conner, which had an attached guest quarters with bunk beds. That particular weekend, Vetter had been alone in the cabin. Investigators believed the blaze started because the fireplace was in use without a screen.

Fellow Divine Light minister Marilee Cronin was quoted: *"My husband Lawrence and I have lost a good friend, and our church has lost one of its founders and guiding lights. I know Eric will continue his amazing work for us in heaven."*

The article pointed out that the Church of the True Divine Light had been in the news lately, due to allegations from some ex-members that the church used brainwashing techniques, blackmail, and extortion.

There wasn't much in the piece about Eric Vetter's personal life. He was survived by a younger brother, an ex-wife (now married to someone else), and a married daughter. He'd been close friends with Scott and Sherry Singleton for twenty years.

Laura wondered why she hadn't heard more about Eric Vetter in the wake of the Singleton murders. After all, here was another prominent figure from the same controversial church who had died just a month before Scott Singleton. It seemed like too much of a coincidence. Then again, why would the police or the press see a connection between the deaths? One man had died in a fire that was easily explained. And a month later, the other died with his family in a mass murder that had two suspects now on the run from the police. Maybe it was a coincidence after all, and maybe she was just trying too hard to find something to help Joe.

She reread the part about the Messengers. The whole thing seemed kind of cultish: recruiting college-age kids in need of scholarships and taking them to some remote cabin in the woods for orientation or indoctrination or whatever. Was that where the alleged brainwashing took place?

Laura wondered if Doran Wiley was a Messenger or a wannabe Messenger. She tried a Google search for Doran, and found only one article—from *The Spokane Spokesman-Review*—which mentioned his name in connection with his participation in a high school football game. Laura couldn't even find a Facebook profile on him. She imagined he was one of those kids who went by another name on Facebook, so potential employers couldn't check their profiles and see how much partying they did.

Laura was starting to get frustrated. Instead of finding some answers, she was just coming up with more questions. And nothing she read seemed connected to Joe.

She tried a search for *Zared* on Google. She figured it might be someone's last name. But the only results she got were for websites on baby names and name-meanings. Zared was a boy's name with Hebrew origins, and it meant "trap" or "ambush."

To Laura, it still sounded like the name of a comic book super-villain—something Joe might have invented. She tried linking *Zared* with the Singletons, Eric Vetter, and Doran Wiley, but didn't come up with anything.

Feeling defeated, she gave up on the Google searches, and instead, checked the latest updates on the Singleton family murders. The top story was still the manhunt for the two fugitive suspects. The police had interviewed Alan Halstead, a psychiatrist who had treated Joe at

Western Washington Psychiatric Institute in Marysville. According to a *Huffington Post* article:

> Halstead maintained that, in his opinion, Joseph Mulroney was incapable of doing harm to anyone—except possibly himself. "At the time of his release, we were confident Joseph would have great success with his medication and outpatient therapy."

But Laura remembered Joe admitting to her that Vic had persuaded him to stop taking his medication.

She scribbled down Halstead's name. She wondered how the psychiatrist could say that Joe was incapable of harming anyone when he'd put that coworker in the hospital. Then again, she'd seen how little Joey had taken abuse from Donald Clapp for weeks and weeks without complaint. Maybe it was the same scenario with this bully of a coworker. Maybe the guy had it coming.

According to the same *Huffington Post* article, even though Vic had been identified as the man in the North Seattle 7-Eleven video at the time of the Singleton murders, he was still considered a "person of interest" in the case. And he was still wanted by the police for escaping from the institute and the attempted murder of a guard. Before his incarceration there, Vic had already accrued a long rap sheet that included robbery, destruction of private property, forgery, reckless endangerment, assault, and assault and battery. The last charge, which had landed him in the Western Washington Psychiatric Institute, was in connection with his "attack" on a seventeen-year-old girl two years ago.

Laura couldn't help wondering if this "attack" might have been a rape that his lawyer had negotiated to a lesser charge. It was certainly a possibility.

And here she'd left her daughter with him.

The police and the press didn't even know what she knew about Vic—that, on top of everything else, he was a murderer.

Laura kept thinking her children might be better off if she went to the police right now. But she remembered Vic's warning. He'd promised that James would be the first to die. She knew he wouldn't hesitate to do it either.

Right now, her only hope was that Joe would realize that she was on his side, and he would somehow intercede. But so far, she'd come up with nothing to help his case, nothing to explain why that whole family was slaughtered and he was spared, nothing to explain how he could have slept through all of it.

The student at the computer next to hers shoved his notebook and Good & Plenty in his backpack and grabbed his jacket off the back of his chair. Then he passed behind her.

A moment later, Laura heard him talking to someone. He sounded a bit curt: "You can use that computer now if you want. You know, the other computers are working as well. Or is there some other reason why you have been standing there staring for the last twenty minutes?"

Laura swiveled around. He was talking to the same

young man who had been staring at her in the cafeteria, the Aryan-looking blond with the pouty lips.

He sneered at the East Indian student, and then locked eyes with Laura's for a moment—that same icy stare as before.

Laura felt herself shrink back.

He turned and walked away. The student who had been using the computer headed off in the other direction.

Laura sat there, afraid to move. The blond man looked too young to be a cop. She wondered if he was a student. Maybe he was one of the church's Messengers.

She glanced around and didn't see him anywhere.

But she knew, whoever he was, he hadn't really gone away.

Tuesday—4:10 P.M.
Lopez Island

" *'Mama said there'd be days like this,' "* Martha muttered to herself as she stepped out of the café. It was one of those old song quotes she sometimes used as a mantra. Martha had thought she'd be finishing work on time at three, but things got crazy with the late-lunch crowd.

Usually she drove to the restaurant, but her car was in the shop. A neighbor had given her a lift this morning, but she'd have to hoof it home. She told herself it was only a little over a mile and at least it wasn't raining. Buttoning up her jacket, she thought about soaking her feet when she got home. That reporter woman was supposed to come by for her big scoop around five-thirty. Martha figured the money she collected from the woman ought to cover the car-repair bill.

At the far end of the restaurant's parking lot, near the recycling station, she spotted a man leaning against a black BMW. He wore a black V-neck sweater and stared at something on his smartphone. As Martha got closer to him, she recognized his face. It was Mr. Pecan Waffle. He'd left the café at least three hours ago. Had he been out here this whole time?

He smiled at her. "Hey, need a ride?"

Martha warily shook her head. "No, thanks." She kept moving.

He started to follow her. "What did you tell that woman reporter earlier?"

"Not that it's any of your business, but I caught her trying to shortchange me." Martha didn't break her stride. There was no sidewalk on this stretch of road, so she started walking on the dirt path near the shoulder. There were some woods on her right.

He was still tailing her. "Did you get the woman's name?" he pressed.

"No, I didn't, and if you don't stop following me, I'll call a cop. And it won't take long to get one here. This island is crawling with them right now." Holding her purse close, she kept walking. She figured she didn't owe this guy anything. He didn't even leave her a very good tip.

She must have scared him off, because he stopped following her.

Martha pressed on. She was relieved. It was starting to get dark out, and the street lights hadn't come on yet. She wasn't too worried about being followed along this roadway, because cars zoomed by pretty frequently. If he'd tried to attack her, someone would have noticed him dragging her into the woods. The side roads were what worried her. They were kind of iffy—with less traffic and just as many dark wooded areas. Of course, Lopez Island had always been pretty safe. It was one of those places where people never locked their doors at night—at least it had been until this past weekend.

She turned down the first side street on her usual route home. There still wasn't a sidewalk, and the dirt path along the roadside was more gravelly. It wasn't easy on her sore feet.

Martha had trudged along for only about a half-block when she heard a car coming up in back of her. She moved a step closer to the trees to clear the way, and then looked over her shoulder.

It was the black BMW, crawling along behind her.

"Crap," she muttered under her breath.

This was the "iffy" area she'd been thinking about earlier. She had the woods on her right, and on the left were a couple of ramshackle houses and the back of a rundown strip mall. Not too many people used this street. It might be a long time before another car came along. Martha told herself to just ignore the guy. *Don't slow down, don't hurry up. Just keep walking.*

Behind her, Martha could hear the engine humming and gravel snapping under the tires. She could see the headlights on the street pavement.

She tried not to panic. What the hell did he want? She wondered if he was another reporter, possibly a competitor of the woman she'd made the deal with. Or maybe he was one of the church followers, maybe even a big shot, since he was at the wheel of a BMW.

Just this morning she'd been thinking, *there are too many strangers on this island right now.*

She kept her purse close to her and reached inside for her phone. Should she threaten to call a cop again—or just call them? If she didn't, she had a feeling this guy was going to follow her all the way home.

Then, just near the end of the block, when Martha was about to turn down another street, she heard the tires screech and the car roared past her. With a squeal, the BMW turned in front of her and sped down the next block.

"Asshole!" she muttered.

But she was thankful he'd moved on. With a shaky hand, she closed her purse again.

Martha walked another two blocks before her heartbeat seemed to slow down to normal and she could breathe right again. She would be home in about five minutes. This was a residential neighborhood. She was safe now. The guy was just being a jerk.

As she turned down her own block, Martha saw the BMW again. It was parked across the street from her townhouse.

She stopped dead.

How did the son of a bitch know where she lived?

It was too late to turn and run. Martha was sure the man could see her from where he was parked. She'd be better off making a mad dash to the front door. If he tried to attack her, she'd scream. The neighbors would hear.

She started walking again, this time at a brisk clip.

As she got closer to the townhouse, she spotted the man in the driver's seat of the BMW.

Martha picked up the pace a little. She opened her purse and reached inside for the house keys so she'd have them ready. She glanced over at the black car again. He still hadn't gotten out.

Approaching the walkway to her front door, Martha had the key in her hand, and she began to run. Was this a mistake? Was it smart to let him know where she lived? But obviously, he already knew, damn it. She would phone 9-1-1 as soon as she got in the front door—if she ever got in the front door. Her hands shook so much she couldn't fit the key in the lock.

Martha kept thinking he was coming up behind her again. But when she glanced over her shoulder, she didn't see anyone.

Finally, she unlocked the door and pushed it open. Hurrying inside, she locked and bolted the door behind her. She grabbed her cell phone and her purse dropped to the floor. A few items spilled out, but she barely noticed. She looked out the window to see if he was coming up the sidewalk to the house. There was no sign of him. The best view of where he'd parked his car was from her kitchen window. Martha headed that way. Maybe she could take down his license plate for the police when she reported him.

She stepped into the kitchen and saw someone in there.

Martha let out a shriek. The phone slipped out of her hand and landed on the floor with a hollow thump.

It wasn't the same man as before.

But he looked sort of like the other one—about

forty-five, tall, dark hair and a dark complexion. He wore a black tracksuit with silver piping. He stood by her kitchen table with a gun in his gloved hand. It was pointed at her.

Martha didn't move.

"Your shift was supposed to end an hour ago," he said. "I've been waiting here a while."

"What—" She couldn't talk. She could hardly breathe. She had her hands half raised in front of her. "What do you want?"

"Let's take it to the bedroom, Martha." He gave her a tiny smile. "What do you say?"

She let out a whimper and shook her head.

"Relax," he said. "I just want to talk a little, and there are too many windows in this room. I don't want the neighbors to know you have company."

Her legs felt wobbly as she turned and headed through the front hallway toward the bedroom. She thought about making a run for the front door, but she'd already locked and bolted it. She reluctantly stepped into the bedroom. It was a bit messy. She hadn't had time to make her bed this morning. The shades were drawn and it was dark in there. But her bathroom light was on. Martha didn't know if she'd left it on this morning or if he'd turned it on.

"Go ahead and sit down on the bed," he told her. "You've been on your feet all day. And take off the jacket."

Martha obeyed him. She stared up at the man with trepidation. Something about his face was familiar. He must have been a customer at the café. "Is that—is that your friend in the car outside?" she asked.

He nodded. "He told me you weren't very forthcoming about the woman reporter who was in the café today. You sure you didn't get her name?"

Martha shook her head. "I didn't, I swear."

"Apparently, she thinks you know some things about the Singletons that no one else knows."

Martha shook her head again. "I really don't know much—just rumors I've heard, that's all. It—it's only gossip. I'm not even sure if any of it's true."

"My friend was watching you very carefully. He thought you might have made a deal with this woman."

Martha's fingers dug into the edge of the mattress. "Well, I—I might have let her believe that I knew something," she admitted.

"Like what?"

"Like Mrs. Singleton was fooling around with the groundskeepers, and someone was paying off the different guys to keep them quiet."

He let out a little laugh—like it was nothing. "So you told her that?"

"No—no, I haven't." Martha glanced over at her nightstand clock. "She's supposed to come here . . ." Martha realized she might be able to use this to her advantage if she only lied a little. "In fact, she—she's due here any minute now, and she said she'd be bringing a work associate, a man . . ."

"In that case, we better not waste any more time," he said. "C'mon, let's move this into the bathroom."

Martha didn't move. "What for?"

"I just said," he whispered, "don't waste any more of my time, bitch."

She still couldn't move.

"Get up!"

Martha stood up and unsteadily made her way into the bathroom. "Please, whatever you and your friend want, I'll—"

"Take off your clothes," he interrupted.

She stared at him. He stood in the bathroom doorway, blocking her escape.

"You heard me," he said.

Martha glanced around her messy bathroom—with its cluttered sink-counter and towels hanging askew on the racks. She braced herself against the sink and kicked off her shoes. "Why are you doing this?" she asked. She could feel her throat starting to close up. Tears came to her eyes.

"Hurry up," he murmured.

With her hands shaking, she unzipped her brown and beige waitress uniform and took it off.

He stared at her, but didn't seem the least bit sexually interested in her.

Martha suddenly realized where she'd seen him before. "You—you're the man in the sketches she showed me."

He nodded. "She showed them to my friend, too. C'mon, take off the slip—and the rest of what you've got on under there."

"Why?" she asked, crying. "Why are you making me do this?"

"Because," said the man, "when they find you in the tub, you should be naked."

CHAPTER NINETEEN

Tuesday—4:28 P.M.
Bellingham

Laura sat there at the computer, uncertain what to do. She didn't see the young blond man anywhere around the library's reserves area, but she felt he was still close by. According to the other student, he'd been standing there and staring at her for at least twenty minutes. And he'd been watching her earlier at the cafeteria. Had he been following her since Mathes Hall? For all she knew, he might have come over with her on the ferry from Lopez Island.

Gathering her things, Laura got to her feet. As she headed through the lobby, she kept looking over her shoulder, expecting to see him. There was no sign of the young man, but she still felt as if she was being watched. Out the library's front windows, she noticed it was getting dark out. The lights along the campus walkways were already on. Laura stopped and waited by the front door. She flagged down two young women and a tall, stocky bearded man who were leaving the library together. "Excuse me, but could I walk out with you? I think there's somebody following me . . ."

"Where?" asked the tall young man. He looked as if he was ready to take on the culprit—wherever he might be.

Laura glanced back toward the lobby. There was still no sign of her stalker. "I don't see him now," she said. "Anyway, I really don't want to make a fuss. I'd just feel better if I left here with a group . . ."

"We're only going as far as Mathes Hall," said one of the girls. She was an attractive brunette with glasses. "Is that okay?"

"Mathes Hall is perfect. I'm parked right near there."

"Well, c'mon," said the young man. "Stick with us."

Laura took one last look at the library lobby, and then headed outside with the trio of students. With all the other people walking around the grounds, she probably would have been fine on her own. But there were also a lot of trees, bushes, and shadowy areas to make her grateful for the company. They were polite kids. The brunette girl asked if she was taking adult continuing-education classes.

"No, I'm not a student," Laura said. "I was just using the library for some research. In fact, maybe you guys could help me. Have you come across any students here who are 'Messengers' for the True Divine Light Church?"

The brunette girl stopped in her tracks. "Are you one of them?"

Laura shook her head. "No, I was just reading about them."

The brunette and the tall man looked relieved. The other girl was looking at her smartphone.

"I understand the church gives scholarships to certain students who help recruit new members," Laura said.

"Freaks," muttered the other girl, still staring at her phone.

"They used to have a booth set up over there outside the union," the young man explained, with a nod toward the Viking Union building to their right. "They handed out fliers about living up to your true potential and finding your spirituality and bullshit like that. The guys were these square-jawed jocks. The girls were really pretty. And every one of them was white, I mean Wonder Bread white. Yeah, the Messengers, that's what they called themselves."

"Are they connected to the university?" Laura asked the young man.

"God, no. We have all sorts of organizations here that aren't affiliated with the university. The only connection is the church privately pays for some of those scholarships—like they do at a bunch of other universities. These True Divine Light freaks are on campuses all over the country. I think there are a few more here in the Pacific Northwest because their headquarters are here."

"Back when the weather was nice, they were out here every day," the dark-haired girl explained. "Then about a month ago, they kind of disappeared, thank God."

"A bunch of fascists," said the girl, still studying her phone.

The tall young man nodded. "Sometimes, they'd show up at parties in pairs or threes. Talk about a buzz-kill. Or they'd be in coffeehouses, ready to pounce on some unsuspecting freshman."

"My friend, Rachel Porter," said the brunette, "she met this super-cute guy at a kegger, and he asked her out on a date. So she meets him at La Fiamma for pizza, and he ended up bringing along two friends who tried to recruit her. They like ambushed her. How creepy is that?"

"Anyway, like we said, they haven't been around much anymore," the young man remarked.

"Maybe we've seen the last of them now that their fascist leader is dead," muttered the girl with the phone.

"That's kind of harsh, Stacy," the young man said, but he chuckled.

They stopped in front of Mathes Hall. "Well, this is us," announced the brunette. "Do you want us to walk you to your car?"

Laura glanced back toward the Viking Commons and the Union. She didn't see the Aryan-looking stranger amid all the students milling about. She smiled and shook her head at the girl. "That's not necessary, but thanks. I'm just in the lot over there. I should be okay. You guys have been really nice. Thanks again."

The tall young man glanced back at her as he headed into the dormitory with the two girls.

Laura waved and started toward the parking lot. She thought about what they'd just said. Eric Vetter had been the force behind these Messengers. Was his death last month the reason why the campus recruiters had vanished? She couldn't figure out earlier why Doran Wiley had been so angry at her for bringing up Eric Vetter and the Singletons. If he'd been a Messenger, maybe he was embarrassed about it now and didn't want anyone to know.

As Laura climbed inside the car, she wondered: *What the hell does any of this have to do with Joe?*

A shadow passed over her, and then someone tapped on the driver's window.

Startled, she gaped out the window and gasped.

With one hand on the car roof, the blond man bent down toward the window to stare at her. "Did I hear you right back in the cafeteria?" he said loudly—so she could hear him through the glass. "Did you tell Doran that you're a reporter?"

Laura glimpsed other students walking around nearby. She told herself she could scream or honk her horn if he tried anything. Close up, he really did look like some pretty-boy Aryan—a Hitler Youth extra out of *Cabaret*; all that was missing was a brown uniform and a swastika armband.

With uncertainly, Laura lowered the window a bit so she wouldn't have to shout. "Who are you?" she asked.

His blue eyes narrowed at her. "You aren't with the church, are you?"

Laura shook her head. "No, I'm not. Why are you following me?"

"Relax, lady, I'm not stalking you. In fact, to be completely honest, I was kind of stalking Doran Wiley." He smiled. "But then I got fascinated with you—and the prospect of talking to a reporter."

"Really?" Laura asked, still wary of him.

He nodded and drummed his fingers on the car roof. "I thought maybe you'd like to know why that son of a bitch freaked out on you back in the commons."

She let out a nervous laugh. "As a matter of fact, I was just wondering about that."

"Your big mistake was asking him about Scott Singleton and Eric Vetter there in front of his dipshit friends—while he was cold sober. Now, if you were alone with him while he was drunk and feeling a little sorry for himself, then he might have told you the whole sordid story, just like he told it to me . . ."

The young man's name was Randall Meacham, and he was a freshman at WWU. For the price of a cup of coffee at the Viking Union, he was all too eager to tell Laura what his former friend, Doran Wiley, was hiding.

They found a café table in the atrium by the VU Market. Students focusing on their laptops or smartphones occupied most of the other tables. A big TV on the wall near some stairs was tuned to CNN, closed-captioned with the volume off.

"I overheard Doran say you were freelance?" Randall asked.

Laura nodded. "I'm trying to get a new angle on the Singleton murders. And I was told by someone on Lopez Island that Doran might have some useful information about Scott Singleton, something that might explain why he and his family were killed."

"Well, whoever told you that isn't too far off," Randall remarked over his coffee cup. "Are you going to sell your story to the newspapers?"

"I'm hoping to," Laura lied, "or maybe some online news publication."

He grinned. "Either way, it'll prove embarrassing as hell to Doran when it comes out, right?"

"I suppose," Laura shrugged. "But I haven't heard your story yet."

Randall nodded pensively. "I wouldn't mind one bit seeing him publicly humiliated when all this comes out . . ." His eyes met hers. "But you need to call me an 'unnamed source' or something like that, because what I have to tell you might piss off some of the higher-ups at the Church of the True Divine Light."

"That's fine with me," Laura said. She dug a pen and some scratch paper from her purse.

"You don't have a recorder?" he asked.

"I like the old-fashioned way. So—how long have you known Doran Wiley?"

"I met him in September, down in the laundry room at Mathes Hall. It was late on a weeknight—and still pretty warm out. He was wearing a tank top and track shorts with these slits up the sides, and I was like—*wow*. He needed quarters for the dryer, and we started talking . . ."

Laura nodded attentively. She hadn't gotten any gay vibe from Doran. She wondered where this story was going.

"Anyway, he invited me to dinner that coming Thursday," Randall continued. "I couldn't believe my luck. I mean, here I was, in college for like two weeks, and this tan Greek god asked me out. I was pinching myself. The night of our big date, I was so nervous. Well, the joke was on me. You know what happened?"

Laura shook her head. She hadn't taken any notes yet.

Randall sipped his coffee and then frowned at her. "Doran took me here for Panda Express . . ." He nodded to indicate they'd come here to the union. "And we met this buddy of his, Ben. At first, I thought this dude was his boyfriend, because he was really good-looking, too. But then, over pot stickers, I realized they're both straight—or at least, that's how they wanted to come off. But I could see some gay potential in both of them—especially Doran. You know, the closeted frat-boy type: *I was so drunk last night, dude, I can't believe we did that.* So I was still hopeful, still stringing myself along. Plus they were friendly as hell to me . . ."

"Because they were trying to recruit you for the church," Laura interjected.

He nodded. "I should've figured that out by the time we ate our fortune cookies. But they hadn't mentioned a thing about the church, and I was really infatuated with Doran. They asked if I wanted to go 'rough it' with them that weekend at their friend's cabin near La Conner."

"Eric Vetter's cabin?" Laura asked.

"Bingo. Anyway, I agreed, and they hit me up for twenty bucks in advance for gas and food. I must have had *sucker* written on my forehead. So Friday afternoon, I was supposed to meet them in front of Mathes Hall and Ben showed up—alone. He said Doran would meet us at the cabin later. Anyway, Ben drove there, and I met Eric Vetter. In him, I could definitely see major gay potential, not that I was interested, because he was like fifty or something. But the other guy, who was Eric's guest for the weekend, he was about a year older than me and kind of hot. I can't remember his name. I wasn't all that interested in him. I was still waiting for Doran to show up. After dinner, Eric announced that Doran wasn't coming until the next day. Then he said he was turning in early, which I guess was a cue for the three of us to go to the guest quarters. It was attached to the cabin, and had an indoor bathroom, thank God. There were also two sets of bunk beds, and a mini-fridge stocked with beer. Now, mind you, so far, nobody had said a thing about the church. Anyway, it was like only nine o'clock, but Ben opened a beer, stripped down to his tighty-whiteys, and climbed into one of the bunks. And I figured that was going to be my big thrill for the dismal night. But then he started telling us this story about skinny-dipping in a creek with this girl and another guy the last time he was in the woods there—and how it turned into a regular orgy. He went into a lot of detail, and I have to admit, it kind of made me horny. The whole thing became this discussion with him asking this other guy and me about the weirdest places we'd had sex or jacked off. He kept handing out the beers and asking questions about our fantasies, and the things we've done that we were the most ashamed of. Well, I came out in high school, so I didn't mind them knowing I was gay. Also I was pretty drunk, so I admitted I was hot for Doran. At this, Ben dared me to get into bed with the other guy and make out with him. By that time, the other guy—why can't I remember his name? Well, the other guy was totally wasted, and both of us were pretty horny. Anyway, cut to the chase. Ben put on his pants and went down the hall to Eric's, so the other guy and I could be alone. And then the two of us messed around." He shrugged. "I hope I'm not shocking you . . ."

"No, please, go on," Laura said.

She still hadn't jotted down any notes yet. She wondered if he'd ever get back to Doran Wiley. She had a feeling Randall had wanted to tell this story to someone for a long time. Maybe he regarded her as a sort of mother confessor.

He finished off his coffee. "So—the next day, guess what?"

"What?"

"Doran didn't show. Eric said he'd texted that he couldn't make it after all. The four of us went hiking, hung out, and ate a big breakfast. It was kind of fun, but I was hung over and disappointed about Doran pulling a no-show. Oh, also, this is when Eric started talking about the church, and the scholarships they offered. He indicated that Doran and Ben were getting a free ride from the church. But I was too stupid to realize they were getting this sweet deal because they were recruiting people like me to become new church members."

"So they were Messengers," Laura said.

"You did your homework, I see," Randall said. "I don't know where they found Ben, but Eric discovered Doran playing football for Mt. Spokane High School. I found out later that Doran hadn't been good enough to get a regular football scholarship. But I'm getting ahead of myself. Where was I?"

"Day two at Eric Vetter's cabin in La Conner."

"Yeah, well, that afternoon, the other guy had to leave, which was fine with me, because he was so damn uptight around me most of the morning. Ben drove him back to wherever. He wasn't at Western. Later, Ben returned with this girl. And after dinner, they wanted to be alone, so Eric told me I could stay in the cabin with him for the night. And well, I suppose you know where I'm going with this . . ."

"You and Eric . . ." Laura asked, raising her eyebrows.

With a sigh, he nodded. "And leading up to it, we talked. He asked me about my family and my relationship with my parents—the things I didn't like about them, my resentments, and all sorts of crap like that. He was good. He didn't even need beer to get me to open up. Eric, he was a great listener, too. He asked me what I wanted to do with my life, and he really seemed to care . . ." Randall slowly shook his head. "God, I fell for it. I really did.

"On Sunday, Ben drove me back to school, and Doran met me and he was all, *'So sorry I missed you, bro,'* and shit like that. He asked if I wanted to drive back there with him the following weekend."

"And you went?"

He nodded. "I went—with Doran. When we got to the cabin, six other people were there—a mix of guys and girls, all college age. Plus Eric. He had a bunch of games he wanted us to play. One had us sitting in a circle and tossing around a *truth ball*. When you caught it, you'd have to tell some secret about yourself. There was a whole bunch of other truth-or-dare type of games. And then we were supposed to write down stuff. *'You have five minutes to write down everything you hate about yourself'* and *'You have five minutes to write everything you love about yourself,'* shit like that."

"They wanted to see if you were a good candidate for the church," Laura said.

"Exactly," he frowned. "We didn't know it at the time, but we were being recorded. It was all personal stuff they could use to get inside our heads and manipulate us. And later, if we wanted to leave the church or bad-mouth them online or on TV, they could use this same information to keep us quiet. They had another secret weapon to keep us in line. But I'm getting ahead of myself again, aren't I? The thing about these games and everything that went on that weekend is that I ended up bonding with all the people there. They were like my new family, because we shared this experience together. It was sort of like a hazing. They wouldn't let us eat—or sleep. All of us had these meltdowns and breakdowns, all of us except Eric and Doran. They spelled each other and got these little breaks: food, coffee, or naps. Doran told me later. By Sunday afternoon, we were all like—euphoric. I don't know how else to describe it. We would have done anything for Eric. One weekend, and we'd become these brainwashed converts. It was crazy . . ."

Laura had had a vague inkling something like this had been going on from the news stories lately about disgruntled ex-members of Scott Singleton's church.

She wondered if Scott and his family—and possibly Eric Vetter—might have been murdered by an angry former church member. It was quite possible Joe had nothing to do with those killings and was guilty only of having slept through them.

But so far, Randall hadn't told her anything that actually helped Joe's case. And he still hadn't talked about Doran Wiley's stint as the Singletons' caretaker. Laura stole a glance at her watch: 4:50. She'd have to leave in fifteen minutes if she hoped to catch the six o'clock ferry.

"So—I was walking on air," he continued. "I had this new family—with Doran, Ben, and the rest of them. There were about twenty of us on campus—and this senior, Courtney Furst, she was in charge, like the queen bee. She was Eric's right-hand girl. She was always working the church table we set up outside the union. We all looked up to her. Anyway, after about ten days of me being in this bliss state, Doran and Courtney sat me down and said they needed two hundred bucks from me—so the church could invest in my *spiritual future*. It was like *insurance for my soul*. Have you ever heard such garbage?"

Laura nodded. She'd heard it just yesterday. Though he didn't tap him for money, Scott Singleton had given the same spiel to Joe on the night of the murders.

"Courtney and Doran said that if I didn't have the money, I should hit up my parents for it," Randall went on. "They had tips and guidelines on what to tell them in an email or phone call. And of course, I wasn't supposed to mention the church. Courtney and Doran had all the inside info on my relationship with my parents—thanks to my heart-to-heart discussion with Eric the night we screwed. They told me how to approach them, and how my parents owed me and *my soul* this money—which I was supposed to hand over to the church."

"What did you do?" Laura asked.

"I told them I'd think about it. My parents aren't perfect, but they didn't kick me out of the house when I told them I was gay, and they're paying for my school. It seemed dishonest hitting them up for this money. My parents deserved better. I felt like I was being ripped off. I kept thinking this was just the start of regular payments the church would demand from me. It kind of popped my bubble, y'know? I came to the realization that Doran and I were never going to get it on. Plus, I wasn't sure I even liked him anymore. He and Courtney kept bugging me for the two hundred, saying if I didn't cough it up, I couldn't be a church member anymore and all my new friends would turn their backs on me. Then, about a month ago, Ben split, just disappeared. A day later, Courtney left school all of a sudden. A couple of days after that, Eric Vetter died in a fire. All of this happened in the same week. Kind of weird, don't you think?"

Laura nodded. "Did you ever find out what happened to Ben or Courtney?"

"That's what I asked Doran the night we got drunk together."

"When was this?"

"About a month ago," Randall said, "a few days after Eric was killed. Doran showed up to my room with a six-pack of beer, a pint of Jack Daniel's, and a bag of Doritos. He wasn't even that drunk when he admitted to me that Ben wasn't a student here. He worked for the church—and for Eric. I never got his last name the three weeks I knew him. The day before he took off, he told Doran that 'some shit was coming down.'"

"What did he mean by that?" Laura asked.

Randall shrugged. "I have no idea. I asked Doran, and he didn't know either. Anyway, Ben told Doran that he was going to Iowa to work on a farm with a friend of his."

"What about Courtney?"

"Her roommate over at Birnam Wood said Courtney left in a real hurry. She packed a couple of bags, but left a bunch of stuff behind. Her roommate said she thought Courtney would be back to pick up the stuff, but . . ." Randall shook his head.

"What did you say Courtney's last name was?"

"Furst, F-U-R-S-T," Randall said. "Without her, our pseudo-family just fell apart."

Laura scribbled it down: *Courtney Furst – Birnam Wood.*

"So—Ben and Courtney took off, while Doran remained here with the rest of you," she said.

Randall nodded. "Right, and Doran was pissed about it, too. See, like I told you earlier, Eric plucked Doran fresh out of high school. Doran spent a few weekends at the cabin—always with a group, and he got snagged the same way I did—an overnight with too many beers, and a lot of sexy stories. He ended up having a three-way with a girl and another guy in that special guest room of Eric's. It was special, because Eric had video cameras set up behind a couple of two-way mirrors in the room. Doran told me that Eric amassed a huge homemade porn collection—starring all these college-age recruits and recruit candidates. It wasn't enough that we'd written down all our deepest secrets, shames, and fears for them, they also had each one of us on X-rated DVDs. Talk about *insurance for your soul.* This was their insurance that none of us would ever publicly talk out against the church. That was what I meant earlier about the other 'secret weapon' they had to keep us in line. Doran was furious as hell when Eric told him that he'd been recorded messing around with that girl and guy—especially the guy." Randall sighed. "God, what I would've given at one time to be that dude . . ."

"When did Eric tell him about these videos?"

"It was after Doran quit working for the Singletons."

Laura stole another glance at her watch. "Yes, tell me more about that."

"Well, Eric introduced him to Scott back in June. This was a big deal. I think Courtney was the only other one of us who actually met Scott. Anyway, Doran already had the church paying his tuition and room and board here. Scott suggested he come work at the family's summer home on Lopez Island. That way, Doran would have some spending money at school. Well, at first, Doran loved it. He said it was the best job ever. He had his own furnished apartment above their garage. He said the Singleton girls were pretty to look at—and flirty. The work wasn't too tough, and there was always something fun going on. But for the first couple of weeks, Scott wasn't there. He was traveling a lot.

"It was like early July when Scott finally came to the summerhouse, and his first night there, he called Doran on the intercom and said he wanted to talk to him in his study. So Doran showed up, and Scott poured him a beer and told him what a *tip-top* job he was doing . . ."

Laura nodded. It sounded just like Joe's experience with him late Friday evening.

"And that was the last thing Doran remembered from that night," Randall said.

Laura leaned forward in her chair. "What?"

Randall let out a little laugh. "Doran woke up in his apartment the next morning, and didn't have a clue what had happened. And can you believe it? The stupid asshole didn't catch on until about the third or fourth time that Scott was slipping him roofies. Mr. Divine Light was doing him while he was totally out of it."

Laura shook her head. No wonder Joe had slept through the murders and couldn't remember anything from that night. She'd suspected Joe was holding back on telling her something about that night. Maybe this was it. Maybe, like Doran, he hadn't caught on that he'd been drugged and raped.

"By the time Doran put together what had happened," Randall explained, "he was too humiliated to tell anyone except Eric. He went to Eric and basically said to him, *take this caretaking job and shove it.* He was kind of soured on the church, too. That's when Eric showed him the video he'd made of Doran embracing his gay potential—or at least, his bisexual potential. Eric said it could go on the Internet at any time. And wouldn't Doran be a lot happier working for the church while they foot the bill for his first semester here?"

Laura kept shaking her head. She told herself that she shouldn't have been shocked, but she was. Scott Singleton, the great defender of the sanctity of traditional marriage, was screwing around behind his wife's back—with drugged-up teenage boys, no less. "How did Scott Singleton handle Doran walking out on the job?" she asked.

"Oh, Eric made sure it was all smoothed over. He told Doran that, no offense, but Scott was getting pretty tired of him anyway. Apparently, old Scott was far more into girls. But he liked to 'spice it up' once in a while. At the same time, he was a big homophobe, and I asked Doran about that—during that night we got drunk together. He said Eric explained that Scott was only interested in handsome, super-straight guys. He hated sissies. Anyway, he got Eric to find him guys and he used roofies to do what he wanted with them. None of them ever lasted long. I'll bet it's because Scott hated to be reminded of that side of himself. Anyway, Eric was always there to make sure the guys were paid to keep quiet. I hear a few of the girls Scott seduced had to be paid off as well. I'm not sure how long each one of them lasted. Doran said Courtney was one of Scott's favorites, so I think the two of them had something going on for a while. He said Courtney also starred in a bunch of Eric's videos."

Laura couldn't fathom it. Then again, until yesterday morning, she never would have guessed her own husband would be spending tomorrow night in a Paris hotel with someone he was passing off as *Mrs. Gretchell*. She still didn't want to believe it.

Randall nodded at the TV over on the wall. CNN was showing Scott's partners in the church, Lawrence and Marilee Cronin, at yet another news conference. Marilee had her flaxen hair in pigtails again, and she wore a dress that looked more like a band uniform. "It's obvious she has no gay friends," Randall said, "because no self-respecting homo would let a girl-friend leave the house in that outfit—unless she was a drum majorette."

Once again, the Cronins gave off a somber and self-righteous attitude for the press. Laura didn't bother reading the closed-captioning.

"I'll bet they're secretly breathing a sigh of relief that Scott is dead," Randall muttered. "Now he's St. Scott, a martyr for their church—instead of a national embarrassment."

Laura stole another glance at her wristwatch. She wanted to talk with Courtney's roommate, and she was already getting down to the wire if she hoped to catch the next ferry from Anacortes to Lopez Island.

"Anyway, back to that night in my room with Doran," Randall continued. "He got hammered, and was really feeling sorry for himself. He thought his friends had deserted him, and he'd just found out the church wasn't paying his tuition next semester. I guess with Eric dead, they dropped their scholarship program. Doran felt really screwed over. He actually hugged me and cried on my shoulder about it—on my bed." Randall held up his hand—the thumb and index finger half an inch apart. "I came *this* close to making a pass. And I probably should have, too. But like an idiot, I kept thinking, *well, now we'll be friends again, so I better not spoil it.* And guess what? The next day, when I saw Doran during lunch at the commons, the bastard totally blew me off. He didn't want anything to do with me. That was nearly a month ago, and he still won't talk to me. He's too cool for me. He looks at me like I was a pest. So—go ahead and please publish everything I just told you. I hope *Vanity Fair* ends up buying the story." He glanced down at the scratch paper. "You haven't taken many notes . . ."

"Ah, I have a really good memory," Laura said. "And I'll get back to you for direct quotes. In the meantime . . ." Opening her purse, she took out Joe's sketches and set them out on the table. "Before we wrap it up here, could you tell me if the man in these sketches looks at all familiar to you?"

His brow furrowed, Randall studied the drawings. "Are they all the same guy?"

"Yes."

He pointed to the detailed one. "This looks like Clint Eastwood."

She nodded. "I thought so, too. But does he look like anyone you might have met through Doran or Eric, maybe somebody with the church? Does he resemble Ben at all?"

"No, this guy looks about fifty. Ben was only like twenty." Randall shook his head. "Nope, sorry, I don't know who this is supposed to be . . ."

Laura started folding up the drawings. "What about

the name, *Zared*. Does that ring a bell—even a distant bell?"

"Zared. Is that a first or last name?"

"Either."

He seemed to ponder it for a moment and then shrugged. "Sorry, it doesn't sound familiar to me. But hey, wait a minute. Maybe that was Ben's last name . . ."

"Maybe," Laura murmured, considering it as a possibility. That gave her even more impetus to track down Courtney Furst and talk with her—if there was time.

Laura stood up, grabbed her coat off the back of the chair and put it on. "Do you have any idea what happened to the DVDs?"

Randall shrugged. "I'm guessing they all went up in smoke when Eric's cabin caught fire." He got to his feet. "Or maybe someone connected to the church found them and destroyed them. Like I say, it must have been quite a porn collection. Doran said he watched a few with Eric, and the quality was damn good."

"And those nights Scott was with Doran, you're sure he slipped him a roofie?"

Randall threw on his jacket. "That's what Doran said."

"Well, that would explain why Joe Mulroney slept through the killings and couldn't remember anything from that night, wouldn't it?"

Laura was hoping this revelation might be enough to prove Joe's innocence.

"Joe Mulroney, he's the caretaker, the guy the police are looking for, isn't he?"

Laura nodded.

"Well, to me, it also explains why this Mulroney guy went berserk and killed Scott—along with the whole family. I mean, maybe he figured out what Scott did to him. Look at how Doran went crazy on you when you just broached the subject—and he's *sane*. He's an asshole, but he's sane. Didn't that Mulroney guy spend some time in a nuthouse?"

Laura just gazed at him. She didn't have an answer.

CHAPTER TWENTY

Tuesday—4:35 P.M.
Leavenworth

"Do me a big favor," Sophie called to Liam in the bedroom. She was on her hands and knees on the bathroom floor, cleaning around the toilet with some wadded-up toilet paper. "Next time James comes in here, would you show him how to aim? He could use a lesson or two. I think he might have missed the floor and accidentally gotten a few drops in the toilet."

At least he'd washed his hands afterward.

She'd been trapped in her bedroom with her two brothers since lunchtime. She and Liam took turns trying to keep James entertained—and quiet. She had a deck of cards, thank God, so they played Slap Jack for a while. Then James colored with her highlighters. Liam sat with him while he took a long bath, and they got him to nap for nearly an hour. But he usually ate a mid-afternoon snack by now, and he was a bit cranky-hungry.

It was ironic how they'd been trying not to make any noise, but Vic had the TV blaring downstairs: *The*

Jerry Springer Show, some game show, CNN, and then ESPN. All of it competed with her radio, which she kept at a low volume. It was *"easy listening shit"* as Liam called it, but at least the elevator music was slightly distracting, and the station broke for news every hour. There were no real updates. The news announcer mentioned that the two Singleton murder suspects were still at large. For the last news break, it was the fourth item they'd mentioned. Sophie couldn't help feeling like it was no longer too important to everyone out there.

She'd tried to read earlier but couldn't really concentrate. Every time she heard a noise, she thought it might be the delivery person. She'd figured that would be their last chance to get help. So Sophie had taken a piece of Kleenex and carefully written on it in tiny print:

> *Singleton murder suspects have taken over house—3 hostages. Tell police be careful. Suspects will kill hostages first sign of interference.*

It had taken her the better part of a half hour to get the note so it was legible and she didn't tear the tissue. Several other attempts had failed and needed to be wet and wadded up so Vic wouldn't discover them later. She practiced with Liam how she would subtly pass the finished product, carefully folded up, to the delivery person as the package was handed off. If she screwed it up and Vic caught on to what she was doing, he'd probably end up pistol-whipping her. And she was pretty certain he'd kill the delivery person. Some poor UPS or FedEx employee's life was in her hands. She pictured some cute, polite guy in the delivery uniform—and Vic slitting his throat. Did she really want to risk it?

She finished cleaning up after James and then flushed the toilet paper down the toilet. As she washed her hands, she glanced at the nailed-shut window and realized it was already nighttime.

Liam suddenly appeared in the bathroom doorway. "Someone's coming up the driveway," he whispered.

"Vic!" she heard Joe yell from downstairs. "I see headlights! It's time!" Then there was muttering, and after a moment, someone came charging up the stairs.

Sophie quickly dried her hands. But they were still damp. She didn't want to try handing off the fragile Kleenex note with damp hands. The tissue would fall apart in her damp fingers.

Liam hurried back toward the window seat. "It doesn't look like a delivery truck," he said, "at least, not from here . . ."

The door squeaked and buckled, and then opened. "All right," Joe said, a little out of breath. He nodded at her. "We need you downstairs. Please, just sign for the package and don't try anything . . ."

"Okay," she said, suddenly out of breath, too. She brushed past him and headed into the hallway. She rubbed her hand on her pants-leg to make sure it was dry. Reaching into her pocket, she delicately pulled out the folded-up tissue. She transferred it to her left hand and made fists of both her hands.

Coming down the stairs, Sophie saw Vic already in

position beside the front door. His back was pressed against the wall, and he brandished a switchblade knife. He almost seemed eager to use it. His eyes narrowed at her. "Don't try to get cute, princess," he said.

At the bottom of the stairs, Sophie could hear the vehicle pulling up outside. Already, she felt her palms sweating. She tried to ignore Vic as she opened the door with her right hand.

She immediately saw that Liam had been right. It wasn't a delivery truck, but rather a silver Toyota Camry. It took her a moment to realize it was her grandmother's car.

A panic swept through her. She wouldn't be able to send her grandmother away as she had Mrs. Bellini.

And Vic wasn't going to let her go.

Helpless, Sophie watched her grandmother climb out of the car. Her mother's mother was a widow in her mid-seventies, with short auburn hair and a fondness for jangly bracelets. She'd survived cancer, and just lately, seemed to be slowing down a little—and filling out a bit. "How's my darling?" she called to Sophie as she shut the car door. "You want to get your brother out here to help me with my bags?"

Sophie quickly shoved the Kleenex note back in her pocket. Leaving the door open, she ran to her grandmother. She instinctively put herself between her grandmother and Vic. She hugged her fiercely. The bracelets jangling and the familiar smell of her grandmother's Chanel No. 5 should have been a comfort, but Sophie found she couldn't hold back the tears. "Oh, Nana . . ." she cried. "Something's happened . . ."

"What in the world . . ." her grandmother murmured.

Sophie turned and looked back at Vic, standing in the door. He still had the knife in his hand. Clinging to her grandmother, Sophie shook her head at Vic. "Don't . . . please . . ."

He stepped onto the front porch, but stopped there.

"This is my grandmother," Sophie explained, wiping a tear away as she stared down Vic. Her voice shook. "If you hurt her, I swear . . ."

She glanced up at her bedroom window and saw Joe leaning over the window seat, holding onto Liam's arm. Her brother seemed to be squirming and struggling a bit. "Joe!" she called. "We need you down here!"

Someone had to run interference with Vic. He probably didn't want another hostage around. In his sick mind, it would probably be simpler just to kill this old woman.

"Where's your mom?" her grandmother asked urgently. "What's going on here? Who are these men?"

Sophie shook her head. She couldn't get the words out. She was terrified that Vic might shoot her—right here, right now.

Her grandmother took a deep breath, and held her close. She stared at Vic. She didn't seem the least bit scared of him.

"What have you done to my daughter?"

Tuesday—5:02 P.M.
Bellingham

Laura was trying to make sense of the directory near the entrance to a maze of tan and brown apartment buildings. They were set on a beautiful wooded property with bridged walkways between the two-story structures. Birnam Wood was the housing complex for upperclassmen. It was also the former residence of Courtney Furst, the "queen bee" among the True Divine Light church's campus converts.

Laura anxiously glanced at her watch. If she hoped to catch the six o'clock ferry in Anacortes, she had about three minutes to find this young woman's apartment and talk to her former roommate—if the roommate was even home.

Randall still had in his smartphone Courtney's apartment number from a potluck she'd hosted back during his brief bliss period. He had Courtney's phone number, too, but said every time he called, he'd gotten a recording saying the customer's voice-mailbox was full. He'd also given Laura directions to Birnam Wood.

While still at the Union, she'd also spotted an ATM. It took two transactions and an added six-dollar fee, but Laura had taken out four hundred dollars. Between that and what she had in her purse, it was enough to pay Martha for the information she was selling.

But Laura was pretty certain Courtney Furst knew a lot more about the Singletons than Martha ever hoped to know.

She flagged the first student to pass by, and asked for help finding Courtney's apartment number. "I can't figure out this directory for the life of me," Laura said.

The young redhead in the blue ski jacket looked at her as if she were a bit crazy. But she politely pointed out the building for her.

Laura practically ran to the building. When she reached the apartment door, she noticed the names over the unit's doorbell:

C. Furst
L. Kim

She rang the bell. Catching her breath, she tried to listen for some activity on the other side of the solid door. It didn't sound like anyone was home. *All this for nothing*, she thought hopelessly. Still, she rang the bell again.

She heard a lock click, and the door opened a couple of inches—as far as the chain lock allowed. "Yes?" the young woman asked, peering out at her through the opening. From what Laura could see, *L. Kim* was a petite, pretty young Asian woman with long black hair parted down the middle.

"Hi, I'm sorry to bother you," Laura said. "My name's Laura, and I was hoping you might be able to tell me how to get in touch with Courtney."

The girl shook her head. "I'm sorry, she's moved away."

"I know," Laura said. She was still trying to get her breath. "But it's urgent I get in touch with her."

The girl looked hesitant. "Are you one of her friends through the church?"

"No. But—well, my son, Randall was, and it's kind of an emergency. I think Courtney's the only one who might be able to help us. I've tried her phone number, and I keep getting a recording saying the voice-mailbox is full . . ." The last part of her story was more or less true. Just to double-check what Randall had told her, she'd tried the number on her way to Birnam Wood, and got the automated recording telling her to hang up.

The girl shrugged. "I'm sorry, but I haven't seen or heard from Courtney in nearly a month. I don't know how I could help you."

"Well, I understand she left some of her things behind. Maybe there's a letter or a bill with some other contact information on it. Do you know where she's from?"

"Lake Chelan," the girl said. She seemed a bit reluctant as she unfastened the chain and opened the door wider. "Her mother lives there. But I just talked with Mrs. Furst two weeks ago, and she doesn't know where Courtney is either."

"Well, has anyone called the police?" Laura asked. "Her mother doesn't know where she is. You're Courtney's good friend, and you don't know where she is . . ."

The girl shrugged. "Courtney and I were roommates, but we weren't very close."

"You aren't with the church?" Laura asked.

The girl shook her head, but she smiled wryly. "I don't think they'd want me for a member. I'm a little too ethnic for them. But you're the first person to ask . . ."

Laura blinked at her. "Beg your pardon?"

"Since she disappeared, three other people have come here looking for Courtney, saying it was an emergency. They claimed not to be with the church, but they never asked if I was a church member. That's how I knew they were lying. Only someone from the church would know not to bother asking, because their church is just about as white as Ivory Snow."

Laura opened her purse and pulled out Joe's sketches. She showed the girl the drawings. "This is all supposed to be the same man. Did any of the people who came looking for Courtney resemble the man in these sketches?"

The girl sighed. "Come on in while I get my glasses."

"Thanks." Laura glanced at her wristwatch as she stepped over the threshold. She looked around the living room—with some rather drab tan wood furniture that appeared to have come with the unit. Colorful posters of chimpanzees and apes decorated one wall. A monkey stuffed animal sat in one corner of the brown sofa in lieu of a throw pillow. "Somebody likes monkeys," she said.

The girl put on her glasses. "That's Courtney. You should see her room. It's a veritable simian museum—everything from a Curious George cuddly to a poster for *King Kong*. She's ape for apes. I still can't believe she left it all behind." She studied the sketches, and nodded at the detailed rendering that resembled Clint Eastwood. "That guy looks kind of familiar."

"Did he give his name?" Laura asked.

"I'm sure he did, but I can't remember."

"Was it *Zared,* by any chance?"

She made a face and then shook her head. "No, that wasn't it."

Biting her lip, Laura put the sketches back in her purse. "You don't still happen to have Mrs. Furst's phone number, do you?"

The girl walked over to a desk on the other side of

the room from the ape posters. She looked something up on her phone, and then picked up a pen. "I'm writing it down for you," she said. "So—do you mind my asking what kind of trouble your son is in?"

Laura sighed. "To tell you the truth, Miss . . ."

"Kim," the girl said. She came over and handed her a Post-it with a phone number on it. "Lisa Kim." She opened the door for her.

"Thank you." Laura slipped the Post-it inside her purse and turned to her in the doorway. "To tell you the truth, Lisa," she said, "it's not just my son who's in trouble. It's my whole family."

CHAPTER TWENTY-ONE

"Hello, Mrs. Furst, you don't know me, but my name's Laura, and I'm a senior here at Western . . ."

Holding the cell phone to her ear, Laura glanced at the speedometer: eighty miles an hour. She'd never been one to talk on her phone while driving. It always made her nervous, and besides, it was against the law. She prayed there were no cops patrolling this winding stretch of Interstate 5. And she prayed she didn't end up having an accident. The section of highway wove through trees and hills, so the reception on the cheap little phone was awful.

"Yes?" Courtney's mother sounded wary.

"I'm looking for a place to live," she explained. "And I understand your daughter, Courtney, moved out of her apartment at Birnam Wood. It's perfect for me. But Courtney left a lot of things behind, a whole collection of monkey and ape memorabilia. Her roommate, Lisa, said she can't get ahold of her. Now Lisa's out of town and I have the key. Anyway, I don't want to throw this stuff out, not without talking to Courtney first."

"I'm sorry, what did you say your name was?"

"Laura . . ." She passed a sign for a highway exit. "Fairhaven, Laura Fairhaven."

"You aren't with the church, are you?"

"What church?" Laura figured it was better to play dumb.

"I thought you might be one of Courtney's church friends calling again," Mrs. Furst said.

"No, Courtney doesn't know me."

"Well, I'm sorry, but I have no idea where she is. I haven't spoken to her in quite a while."

Laura had a feeling she was covering for her daughter. "Well, I'm already half-moved in," she said. "And I'd really like to pack up this stuff of Courtney's and move it out. A lot of it looks kind of personal. If by any chance you hear from Courtney, could you please have her call me at this number—just as soon as she can? Do you have a pencil and a piece of paper handy, Mrs. Furst?"

"Well, I really don't think I'll hear from Courtney anytime soon, but if you'll hold for a minute, I'll take your number down . . ."

When Mrs. Furst got back on the line, Laura gave her the number of the pay-as-you-go phone. "Please, if you figure out any way to get in touch with your daughter, could you have her call me?" Laura pressed. "I'd really hate to throw all her things away and find out later that she was coming back for them."

"I have your number, Laura," Mrs. Furst said. "If I

hear from Courtney, I'll pass along the message. Good-bye."

Through the cheap phone's static-laced reception, Laura clearly heard the click on the other end.

"Oh, my God, really? Are you really slowing down for a green light? What is your problem? Are you try-ing to torture me?"

It was all Laura could do to keep from honking her horn at the painfully slow driver in the SUV in front of her. This was the last stoplight on Commercial Street before the Anacortes ferry terminal. She'd been stuck behind the SUV for at least two miles, and she'd tried not to tailgate. But that didn't stop Laura from talking to, pleading with, and now yelling at the stupid driver who was going to make her miss her ferry.

The dashboard clock read 6:01. Laura was con-vinced that by the time she pulled into the terminal, she'd see the ferry leaving the dock. And the next ferry wasn't until 8:25.

She made it through the intersection just as the light turned yellow. She saw the tollbooth about a block ahead. She'd had her money out and ready since pulling off the Interstate twenty minutes ago. And now she had her window down.

The idiot in the SUV finally decided to turn right—without a signal, of course. Laura sped up, pulled into the terminal area and stopped at the booth. "Am I too late for the six o'clock?" she asked the woman.

"Lane two," the woman said, handing Laura her ticket and change.

Laura realized the woman had probably been instructed not to tell people to hurry, because it could lead to accidents. As she drove down lane two, she didn't see any cars waiting in front of her. She spotted the ferry worker grabbing the chain to block access as they got ready to raise the ramp.

Laura tapped the horn and frantically waved out the window. "Oh, please, please, please . . ." she whispered.

The ferry worker saw her and waved her on.

She slowed down a bit as she approached. "Thank you so much!" she cried out to him. "I'm sorry to honk! Thank you!"

On the vessel, a crewmember waved her into a parking lane on the deck. Laura parked, raised her window again, and turned off the engine. She just wanted to break down and cry. But she still felt on edge. Her stomach was still clenched. She knew she wouldn't feel any relief at all until she called home and talked with Sophie.

She thought it might help if she got out of the car and stretched her legs. She took her purse with her as she weaved through the cars to the railing on the parking deck. The fresh, chilly sea air felt good. She looked out at the dark sky and the silvery ripples on the black water.

The ferry started to pull out of the dock, and she waited a few moments for the din to die down while people climbed out of their cars to go to the upper decks. Once all the door slamming, car alarm-check beeping, and passengers' chatter finally subsided, Laura dialed her smartphone number. It rang three times, and then Vic picked up: "Yeah?"

"Could you turn down the TV and put Joe on, please?" she asked.

She heard Vic muttering, and the TV went mute. Then Joe's voice came on the line: "Mrs. Gretchell? Have you met with Martha yet?"

"No, but I'm on the ferry for Lopez to go see her right now," she said. "First, I wanted to tell you that I talked to a student up at Western who knows Doran Wiley. It's made me realize that your escape with Vic was a terrible mistake. It's made investigators focus more on you than anything or anyone else. To them, your disappearance is like an admission of guilt . . ."

"Are you going to tell us something besides your stupid theories?" Vic cut in.

"The point I'm trying to make is—as far as I know, the police haven't really explored any other possible explanations for the Singleton killings. You're it, Joe. But after talking to some people this afternoon, I think the Singletons might have been murdered by a disgruntled ex-member of that church. Joe, remember I asked if you knew Eric Vetter?"

"Yes?" Joe said, sounding uncertain.

"Well, he was a good friend of Scott Singleton's, and he died in a mysterious fire about a month ago. Around that same time, a few of his church associates on the campus just disappeared or scattered. It turns out the church had some pretty unscrupulous, secret ways of recruiting new members and keeping them in line. Right now, I'm trying to track down a young woman who was close to Eric and Scott. Her name's Courtney Furst. Does that name sound familiar to you?"

"No," Joe replied.

"Well, I believe she might know a lot more about Scott Singleton than Martha knows. She might be able to help clear your name. But the trouble is, she seems to be in hiding. I tracked down her mother and left a message with her. But I don't want to get your hopes up. I don't think Courtney will call me back."

"So—in other words, you don't have a goddamn thing," Vic said.

"No, I have a possible explanation for why Joe slept through all the murders—and why he doesn't remember anything. According to a former friend of Doran Wiley's, when Doran was caretaker at the Singletons' summerhouse, on Scott's first night there, he asked Doran to come to his study, where he poured him a beer and told him what a good job he was doing. Does any of this sound familiar, Joe?"

"Yes, that's just how it happened with me."

"And that was as much as Doran could remember from that night. The rest was a blank. It took a few more nights just like it before he realized Mr. Singleton had been slipping roofies into his beer."

"Wait a minute," Joe murmured. "Roofies, that's the date-rape drug, isn't it?"

Laura could hear Vic cackling on the other end of the line.

"It's not funny!" Joe said angrily.

"It isn't," Laura agreed. "Joe, do you think it's possible he . . ."

Vic was still laughing. "Jesus, that whole time at the country club, you were so worried about someone trying to rape you, and here you finally get out of there, land this great job with this holier-than-thou, self-ordained linebacker, and . . . wham . . ."

"Shut up!" Joe said. "I—I really don't think anything happened, Mrs. Gretchell. I'm pretty sure I'd know."

"Well, on one hand," Laura said, "it explains to the police why you slept through everything that night and can't remember much. It proves you weren't lying. On the other hand, it also gives the police a motive for you killing Scott and his family. They might say you figured out what he'd done to you and went a little crazy . . ."

"But I don't think he did anything to me, I really don't!" Joe sounded so torn up. "And I didn't kill anybody! It was Zared, I'm sure of it. Show my drawings to Martha, I'll bet she recognizes him. I'll bet she—"

"Joe, I already showed your sketches to Martha, and she didn't recognize the man. I told you that already."

"Well, show her the pictures again!"

"Okay, I will. Please, Joe, calm down. Listen, there's some positive news. This Courtney, her roommate said the man in one of your sketches looked very familiar. She thought he was someone associated with the church."

"Then you have to find this Courtney person!" Joe insisted.

"I've tried," Laura said. "I'm hoping she calls me back. But like I told you, I doubt I'll hear from her."

"You've got to! This Zared is the killer, I just know it. I'm sure of it . . ."

"Okay, chill, for Christ's sake," Vic piped in. "Nice going, Teach. He'll be bouncing off the walls for the rest of the night over this rape thing. You got any more jolly news for us?"

She took a deep breath. "Joe stepped away from the phone, didn't he?"

"Yeah, he just went outside for some air."

"Then I'd like to talk to my daughter now."

"Yeah, I figured," he muttered. "I'm headed upstairs right now."

"Have they been locked in Sophie's room all this time?" she asked.

"Yep, best place for them."

Laura nervously drummed her fingers on the deck railing. She hated to think that Vic might be right. She'd seen last night how irritated he'd become around the children. They were probably safer locked in that room—out of sight, out of harm's way.

"We got a little surprise with that delivery this afternoon," he said drolly. "I'll let the prom queen tell you about it."

Laura wondered what he was talking about. She heard rustling and creaking in the background, and then Vic's voice—a little distant. He must have been talking to them: "Holy hell, it's hot! And it stinks in here. Did the kid crap in his pants?"

"What's going on?" Laura asked.

"Four people in a warm room and we can't open a window," Sophie said on the other end, "that what's going on."

"Four?" Laura repeated. "Wait. Okay, first, Sophie, how are you? How is everyone?"

"We're okay, Mom," her daughter said. "We're *tired*, but okay. And Nana's here."

"What?" Laura said.

"You got a minute, lady," she heard Vic mutter in the background.

"Laura, honey?" her mother said.

Hearing her mother's voice at this point was just too much. She couldn't hold back the tears. "Mom? What are you doing there?"

"It was supposed to be a surprise," her mother explained. "Sean set it up. I was the special delivery. I was going to help you pack and take you to the airport. You had a six-forty flight to Seattle, and then a connection to Air France. I was going to stay with the kids for the next six nights while you and Sean did Paris. It was a big secret. Even the kids didn't know about it."

Laura just listened and cried. All the horrible things she'd been thinking about her dear, sweet husband.

"Anyway," her mother said—with a sad little laugh. "Surprise . . ."

"Oh, Mom, I'm so sorry," she managed to say. "I'm sorry you got caught up in this . . ."

"Honey, so far, we're all okay—"

"Gimme," Vic interrupted. His voice was slightly muffled as he spoke to her mother.

"She already knows that. The girl already told her."

"Mom?"

"Your husband thinks you're on your way to Paris," Vic said. "I sent him a text from your phone—with your trademark 'Hey you,' at the start and your little X's at the sign-off. It was a very romantic little thank-you note, and he bought it. He's probably fast asleep, dreaming about you right now. Don't go spoiling things by trying to phone him, because there's nothing he can do, and you'll just end up with a houseful of dead people."

"I won't," Laura heard herself say.

"Call us after you've talked to the waitress," Vic said. "And you better have something *substantial* to tell us—and not just your bullshit theories."

He hung up.

Laura stood there, leaning against the railing for a few moments. She couldn't see the lights on the shore anymore—just the dark horizon. It was three in the morning in France, but she wanted so much to call Sean right now. She wanted to tell him everything. But that wouldn't do any good. He was practically on the other side of the world. What could he do?

At this point, all she could do was hope that Martha could tell her something, the *something substantial* Vic and Joe wanted to hear.

The wind cut through her. Laura hiked up the collar of her jacket and shuddered violently.

She had a feeling her poor, dear husband would never see his family alive again.

Slipping the smartphone into his pocket, Vic headed out of the bedroom. But he stopped in the doorway and turned around.

Sophie felt a wave of dread as he looked her in the eye and crooked his index finger, beckoning her. "Come with me," he muttered.

"What for?" she asked.

"What do you want with my granddaughter?" her grandmother asked. James had been hiding behind his nana ever since Vic had stepped into the room minutes ago. She took hold of Sophie's arm.

"Not that it's any of your fucking business, old lady, but she needs to call her boyfriend."

"Don't talk to my grandmother like that," Liam warned.

Vic just chuckled, dismissing him. Then he locked eyes with Sophie again. "C'mon, move your ass."

"It's okay, Nana," Sophie whispered to her grandmother. She followed Vic out to the hallway.

Shutting the door, he picked up the crowbar, which was leaning against the wall. He shoved it between the door and the doorframe. "I guess Lucky Matt just can't get enough of you," Vic said. "He must want it bad. He keeps texting. And a few minutes ago, he left a voicemail saying he's coming over. You need to put a stop to that, princess."

He led the way down the hall toward her parents' bedroom.

"Where's Joe?" Sophie asked. She'd thought it was strange that he hadn't come upstairs with Vic earlier, when they'd talked to her mother on the phone.

"Joe's outside having a little much-needed alone time." Vic stepped into her parents' room, which was still a mess. He swiped her phone off the bed, which Sophie thought was a strange place to leave it. The nightstand lamp was turned on. He sat down on the bed, patted the spot next to him, and held the phone out to her. "Sit. Give Romeo a call . . ."

Sophie took the phone from him. "I can talk to him standing up."

"Sit down!" he growled. "Don't be so goddamn full of yourself. You know the drill. I need to be in on this conversation."

Sophie didn't budge. "My mother and I had a long talk last night. She said you pulled this same routine with her when she talked to my dad. She said you practically felt her up. I'd just as soon stand, thanks."

He let out a snort. He seemed to focus on her breasts. "I see you changed your shirt for me," he whispered. "Nice. Your tits look good. You shouldn't cover them up in those loose sweaters . . ."

"Charming," Sophie muttered. She crossed an arm in front of her. "I'm wearing a T-shirt because it's hot and muggy in that bedroom, and you've nailed shut the windows. So—what do you want me to say to Matt?"

He adjusted himself at the crotch and then stood up. "Tell him the same thing you told that nosy neighbor this morning. You're sick to your tummy, and you don't want company." He inched up close to her and put a hand on her shoulder.

Sophie could smell his foul BO. She moved her shoulder to discourage him from touching her. His hand swept down across her back and grazed her buttocks.

She speed-dialed Matt's number.

He answered after two rings: "Hey, I was beginning to think you were mad at me or something. What's going on? Are you feeling any better?"

"I'm afraid not," Sophie said, hating that Vic was listening in. He stood so close that he was practically pressed against her. She felt his hand on the small of her back.

"Well, what's wrong?" Matt asked.

"I think we got some food poisoning from the fish we had for dinner last night," she said.

"Oh, God, that's awful. Have you been—like hurling and everything?"

"Yeah, it's a regular barf-fest here. Anyway, we're all still pretty sick. My mother talked to the doctor, and he said that with this kind of food poisoning, we'll probably be feeling crummy for at least twenty-four hours."

"Did he prescribe anything?" Matt asked.

"Yeah, and it's helping a little. Listen, I really can't hang on the phone. But you were sweet to leave those messages and the texts earlier. I just wanted to tell you not to come over. I really don't want you seeing me like this. It's not pretty."

She tried to take a step away from Vic, but he stuck by her—until she was sandwiched between him and her mother's dresser.

"You sure I can't bring you anything?" Matt asked. "Chicken soup? I've got this great recipe. I open up the can of Campbell's and pour it in a pan . . ."

She let out a weak chuckle. "No thanks, Matt. I—I couldn't keep it down. I probably won't be in school tomorrow, but why don't we talk around lunchtime? Okay?"

"Well, all right," he said, sounding a little forlorn. "Feel better soon, okay?"

Vic put his hand on her shoulder again.

"Thanks, Matt," she said into the phone.

"I really missed you today, y'know?"

"I missed you, too. Matt," she said hurriedly. "I've really got to go. Take care."

She clicked off—just as Vic started stroking her hair. She tried to push him away, and the phone dropped out of her hand.

Vic reached over and pushed the bedroom door shut. He lunged at her, knocking her against the dresser. A couple of perfume bottles fell off the dresser top and hit the floor with a clatter. He started pawing at her.

"Stop it!" Sophie shrieked, fighting him off. "Joe! Joe, help!"

All at once, Vic lifted her up and hurled her onto the bed. She didn't realize how strong he was. Before Sophie could get a breath, he grabbed her leg and spun her toward him. He started to climb on top of her.

Sophie kicked and screamed. She slapped his face—hard.

But he didn't let up. He was relentless. He grabbed her arms and pinned her to the bed.

As she squirmed beneath him, Sophie heard her grandmother and Liam down the hallway, banging on her bedroom door.

"What are you doing to her?" her grandmother yelled.

Liam was shouting for Joe.

"Stop it, Vic!" Sophie screamed. She thought if she used his name, he'd actually listen. "Vic, think about—think about what you're doing. If my mother finds out about this, she—she won't help your friend . . ."

"I don't give a shit," he grunted, hovering over her. His face was almost crimson. He let go of one of her arms for a moment and then reached for the front of her jeans.

Sophie slapped him again. She tried to gouge his eyes, but he turned his head just in time. She felt his hand fumbling for the button and zipper on her jeans. But she kept wiggling underneath him. *This isn't happening*, she thought, still trying to fight him off.

With him panting over her—and all the shouting and thumping from her grandmother and brother in her room down the hall—Sophie didn't hear anything else. She didn't hear Joe running up the front stairs. She didn't see him until he'd already burst into the master bedroom. But what she saw was him grabbing the vase-lamp from her mother's nightstand.

He slammed the lamp over Vic's head. Sophie turned her face away and heard a crack as the lamp broke. The lightbulb went off with a pop, and the lampshade rolled across the rumpled bed. The room was suddenly dark.

Stunned, Vic let out a groan and started to slump. But Sophie pushed him off her and he sank down to the floor. Pulling herself off the bed, she staggered to her mother's dresser. She grabbed the first solid object she saw: a heavy, globe-shaped glass paperweight with a rose inside it. She wanted to bash Vic's head in. She turned and rushed toward him, raising the glass paperweight in the air.

"No!" Joe yelled.

Before she knew what was happening, Joe snatched the paperweight out of her hand and grabbed her around the waist. Sophie struggled as he carried her down the hallway and pulled the crowbar out of the doorway.

Her grandmother and Liam were still yelling and pounding on the door—until Joe flung it open. He hauled Sophie inside and set her down on her feet.

She was so unhinged and enraged, she wanted to hit him. It didn't matter that he'd just saved her. What mattered was he hadn't let her kill Vic—or at the very least, knock him unconscious and put him out of commission.

Joe stopped to stare at her for a mere second. Then he swiveled around and hurried out to the hallway. The door slammed shut, and to Sophie, it felt like a sudden punch in the stomach. She heard the squeaking noise and watched the door buckle. She knew he was fastening the crowbar back in the doorway. She couldn't believe it.

Even after he'd seen what his friend had tried to do to her, and even with Vic dazed and subdued in the other bedroom, Joe was still letting that son of a bitch call all the shots.

"My God, Sophie, are you all right?" her grandmother whispered. "Did he hurt you?"

She stood in the middle of the room with a hand over her heart, trying to catch her breath. She felt sick. She shook her head. "No, I'm all right," she lied. "He just—he just mauled me a little."

James took ahold of her hand. She sank down to her knees and held him.

Down the hallway, she heard angry muttering between the two men.

She'd thought that once Vic was overpowered, Joe would somehow come around to helping them. After all, her mother had practically saved his life back when he was a kid—even to the point of making an enemy who slashed up her face. For a brief minute or two, Joe could have put a stop to all this. Instead, he threw her back into this bedroom and barred the door. He might have saved her from Vic's assault, but she still felt betrayed. And she knew they couldn't count on him anymore.

"What the hell is wrong with you?" she heard Vic bellow.

She couldn't make out any words in the apologetic muttering from Joe.

Then it was Vic again: "Goddamn it, your old teacher isn't going to find anything on Lopez! Why are you wasting our time here? What the hell is the point? I know, you know, everyone knows—you killed them all. Jesus, Joe! You're not fooling anybody . . ."

CHAPTER TWENTY-TWO

Tuesday—6:55 P.M.
Lopez Island

Martha's block didn't have any sidewalks, and the houses looked borderline ramshackle. But it also looked rather homey, with bikes out on some of the neglected front lawns and Christmas lights already up and blinking. The shiny black BMW parked across the street from Martha's townhouse didn't seem to belong there. People on the block were probably wondering who had a rich relative visiting.

As she hurried out of the car and headed toward the front door, Laura noticed a few lights on inside the townhouse. She took that as a good sign.

She'd been worried no one would be home. Martha had told her to come by at five-thirty. And here she was nearly ninety minutes late. Laura didn't have Martha's phone number. All she'd gotten was an address scribbled on the back of a grease-stained restaurant check.

Laura knocked on the townhouse door, and then waited. She didn't hear any footsteps. She knocked again. She only had about five minutes to talk with

Martha and pay her for the information, then turn around and catch the 7:10 ferry. She hoped Martha would be less chatty than Randall.

Laura still didn't hear any activity inside the house. The waitress had already taken her for forty bucks. Was it possible Martha had given her a bogus address?

By the doorway, Laura noticed a mailbox with a little window in it. She could see mail in there. She reached inside and pulled out a Comcast bill addressed to Martha Dressler. So at least she was at the right address. Laura tucked the envelope back in the mailbox and wondered why Martha hadn't picked up her mail this afternoon.

She knocked again, harder. The door squeaked and gave a little.

It wasn't locked, and hadn't even been closed all the way.

Laura pushed it open farther and peered into the empty front hallway. "Hello?" she called. "Martha? Your front door was open . . ."

With uncertainty, Laura stepped inside. From the smell, she knew Martha—or maybe someone who lived with her—was a smoker. One light was on in the living room, which was messy. The furniture looked like early, long-ago-expired stuff from Ikea. A string of Christmas lights was hung over a brick and wood bookshelf but wasn't plugged in.

Laura never would have barged into a stranger's home like this, but she was desperate. She could hear water running in another part of the townhouse. She peeked into the darkened kitchen and looked at the sink. Nothing.

Following the sound, she wandered to the bedroom and stopped in the doorway. The nightstand lamp was on, harshly illuminating a full ashtray just beside it. Clothes were strewn over a chair, and the bed hadn't been made. The bathroom door was open a crack. Laura could hear the shower going. A trail of steam wafted into the bedroom.

There was no time to be tactful, tiptoe away, and come back later.

"Martha!" she called, still tentatively standing in the bedroom doorway. "Martha! It's Laura—from the café today!"

She didn't want to walk through the bedroom and knock on the bathroom door. Part of it was politeness. But there was another reason for her hesitation. Laura felt as if someone was watching her. It was a strong, overwhelming sensation, and for a few moments, it paralyzed her. She called out to Martha again, but there was no response—just the constant roar from the stream of the shower water.

Finally, Laura stepped into the bedroom and approached the bathroom door. This close, she could see the brown and beige waitress uniform in a heap on the bathroom's tiled floor. She rapped loudly on the doorway frame. "Martha? Your front door was open . . ."

She didn't understand why the woman still couldn't hear her. She was only a few feet away. Of course, she also couldn't understand why anyone would take a shower while alone in the house and leave their front door open.

Laura reluctantly moved past the bathroom door. It squeaked as she opened it farther. The shower had a semi-transparent curtain, closed all the way. But no one seemed to be standing on the other side of it.

With trepidation, Laura pulled the shower curtain open a few inches.

She gasped at what she saw.

Martha's nude body was curled up in the tub. Her head was close to the drain, resting on her bent arm—the one with the Winnie-the-Pooh tattoo. The shower's spray washed away the blood that leaked from an ugly gash in her forehead. Her eyes were half open, and Martha had a listless, dazed look on her face.

It looked as though she must have slipped and hit her head—maybe on the faucet.

But was it really an accident?

Horrified, Laura couldn't move or breathe. But then, behind her, she heard a door squeak.

She swiveled around. The closet door in the bedroom was half open. It wasn't like that before. She was practically certain of it.

Laura bolted out of the bedroom, through the front hallway and out the door. She shut the door behind her. But she was convinced someone was still chasing her. She could almost hear the footsteps in back of her. Racing down the walkway, she frantically groped inside her purse for her keys. One of the twenty-dollar bills flew out, but she didn't care. She just kept running. She unlocked the car with the device on her key fob, opened the driver's door, and jumped inside.

With her heart pounding furiously, she peeled away from the curb and sped down the street. In her rearview mirror, she didn't spot anyone following her. But she didn't slow down—not for several blocks, not until she was practically at the ferry terminal. She checked the rearview mirror again and didn't see any cars—not yet, at least.

Up ahead, the 7:10 ferry was already loading.

Laura didn't know what to do. If she went to the police right now, she'd end up endangering her family. But she couldn't just drive away. She paused at the ferry terminal entrance.

She wasn't certain anyone had actually been chasing her. But she was almost positive that Martha's death was no accident. The timing was just too much of a coincidence.

Up ahead, only four cars were left in the line of vehicles driving onto the ferry to Anacortes.

Wincing, Laura pulled forward to the ticket booth. With a shaky hand, she pulled out her round-trip ticket and showed it to the man.

Mr. Pecan Waffle was the last one to board the ferry, and he took his time about it. He waited until one more traveler—in a minivan—drove onto the vessel after the woman in the Toyota Sienna. Then he pulled up to the booth, paid for his ticket, and cruised onto the car deck. He stayed inside his BMW. He was pretty certain she couldn't see him parked behind the minivan.

In the cup holder, he had his smartphone on speaker. From the license plate on the Sienna, his work partner already had the driver's name and address: Laura Gretchell on Rural Route 17 in Leavenworth. Google gave even more information on the woman, thanks to a fluff piece in the *Wenatchee World*. She was Mrs. Sean

Gretchell, formerly of Seattle. She and her husband had three children, and they'd recently purchased a winery in Leavenworth. Laura was a former teacher.

"The article doesn't say anything about her being a reporter," his friend told him.

That meant she had been lying to him—and lying to the waitress at the Last Sunset Café.

Of course, he'd lied to her, too, especially when he told her that he didn't recognize the sketches of his work partner.

This Gretchell woman had slipped away from him once before. He wasn't going to let it happen again.

He intended to keep following her—even if she took him all the way back to the winery in Leavenworth. She'd told him that she hadn't sketched those pictures, so he needed to find out who had drawn them. Those pictures were worth a lot to him and his partner. He wanted them. And like many serious art collectors, he considered it advantageous to deal with work by artists who were dead.

They couldn't afford any loose ends. It was why they'd gotten rid of the waitress.

With this one—and maybe her artist friend—he'd make it look like another accident.

"No, you're not calling the cops," Vic said on the other end of the line. "I thought I made that clear."

Parked on the car deck, Laura sat at the wheel of her Sienna. She had the cell phone to her ear. The ferry had left the dock about five minutes before. "Vic, listen to me," she said. "I just want to call nine-one-one, give them Martha's address, and tell them she's dead. Then I'll hang up. We can't just leave her lying there in the tub."

"Why the hell not?" he said. "If you call the cops, they might be able to trace the location of your cell. You could end up having a reception committee waiting for you when the ferry pulls into Anacortes. Forget it."

"Is Joe there?" she asked. "Is he listening in, because this is more for him than you."

She heard muttering. Then Joe came on the line: "Is it true about Martha?"

"Yes, I'm afraid so. Joe, I know you were hoping she had some proof that you didn't kill the Singletons. But her dying this way just when she was ready to sell me information about the murders, it's too much of a coincidence. It proves what you said. Between the so-called accidents that killed Eric Vetter and now Martha, and Scott Singleton's penchant for using roofies on unsuspecting teenagers, there's obviously some sort of cover-up going on. This church Messenger, Courtney Furst, has disappeared, so either she's dead or she's in hiding. If the police knew about this, they wouldn't be so quick to assume you're guilty of the murders. Don't you see, Joe?"

"I just can't believe she's dead," he murmured.

"Joe, even your doctor from the institute thinks you're innocent. I read an article while I was at the university library this afternoon, and he said he couldn't see you intentionally harming anyone except yourself."

"Dr. Halstead said that?"

"Yes, he did. If you turn yourself in and let me talk

to the police, they'll probably start searching for Courtney. They'll start investigating other reasons for the Singleton murders, reasons that have nothing to do with you."

"What about Zared? He's the one who killed them, I'm sure of it . . ."

"The police would start looking for him, too—if you turned yourself in. Courtney's roommate said the same man in your sketches came looking for Courtney. She'll be able to back up your story."

"He's not turning himself in," Vic piped in. "And we don't need your goddamn advice."

Laura clutched the steering wheel with one hand and took a deep breath. "Vic, take anything you want from the house. Take my mother's car and go. Just leave my family alone. Joe will stay behind and make sure no one calls the police for as many hours as you need. And once we know you're far enough away that the police can't find you, Joe will turn himself in. It's a good deal for everyone, Vic. If you really care about Joe—"

"Screw that, and screw you," he barked.

"I get it, Vic," she said. "You don't want to be alone. You were a fugitive alone after you broke out of the institution. But then you helped Joe escape from that hotel where the police had him. To hear Joe tell it, you *made* him escape, and then you weren't alone anymore. You had a partner. You were on the lam with your friend like a couple of outlaws, like Butch and Sundance. You've gotten him deeper and deeper into trouble so you won't have to be alone . . ."

"Vic, what's she talking about?" she heard Joe ask.

"She sounds like one of those quacks at the country club," he said. "Who do you think you are, analyzing me? You were spouting the same bullshit yesterday. You want to hear what sounds like a sweet deal to me, lady? I take what I want, I kill everyone in the house, and then Joe and I hit the road in the old bag's car. Same plan, but no witnesses."

"You can't do that," she said, trying to hide the panic inside her.

"What's stopping me?"

"Me," she heard herself say. "As long as I'm out here, you can't touch me. And I'm cooperating with you—*for now*. But if you hurt my family, Vic, I'll have the police on your ass so fast, you won't know what hit you. If you're smart, you'll consider that deal, just the way I offered it. Think about it, Vic. Now, please put my daughter or my mother on the phone."

There was silence on the other end.

"Vic?"

Another moment passed. Laura wondered if the very next thing she'd hear would be a gunshot.

She clutched her stomach. "Vic?"

Someone came on the line. "Laura? Honey, are you okay?"

"Mom? Oh, Mom, for a minute there, I thought . . ." she trailed off.

"The kids and I are all right. We're hanging in there. How are you?"

"Oh, God, Mom, I'm such a wreck. I was just in this woman's house. She said she had some information for me . . ." Laura realized her mother didn't need to hear about a murdered waitress—not now. She had enough on her plate at the moment, looking after three terrified children.

Laura took a deep breath. "I can tell you about it when I see you. I should be home in about three hours, maybe closer to four if the pass conditions are bad. How are you really? Have they still got you all locked up in Sophie's room?"

There was no answer. Laura realized she'd been talking to no one for a while. It was a horrible feeling.

"Mom?"

She didn't hear anything for another few excruciating moments.

Vic came on the line. "Y'know, we asked you to do one simple thing for us today, and you failed miserably."

Then he hung up.

Laura clicked off. She closed her eyes and rubbed her forehead.

Every time she hung up after talking with her family, she thought it might be the last time.

She wanted so much to call the police about Martha, and yet she couldn't. She hated to think that Vic was right. But if she called the police and they tracked her down, they'd never let her go home. Martha was dead and there wasn't anything Laura could do for her.

She had to think about her family.

Her only hope at this point was Joe. She told herself that Joe would never let Vic hurt any of her children—or her mother. If only she could get through to him about turning himself in to the police.

Maybe someone else could get through to Joe.

Laura grabbed her purse and climbed out of the car.

Locking the Sienna with the device on her key fob, she hurried up the narrow, gray stairwell toward the passenger deck. Just minutes before, she'd been worried someone was following her. But she'd forgotten about that for now.

On the passenger deck, she saw a heavyset, pretty young woman with long brown hair sitting alone, staring at her smartphone.

A bit out of breath, Laura plopped down in the seat across from her. The girl looked up.

"Hi," Laura said. "Would it be possible to borrow your phone for just five minutes? It's kind of an emergency. I need to look something up, and all I have is this thing . . ." She took the pay-as-you-go phone out of her purse and showed her.

The girl seemed hesitant.

"If you don't trust a total stranger with your phone, I understand." Laura reached into her purse again and pulled out two twenties. "Tell you what. I'll give you forty bucks if you look up a couple of things for me . . ."

The girl stared at the money. "What do you want me to look up?"

"I need the contact information for a Dr. Halstead at the Western Washington Psychiatric Institute in Marysville. And then I need directions to the Institute."

The girl stared at her for another moment—as if Laura might want to check herself in once she'd driven to the institute. Then with a sigh, the girl reached across the table and took the forty dollars. She started working her thumbs over the keypad of her phone. "How do you spell Halstead?" she asked.

CHAPTER TWENTY-THREE

Tuesday—7:26 P.M.
Leavenworth

"You got me into trouble," Vic said, smirking at her. He rubbed the back of his head. "I've got this goose egg, and nobody's talking to me—all because of you."

Sophie said nothing. She set a basket of bread and a plate of butter on the lazy Susan in the center of the round breakfast table.

Vic sat there alone, drinking expensive wine from a juice glass. The table was set for six, because he'd insisted they all eat dinner together—like a family. Obviously, he hoped to amuse himself in some perverse way, the sadist.

Sophie's grandmother was just taking the chicken casserole out of the oven. Joe, Liam, and James were in the family room watching *Who Framed Roger Rabbit?* on some cable station with tons of commercials. But that didn't matter, just as long as the movie kept James entertained and quiet.

Since assaulting her, Vic had been more intolerable

than ever. He'd been acting like what he'd done was nothing. To him, it was all just a little misunderstanding. A half hour after attempting to rape her, he'd let everyone out of the bedroom so she and her grandmother could get dinner started.

"Hey, now, don't get all pissy with me just because I wanted to have a little fun," he'd said, grinning at Sophie as she'd passed him in the hallway. She'd barely been able to keep from spitting in his face. She'd kept moving toward the stairway and refused to even glance at him.

The whole family had been giving him the silent treatment. "Well, looks like I'm in the doghouse with everybody here," he'd announced at one point—like a dad who had just announced the family vacation had been canceled.

Sophie and her grandmother had been in the kitchen getting dinner started when her mother had phoned. What Sophie had understood from hearing one end of the conversation was that someone had been killed, someone who was supposed to have given her mother information that would have cleared Joe's name in the Singleton murder case.

It had come as a shock to Sophie.

Until hearing about this new death, her one solace had been that at least her mother wasn't in danger. As long as she wasn't stuck here inside the house with these two murderers, her mom would be okay.

But that really wasn't true anymore.

Vic had allowed only her grandmother—and no one else—a few seconds on the phone with her mom. Sophie wished she'd gotten a chance to talk with her. Un-

fortunately, her grandmother didn't realize how important each phone call was. She didn't know about the
word codes Sophie and her mother had worked out together.

Now, Sophie had no idea what to do.

Maybe her mother was ready to "say a prayer" for
them. But Sophie couldn't imagine her mom calling
the police without bracing her for it first.

At this point, Sophie felt their chances for survival
didn't look good at all, way below the twenty percent
her mother had projected last night.

Sophie didn't want to believe it, but from what
she'd overheard Vic say, it sounded as if Joe had indeed murdered that whole family. Now, every time she
set eyes on Joe, she thought: *he's a murderer*.

She glanced at him in the family room, sitting alone
on one end of the sofa, a look of concentration on his
handsome, boyish face as he watched the television.
James was squeezed in next to Liam on the other end
of the couch. Even her baby brother now seemed to realize the guy was poison. It was strange to see the three
of them looking so serious while cartoon voices and
zippy music filled the family room.

Vic was now on his third glass of cabernet. As Sophie left him alone at the table and started back into the
kitchen, she had a feeling he'd only become more
surly and dangerous if he kept up the drinking. Then
again, maybe they'd get lucky and he'd pass out.

"Dinner's ready," her grandmother announced.

"Get in here, guys!" Vic called. "Leave the TV on!"

In the kitchen, Sophie's grandmother heaped hearty
portions of chicken casserole on each plate. It had

pasta, a Frito crust, and a ton of butter—heart-attack comfort food. Maybe her grandmother thought Vic would mellow out and fall asleep if he had a full stomach. Sophie carried the first two servings around the counter to the breakfast area. She put the plates down at Vic's and Liam's spots. Then she stopped to help James into his booster chair. Joe sat down next to Vic on one side, and Liam had volunteered to occupy the chair on the other side of him. Sophie knew he was doing it so that she wouldn't have to sit next to the son of a bitch.

"Hey, Lee-ham, get me a glass of water," Vic said.

"I'll get it," Sophie murmured.

"No, let Lee-ham fetch it. I don't trust you, princess, not anymore. You'd spit in it."

Liam got up from the table and went into the kitchen with her. "I'll spit in it for you," he said under his breath.

"No, don't take any chances," she whispered.

She heard Vic clear his throat. "Joe, on second thought, go turn off the TV," he said. "That cartoon shit's getting on my nerves."

Sophie heard the TV go off. She, Liam, and their grandmother came around the kitchen counter at the same time Joe returned to the table. Vic was already eating—and guzzling his wine. Liam set the glass of water on his place mat.

Everyone sat down, and Sophie's grandmother made the sign of the cross. Sophie's family usually didn't say grace unless it was some kind of sit-down dinner with her grandmother. So she and Liam went along with their grandmother as she prayed out loud: *"Bless us, our Lord, and these, thy gifts . . ."*

Joe looked embarrassed that he'd already started eating. With his mouth full, he sat there, not moving and not chewing until her grandmother said, *"Amen."*

But Vic kept stuffing his face throughout the prayer.

"This is really delicious, ma'am," Joe said after finally swallowing the mouthful of food.

Her grandmother seemed to force a cordial smile for him, and then she started eating. Except for the clanking of silverware, it was quiet for a few moments.

Sophie noticed Vic smirking.

Something was wrong. For a few moments, he'd been alone at the table with James—and two plates of food: his own and Liam's.

"Isn't this tasty, Vic?" Joe asked.

Liam dropped his fork on the plate. It made a clang. He grimaced, "It's crunchy. There's something crunchy in this . . ."

Vic started to snicker.

Liam coughed and put a hand up to his throat.

Sophie suddenly realized what was happening. She gaped at Vic. "Did you put something in his food?" she asked in a shrill voice. "Did you put nuts in there?"

Vic covered his mouth as he giggled.

Liam started choking. He pushed himself away from the table. His eyes rolled back.

Sophie jumped up from her chair, raced around the counter into the kitchen, and pulled open the junk drawer. She found an EpiPen, snatched it up, and hurried back to the table. "Hold on, Liam! Hold on!"

Liam was going into convulsions. His whole body shook and he made a horrible raspy, choking sound.

James started to scream. Joe got to his feet.

Her grandmother ran to Liam and held him down in the chair.

Sophie snapped off the EpiPen cover and plunged the needle into Liam's thigh. She kept it there for a moment. Her brother gasped and then started coughing. The violent tremors that racked his body seemed to subside, but he was still shuddering with little aftershocks. His eyes seemed unable to focus.

Crouched at his side, Sophie watched him and waited to make sure the dose was working.

"Can I do anything?" Joe asked. "What can I do?"

Sophie glanced over at Vic. He took a swig of wine. "I had some nuts in my backpack," he sniggered. "I thought they might spice up his meal."

Sophie suddenly became unhinged. She still had the EpiPen in her hand. With a yell, she swung the needle device toward Vic and plunged it into the side of his neck.

Stunned, Vic dropped his glass and shot up from his chair. It tipped over behind him. The pen dropped from his neck onto the floor. A thin trail of blood rolled down to his shoulder. He slapped a hand over the wound. Wide-eyed, he helplessly staggered back—until he hit the curtains at the edge of the sliding glass door. It seemed to jar him out of his stupor.

He took his hand away for a moment and looked at the blood on his fingers.

"Goddamn it!" he bellowed. He blinked several times, and then his rage-filled eyes locked onto her. "You little bitch . . ." He charged toward her.

Sophie reached for a fork from the table to defend herself.

But it was too late. Vic grabbed the front of her T-shirt and yanked her up. With his fist, he punched her in the face. The force of the blow sent her crashing against the fallen chair. The pain was excruciating. She didn't know what was happening. Past a loud ringing in her ear, she could hear her grandmother and James screaming.

"God, Vic, no!" Joe yelled. "Stop it!"

Sophie couldn't see anything—just little white explosions.

But she knew it wasn't over.

She listened to Vic grunting. There was the sound of plates being knocked over, and more shouting. Joe was still pleading with him to stop.

Then there was another bone-crunching smack as Vic hit her in the face again.

It was the last thing Sophie heard.

CHAPTER TWENTY-FOUR

Tuesday—8:53 P.M.
Marysville, Washington

" I 'm here to see Dr. Alan Halstead," Laura said. "I called earlier."

She gazed up through the car's open window at the middle-aged uniformed guard. He had silver hair and a ruddy complexion. He leaned out of the window of his little booth by the front gate. The badge on his blue jacket caught the bright security lights from overhead.

"Can I see some identification, please?" he said. His breath was visible in the cold night.

Laura handed him her driver's license. She was glad she hadn't given him a fake name when she'd first rolled down the window.

"One minute, please," he said. Then he turned and picked up a phone. There was a row of small TV monitors just above the window in front of him, security cameras obviously. But one of them was showing an old *Happy Days* rerun. Laura recognized Fonzie.

One of the cameras was in evidence by the chain-link front gate. The tall fence was also chain-link, with a section of barbed wire along the top. It encircled the parking lot and the long, rambling three-story brick building. All but a few of the windows had been covered with chain-link screens—just like the fence. Laura guessed the place was built in the thirties. But the entrance in front appeared to have been added on in the eighties or nineties. The sign by the entrance had shiny white lettering with a blue background, and seemed kind of cheap. It had either been hastily set up or was temporary. It said WESTERN WASHINGTON PSYCHIATRIC INSTITUTE.

Joe and Vic's former home was in Marysville, not far from the center of town. It was fifty minutes south of Anacortes, a brief stop for Laura on the way to Highway 2 and home. She hadn't lied to the guard. She'd called earlier. She'd gotten the phone number and directions from the ferry passenger, who had taken her forty bucks for five minutes of research. Laura had talked with an operator at the institute. She'd asked if there was any way to get ahold of Dr. Halstead. She'd said it was an urgent, personal matter concerning a former patient. The woman had told her that Dr. Halstead was with a patient at the moment, but she could leave a message. Laura hadn't expected him to still be at the institute when she'd called at 7:30 at night. But the woman had told her that he was working the late shift until eleven tonight. Laura had thanked her and hung up without leaving a message. She'd figured the chances of him calling her back were about as good as the chances of Courtney Furst calling her back—infinitesimal.

The guard had slid his window shut—probably to keep out the cold and also keep her in the dark about what he was saying on the phone. Now he slid open the window again. "What's the purpose of your visit?" he asked, sounding officious.

"It's in regards to a former patient of Dr. Halstead's," she replied.

He half-turned away and muttered her response into the phone. Then the guard turned to her again. "Are you a reporter? Dr. Halstead isn't seeing any reporters."

"No, I'm—or I *was* a teacher. Tell him that I was Joseph Mulroney's third-grade teacher, back when he was Joey Spiers."

That did the trick. The guard gave her a guest-pass badge and something for the dashboard of her car. He pointed out the guest parking area of the well-lit, near-empty lot. Then he hit a button, and with a loud rattle and hum, the gate slid open.

After she parked the car, Laura hurried toward the entrance. She hoped Halstead could tell her how to deal with Joe—and get him out from under Vic's influence. Maybe he could even talk to Joe himself. She was running out of options.

At the entrance was a glass door. Laura saw another guard in a Plexiglas booth in the vestibule. She was buzzed in. The woman guard, who looked bored, nodded at her to proceed through another glass door, which buzzed and clicked when she pushed it open.

On the other side of the door, in a drab hallway, was a large man with receding hair, a gray-black beard, and thick glasses. He wore a doctor's white lab coat over an ugly yellow-and-green striped shirt. Laura put on a cordial smile, and approached him.

But he was frowning at her. "You're not Joe's teacher. She . . ."

Then he bit his lip as Laura stepped closer.

"Pardon?" she asked.

"Nothing," he said, working up a smile. He looked embarrassed. "What did you want to see me about, Ms. Gretchell?"

Laura realized he hadn't noticed the scars on her face until she was nearly right in front of him. For a moment there, he must have thought she was a phony. It confirmed what she'd surmised. Joe must have told him what had happened back in third grade.

"I won't take up much of your time, Dr. Halstead. Is there someplace where we could talk?"

"Well, I'm on a break right now. Let's see if the staff break room is empty."

The break room was just a few doors down in the fluorescent-lit hallway. Its beige-painted cinderblock walls were without windows—just a bulletin board covered with fliers, postcards, and take-out menus. There were three café tables with chairs, two vending machines, a sink, a microwave and a large refrigerator that hummed. The place smelled like slightly bad baloney.

"Grab a seat," Dr. Halstead said as he headed for the refrigerator and opened it. "There's some yogurt in here with my name on it—if one of my thieving coworkers didn't abscond with it. Good God, look at all this. There's food in here from before the Fourth of July. Can I get you anything?"

"No, thanks," Laura said. She sat down at one of the tables.

During the drive down from Anacortes, she'd thought about how much she should tell him and how much she should lie. "Joe called me today," she said.

He turned to stare at her. "Really? Out of the blue?"

She nodded. "Out of the blue."

"Did he say where he was?"

She shook her head. "The Caller ID said *Caller Unknown*."

"Did you tell the police about it?"

"Joe made me promise not to. I thought if I talked to you, you might advise me on how to persuade him to give himself up. He mentioned you, Dr. Halstead. He spoke very highly of you. I want to help him. We—we have some history, as you must know. I asked him to call me back, and he said he would."

"All the more reason to let the police in on this," Dr. Halstead said, still standing in front of the open refrigerator.

"No," Laura said. "He trusts me, and I don't want to betray that trust by going to the police just yet. I think he's innocent. No one else believes that, because he ran away—with this Victor person. Unfortunately, Joe's still with him. This Vic seems to have a lot of influence over him."

"A lot of bad influence," Dr. Halstead said.

The open refrigerator behind him started to hum more loudly. With a perturbed look on his face, he turned and shut the refrigerator door. Then he came and sat down with her at the table. "At the risk of repeating myself, I still think you need to contact the police."

She shook her head. "I can't. But maybe you could tell me what to say to him when he calls back. I think Joe would like to turn himself in, but this Vic person won't let him. I know they became friends here. Is there something you can tell me about their relationship, something that might help?"

"Do you know why Joe ended up in this place?" Dr. Halstead asked.

Laura nodded. "He mentioned that he'd beaten up a coworker who had been bothering him at work."

"I still remember the guy's name, Larry Rumble," Dr. Halstead said. "From everything I've read about the incident, the guy had it coming. He was a bully. All of Joe's coworkers said so. No one liked him. But it was the way Joe kind of went crazy on him—and then Joe's PTSD reaction. That's what landed him in this place."

"Yes, he told me that he put his hand through a window," Laura murmured.

"He had a breakdown. You know, he didn't have to come here. He settled out of court and agreed to it. His grandmother had just died. And I think he figured he really needed some help. You obviously know something about the way Joe has always been so passive, sort of a natural target, bully bait . . ."

"He was always so defenseless back when he was a child," Laura added. "Like a little deer."

"Well, he was that way when he was an adult, too. I could talk about all the damage his mother did, but we'd be here half the night. Besides, you already know about it. You rescued him from that. I can understand why he turned to you now. And I know why he's so dependent on Vic." Dr. Halstead leaned back in the chair and sighed. "I shouldn't be discussing a patient with you, but desperate times and all. Joe was very much alone when his grandmother died, alone and defenseless. So he sort of invented another personality for himself, someone who basically wasn't going to take anybody's shit. It was a part of him that he'd been afraid to let out, sort of a dark avenger. Joe invented him to survive." Dr. Halstead chuckled. "Believe me, it's not quite as schizophrenic as it sounds . . ."

Laura just nodded attentively. But she kept thinking it sounded pretty schizophrenic to her.

"Anyway, it was this avenging side of Joe's personality that went berserk and put Larry Rumble in the hospital. When Joe came here, he started getting picked on again. But he didn't want to dredge up this avenger alter-ego that had gotten him into trouble. Besides, he didn't need to, because he found him in Victor Moles. He had someone defending him and watching his back. Unfortunately, that someone was a manipulative sociopath . . ."

"And Joe's convinced he can't survive without him," Laura said. "You know, from what Joe told me, this running away—this escape from the police—it was all Vic's idea, something he made Joe do."

Dr. Halstead sighed. "I suspected as much. Joe never would have done that on his own."

"I think it's made the police automatically assume he's guilty," Laura pointed out. "They aren't even looking at other possible suspects in the Singleton murder case. I've done some research since Joe's call this afternoon. There are all sorts of corrupt, criminal goings-on with that church. Joe told me that a few weeks ago, he saw Scott Singleton in his driveway at the summer house having an argument with a man who threatened to destroy him—and his family. Joe told this to the police, but they didn't seem to believe him. But I do. Joe's convinced this is the man who killed the Singletons. But nobody's looking for him. I told Joe I'd do what I could . . ."

Laura thought about pulling out the sketches to show Dr. Halstead. Maybe they resembled someone else in Joe's life, someone threatening. But she thought better of it. If she showed Joe's sketches to the doctor, he might recognize Joe's drawing style from an occupational therapy class or something. He'd know that she'd met with Joe in person.

"Did Joe say when he'd call you back?" Dr. Halstead asked.

"I think within an hour or two," Laura said.

"Well, listen, why don't you stick around here? I could talk to him for you, and I'd like to get the police in on this."

She shook her head emphatically. "No, as I said, I promised Joe, no police. I want to talk to him one more time before going to the police. And I can't stay. I'm sorry. I really need to get back to my family in—in Seattle." If she could make it a little more difficult for the doctor and the police to track down where she lived, then all the better—at least for now. "I've left my kids alone in the house, and they're pretty nervous about it—what with the murders and everything. If I could get your phone number, maybe I can have Joe call you."

"I think you're making a big mistake not getting the police involved," Dr. Halstead said. But he took a business card out of his lab-coat pocket, along with a pen. He scribbled his phone number on the back of the card. "Can I ask you something?" he said, holding back the card.

"Of course," Laura replied, a bit apprehensive.

"Are you being completely honest with me about Joe calling you out of the blue? Somehow, I feel I'm not getting the whole story here. I think there's something more you're not telling me."

Laura quickly shook her head. "No, I—I've told you everything."

It was killing her not to tell him the truth. And maybe it was a huge mistake not to.

Dr. Halstead slid the card across the table to her.

"Thank you," Laura said, slipping it in the pocket of her pea jacket. "I'll call you with an update as soon as I hear from Joe—and I'll ask him to call you. I hope you understand about the police. I promised Joe I wouldn't contact them and that I'd do my best to track down this Zared person he says killed the Singletons."

Dr. Halstead's eyes narrowed. "Joe told you the Singleton murderer is someone named Zared?"

She nodded. "Yes, Joe practically insisted . . ."

Dr. Halstead frowned. "Mrs. Gretchell, Zared is Joe. That's the name he gave to his avenging alter-ego."

CHAPTER TWENTY-FIVE

Laura stepped out of Mort's Munitions, Guns and Ammo Emporium on Highway 2. She'd just purchased a Cobra Arms Freedom .380 semi-automatic pistol.

She knew the waiting period for a background check in Washington State was five to ten days. But she'd recently read an article by a Seattle reporter who, one week after yet another mass shooting, walked into three local gun stores and, each time, walked out with a gun—without any background check.

While the short, dumpy forty-something clerk had copied down her driver's license information, Laura had told him, "I need the gun tonight. Is that possible?"

From the other side of the glass counter, he'd looked up from his paperwork.

She'd pointed to the bruise on her chin. The makeup had worn off. "I didn't get this running into a door," Laura had said. "I have a problem at home, and I could really use something so I can defend myself—if you know what I mean."

He'd nodded. "If you have an extra fifty in cash, I can—uh, expedite things for you."

"You're very gallant," Laura had said, reaching into her purse for some cash. The irony in her tone seemed to have eluded him.

He'd shown her how the gun worked and even loaded the clip for her. She'd also bought a small canister of pepper spray.

There were only two other cars in the small parking lot of Mort's Emporium at this hour. One of them was a black BMW. It was parked under a streetlight, which glared off the windshield and the driver's window, so Laura couldn't quite see if anyone was sitting inside. She remembered the black BMW parked across from Martha's townhouse, but that was nearly three hours ago—on Lopez Island. She told herself it was probably just a coincidence. After all, it wasn't as if black BMWs were a rarity on the highways.

But that BMW didn't seem to belong on the slightly run-down block on Lopez any more than this BMW seemed to belong in the parking lot of a guns and ammo shop in Monroe.

Laura hurried to the car and checked the backseat before she climbed in. She tossed the bag with the gun in it on the passenger floor, set the pay-as-you-go phone in the cup holder, and then started up the car. After pulling onto the highway, she kept checking her rearview mirror. At the third glance, a pair of headlights came into view. But then the trailing car passed under a streetlight, and she noticed it was a Volkswagen bug.

A car horn blared, and Laura realized she'd been drifting into the oncoming lane. She quickly jerked the wheel to one side. The car made a little screech as she veered back into her lane. "C'mon, wake up," she muttered to herself, straightening in the seat. "You still have an hour and forty minutes until you're home."

Getting home, that was all she'd been thinking about for the last forty-five minutes.

When Dr. Halstead had told her that Zared was Joe, he'd broadsided her. Laura couldn't quite hide her astonishment and panic. "Well, I—I'm sure I must have heard Joe wrong then," she'd stammered. "Or maybe Joe got confused when he—when he told me about the altercation in the driveway between Scott Singleton and this other man."

Perhaps Joe had assumed the man's name was Zared, because of his threatening nature. There were a number of possible explanations. It didn't necessarily mean that Joe had gone berserk and let his dark avenger alter-ego take over and murder the Singleton family.

She'd made her excuses to Dr. Halstead and bolted out of the employee break room. She'd been convinced that Halstead would call the guard at the door and instruct the woman not to let her leave. But both doors had opened in the vestibule. Then as she'd hurried to her car, she'd been certain the guard at the gate would be the one to stop her. But he'd collected her guest passes and opened the gate for her with a friendly nod.

During the drive along Interstate 5 to Monroe, she'd wanted to call home and check on everyone. But she'd had nothing to report—except that she'd seen Joe's doctor at the institute. And as far as Vic was concerned, that was practically the same thing as going to the police.

There was a very real possibility Dr. Halstead had already phoned the police about her. But Laura had tried to put it out of her mind. All she could think about was getting back to her children and her mom—and saving them.

That was why she'd bought the gun and the pepper spray. She was her own version of Zared, the great avenging super-mom, armed and ready, rushing home to defend her family.

Then again, Vic would probably search her the minute she came through the door. Or maybe Joe and Vic wouldn't even be there at all, and she'd come through the door to find her mother and children slaughtered.

Laura pressed harder on the accelerator. In the rearview mirror, she watched the gap grow between her and the VW behind her. Some other cars were in back of the Volkswagen, unable to pass it on the two-lane highway. She wondered if one of them was the black BMW.

A few raindrops hit her windshield, and she thought about the mountain pass ahead. She'd just see how bad the snow was when she got there.

Her phone rang, startling her. Obviously, something had happened at the house. Was one of the kids hurt?

Without taking her eyes off the road, she reached for

the phone in her cup holder. She had to hold it up to her face so she could see where to switch it to talk mode. "Yes?" she said anxiously.

"So—which are you?" a woman asked.

"Pardon?" Laura didn't recognize the voice. "Who is this?"

"Which are you?" the woman asked again. "Are you Randall Meacham's mother—like you told my roommate? Or are you Laura, the girl who's moving into my room at Birnam Wood—like you told my mother? Funny, you both seem to have the same phone number. So which one are you?"

Laura tightened her grip on the wheel. "Courtney?"

There was silence—and a little static—on the other end.

"Listen, I'm sorry I had to resort to lying," Laura said. "It's just that I've been desperate to talk to you."

"Well, you're not a very good liar," Courtney said, her tone still icy. "You told my mother that my roommate was going out of town. All it took was one call to Lisa to find out that it wasn't true—and that she'd had a visitor this afternoon."

"I'm not with the church," Laura said.

"That's what Lisa told me. So—who are you and what do you want?"

"Well, Laura is my real name," she said, watching the road ahead. Raindrops accrued on the windshield, but not enough to switch on the wipers yet. "I'm trying to find out who killed Scott Singleton and his family. I don't think it's this Joe Mulroney the police are after. I believe it might have been someone connected to the church. Maybe it's somebody with an ax to grind or a cover-up of some kind. People associated with that church have been dying or disappearing for a month now. And I think you might know something."

"If you're not with the church, who are you? Are you with the police?"

"No, I—"

"Then why does it concern you so much?"

"I was Joe Mulroney's teacher back when he was a child," she said. "I helped him once. He got in touch with me, hoping I'll help him again. He says he's innocent, and I believe him. At least, I want to believe him."

"Where are you right now?" Courtney asked. Her voice came through a bit choppy.

Laura hesitated. For all she knew, this Courtney person could still be in cahoots with the church. She could have had a direct connection to the deaths of Eric Vetter, the Singleton family, and maybe even Martha. Laura squirmed in the driver's seat. "Why do you need to know where I am?" she asked warily. "Can't we just talk over the phone?"

"No, we can't."

"Why not?"

"Well, for one, the reception's shitty," Courtney said. "I can hardly hear you. And second, I'm not telling you a thing over the phone. I'll meet you someplace. It sounds like you're in your car . . ."

"Yes," Laura admitted. She checked the rearview mirror again. She realized she must have slowed down, because the vehicles behind her were catching up. "I'm on my way to central Washington."

"So where? Moses Lake? Wenatchee?"

"I'm about two hours away from Wenatchee," Laura

said. "I couldn't get there until eleven-thirty at the earliest."

"Well, that's fine with me. I'm not sleeping much lately anyway. There's a bar called Irv's Lounge on Wenatchee Avenue, and it's open late. I'll meet you there at eleven forty-five."

Laura thought about how this meeting would delay her return home. At the same time, if Courtney could tell her something that would prove Joe's innocence, then it might save her family. "All right," Laura said. "I don't know what you look like, but I have on a navy blue pea jacket and—"

"Lisa told me what you look like," Courtney interrupted. "I'll find you."

"Before you hang up, could you tell me something?" Laura asked.

"What is it?"

"Do you think Joe Mulroney is innocent?"

"Put it this way," Courtney replied. "If I thought the Singletons were randomly murdered by some nutcase who was their caretaker, I certainly wouldn't be in hiding now—and I'd be sleeping a lot better. See you in a couple of hours."

She hung up.

Tuesday—10:17 P.M.
Leavenworth

On the other side of the door, Joe could hear the little boy still crying.

He stood in the hallway, outside Sophie's bedroom. The crowbar was wedged in the doorway frame. The three kids and the grandmother had been in there for the last two and a half hours.

"Please, we have to get Liam to a hospital!" he heard the grandmother plead. "For God's sake, he needs a doctor. He keeps having these convulsions—and his breathing . . ." She started to cry. "I'm worried he might slip into a coma. *Both* of these children need a doctor. Sophie's eye is practically swollen shut. Are you even listening to me?"

"I—I hear you, ma'am," he replied, leaning close to the door. "I need to check with Vic."

"He's the one who did this to them! Can't you think for yourself? My daughter helped you once, and it cost her dearly. How can you sit still and let this happen to her children?"

Joe closed his eyes and winced. "I'll see what I can do!" he called. Then he turned and hurried down the hallway toward the stairs.

He knew the boy wasn't well. Joe had carried him up the stairs earlier. And it was true what the grandmother said about his breathing. It sounded like a death rattle. Both the grandmother and Sophie had told him that the EpiPen was just a temporary fix for someone going into shock. Joe had given Sophie a Baggie full of ice for her eye, and helped her up the stairs. Her walking had been a little wobbly. Over little James's terrified screams she'd kept saying that Liam needed to go to the hospital.

But Vic had refused to let anyone leave the house.

Joe found him downstairs in the dining room, crouched over the lower cabinet of the built-in hutch. He was loading items into a Safeway grocery bag.

"Look at this thing," Vic said, holding up a small silver tray. " 'Sterling,' it says on the back. You know what that means? Big bucks, that's what. We're sitting on a gold mine, here—or a silver one. Some of this crystal shit is worth a lot of money, too."

Joe was a little out of breath. "Vic, we need to let the grandmother drive Liam to the hospital. He could die."

Vic shoved the tray in the grocery bag, which clanked when he moved it. "You know, I don't feel so hot right now either. When that little bitch stuck me with that pen, some leftover shit might've still been in there. I read the warning label on the other pens in the kitchen drawer, and they said if a normal person gets stuck with one of those needles, they need to go to the hospital, too. I feel woozy, but I'm riding it out here. The kid can ride it out here, too. I mean, he wasn't even bleeding. And I was bleeding like a stuck pig for a while there . . ."

"You weren't bleeding that much," Joe murmured. He figured if his friend was really feeling *woozy*, it was because he'd had four or five glasses of wine. "Vic, we've got to let the grandmother and Liam go. They won't say anything to the police—not if Sophie and the little boy are still here."

"God, listen to yourself, worried about some stupid brat," Vic said, inspecting a fancy, cut-glass bowl. "Hell, what difference does it make? He's going to die anyway . . ."

"What do you mean?" Joe asked.

"Oh, come on, kiddo. It's over." Vic tossed aside the glass bowl and examined a pair of silver salt and pepper shakers. "Your old teacher played her last card. She didn't talk to the waitress. Hell, for all we know, Martha's just fine, and your precious Mrs. Gretchell is lying through her teeth. Either way, she didn't live up to her end of the bargain. It's just a matter of time before she realizes she's lost all her bargaining power, and she'll call the cops. Once we get the old bag's car loaded, I'll go upstairs and shoot them. You don't have to be a part of it. You can wait in the car—"

Joe shook his head. "No, I won't let you. Why are you so bent on killing them? It wasn't supposed to be this way. We came here for help. Mrs. Gretchell practically saved my life when I was a kid—"

"How many times do I have to hear about that?" Vic groaned. "I saved your ass plenty of times at the country club. I sprung you from that hotel, where the cops were putting the screws to you. I'm in a lot of deep shit because of you . . ."

"No, I'm in deep shit because of *you*!" Joe argued. "Mrs. Gretchell was right about that. Why didn't you take her up on her offer? It was a sweet deal, Vic. You could make a clean getaway with a huge head start over the cops. And no one would get hurt . . ."

Joe heard someone pounding again on the bedroom door upstairs. The grandmother cried out to him.

"Shut the fuck up!" Vic shouted at the top of his voice.

It turned quiet.

Vic turned to him again. "If you let me handle everything, we can be out of here within fifteen minutes. Three hours from now, we'll be in Montana or Idaho, a couple of amigos on the run . . ."

The phone inside Vic's pocket rang.

With a sigh, he pulled out Mrs. Gretchell's smartphone and answered it: "Yeah, what?"

Joe leaned in close to Vic so he could hear her, too.

"I'm approaching Stevens Pass, and it's snowing," she said—through some choppy static. "Can you hear me?"

Joe spoke up: "I can hear you, Mrs. Gretchell."

He wondered what he would tell her when she asked to talk to her mother or one of the kids.

"I got a call from Courtney Furst," she said. Her voice kept going in and out. "She's agreed to talk with me. We're meeting in Wenatchee in about ninety minutes. Joe, she thinks you're innocent. Did you hear me? I'll try to persuade her to go to the police. And even if . . ." They lost the connection for a moment.

"Mrs. Gretchell?" Joe said.

". . . I can still talk to the police on your behalf. They'll have to listen. It's good news, Joe."

"Show her my sketches," Joe said.

"What did you say—*sketches*?" Mrs. Gretchell said. "We have a terrible connection. Yes, I'm going to see if she recognizes the man in your sketches—if that's what you just said."

"Good," Joe said. "Thank you . . ."

"Joe, about the man in your drawings, are you sure his name was Zared? I mean, did you actually hear Scott Singleton call him by that name?"

Joe hesitated. He wasn't sure what she was getting at.

"Joe, you seemed so sure someone named Zared killed the Singletons. And I have a feeling that's not the man's name—or the killer's name. Is it possible you were confused?"

"Maybe," he shrugged. "I—I guess I'm not so sure anymore."

"If he told you that was the guy's name," Vic jumped in, "then that was his name. What is this bullshit?"

"It's good news for Joe, that's what it is," she replied through the static. "Can I talk to Sophie, please?"

Joe cringed and turned to his friend. "Well, Mrs. Gretchell, before you talk to her, I need to tell you that something happened . . ."

Glaring at him, Vic shook his head.

"Joe?" Mrs. Gretchell said. "You're . . . in and out. I can't hear . . . this stupid phone . . . Joe, are you . . ."

Then the line went dead.

Tuesday—10:22 P.M.
Stevens Pass

Laura held the cheap little phone near the steering wheel so she could press redial without taking her eyes off the road. Maybe it was her frayed nerves or the awful reception, but she'd had a feeling something had happened at home. She needed to call back and hear Sophie's voice. She wanted her daughter to tell her that she was *tired*.

But in the little window on the phone was the message: *No Service*.

A horn blared as a car sped past on the left and then cut in front of her.

Laura didn't realize until now how much she'd slowed down.

"I'm sorry, I'm sorry, I'm sorry," she whispered

anxiously. She set the phone back in the cup holder, and then she pressed harder on the accelerator.

The winding, narrow road was covered by a light blanket of snow with little land mines of black ice. Her headlights didn't catch the icy patches. They just sort of snuck up on her, and then she'd suddenly feel the car sliding out of control for a few seconds. The snow came down thick—not quite blizzard conditions, but close. The wipers and the defroster kept most of the windshield clear, but flakes had accumulated to create blind corners on both sides. At her right were tall snow-drifts and the mountain wall. At the left, the oncoming traffic seemed to speed by, the headlights momentarily blinding her. The cars were few and far between, thank God. There weren't too many people stupid enough to attempt the pass under these conditions right now. On the other side of the westbound lane was a low, snow-capped guardrail along a precipice—and beyond that, Laura could see the white-trimmed treetops of tall evergreens.

Both hands clutching the wheel, she checked the rearview mirror. There were only a couple of cars be-hind her in the distance. The second vehicle looked like a black BMW, but she couldn't be certain.

She sped up a little, and heard the slush spraying under her tires. The engine hummed louder as she climbed up toward the summit. She glanced at the speedometer: fifty-three miles per hour. She felt like she was pushing the envelope. Any minute now, she could hit another patch of ice and spin out.

Laura felt sick to her stomach and her head throbbed.

Most of it was tension. Or maybe it had something to do with the fact that the last thing she'd eaten was the bowl of scalding chicken noodle soup Martha had served to her over ten hours ago.

She remembered the man at the nearby table, the one with the pecan waffle. What had made her think of him now?

Up ahead, she saw a car on the narrow shoulder, spun out and half in the ditch. Its hazard lights were blinking. Laura slowed down to pass it.

In the rearview mirror, she noticed the first car behind her closing the gap between them. She tried to get a better look at the vehicle in back of it. "Shit," she murmured.

It was definitely a black BMW. She couldn't see any other cars behind it.

She sped past a sign by the snowdrifts: *Passing Lane – 1000 Feet.*

As the lane opened up, she noticed two more vehicles had either spun out or pulled over. Laura signaled, and then steered over into the slow lane. The car trailing her pulled forward and zoomed past on her left. Biting her lip, Laura checked the mirror again. The black BMW seemed to be gaining speed.

"Pass me," she whispered, slowing down. "Please, just pass me."

The BMW's headlights loomed closer and larger in her side mirror. But then—just as it pulled up two car-lengths behind her, the BMW seemed to lock in position. It hovered there in the passing lane.

"What are you doing?" Laura murmured, checking

in the mirror again. She slowed down to forty-five miles an hour. "Why don't you pass me? What are you trying to do?"

Then she realized what the driver was trying to do. He wanted to keep following her—maybe even run her off the road.

Passing Lane Ends – 1000 Feet, said the sign ahead.

Laura pressed harder on the accelerator. She hit an ice patch and felt a little skid that made her stomach lurch. But she kept a tight, white-knuckle grip on the wheel until the car seemed to right itself. Then she signaled.

In the side mirror, she noticed the BMW speed up.

"Son of a bitch," she muttered, pressing harder on the gas. The pedal was almost against the car floor. She was running out of road ahead.

The engine roared as she turned the wheel and swerved in front of the pursuing BMW. The snow hurtled toward her windshield almost faster than the wipers could brush it away. It felt like the tires were gliding on ice—toward oncoming traffic in the other lane. Laura was certain she'd smash into an SUV heading her way. Squinting at the headlights, she rode out the skid and moved back into her lane. All the while, her heart felt like it was about to explode in her chest.

Laura glanced at the rearview mirror again. The BMW was closing up the small gap between them.

It was the same car she'd seen at the gun store in Monroe, the same car she'd seen by Martha's townhouse on Lopez Island. Laura was almost certain now. She remembered Martha in her bathtub—with her head bashed in. Did they have something like that in mind for her? Was she slated to die in some "accident" on Stevens Pass?

The fire that swept through Eric Vetter's cabin last month and killed him—that had been an *accident*, too. These people were experts.

The BMW's brights went on. The harsh light seemed to illuminate the interior of her Sienna. It reflected off her windshield, too. In her mirrors, she couldn't see anything but a blinding glare. The BMW sped up again—so close that Laura suddenly couldn't see its headlights anymore.

All at once, the BMW slammed against her rear bumper. Laura felt the car jolt—and once again, she had no control over it. The BMW was in command, steering her toward the oncoming lane.

Stiff-armed, Laura held on to the wheel and pushed down on the gas. Her car lurched forward and she swerved back toward her lane. But she hit some ice. The car kept veering toward the side of the mountain. She grazed the snowbank and winced at the scraping sound. A spray of snow and ice hit her windshield.

She steered back into her lane and checked the mirror again.

The BMW wouldn't give up. The light from its high beams filled her car again. Then she felt another jolt as the vehicle hit her rear bumper once more. She heard its engine whining and the tires humming.

"You goddamn son of a bitch!" Laura screamed.

In the westbound lane, a semi-truck came around a curve in the road and barreled toward her.

The BMW pushed her across the yellow line into the truck's path.

The semi's horn blared like a siren.

With tears in her eyes, Laura jerked the wheel to one side. She overcompensated and felt the car buck and shake as she brushed against the snowdrifts again.

The BMW careened past her, hurtling out of control. With its tires screeching, the black car slammed into the truck at full force. Over the semi's wailing horn, there was a loud, sickening crunch of metal and glass.

Laura didn't know what instinct kept her from stopping the car. She merely slowed down and stared in the side mirror at the wreckage blocking the highway behind her. What she saw of the BMW wasn't even recognizable—just a huge mass of twisted metal affixed to the dented cab of the semi. Smoke spewed from the rubble. All the while, the snow kept falling, quiet and constant.

Laura could hardly breathe, she was so rattled. She wanted to stop and call 9-1-1.

But then she remembered she couldn't get a signal on Vic's pay-as-you-go phone. And she couldn't afford to stop—or involve herself with the police.

Laura pressed on, practically alone on the mountain highway—except for an occasional car in the westbound lane.

It was ten or fifteen more minutes until she heard the ambulance and police sirens. The emergency vehicles sped by in the oncoming lane—as much as they could speed through the snow and ice.

With a shaky hand, she tried the cell phone again but still couldn't get a signal.

For a long while, Laura was entirely alone on Highway 2. She realized they must have closed off traffic in both lanes because of the accident. It was an eerie, unsettling feeling—as if she were completely alone in the world.

And all she could think about right now were her children and her mom.

CHAPTER TWENTY-SIX

Tuesday—10:51 P.M.
U.S. Highway 2

"Honey, you and Liam both need to go to the hospital," Laura said into the phone.

Hearing what Vic had inflicted on her two children left her rattled—even more so than the highway smashup that had almost taken her life some twenty minutes before. Laura couldn't stop shaking. She tried to stay calm and focused on the road ahead. She had one hand tightly gripping the wheel while she held the phone to her ear.

"Mom, I'm okay," Sophie said. "I'm banged up and *tired*, but I'm okay—only I can't see out of one eye. So I can't drive anywhere. And somebody needs to stay here with James. They're not going to let him go . . ."

"But you could end up with some damage to that eye—"

"Mom, Nana needs to drive Liam to the hospital, it's the only way. You just need to tell her so. Here, let me put her on . . ."

"Wrap it up!" Vic yelled in the background. It

sounded like he wasn't handling the phone as he had been in the previous calls. Laura guessed he was standing in Sophie's bedroom doorway—or perhaps in some far corner of the room—while Joe passed the phone around.

"And no one's leaving this house!" Vic added.

"Honey?" Laura's mother said on the other end. "What's this about a car accident?"

"I'm okay, Mom. I'll tell you later. Listen, Sophie's right. You'll have to drive Liam . . ."

"It's no good. He won't let us go . . ."

"Yes, he will. So like I say, you'll have to drive Liam to the hospital, Mom. Sophie will stay . . ." She started crying. "Tell her I'm proud of her, will you?"

"Oh, sweetie . . ."

"I love you, Mom," she said. "Now, put Joe on and listen in to what I tell him . . ." She quickly wiped her eyes with the back of her hand that held the phone.

Putting the phone to her ear again, Laura heard some murmuring. Then Joe came on the line: "Mrs. Gretchell?"

"Joe, my mother's going to take Liam to the hospital *now*," she said steadily. "I don't want any argument. He's going to die if he doesn't get some medical attention soon. You tell that son of a bitch friend of yours it's the way it's going to be. I'm risking my life to help you, Joe, and I left my children in your care. Neither Liam nor my mother will say anything to the police. And they won't say anything to the doctors to give you away . . ."

"What's she talking about now?" Vic asked in the background.

"I want you to carry Liam out to my mother's car, Joe," she continued. "I'll be passing through Leavenworth in about twenty minutes. I'll check at the Cascade Medical Center, and if they aren't there, I'm not going to Wenatchee. I won't talk to this Courtney person for you. I'll talk to the police. Do you understand me?"

"Yes, ma'am," he muttered. "This wasn't supposed to happen. I'm really sor—"

"Don't apologize, Joe. Just do it," she said.

And for a change, she hung up on them.

Liam sat up on the bed, still rasping and shuddering. But for a few moments, he seemed to focus on his sister as she helped him put on his jacket. He winced. "God, you look like Robert De Niro in *Raging Bull*," he muttered.

"Thanks, I love you, too," Sophie said, buttoning his jacket for him.

Joe could hardly look at her—this pretty girl with a red, swollen, slit-of-an-eye and the harsh, purplish bruise already forming on her cheek. Meanwhile, her brother was helpless, his body racked with tremors. Joe felt responsible for it all.

The grandmother was already outside, warming up the car.

Amazingly, throughout everything, the little boy remained asleep in the other twin bed.

Vic stood in the hallway, glowering in at him. He had the crowbar in his hand.

Joe came to the bed and scooped Liam up in his

arms. He watched the boy's head as he carried him through the doorway. Before turning down the hall-way, he glanced at Vic.

"I don't see why you're letting that bitch call all the shots," his friend muttered. "She's not your teacher anymore. You're a grown man."

"It's the right thing to do, Vic," Joe said. He looked back at Sophie, who tiredly plopped down on the bed. She stared back at him with her one good eye.

Vic shut the door. "It's just fine with me," he said under his breath. "I didn't want those other two around. They were just in the way."

"What are you talking about?" Joe whispered.

Vic wedged the crowbar in Sophie's doorway. Then he turned and gave him a tiny smile. "The one I'm really interested in is still here."

"Liam's doing much better, Mrs. Gretchell," said the chubby, sandy-haired twentysomething nurse. He wore blue hospital scrubs and carried a clipboard. He walked Laura down the short corridor in the Urgent Care Unit of the Cascade Medical Center. "We want to keep him here for the night just to be on the safe side," he continued. "The doctor's with another patient right now, but she'll come talk to you in just a few minutes. Here we are . . ."

Laura stepped into the small, dimly lit room. Liam was sitting up on a gurney-bed. He wore a pale green hospital gown and his left arm was hooked up to a com-puter monitoring his vital signs. The large machine on wheels stood on one side of him. On the other side sat her mother—with Liam's clothes folded up in her lap.

Liam looked pale, but he gave her a smile. "Hi, Mom."

Unable to hold back the tears, Laura rushed to his side and embraced him. At the same time, she knew he was sort of fragile. And she was careful not to dislodge the cuff around his arm or the metal clip on his index finger. "Oh, my baby . . ." she cried.

"God, Mom, don't . . . I'm okay . . ."

"He's going to be all right, Mrs. Gretchell," she heard the nurse say.

The young man had no way of knowing just why she was this upset.

Laura had been alone in the car for most of her previous teary breakdowns. She knew she should be holding it together for Liam and her mom, but she couldn't help it. She was just so thankful to see them here—out of harm's way at last. And of course, she couldn't help thinking of Sophie and James, still at the house, still at the mercy of that monster.

"I'll tell the doctor you're here," the nurse said. Then he retreated down the corridor.

Laura hugged her mother fiercely. She felt her mom's warm, familiar caress on her back and listened to the sound of her jangling bracelets.

"The doctor said Sophie saved his life with the EpiPen," her mom said. Then her voice dropped to a whisper. "We haven't said anything. We told the doctor a friend of Liam's came over for dinner and slipped the nuts into his food as a joke."

Laura dug some Kleenex out of her purse and blew her nose. "How are Sophie and James?"

"Her eye looks really scary," Liam said.

Laura's mother nodded. "It's true, the poor thing. When I think of her and James there at the house with those two . . ."

Laura didn't want to think about it, because she'd probably have another breakdown and not want to go on with what she needed to do.

"I just wish I'd seen her stick my EpiPen into that creep's neck," Liam said. "I'd give a million bucks for a recording of that . . ."

"You and me both, sweetie," Laura said. She took hold of her mother's hand. "Listen, Mom, I need you to stay here with Liam. If you can't stay in the room with him, I want you to sit in the lobby."

"Are you headed back to the house?" her mother asked.

She shook her head. "I'm going to Irv's Lounge in Wenatchee to meet this woman. And to be completely honest, I'm not exactly sure what I'm walking into. For all I know, this young woman could be setting me up . . ."

Her mother shook her head. "Oh, Laura, honey, then don't go . . ."

"I've got to," she said. "If everything goes well, I'll call here at twelve-fifteen and let you know that I'm okay. If I haven't phoned by then, you call me . . ." Laura bit her lip. "Oh, but you don't have the number, do you?"

She took out her phone and a pen and then scribbled the cell number on the back of a reminder card from her dentist. She handed the card to her mother. "Here, Mom. If I don't pick up, it means you'd better get ahold of the police. But first call my regular phone. You know the number. Make sure they let you talk to Sophie. Tell her that I said *I'm praying for her*. It's code, Mom. If she hears that she'll know the police are on their way."

Her mother nodded nervously. "*You're praying for her*. Okay."

"As soon as you hang up with Sophie, call the police and tell them everything."

Her mother grimaced. "Laura, honey, don't you think it would be safer just to call the police now? Have them meet with this woman in Wenatchee . . ."

Laura shook her head. "If Courtney's on the level, I don't want to scare her off. She might be the only one who knows who killed the Singletons and why. Besides that, I don't want to send the police to the house. Vic said the minute he sees a policeman on the property—"

"Yes, I know," her mother interrupted, frowning. "I heard him say it a couple of times . . ."

"You've been around him for most of the day. Do you believe him?"

Her mother hesitated, then sighed and squeezed her hand. "Be careful, sweetie."

Laura kissed her mom good-bye. "Tell the doctor I'm sorry I missed her."

After she hugged and kissed Liam, she hurried back to the nurse at the front desk. She asked for the phone number there so she could check in later. She grabbed a flyer about flu vaccines off the desk and scribbled the number on it.

Laura's next request got a puzzled look from the woman at the desk. But she turned to her computer, typed something on the keyboard, and then gave Laura directions to Irv's Lounge in Wenatchee.

A few minutes later, Laura was driving through Leavenworth's town center—all aglow with white Christmas lights. It was snowing gently, but the roads were still clear. Laura reached the intersection on Highway 2 where, from this direction, she usually took a left to go home. The house was just ten minutes away.

It took everything in Laura's power not to make that turn.

Instead, she continued straight and pressed harder on the accelerator.

Wenatchee was a half hour away.

"We've only got about an hour," Vic said. He set the glass of beer down on the kitchen counter-bar. "So drink up, we still have a lot to do . . ."

On the other side of the counter-bar from his friend in the kitchen, Joe warily gazed at the beer. Vic had said something earlier about how he should take the edge off, sit down, and have "one for the road." But Joe couldn't sit down. He was too stressed. And he was an extreme lightweight when it came to drinking, Vic knew that. Joe wanted to keep his wits about him for the next few hours. So he merely took a sip.

"I don't think the old bag or the kid will talk to the cops for a while. So we're safe." Vic took a swig of his beer and then set down the glass. "I say we load up the dead guy's pickup. It's a piece of shit, but it should get us to Spokane or Yakima. Once we're there, I can steal a car for us. You know those pills I got that calm you down when you're freaking out? We'll give one to the little brat to knock him out. And we'll tie the girl to the bed. No one will get hurt. By the time Teach gets back from Wenatchee, we'll be well on our way."

"But she's going to Wenatchee for me, Vic," Joe said, pacing back and forth the length of the counter-bar. "This Courtney person might have information to prove I'm innocent."

Vic rolled his eyes. "Oh, Jesus, would you just own up to it? I don't care if you killed them. You don't have to lie to me. Go ahead and lie to your old teacher and send her on this *snipe hunt* for a witness who'll clear your name. I get it. You don't want her to think you're a bad guy. But I know you killed those people . . ."

"I don't think I did, Vic," Joe said.

"Man, it doesn't make any difference to me if you offed some family. You had just cause. That Singleton guy drugged and raped you. Hell, until I heard about that today, I wasn't really sure why you'd killed them all. But damn, now it makes perfect sense."

Joe shook his head. "Vic, I think I'd know if something happened—even with the drugs and all. I think I'd know if I'd been violated."

Vic snorted. "Huh, *violated*."

"It's not funny," Joe said. "Okay, so Mr. Singleton drugged me, and that explains why I slept through everything. And maybe he wanted to rape me or whatever. But I think before he actually did anything, this guy broke in and killed everybody. I don't think Mr.

Singleton even left the study. That's where I last saw him that night, and that's where I found his body the next morning. And another thing, Vic, when I woke up that morning, I still had my clothes on from the night before. I swear, I don't think he ever touched me."

Vic frowned at him. He actually looked disappointed.

"To be totally honest," Joe murmured. He stopped pacing. "When I found them all dead the next morning, I thought you might have done it, Vic."

His friend took another gulp of his beer. "You saw the Seven-Eleven video . . ."

"Yeah, but for a while, I thought you could have done it."

"Well, that video clears me." Vic chuckled. "I think of all the crap you gave me about not shoplifting or causing trouble while I was in town on Lopez. Well, stealing those beers and making trouble on camera in that Seattle store got me out of a murder rap—and I didn't even know it. What a stroke of luck. They could have framed me, too. My prints are all over that house, and like you were constantly reminding me, people in town on Lopez saw me hanging around." He raised his glass. "Let's drink to luck . . ."

Joe hesitated. But then he raised his glass and sipped the beer.

"C'mon, you can do better than that," Vic said. "Chug it."

But Joe put the glass down, and he started pacing again. He wondered how his friend could be so calm when, according to him, they had less than an hour to get out of there. It didn't make any sense. With everything happening right now, Vic wanted to stand there, drink beer, and chew the fat.

Didn't Vic feel the time crunch? Joe felt it, because he didn't want anything going wrong when Mrs. Gretchell returned. He wanted Vic out of the house and long gone.

He wanted *Vic* out of the house.

Joe suddenly realized that he really didn't want to go with him.

"Vic, Mrs. Gretchell was right," he said. "The deal she offered you was really nice. We—we need to split up, you and I. It's the only way. Why don't you take that dead guy's car and hit the road now. It'll give you a head start. I'll stay here and make sure no one calls the cops for two or three hours, however long you need."

"Shit, you really must be crazy, kiddo. You think the police will go easy on you? You'll get into a shit-load of trouble for aiding and abetting. And that's just for starters."

"I don't care," Joe said, "as long as it's not murder."

"Sit still for a couple of minutes. Finish your beer."

Joe shook his head. "I can't."

Vic frowned. "So—after all I've done to save your ass, you're ready to split up, just like that?"

Joe finally stopped pacing and gave him a weak smile. "It would be the last time you'd have to save my ass, Vic."

His friend stared at him, and then laughed. "Okay, yeah, sure, fine." But the smile ran away from his face. "Only you have to promise me a few things. Before I leave, I'm taking some of the silver and crystal. I'll need to hock it for cash later. Also, like I said before, we'll have to slip the little brat a downer—or at least half a pill—just to make sure he doesn't wake up and start bawling before mama gets home. And his sister upstairs, the princess, we still need to tie her up. Once I leave, you've got to promise me that the bedroom door will stay closed and barred. I don't want you talking to her or anything. You're such a sap. I can see her luring you into the room and using the kid as bait. *He's sick,* or some such shit—and *bam*, she'll clobber you over your fat head with something. And she'd have the cops here before I even reach the highway. She's a sneaky, resourceful little bitch. So promise me, she stays tied up until her mama gets home. And for the duration, you stay clear of her. That's non-negotiable."

Joe balked at the idea of doing anything else to the poor girl. She'd been through enough. But if it got Vic out of the house, then Joe would help tie her up.

He looked at his friend and nodded. "Okay, I promise."

"Drink up!" Vic said. He opened a couple of drawers until he found the dish towels. He grabbed a bunch and set them on the counter. Then he pulled out his switchblade, clicked it open, and started cutting strips from the towels.

Joe realized Vic was fashioning restraints out of the rags—for Sophie.

"Why aren't you drinking?" Vic asked. "You aren't going to have one last beer with me?"

Though he didn't want it, Joe took a big gulp. "Um, I—I thought I heard a car," he lied. "But maybe not . . ."

Vic stopped working on the towels and headed toward the front of the house.

Joe quickly moved into the kitchen and poured his beer down the sink drain.

"False alarm," Vic announced, returning to the kitchen.

Joe was holding the empty glass to his lips. He set it on the counter. "Boy, I shouldn't have drunk that so fast," he murmured.

"Pussy," Vic chuckled. With his knife, he went back to making strips from the dish towels. "We weren't thinking ahead. We knew we'd probably have to tie up a few people. Before we came here, we should have bought some rope—and tape."

Joe listened to the ripping sound as his friend tore up the towels.

"I'll bet they have rope and tape down in the basement," Vic continued, with his back to him. "We should have looked for some before I nailed shut the door. Oh, well, last time we ever make that mistake . . ."

Joe gazed at his friend hunched over his work.

"Yes," he murmured. "The last time . . ."

CHAPTER TWENTY-SEVEN

Tuesday—11:48 P.M.
Wenatchee, Washington

I rv's Lounge was a dive.

Walking into the hole-in-the-wall tavern off Wenatchee's main drag, Laura wasn't sure who she should be looking for. She didn't see any college-age girls at the bar, at the tables, or in any of the booths—at least not at first glance. There weren't any women over near the two pool tables either. The tavern's cheaply paneled walls were decorated with neon beer signs and tinsel garlands of red and green that had seen better days. Several of the mini-bulbs were burnt out on the strings of Christmas lights strung around the bar. The place looked pretty dead.

Yet Laura could hear people laughing and hooting, and a woman singing a drunken, off-key rendition of Linda Ronstadt's "You're No Good." Someone yelled at her, "*You're* no good!" That got a big laugh. Laura couldn't tell where all the noise came from. The TV by the bar was showing a foreign soccer game on mute.

She was a few minutes late, but wondered if she'd

made it there before Courtney. Or maybe Courtney never had any intention of meeting her—and this was just a waste of time.

Laura had been standing by the door for so long that a skinny, middle-aged waitress approached her. She had a bad perm and smelled like cigarettes. "If you're here for karaoke, it's upstairs."

"Oh, thank you," Laura said. "Actually, I was looking for a girl—around college age . . ."

"So's most every guy in the joint, honey," said the waitress. She nodded toward the pool tables at the other end of the bar. "Try upstairs."

Laura glanced over at the booths as she walked toward the alcove on the other side of the pool tables. She didn't see anyone—except a sad-looking older couple who were drinking and not talking to each other.

In the dark alcove, Laura passed by the restrooms and headed up a grimy stairway. She kept thinking that Courtney might have set her up. Maybe instead of finding Courtney here, a man looking very much like "Zared" from Joe's sketches would find her. Laura kept thinking about her conversation with Courtney earlier tonight—along Highway 2. While the black BMW must have been following her for quite a while, it didn't start to approach her until minutes after she'd told Courtney where she was.

Then again, maybe that was just a coincidence.

The second floor of Irv's was where it was all happening. The place was crowded and noisy with drunken patrons. At the standing microphone on the karaoke stage, a stocky, middle-aged man in a cowboy hat had taken over for the woman who had been butchering "You're No

Good." He sang a passable rendition of "Ring of Fire." The room had its own bar, more neon beer signs on the walls, and more tacky Christmas decorations.

Laura scanned the faces of the patrons sitting at the bar and at the tables. She didn't see any college-age girls. Nor did she see any men who looked like the subject of Joe's drawings.

"Buy you a drink, pretty lady?"

Laura turned and stared at the short, balding, middle-aged man who looked like Danny DeVito. He'd snuck up to her side.

"No, but thank you," Laura said. "I'm here looking for a friend."

"Aren't we all?"

Laura worked up a weak chuckle and then turned away. She figured she was better off waiting for Courtney downstairs.

Halfway down the steps, she heard someone behind her. "Are you Laura?"

She swiveled around to see a woman in a blue eiderdown vest, skinny jeans, and a knit cap. With one hand on the banister, she stared down at her.

"Courtney?" Laura asked.

She nodded. "Are you here alone?"

"Yes."

"Anyone follow you here?"

"I don't think so," Laura said. "At least, I haven't noticed anyone for the last half hour or so."

"Good. Let's talk downstairs. There are more exits— in case I need to leave in a hurry."

They sat in one of the booths. Courtney wanted to be facing the front door so she could check any new arrivals. She seemed extremely nervous. The waitress took their drink orders. Laura asked for a club soda. Courtney ordered a gin and tonic, then sat back in the booth and unzipped her eiderdown vest. But she left the knit cap on. Some of her blond hair wasn't completely hidden by it. She didn't seem to be wearing any makeup. She looked a bit rough around the edges. But Laura imagined Courtney with her hair down and just a little mascara and lipstick—and she was probably a knockout.

"So—did you really know Joseph Mulroney when he was a child?" she asked.

Laura nodded. "As I told you, I was his teacher. I was pretty surprised to hear from him out of the blue this morning."

Courtney let out a little laugh. "I'll bet. So—what did you want to ask me?"

"Joe insists he didn't kill the Singletons. I thought you might have a pretty good idea who did."

"Maybe," Courtney allowed. "My roommate, Lisa, said you claimed to be Randall Meacham's mother. So I'm guessing you talked to some kids at Western and ended up getting an earful from Randall. Is that how you heard my name?"

Laura nodded. "He said you handled a lot of the recruiting for the church and you were—pretty intimate with both Eric Vetter and Scott Singleton."

As soon as the words had come out of her mouth, Laura regretted it. If Courtney was still working with the church, if she was involved in any of the recent deaths, how long would it be before Randall had an unfortunate, fatal accident?

"Well, that Randall sure likes to talk, doesn't he?"

Courtney said. "But he's right. I met Eric and Scott four years ago. They were at Lake Chelan for some conference. I was working as a maid in the resort where they stayed. I guess you could say Scott just sort of swept me off my feet. Eric made sure I was comfortable and well provided for. Through the church, Eric set me up with a scholarship to Western, and even paid my room and board. Then I started working for the church. I guess Randall told you a bit about how we recruited some of the college kids."

Laura nodded.

"Well, that's how Eric recruited me. Did Randall tell you about the home movies?"

She nodded again. "Yes."

The waitress returned with their drinks. There was a small, decorative plastic monkey with its tail curled over the rim of Laura's glass.

"How come I didn't get one of those?" Courtney asked no one in particular, since the waitress had already left. She nodded at Laura's club soda. "Could I have the monkey? I kind of collect them."

"Of course." Laura handed it to her.

"Thank you," Courtney said, carefully setting the plastic trinket on the table in front of her. She sipped her gin and tonic. "Anyway, about the movies, I starred in several of them. With the first two, I didn't know I was being filmed at the time. But then Eric told me, and I went along with all the others. I know what you must think. But I would have done anything they wanted me to do. They were paying for my school, and I was crazy about Scott. He told me he enjoyed seeing me with other guys. And Eric, well, he was like a father to me. I never had a father. They were like family, kind of a dysfunctional, incestuous one—but a family just the same . . ."

She stopped talking to study a couple coming into the bar. They walked past the booth and headed to the alcove on the other side of the pool tables. Upstairs, a tone-deaf woman was trying to channel Annie Lennox with her version of "Sweet Dreams (Are Made of This)." At the pool table, someone just broke a new rack of balls.

Courtney squirmed a bit and took another sip of her drink. "Do you know who Lawrence and Marilee Cronin are?"

"They're—or they *were*—Scott Singleton's partners in the church."

"Co-ministers," Courtney said. "They came into the picture about three years ago. They pretty much made Scott and his church into the multimillion-dollar business it is. They knew how to cash in on Scott's name. Eric thought they were a couple of parasites. He never liked them. And Scott, he loathed Marilee. Anyway, Lawrence and Marilee aren't as stupid as they come across on TV. It didn't take them long to figure out what Eric and Scott were doing with some of the college students they'd recruited. They thought Eric was a major liability to the organization, and decided to nip it in the bud by offering him a big chunk of money to dissociate himself from the church—and from Scott. Eric was insulted. But Scott backed the Cronins and told his friend to take the buyout. I remember Eric telling me, 'I'm not taking that hush money and just disappearing like one of his fast fucks.'" Courtney shrugged and took a swig of her drink. "Pardon the language. I usually don't swear . . ."

"It's okay," Laura murmured. It struck her as odd that this young woman who starred in homemade porn movies and drank then apologized for cursing. Maybe that was the side of her that had embraced the church for a while.

Laura stole a glance at her wristwatch. She had to call her mother at the hospital in fifteen minutes. "Please, go on," she said.

"Well, I was very disappointed in Scott," Courtney said. "He sort of dropped me and Eric around the same time. He could have stood up for his friend, but he didn't. He told me that he was going to clean up his act, and I thought, 'Oh, yeah, like fun you will.' I knew he'd go on doing whatever—and whoever—he wanted. He thought he was invincible. He thought the Cronins wouldn't touch him. After all, he was their golden boy. The church would fold without him."

She sipped her drink. "Anyway, so Eric was on his way out. Not only was he a potential embarrassment, but his college recruiting program with the scholarships cost the church a lot more money than it made. The Cronins planned on dropping the program as soon as they got rid of Eric. But Eric wasn't going quietly. He demanded more money—and told Lawrence and Marilee about the DVDs, some of them featuring their golden boy in all sorts of—compromising positions. He told them that some of us Messengers who worked for him could be persuaded to testify that everything we did—however unscrupulous or scandalous—we did for the church."

She sighed and gulped down the rest of her gin and

tonic. "Anyway, it was a dumb move on Eric's part. He didn't know just how deadly serious Marilee and Lawrence were. They have a couple of goons who work for them. Eric called them the two Teds—Ted Houser and Ted Flint. He could never keep straight which one was which. They handle security . . ." Courtney paused to give the word *security* air quotes. "The Teds took care of all sorts of things for the Cronins and the church. They collected money and intimidated former church members to keep their mouths shut. They did the bribing and extorting, and occasionally made certain troublesome people disappear."

"They sound like hit men," Laura said.

Courtney nodded. "That's basically what they were. Not long after Eric told Marilee and Lawrence what to do with their buyout offer, the two Teds paid me a visit at Birnam Wood. They threatened to kill me. They said it would look like an accident." Courtney's voice started quavering. "They said they knew where my mom lived, and they'd pay her a visit if I didn't cooperate. They asked me if I had any of the DVDs. They scared the you-know-what out of me. I told them that Eric and Scott were the only ones who had access to the porn. I said the DVDs were probably at Eric's cabin near La Conner. I promised I wouldn't say anything to anybody. That night, I packed up what I could and left school. I just had to get out of there . . ."

Laura remembered what Randall had told her about a conversation between Doran Wiley and the other recruiter, Ben, that had occurred shortly before Eric Vetter was killed. "Some shit's going down," Ben had said—or words to that effect.

"This was before Eric was killed in the fire, wasn't it?" Laura asked.

Courtney winced and a tear slid down her cheek. "Two days before," she whispered. She wiped her cheek. "I—I can't help thinking I practically sent the Teds to him. I could have lied about where Eric kept the DVDs. Anyway, I'm almost positive that's why they decided to burn the cabin down with him in it. You know, *two birds*, and all . . ."

"It sounds to me like you didn't have any choice," Laura said.

Courtney gave a sad little shrug. "Anyway, I've been pretty much hiding and watching my back ever since. On Saturday, when I heard the news about Scott and his family, I knew who was behind it. Your former student, Joe, I'm sure he didn't do it. The police could've found him covered in blood, holding a knife and standing over Scott's dead body, and I'd still say they had the wrong guy. He couldn't have done it—unless Marilee and Lawrence put him on their secret payroll."

"So—it was the Teds," Laura said, reaching for her purse.

Courtney nodded. "Working for Marilee and Lawrence Cronin."

Laura took out a pen. "What did you say the Teds' last names were?"

"Ted Houser and Ted Flint."

Laura scribbled the names on her cocktail napkin.

"Your former student is innocent." Courtney said. "I mean, for starters, how could he have tied up all those people by himself? And why would he torture Scott?

That's how one of the newscasters described it. They said he was beaten up. I heard that, and I knew. The Teds had to beat it out of him. Most of the DVDs burned in Eric's cabin fire, but Scott still had some. If any of them had been found, it would have been a huge embarrassment to the church. It was like the Cronins sent the Teds to clean Scott's house for them. I could imagine Scott telling them to go to hell when they asked him to surrender those DVDs. I'm sure he finally told them where the DVDs were once they threatened to start killing the wife and kids."

She picked up her glass and shook it. The ice cubes rattled. She slurped down what was left at the bottom of the glass. Upstairs, several people were singing a slightly off-key rendition of "Piano Man."

"Lawrence and Marilee played it really smart," Courtney said. "Scott died a martyr—with an unstained reputation. His children were sacrificial lambs. The church was saved any potential embarrassment. I'm sure donations have gone up since the weekend. The church will continue to be profitable with the Cronins in charge—evoking the memory of *St. Scott*. And your friend—this caretaker with an unstable mental history—he was a bonus they didn't expect, a little gift from heaven."

Laura took Joe's drawings from her purse and unfolded them. "Does this look like either one of the Teds?"

Courtney nodded. "That's him, especially in this one . . ." She pointed to the most detailed sketch. "Those are his eyes, kind of dead and cold. I can't say which Ted it is. I couldn't really tell them apart any more than Eric could. He pointed them out to me at some conference last year. The next time I saw them was when I came home from classes last month, and they were in my living room at Birnam Wood, waiting for me. Like I say, that was the last time, and I hope to never see them again."

Laura folded up the sketches. "Do you know if either of them drives a black BMW?"

"I remember looking out my window at Birnam Wood after they left," Courtney said, staring at her, wide-eyed. "They both got into a shiny BMW and it was black. Why do you ask? Did you recently see a car like that?"

"Yes, earlier today—".

Courtney flinched and gaped at something toward the front of the bar.

Laura glanced over her shoulder and saw that two men had just walked in. They were both around thirty with solid builds. The duo looked like a couple of working-class guys getting off a swing shift someplace. Neither one resembled the man in Joe's sketches. The men headed toward the alcove, but slowed down at the booth to check the two of them out. One smiled at Courtney. But they kept moving and headed into the alcove.

"I'm starting not to feel very safe here," Courtney whispered. She picked up her plastic monkey trinket and slipped it inside the pocket of her eiderdown vest.

Laura nodded and took some money out of her purse for the bill. "If it's any help, I was about to explain that earlier today I saw a black BMW on Lopez Island. I had an appointment with a waitress who said she had information about the murders. The BMW was outside of the waitress's townhouse—and inside, in the bathroom, she was dead. It was made to look like an accident, like she'd slipped in the tub . . ."

Courtney let out a dazed laugh. "How is this *helping*?"

"I'm pretty sure the same BMW followed me all the way to Stevens Pass," Laura explained. She left ten dollars on the table. "A few minutes after I talked to you, the car tried to run me off the road. But it ended up smashing head-on into a semi. The BMW was totaled. If anyone inside that car managed to walk away after what happened, it would be a miracle."

"I'm still a very religious person," Courtney said. "I believe in miracles."

"Does that mean you wouldn't be willing to come forward and tell your story to the police or the press?" Laura asked. "People's lives depend on it, Courtney."

"My life depends on it, too," she replied in a hushed voice. She leaned forward. "I can't pretend that I'm not a little relieved to hear that one or both of the Teds are now facing their final judgment. But they're mere errand boys, following orders from Lawrence and Marilee. If they killed a waitress today, it was because the Cronins wanted her dead. If they tried to run you off the road tonight, it's because Lawrence and Marilee want you out of the way. If the Teds are really gone, they'll just get replaced by another couple of 'security' men. So—as long as Marilee and Lawrence are free and drawing breath, I won't feel safe."

Courtney leaned back and zipped up her eiderdown vest. "And neither should you . . ."

CHAPTER TWENTY-EIGHT

Wednesday, November 29—12:16 A.M.
Leavenworth

"What is that? What are you giving him?"

In her bedroom, Sophie hovered behind Joe, who had a glass of grape juice in one hand and a prescription bottle in the other. He crept toward little James, still asleep in one of the twin beds.

"It's just to make sure he stays asleep for the next hour or so—until your mom gets home," Joe whispered. He set the glass down on Sophie's nightstand and unfastened the top of the bottle. He seemed to have a bit of trouble getting it open. "It's perfectly safe, over-the-counter medication. Vic gives it to me whenever I get too stressed. Don't worry. I'm only giving James a half-dose."

"Well, if it's over-the-counter, why is it in a prescription bottle?" She started to reach for the little container.

"Sit down and be quiet," Vic said with a calm authority that was very out of character for him. His hands behind his back, he leaned against her bedroom door frame. "Joe is James's buddy. He wouldn't do anything to hurt him. This is just to make sure James doesn't wake up and get scared when he sees that you're—incapacitated."

Incapacitated. That was a nice way of saying bound and gagged.

When Joe had first come in and told her a few minutes ago that Vic was leaving, she'd been elated. Vic had agreed to go along with her mother's proposition: he'd hit the road and get a few hours' head start before Joe called the police to turn himself in. The only stipulation was that Sophie had to stay tied up in her room with the door barred for the next forty-five minutes— until her mother came home. "I don't want you pulling any fast ones with Joe once I'm gone," Vic had explained while lurking in her doorway. "With you tied up in the bedroom here and him downstairs, you won't be able to take advantage of his good nature. We all know he's a soft touch. Even Joe knows it, don't you, Joe?"

Sophie loathed the idea of being tied up and helpless. But she'd been so relieved to learn Vic was leaving that she probably would have agreed to be hung upside down from a meat hook for forty-five minutes just to watch him go out the door. Plus, she'd realized, as Joe had nervously laid out the plan, they weren't really asking her permission to do any of this. They just wanted her cooperation. If she didn't go along willingly, Vic probably wouldn't hesitate to knock her unconscious so they could tie her up. With that in mind, Sophie decided to cooperate. Her head had been battered around enough for one night.

That had been only a couple of minutes ago—a couple of minutes to get used to the idea. Joe had left just long enough to run down the corridor, where he must have had the juice and the pills on the table at the end of the hall. Vic had remained in the doorway. He hadn't actually stepped inside her bedroom since punching her in the eye at dinner. Maybe this was so she wouldn't feel threatened. But it had just the opposite effect on Sophie. Seeing him so calm and restrained was truly frightening, because, by now, she knew him. She knew he might be up to something.

Sophie did what she was told and reluctantly sat down. Biting her lip, she watched Joe gently wake up James. Her baby brother was in a stupor and didn't resist as Joe fed him the half pill and had him wash it down with some grape juice. A part of her wondered if it was poison. Were they showing mercy on the young one—and making his death as peaceful as possible?

"See? That wasn't so bad," she heard Vic say. Sophie's back was to him.

She watched little James set his head back down on the pillow and go to sleep again. Joe gently stroked his hair.

Sophie wondered if her little brother would ever wake up.

"Now he'll stay asleep, and there's no risk of him getting up and accidentally hurting himself," Vic said.

Sophie nervously rubbed her arms. Vic's words weren't reassuring at all, not coming from him.

Joe slipped the prescription bottle into his pocket and then turned to her. "I think it's best if you lay down on the bed," he said quietly.

Glancing over her shoulder, she saw Vic with his hands still behind his back. "Facedown," he added. Then he brought his hands out in the open. He had a small bundle of strips fashioned from her mother's dish towels. Some were tied together to create a long, makeshift rope.

In a panic, she turned to Joe and shook her head at him. "No . . . please . . ."

Gently, he put his hands on her shoulders and pushed her down on the bed. "Once I finish tying you up, I'll turn you on your side so it's more comfortable and easier for you to breathe."

Sophie resisted. She kept imagining him saying the same thing to one of the Singleton girls before tying her up and stabbing her to death.

"Don't fight it, Sophie," Vic whispered. "Joe doesn't want to make this unpleasant for you, do you, Joe?" He stepped into the room to hand Joe a few of the long, thin rags they'd tied together.

Joe dropped the first batch of rags, and Vic gave him another handful.

"It's only going to be forty-five minutes," Joe said, taking hold of her wrist.

"Please, wait," she begged, squirming away from him. She was half-sitting up. "I promise, I'll just sit here and not say a word. You don't have to tie me up . . . please . . . don't . . ."

"Now, now, c'mon," Joe said, sitting down beside her. His voice sounded a bit listless. His grip on her wrist slackened, and he seemed to fumble with the makeshift rope. "Don't struggle . . ."

"Look at you, Joe," Vic said. "You're all thumbs. You don't know what you're doing. Let me . . ."

Panic-stricken, Sophie tried to recoil. But Vic grabbed her by the arm and yanked her over on her stomach. All at once, she was facedown on the bed, helpless. As he pulled her hands together behind her, Sophie thought he might break one of her arms or pull it out of its socket. His knee pressed against her back.

"God, Vic, don't hurt her," Joe whined.

Sophie had once seen a YouTube clip of cowboys roping a calf, tying its hooves together with speedy efficiency. It had made her squeamish. Sophie thought of that video clip now as Vic held her down and quickly wrapped the rag-strips around her wrists and ankles. He was so expedient about it, and so powerful. She couldn't move or struggle.

It was over within a couple of minutes.

"Well, that's that," she heard him grunt. He gave a tug at the restraints around her ankles, and then another pull at the rags around her wrists, tied behind her back. It hurt as he suddenly yanked her hands up behind her to test his work one more time. Sophie let out a sharp cry.

The restraints were so tight that they pinched her skin. It felt as if he'd cut off the circulation in her hands and feet.

"Are you okay?" Joe asked. "Did he hurt you?"

"She's fine," Vic answered for her. "C'mon, let's go . . ."

He switched off the overhead light in her bedroom.

Arching her back, Sophie turned her head to see Joe and Vic stepping out into the hallway together. Joe seemed a bit out of it, almost like he was dizzy or drunk. Vic shut the door, and suddenly, Sophie was swallowed up in darkness.

Her heart was racing, and she tried to get a breath. She listened to their footsteps as they headed down the hallway.

"Hey, watch your step there, buddy," she heard Vic say. "You better come in here and sit for a minute. Are you a little light-headed?"

It sounded like they were in her parents' bedroom. Past James's breathing, she thought she heard her parents' mattress squeaking.

"There, take a load off," Vic said. "How do you feel?"

"I'm so tired all of a sudden . . ."

"Why don't you just lie down there for a while?"

"Did you—did you give me something?" Joe asked. Sophie could barely hear him. "Did you slip me—slip me one of those pills we just gave the boy?"

"No, those just chill you out and make you drowsy," Vic answered. "But I have a confession, kiddo. I did put something in your beer earlier. You know how many times I've been in that house on Lopez Island? Well, I knew in swanky digs like that I'd come across some good pharmaceuticals if I only looked hard enough. Well, I found Scott Singleton's private stash in his study. I took down the name on the bottle and collected a few pills for future use. Man, was I surprised when I discovered they were roofies. Shit, until your old teacher said something today, I had no idea he'd slipped you one. Anyway, I held on to them. I figured they'd come in handy someday. So—why don't you just lie down for a few minutes while I take care of some unfinished business down the hall?"

"Wait a minute," Joe muttered. "You gave me a roofie? You said you weren't going to hurt her. No . . ." Then he raised his voice. "No, Vic!"

Vic shushed him.

Horrified, Sophie started squirming on the bed. She tried to jerk her hands free from the cloth restraints.

"Just chill," she heard Vic whisper to his friend. "This way, you won't remember a thing. By the time that stuff completely kicks in, you might even want to join me . . ."

"No, Vic, you promised . . ." His voice sounded weak.

"I know what you're thinking. But I don't care if her face is a mess. I've been itching to get at her ever since I first set eyes on her yesterday . . ."

Sophie kept tugging at the rags around her wrists. She started to cry. The skin under the restraints felt raw from all the friction. Struggling only seemed to tighten the knots Vic had tied. She couldn't feel her fingers.

The pillow under her head became wet with her tears and snot. She kept squirming, and all the while, she could hear him down the hall.

"I'll be doing the little bitch a favor," he said. "I'm sure she doesn't want to die a virgin. And by the time I'm done with her, Mama will be home. I'll kill them both. You won't have to do a thing—just help me load up the car. You won't remember any of it tomorrow. We'll be on the road, Joey, just a couple of outlaws . . ."

* * *

Laura kept checking her rearview mirror. Talking to Courtney had made her even more worried that someone might still be following her. But in the rearview mirror, she didn't see any cars. Highway 2 between Wenatchee and Leavenworth was nearly deserted. Her headlights caught the gentle snowfall and the dark, winding road. Very few people were crazy enough to be out this late at night in this weather.

The drive was lonely and creepy—and she felt as if it might take forever for her to get home. Every few miles, she hit a little patch of ice, jolting her out of the monotony—as if her nerves weren't already frayed enough. She'd had a brief reprieve from the awful loneliness and dread when she'd called the hospital and talked to her mom.

Liam was fine and sleeping in a private room. Her mother had sweet-talked the doctor into letting her sit up with him. They'd offered to get her a cot, but she knew she wouldn't be able to sleep. There was a comfortable chair in the room. And from the lounge, she'd found a magazine with a challenging crossword puzzle to keep her mind off things.

Her mom had asked if she was going to call the police.

"After talking to this girl, I think I have enough information to steer the investigation away from Joe," Laura had told her—through the choppy phone reception. "This girl is ninety-nine percent sure the Singletons were killed by a couple of hit men named Ted. She says Joe had nothing to do with the murders. I think I might be able to persuade him to split with Vic and turn himself in. But I don't know about Vic. I should be home in about a half hour. So—if you don't hear from me in forty-five minutes, call the police and tell them everything."

Before they'd hung up, her mother had kept saying she had a "bad feeling" about what Laura was about to do.

Laura didn't feel too good about it either. But she knew Vic would be true to his word about executing everyone at the first sign of a cop on the property. Her children had a much better chance of surviving if Vic was given a car and a few hours' head start before Joe called the police to turn himself in.

At the same time, she hated the notion that Vic would be out there somewhere, possibly hurting someone else.

Laura hit another ice patch on the road. Her stomach lurched as she felt the car skid for a second. She glanced at the clock on the dashboard: 12:27 P.M. She would be home in about fifteen minutes.

She passed a temporary sign near the turnoff to Highway 97 and Blewett Pass:

**ROAD
CLOSED
AHEAD**
Use Alternate Routes

The orange DETOUR sign alongside it had an arrow directing drivers to Highway 97. Laura figured the police were probably still investigating the head-on collision about forty miles ahead on Stevens Pass.

After that point, she was the only one on the road for a few minutes. She felt a tiny bit better as she passed her regular Safeway. After the long, bleak, dark highway, here was civilization—and something familiar, close to home. She reached over for the phone and punched in her number.

Laura counted the ringtones on the other end. Then her greeting came on. She felt her stomach lurch again—harder this time. All the icy patches along the highway were nothing compared to the helpless feeling she had now. What had happened? Why wasn't anyone picking up?

The beep sounded.

"Joe? Is anyone there?" she said, though she knew her message was going straight to voicemail. "Joe, I had a meeting with this Courtney, who knew Scott Singleton. She's convinced you're innocent, and the murders were committed by a couple of hit men working for Marilee and Lawrence Cronin. Once the police know about this, you'll be off the hook . . ."

Laura was about to say that she'd be home in ten or fifteen minutes. But she hesitated. Maybe she was better off not telling them when she was coming home. "Um, call me, okay?"

She clicked off.

Something had happened. Until Joe called back, she'd have to prepare herself for the worst possible scenario. At the same time, it might be too soon to call the police.

Laura pressed harder on the accelerator. She just needed to get home. She didn't have a plan. But she had the gun and some pepper spray. And since they had no idea how soon she would be there, she had the element of surprise on her side.

So how come she felt as if she was the one in for a horrible surprise?

In the distance, up ahead, she could see the town center with all the white Christmas lights sparkling.

Laura slowed down for the turnoff that led to Rural Route 17—and home.

Lying on her bed in the dark, Sophie listened to Vic moving around the house. He trudged up and then down the stairs. She wasn't sure if he was checking on Joe or stealing more valuables to take with them.

As soon as the two of them had left her alone with James, Sophie had rolled over so that she was on her side. She faced the closed door and kept wiggling her hands and feet. But it still didn't seem to do any good. The restraints were as tight as ever, and the constant tugging only chafed her skin until it burned.

She might have rolled off the bed and tried to find something to cut at the rag-restraints, but Vic had already removed all sharp objects from her bedroom and bathroom. There was nothing she could do but keep struggling—even if it was in vain.

At one point, Vic turned on the TV again—at a normal volume for a change. Sophie could hear some comedian talking and laughter from a studio audience. For a minute, she thought Vic might have parked himself in her father's chair in front of the TV again.

But then she heard the back door open and shut. After a few moments, a car engine started up. She remembered her mother saying that Dane's pickup was parked behind the garage. Sophie realized Vic was getting the vehicle ready for their getaway. It made sense. The police would be looking for her mother's Sienna, not Dane's pickup.

She realized something else. This was probably her only chance to get some help while Vic was out of earshot.

"Joe?" she cried. "Joe, please, wake up!"

Right now, he seemed like her only chance. She tried to lift her head up from the pillow. "Damn it, Joe! Please!" she yelled. "Help me!"

In the twin bed across from her, James stirred and groaned a little.

Sophie heard the pickup's engine purring as Vic pulled up somewhere near the front of the house. She kept calling for Joe, even louder. She knew he'd been drugged. But how could he not hear her? He was just down the hall, and she was screaming.

She remembered all the news stories about how Joe had slept through the Singleton murders—and the shooting that had occurred just below his garage apartment window. Still, she kept crying out his name until she heard the pickup's engine stop.

The vehicle's door opened and shut. A few moments later, she heard the kitchen door slam. Vic was back inside the house.

On the TV, there was another big wave of laughter from the studio audience.

Sophie held her breath and listened.

He was coming up the stairs again. "I'm going to finish what I started with you, girlie," he called softly—in a strange singsong way that made her shudder.

She listened to her bedroom door squeak as he removed the crowbar from the frame. "'Hey, Joe, help me!'" he whispered, imitating her. "'Please, Joe . . .'"

Vic opened the door, and the light from the hall poured in from behind him. Sophie saw his silhouette in the doorway. He held up the baby monitor.

"'Hey, Joe!'" he whispered again. Then he cackled.

"He didn't hear you, Sophie. But I was listening. In fact, I have to admit, it got me kind of hot. So go ahead and scream. I want you to. No one will hear you, except me . . ."

Approaching the driveway, Laura slowed down and switched off her headlights. She leaned in close to the wheel and watched the road ahead. There were no other cars along the route. She navigated in the dark for a few moments until she reached the driveway. After she made the turn, Laura braked for a moment and studied the house in the distance.

Dane's pickup was parked in front. Laura guessed Vic was getting ready to leave—but with or without Joe?

And what about her children?

Everything looked quiet. The living room light was on. Upstairs, the lights were off in Sophie's room and in the master bedroom. But the upper windows weren't completely black, so she figured the upstairs hall light might have been left on.

Laura pulled the car into the driveway, then turned and parked in front of the winery's tasting cottage. She couldn't see the house from here, but they couldn't see her either.

Switching off the engine, she reached for the cell phone and started to dial her number. Maybe they'd answer this time, and maybe Sophie would get on the line and tell her that she was *tired*. Then perhaps they could get through this night without anyone else getting hurt.

But the phone screen light flickered on for a moment, flashing the message: *Low Battery*. Then the light went out. She wasn't even getting a signal.

"What?" she whispered. "Damn it . . ." She hadn't been paying attention to the power grid along the top of the phone screen. She'd figured it had been charged up for the day. Why hadn't she gotten more warning? Her last call had been just fifteen minutes ago. Was that how long the phone had been dead?

For all she knew, Vic or Joe may have tried to call her back. Maybe when they hadn't gotten an answer, they'd thought she had gone to the police.

Laura remembered the old landline in the cottage's closet. She could call them from there.

But Vic wasn't about to pick up a random call—unless he figured out that it was her home phone number. And then she'd only be giving herself away. The whole point to calling was to check on her kids without letting Vic know how close she was. If she called from the cottage, she might as well just walk up to the front door and knock.

Laura decided if she was to use the phone in the cottage, she'd use it to call the police.

But first, she had to know what to tell them. She needed to know what was going on inside her home.

She needed to know exactly where her children were—and if they were still alive.

Laura transferred her house keys from her purse to her coat pocket. Then she reached into the bag on the floor of the passenger side and took out the handgun and the pepper spray. The gun felt so strange in her trembling hand. She carefully slipped it inside the pocket of her peacoat, and tucked the pepper spray into the pocket of her jeans.

The cold night air hit her as she climbed out of the car. A light flurry descended from the dark sky. Laura quietly closed the car door. Then she took a few deep breaths and started to skulk up the long driveway toward the house.

There was just enough light from the hallway for Sophie to see the grin on Vic's face. He stepped into the room, set the baby monitor down on her dresser top, and then reached back for his gun. He put that on the dresser top, too, and sauntered toward her.

Lying on her side, Sophie squirmed helplessly. The mattress squeaked. She lifted her head from the pillow and glared at him. "I know you don't give a damn about waking up my little brother and what he might see, but you don't want Joe hearing us. He's right next door. My mother's out there, helping to prove he didn't kill those people. Do you really think he'll let you do anything to me? I don't care how drugged up he is. He'll stop you, Vic. He might even kill you . . ."

He stood over her in the darkness. "Joe's asleep, honey. He's dead to the world. And he won't remember any of this. Just a few minutes ago, you were screaming for him to help you. I heard you on the baby monitor. He didn't wake up then. He won't wake up now . . ."

"You heard me on the receiver, because the monitor's under my bed," Sophie said, looking Vic in the eye. "But you couldn't hear him answer me—twice. He's half-awake, and if he realizes what you're doing in here, he'll never want anything to do with you . . ."

She kept staring at Vic and wondered if he believed her lie.

Vic said nothing for a moment. He turned and grabbed his gun off the dresser top and tucked it back under his shirttail. Then he came over to the bed, and with one yank, he turned her on her stomach. Then he grabbed her under the arms, pulled her up, and dragged her to the door.

Sophie struggled as he hauled her down the corridor. With her hands and feet tied, she was powerless. Towels and sheets that had been pulled from the linen closet tangled around her feet and left a trail as he kept dragging her along. Just outside the open door to her parents' bedroom, she screamed: "Joe, help! Please . . ."

Vic slapped his hand over her mouth. Sophie tried to bite him. But his hand pressed against her lips so tight she could barely move her jaw.

At the top of the stairs, she tried to throw herself under him in an effort to trip him. Vic merely stumbled. He let go of her and sent her tumbling halfway down the steps. Sophie let out a cry as she landed on her side and bashed her shoulder. It knocked the wind out of her. But the fall had done nothing to loosen her restraints. And the pain was nothing compared to her frustration.

From the second-floor landing, Vic smirked down at her. He wasn't even angry. It was as if he wanted her to put up a fight, and this was just foreplay for him. "Joe's still asleep, Sophie," he said. "But I like your idea of doing it down here in the front room, so I can keep an eye out for your mom. Is that where you and Matt do it when you're alone here?"

Sophie gazed up at him with her one good eye. She shook her head. "Joe!" she screamed at the top of her voice.

Before she could scream his name again, Vic rushed down the steps. Then he gave a little kick and sent her toppling down to the bottom of the stairs.

Laura snuck up to the kitchen window—the one above the sink. She could still see the smudge marks from when she'd wiped away the message she'd written in the steam yesterday morning. That seemed like a week ago.

The kitchen was empty. Vic's backpack sat on the counter-bar. In the family room, the lights were on, and Laura could hear the TV. The sliding glass door's curtains were open, and the darkened glass was like a mirror for the entire room. Sean's recliner was unoccupied. The television was playing to an empty room.

Past the sound of some comedian's spiel on TV, Laura heard a sudden rumble and then a crash. The sounds seemed to come from one of the rooms near the front of the house.

Hurrying over to the kitchen entrance, she pulled at the old screen door. The flimsy little hook lock was fixed in the holder. Laura couldn't believe someone had actually locked the screen door—unless it was Vic, trying to trip up one of her kids in case they attempted a quick escape.

She could hear him now—past the TV. He chuckled. He was talking to someone, but Laura couldn't make out the words.

From her coat pocket, she pulled out her keys and looked at the little replica of a Washington State license plate that spelled MOM. She tried to slip it between the old screen door and the doorframe. But her hand was shaking. "C'mon, c'mon . . ." she muttered impatiently. She finally squeezed the thin plastic trinket through the crack in the door.

Just then, she heard Sophie scream.

For a moment, she was paralyzed.

What was Vic doing to her? She wondered where Joe was—and why he wasn't doing anything to help her daughter.

Tears in her eyes, Laura worked the mini license plate up through the crack and lifted the hook out of its holder. She swung open the screen door and then fumbled with the key in the lock. She knew she had to be as quiet as possible. At the same time, it was all she could do to keep from taking out the gun and shooting off the lock.

She thought she heard a car in the distance, but she

wasn't sure. Practically everything was muddled in her head right now.

Only one thing was clear: Sophie was in there with that animal.

Vic threw Sophie on the sofa, and she screamed.

Again, she landed on her side, banging her other shoulder this time. The restraints continued to chafe and burn the thin skin around her wrists and ankles. She squirmed and writhed on the sofa as Vic hovered over her. He brought his face down close to hers, and she could smell his breath.

Then, past the noise from the TV, Sophie thought she heard a car. It sounded like someone turning into the driveway, but she couldn't be certain.

Vic seemed to hear it, too. He glanced toward the window for a second.

Sophie saw he was distracted, and she knew she had to grab this opportunity. She reeled back and slammed her head into his. She heard an awful crack.

He howled in pain and pulled away.

Sophie struggled to get to her feet but couldn't get her balance. The head slam had her seeing stars. Her ears were ringing. Helpless, she fell back onto the sofa again. The ringing stopped, and she heard the TV—a roar of audience laughter. She heard Vic groaning and grunting.

He came into focus again. Undeterred, he climbed on top of her once more. Blood dripped onto her face.

As Sophie wriggled beneath him, she realized she must have broken his nose. The blood gushed down over his mouth and dripped off his chin. But it didn't stop him. He was almost trancelike in the way he couldn't be stopped. He had a blank expression on his messed-up face as he started to paw at the neck of her T-shirt. His eyes were dead.

"Get away from her, you son of a bitch."

It was her mother talking.

As Vic turned, Sophie peered over his shoulder at her mother. She stood in the front hallway with a gun pointed at him. But Vic didn't move. The blood from his nose dripped onto the front of Sophie's T-shirt.

Her mother nodded toward the front door. "Move away from her now," she said steadily.

Vic laughed—a low, defiant snicker. But he pulled away from Sophie and took a couple of steps toward the hall. He wiped the blood from his face with the back of his hand. "You aren't going to shoot me, Teach."

The gun was shaking in her mother's hands. She glanced at Sophie for just a second. "Where's your brother? Where's Joe?"

Dazed, Sophie stared at her. "Uh, upstairs—asleep," she heard herself say. "He—he drugged them both."

"Keep your hands where I can see them," her mother said to Vic.

He stopped and held his hands out in front of him at waist level, palms up, as if he was about to catch something. He chuckled again. "I saw what kind of *markswoman* you were yesterday," he said. "Even if you tried to shoot me, you couldn't hit me. And by the way, that gun you've got is a piece of shit."

"Open the front door," her mother said, standing her ground. "Open it!"

As Vic slowly turned toward the door, Sophie saw the smirk on his blood-smeared face. He didn't seem at all intimidated. Still, he opened the door. Then he turned toward her mother.

"Now get out of my house," she whispered.

He didn't move. He just laughed again. "Oh, I'll bet you've been just dying to say that since yesterday morning. Did it feel good, Teach?"

She stared at him. "It sure as hell did, you worthless scum."

He still had a tiny smile on his face as he turned his body to one side and edged out the door. Sophie saw him move his hand toward his back. "Mom, he's got a gun!" she screamed.

Vic lurched forward in the doorway and aimed the gun at her mother.

Sophie screamed. She tried to get up from the sofa.

She heard two shots go off.

Her heart stopped. She fell to her knees and gazed at her mother.

With a stunned look, her mom clutched her stomach and backed away until she bumped into the wall. All the while, she stared wide-eyed at Vic.

He stood in the doorway, the grin still plastered on his crimson-smeared face. He cackled—and then started coughing. A spray of blood came out with every cough. His hand dropped to his side and the gun fell to the floor. He tipped his head to the left, and that was when Sophie saw the blood gushing from a hole in his neck.

"My God," her mother gasped. She was still in shock, still leaning against the wall. There wasn't a drop of blood on her.

Vic stumbled back and collapsed on the front porch. He was out of their house at last.

Her mother looked at her and winced. "Oh, look at what he did to you . . ." she murmured, out of breath. "Sweetie, are you all right?"

Sophie nodded. "Are you?"

Her mother nodded back. She even smiled a little.

Then she staggered over to the door and shut it.

CHAPTER TWENTY-NINE

Wednesday—12:57 A.M.

It felt good to shut the door on Vic—for a few minutes.

Laura didn't have to see his corpse lying on their front porch while she frantically searched for a knife or scissors to cut Sophie's restraints. She kept thinking of James upstairs. Sophie had said that he and Joe were asleep. As much as Laura wanted to see him and hold him, she reminded herself that Sophie was the one who needed her help right now.

Laura realized Vic had collected all the sharp objects. The scissors and cutlery were in a garbage pail somewhere out in the garage. So she went through his backpack, which he'd left on the kitchen counter-bar. But she couldn't find anything of use in there. She thought she might discover one of the phones, but no such luck.

Then it finally dawned on her where she could find a knife.

She hurried back to the living room, where Sophie sat on the edge of the sofa—her hands still tied behind her. It hurt just to look at her daughter, so battered—with her bruised eye swollen shut. Sophie squirmed and restlessly tapped her feet. "Mom, I'm going a little crazy here," she murmured.

"I'm sorry," she said, heading for the door. "I know where there's a knife."

"Did you call the police on your way here? I thought I heard a car in the driveway earlier . . ."

Laura hesitated at the door. "No, I haven't called them yet."

"Well, maybe it was your car I heard." Wide-eyed, Sophie looked at her. "Wait a minute. Where are you going? You can't just leave me here . . ."

"I'm just getting a knife," Laura said. She took a deep breath and opened the door.

She'd probably seen too many horror movies, because a part of her had almost expected to find the porch empty—with Vic gone. But he was still there—and quite dead. A large puddle of blood bloomed on the porch beneath his head. His eyes were half-open in a lifeless stare.

Grimacing, Laura crouched down and hovered over him. She was careful not to step in the blood. With apprehension, she reached into the pocket of his cargo pants.

"Oh, God, Mom, I'm sorry," Sophie called.

Laura glanced over her shoulder and caught Sophie's reflection in the living room mirror. Her daughter could see what she was doing. "He—he's got our phones on him, too," Sophie called.

Laura found the switchblade in one of his lower pockets, but he didn't have any phones on him. With the knife in hand, she ducked back inside and shut the door again.

Both she and Sophie were trembling as she tried to cut away at the cloth restraints around Sophie's wrists. "I couldn't find a phone," Laura said, careful not to nick her.

"I think he was loading stuff in the pickup earlier," Sophie said. "Maybe that's where they are."

Past the noise from the television, Laura heard James crying softly upstairs.

"Just hold still, honey," she whispered to Sophie, struggling to sever the cloth restraints. "I've almost got it . . ."

At last, she cut through the knotted cloth.

Sophie let out a grateful moan as her hands were freed. Her wrists were red and raw-looking. "Thanks, Mom," she gasped. "I can get my ankles. I'm okay now. Go to James . . ."

Laura handed her the knife. She kissed Sophie's forehead. "Remind me later to tell you how proud I am of you."

She turned and started for the stairway but balked.

She saw James—with Joe—sitting at the top of the stairs. Both of them were sort of curled up on the landing. Joe had his arm around her son, holding him like a frightened child might clutch a stuffed animal. Joe looked tired, scared, and disoriented.

As Laura hurried up the steps, James reached out to her.

Joe lifted him up and handed him to her. Standing on the steps, she held James close. "It's okay, sweetie," she whispered, kissing James's soft, wet cheek. "I'm here . . ."

He whimpered and tried to talk, but it came out as gibberish. For a few moments, he squirmed restlessly in her arms, but then his sturdy little body seemed to relax. His blond head found that familiar spot on her shoulder.

Laura turned to Joe. "Stay here, will you, Joe?"

With a dazed look, he nodded at her.

She retreated down the stairs. Her daughter was no longer in the living room. "Sophie?" she called, looking at the pile of rag restraints on the sofa—along with the switchblade knife.

"In here, Mom."

Laura found her in the kitchen, going through Vic's backpack.

"I already tried that," she said. "The phones aren't in there . . ."

"Yeah, but your pearl necklace is here—along with some other pieces." She pulled out an expensive brooch from the bottom of the backpack and set it on the counter with some of the jewelry.

"Listen, I want you to put on your coat and whatever shoes are down here in the closet," Laura said. "Take James to the cottage and call the police from there, okay?"

Sophie numbly gazed at her.

"Honey, do you understand? You remember where the keys are, don't you?"

Sophie nodded.

Laura hurried to the front hall closet and got out a coat and boots for James. She sat him down on the sofa to put the jacket on him. He was half asleep. "Don't come back to the house," she told Sophie, who was by the closet. She'd already put on her ski jacket, and was now lacing up a pair of tennis shoes.

"Stay in the cottage," Laura continued. "And tell the police you'll be there. Tell them I don't think Joe will give them any trouble."

She finished putting James's boots on his feet, then looked up at Sophie, waiting by the front door. Laura shook her head. "No, the back way," she whispered. "I don't want him seeing . . ."

Sophie nodded and followed her to the kitchen door.

"You better carry him," Laura said. "He always trips in these boots. Can you manage?"

"Yeah," Sophie said, taking James into her arms. "Are you going to be okay with Joe? Why don't you come with us?"

Laura opened the kitchen door and shook her head. "I don't want to leave him alone," she said. Then she took the keys from her coat pocket and handed them to her. "It might be warmer in the car—if you want to wait there. Just let the police know where you are . . ."

With James in her arms, Sophie stepped out the door, but then she turned to her. "Mom? I'm pretty proud of you, too."

Laura kissed her and James, then gave them a gentle push. She watched them hurry off in the direction of the cabin until they disappeared in the darkness. With a tiny lump in her throat, Laura closed the kitchen door and headed toward the front of the house. She passed the half-table in the hallway where she'd left the gun earlier. She told herself she wouldn't need it.

At the same time, she hadn't wanted Sophie or James in the house while she tried to talk Joe into surrendering to the police. Despite everything Courtney had told her—and everything else she'd learned today that pointed toward Joe's innocence—Laura still didn't want to take any chances with her children.

She left the gun where it was and started up the stairs.

Joe was still sitting on the top step, hunched over, with his arms folded in front of him.

Laura paused on the fourth step from the landing—so that they were almost eye to eye. Catching her breath, she held onto the banister. "The police will be here soon," she said quietly.

"I know," he murmured. "What happened? I heard gunshots . . ."

Laura swallowed hard. "Yes. Vic—he's dead."

Joe's tired, stupefied expression didn't change. He just nodded. "Is everybody else okay?"

"Yes, we're all okay. I talked to that Courtney woman who knew Scott Singleton and Eric Vetter. She said you couldn't have killed the Singletons, Joe. I think I can get her to come around and talk to the police for us. She said the man you sketched was a hired killer. I'll ask the police to send your sketch to the hospital in Anacortes, where they've got that college student who was shot. You know, the one whose life you saved? I'll bet he identifies the man in your drawing as the one who shot him."

Joe's expression didn't change. "Vic gave me a beer that was drugged, but I—I didn't drink much of it. Still, it knocked me out for a while. The gunshots woke me up. This time, the gunshots woke me up. I'm still a little loopy though." He blinked at her. "I'm so sorry about everything, Mrs. Gretchell. Are you sure the kids are okay?"

She nodded, then reached over and touched his arm. "Yes—"

A sound from downstairs silenced her. Then she heard the screen door slam.

Laura knew the police couldn't be here already. It didn't sound like the TV. She wondered if Sophie had trouble getting into the cottage. She turned and started down the steps. "Sophie? Honey?"

With Joe trailing after her, Laura headed through the front hall and passed the empty living room. She could hear shuffling. There was definitely someone in the house. For a crazy moment, she wondered if it was Vic—if he was somehow still alive.

"Sophie?" Laura stepped into the family room and gasped.

Holding James in her arms, Sophie stood trembling in the middle of the room. Little James looked utterly terrified—too scared to scream or cry. His lower lip quivering, he clutched at the front of Sophie's jacket and gaped at the man who stood on the other side of her. The stranger had her by the arm. He held a gun in his gloved hand and pressed the barrel against Sophie's jaw.

"We—we didn't make it to the cottage," Sophie said in a shaky voice. A tear slid down from her swollen eye. "We didn't get to call the police. I'm sorry, Mom . . ."

Paralyzed with fear, Laura stared at the man—and her two children.

The stranger wore a black tracksuit. In addition to the gloves, he had on a pair of plastic shoe coverings. It was obvious he didn't want to leave behind any evidence of having been there.

It took Laura another moment to recognize the man from Joe's sketches. She realized it must have been his car that she and Sophie had heard earlier. Had he followed her from the bar in Wenatchee—or did he and his partner already have her address?

"Well, isn't this perfect?" he said, grinning. He nodded at Joe, standing behind her. "The psycho-case is here. The police are looking all over for you, friend. Isn't that your partner, lying outside on the front porch? Well, that's everything all wrapped up with a nice, pretty bow on it. The police will find you here with the bodies—all of them shot with the same gun I used on that kid in the Singletons' driveway . . ."

He brandished the gun for a moment and then jabbed it under Sophie's chin again. She gasped. James let out a little cry and seemed to hold his sister tighter.

"But it's going to be your prints on the gun, friend," he said. "It'll confirm everything the cops suspected. You and your buddy holed up here and took some hostages . . ."

Laura heard Joe behind her, whimpering anxiously.

The man nodded at her. "You bought a gun tonight at an ammo shop in Monroe. Did you use it to shoot the guy outside?"

Laura stared at him. "How did you know about the gun?"

"An associate of mine was tailing you. He's kept me informed of your every move. So—you shot his friend with your new gun. They'll say he saw what you did, and he went nuts again. He shot you and the kids. Then he killed himself. That's how it'll look to the cops. Like I told you, one pretty package—all wrapped up."

"No," Laura heard herself say. "There are too many loose ends, *Ted*."

The smile faded from his thin face. "How do you know my name?"

"Your partner," she said steadily, "the other Ted, does he drive a black BMW?"

"We both do. How do you know about us? Who told you?"

Past a loud commercial on TV, Laura heard sirens in the distance. They seemed to be getting closer. Since moving out here, they almost never heard sirens anymore. It wasn't like living in the city. She wondered if her mother had phoned the police already. And she wondered if Ted noticed.

Laura took a couple of deep breaths, but her heart was still racing. "Your associate killed Martha, that waitress on Lopez Island, didn't he?"

"No, *you* killed her," he said. "She was dead the minute my partner heard you talking to her in the café. You said she knew things about the Singletons. And you wrote your own death sentence when you showed him those sketches of me."

Laura realized the Pecan Waffle man was the other Ted. "Did Marilee and Lawrence Cronin decree these death sentences?" she asked.

"Very smart, lady," Ted chuckled. "Let's just say we got the nod of approval from someone above." His smile faded again. "So—tell me, how did you get so smart? Who else knows about us?"

"Your partner's dead," Laura said—over the sound of the sirens getting closer. "His BMW was in a head-on collision with a semi on Stevens Pass."

Shaking his head, the hit man looked bewildered. "No . . ."

Laura wasn't sure if he was distressed over the news of his associate's death or the sound of the approaching squad cars.

With the gun, he gave Sophie's chin another jab.

She let out a frightened gasp. Squirming in her arms, James started to cry.

"I thought I heard this little bitch say she didn't get a chance to call the cops . . ."

Laura was terrified. This was just what she'd been hoping to avoid all day—some kind of standoff with the police, and her children as hostages. She reached out to her daughter.

"My friend left the phones with me," Joe said quietly. "I called the police fifteen minutes ago and turned myself in."

His voice was almost drowned out by the sirens blaring and tires screeching.

Laura turned to gaze at him.

"Goddamn it!" Ted muttered.

Laura heard murmuring outside—and someone talking over a static-laced police radio. Behind Ted, through the sliding glass door, she saw a pair of policemen with their weapons drawn, creeping toward the house.

"I still have one of the guns, too," Joe said. His voice was a little foggy. "And I can still be Zared . . ."

Ted must have heard the policemen in the backyard, because he glanced over his shoulder for a second.

Sophie slammed against him, wrenched away, and dropped to the floor with James.

Before Laura realized what was happening, Joe shoved her out of the way. He fired the gun three times.

Ted cried out as the bullets ripped through him. The gun flew out of his hand and he keeled over, crashing into one of the TV tables.

Laura looked up in time to see Joe standing there with the gun still in his hand. All at once, she realized how it must look to the policemen in the backyard.

"No!" she screamed. "Joe, drop the gun!"

But she was too late. A series of blasts resounded, and the glass in the sliding door shattered. Joe was hit—at least two or three times, from the way his thin body recoiled. Then he collapsed onto the floor.

In a panic, Laura crawled through bits of glass to Sophie and James to make sure they weren't hurt. She wrapped her arms around them. She heard doors slamming open. The cold November night air swept into the room as a swarm of policemen invaded the house.

"I'm all right, Mom," Sophie said, talking loudly over all the noise. Still crouched down on the floor, she rocked James in her arms. He was crying, but he didn't look injured—just scared. Laura patted his head and gazed at her daughter.

"We're okay," Sophie said, catching her breath. "How's Joe? You should go to him, Mom . . ."

Lying on the floor, he was surrounded by police.

One of the cops was calling for medical assistance. Still on her hands and knees, Laura scurried over to Joe. She could see he'd been hit in the shoulder and stomach. The shirt he'd borrowed from Sean's closet was spotted with blood.

He saw her and smiled.

"Hang on, Joey," she said.

She was barely aware of the policeman standing over her—until he took hold of her arm and gently pulled her up.

"You saved my life, remember?" Joe whispered.

Laura nodded.

"I owed you," he said.

The policeman started to lead her away. Another cop stepped between her and Joe. Laura noticed a couple of paramedics came in from the front hallway with a stretcher. They hovered around Joe. Sirens were still blaring outside as more emergency vehicles seemed to be arriving. She heard someone upstairs, running around from room to room. There must have been at least a dozen cops in the house, maybe more. One of them started shouting questions at her—about Joe, Vic, and the other man.

Amid all the chaos, Laura broke away from the cop.

Then she rushed back to her children.

EPILOGUE

Wednesday, November 29—1:47 A.M.
Anacortes

In a preliminary search, investigators couldn't find any photographs of Ted Houser or Ted Flint in the police files. So they faxed Joe's detailed sketch to Island Hospital in Anacortes. There, Wes Banyan, the nineteen-year-old survivor of the Singleton murders, was woken out of a sound sleep and shown the sketch.

In the last few days, Wes had viewed hundreds of mug shots. Into each batch, the investigators had slipped photos of Joe Mulroney and Victor Moles. It got so Wes was expecting to see those same two guys every time he looked at a new series of mug shots. He had a TV in his room at the hospital. He knew those two were the main suspects in the murders. He knew the cops were frustrated he hadn't yet labeled either one as the man who had shot him. The police were especially keen on getting him to identify Mulroney as the shooter: "From zero to one hundred, what are the chances that this is the man who shot you?"

Wes had met Mulroney over Thanksgiving and felt the chances were no more than fifteen percent that he was the shooter. But the cops kept showing him Mulroney's photo anyway.

When the night nurse had woken him, Wes had thought she was going to give him another pill or change his IV. They always had one reason or another for ruining his sleep—and wrecking some perfectly wonderful dream in which he wasn't stuck in this hospital bed. But this time, the nurse had a policeman with her, and the cop had a sketch he wanted Wes to look at.

As the nurse raised the hospital bed and adjusted the nightstand light, Wes half-expected to see a drawing of Joe Mulroney.

Instead, they showed him a sketch of the bastard who had shot him.

Monday, December 4—10:40 A.M.
Spokane International Airport

His crutches were wedged between his carry-on bag and the seat he occupied in the boarding area. Except for some idiot who stood directly in front of him, talking on his phone for a few minutes, Jason Eichhorn had an unimpaired view of the gate—and the TV bracketed high on a structural post. He had another half hour before his flight started boarding. It was one of those "puddle jumpers." He'd taken a lot of them lately. This time, he was on his way to Bozeman to interview some former True Divine Light Messengers at Montana State University.

"There isn't an ill wind that doesn't blow someone

some good," his mother-in-law was fond of saying. Jason was pretty sure she'd gotten the axiom from her mother or grandmother. Anyway, whoever had originally said it, they were right.

After his nightmare carjacking ordeal with the two Singleton murder suspects, Jason had spent one night in the hospital, and the next day trying to recover at home. He had a broken arm, a sprained ankle, and nineteen stitches in his head. He also had dozens of fellow journalists foaming at the mouth to talk with him—and that included some of the heavy hitters he'd been trying to impress over dinner Sunday night at the Rumor Mill on San Juan Island. But Jason decided to write his own account of the carjacking. *The Seattle Times* and the national wire services picked it up.

By the time he'd finally gotten his car back—nearly a week after it had been stolen—Jason was in high demand. He decided to follow up his success with an investigative piece on the Church of the True Divine Light. With a bandage still on his half-shaven head, a cast on his arm, and a pair of crutches, he flew to universities all over Washington, Oregon, and Idaho, interviewing former Messengers for the church. One of the wire services was picking up his transportation tab, which included a chauffeur service. It was very helpful, since Jason couldn't drive. Some of the college kids he talked to were still so brainwashed that they refused to say anything negative about the church. But most of the students were very forthcoming—especially Courtney Furst and Randall Meacham. The name Doran Wiley kept cropping up in Jason's conversations with church recruits at Western Washington University.

For a couple of days, the media spotlight had been on Doran, because he'd been the Singletons' caretaker for a while, an unwitting victim of Scott Singleton's predatory ways, and a recruiter for the church. He was also very handsome. It looked like he might be the Kato Kaelin of the Singleton murder case. But in interviews and on TV, he'd been so uncooperative and had come across as such a snarky homophobic ass that the press and the public quickly tired of him. His "fifteen minutes of fame" lasted about four days. Jason had tried to interview Doran for his first piece on the church's recruiting programs in several colleges. But Doran had refused to talk to him unless he was paid.

Jason's exposé was so successful that it helped launch further official investigations into the church's nefarious activities. The Church of the True Divine Light seemed ready to implode. Marilee and Lawrence Cronin were already being investigated for their connection to the Singleton murders and several other crimes.

Jason's trip to Montana was for a follow-up story he was pursuing.

The woman at the gate desk announced that they'd be boarding the Bozeman flight soon—and she went into the usual spiel about the limited space for carry-on bags.

Jason checked his phone messages. Someone from AP had called, and there was yet another message from Doran Wiley. This was the sixth time he'd called in the past week. Even though his scholarship had been revoked and he was in desperate need of money, Doran said for the sixth time that he was willing to talk to him now—without charging a fee.

Jason deleted the message—as he had the other voicemails from Doran Wiley.

Slipping his phone back in his pocket, Jason glanced up at the TV. CNN was showing footage from the weekend's big news story. It was a scene at another airport—Hartsfield-Jackson International in Atlanta—that showed the cops yanking Lawrence and Marilee Cronin off a plane to Honduras. In the footage, Lawrence was yelling at the airport police, and Marilee was covering her face. But anyone could see it was her from the blond pigtails and her royal blue dress, which resembled a doorman's uniform, right down to the epaulets.

She and her husband were being detained after trying to escape the country and pending indictments.

Jason perked up as the woman at the gate announced that they were ready to board the short flight to Bozeman.

With a smile on his face, Jason Eichhorn grabbed his bag and his crutches. Then he hobbled toward the gate.

Friday, December 15—5:22 P.M.
Leavenworth

Sophie sat in the children's section of the Leavenworth Public Library. She had an audience of five toddlers seated around her. She'd just finished reading to them a picture book called *The Christmas Crocodile* by Bonny Becker. It was a hit with the kids.

A couple of them had asked why she was so dressed up. The librarian had asked as well.

Sophie had a date with Matt tonight—dinner at a very fancy, expensive resort, The Sleeping Lady. He'd be picking her up here at the library. It was Matt's early Christmas present to her.

Sophie had come home from school that afternoon, showered, and then changed into a black, sleeveless cocktail dress, very Audrey Hepburn in *Breakfast at Tiffany's*. She'd bought it online specifically for tonight's dinner. From her mom, she borrowed a black cardigan with a design in black and silver sequins.

Sophie was happy with the ensemble. Even Liam said she looked very pretty: "real sophisticated-like." All that remained of her swollen black eye—courtesy of Victor Moles—was a slight bruise, which she'd camouflaged with makeup.

Her dad had been ready to drive her to the library when her mom came downstairs with the pearl necklace that had been in her family for eons, the same pearl necklace Victor Moles had hoped to steal.

"You're letting me borrow the pearls?" Sophie asked.

Her mom smiled. "No, I'm giving them to you, honey."

"But you're not supposed to give those to me until I get married or turn twenty-five or something."

"Or something," her mother said, leading her to the mirror in the living room. She stood behind her and put the string of pearls around her neck. They really looked elegant with the black dress. "You should have them now, because you're a grownup, Sophie." Her mother's voice got a little quaver in it. "You've proven that to me, my brave, beautiful grown-up daughter."

The two of them had a little cry and hugged. Sophie needed to reapply some makeup over her bruised eye.

In the car, her dad even cried a little, too—though he tried to hide it.

He'd promised her mom a trip to Paris next year to compensate for the one she'd missed. Then again, they might not be able to afford the trip next year. They'd had several unexpected expenses recently. The sliding glass door in the family room had to be replaced. Her parents also bought Liam a new camcorder. And they bought a new easy chair for her dad.

No one could stand looking at the old recliner after Vic had made it his for that short period of time. It was almost as bad as viewing the patch of land in the vine-yard where the police had excavated Dane's corpse. So her father's old recliner went to Goodwill. The new one looked nothing like it. Her father put the replace-ment in a different spot in the family room—just to lift the curse off it.

For a while, Sophie had to endure countless questions from her classmates about her ordeal. She avoided going into the gory details. Matt, however, heard everything. After a few days, the hubbub died down. Sophie had been sort of a mini-celebrity for a while, but she didn't mind one bit when the notoriety wore off.

Liam, on the other hand, was wildly popular in his class now. Older kids had actually volunteered to be in his *Psycho* remake—or help with the production. His friends came over to the house, all agog as if it were a museum or some fun-house chamber of horrors. Liam seemed to take it in his stride.

Sophie put *The Christmas Crocodile* back on the library shelf. She peeked out the front window and saw Matt's beat-up Toyota Corolla pull into the lot.

With a small bouquet of flowers, he met her at the library door. He looked pretty cute in his tie and jacket. And she liked the way his eyes lit up when he stared at her. "God, thank you," he murmured, opening the door for her.

"What for?" she smiled.

"For looking the way you do," he said.

As they drove past the town center with all its holiday lights on the chalet-storefronts, Sophie thought about this Christmas. Her parents had said it would be sort of a lean holiday, because of all the recent expenses. James would never know the difference, of course. And it really didn't seem to matter to anyone else.

Her dad had gotten a replacement recliner—just as Liam had gotten a replacement camcorder. Her mother had gotten the promise of a trip to compensate for the one she'd just missed. And Sophie had received a string of pearls she'd always known she'd get. Everything they'd gotten they'd sort of had before.

Only now, it seemed to matter much, much more.

Thursday, December 21—1:20 P.M.
Marysville

The visitors' center at the Western Washington Psychiatric Institute was a large, cold room with three long tables, two vending machines, and a view of an empty courtyard through the chain-link-screened windows. A small Christmas tree with blinking lights stood on a table in the corner. It looked lonely and pathetic.

While they waited for Joe to arrive, Laura and Sean had the place to themselves—except for a guard who stood by the door. According to Dr. Halstead, the guard was just a formality for patients like Joe, who was doing much better there this second time around.

Joe had been transferred to the facility from the hospital the first week in December. His condition had been critical for a while. His left leg had been grazed by two bullets. Two additional bullets had done major damage to his stomach and his rotator cuff.

Laura had visited him in the hospital in Wenatchee. She'd asked Sophie and Liam to send him Get Well cards, and they'd done so with slightly mixed feelings. However, James happily drew a picture for him. It showed a stick-figure man in a hospital bed with his arm in a cast.

This was Laura's first visit with Joe here at the institute. It was also Sean's first meeting with him ever. He, too, had mixed feelings about Joe. On the drive to the institute, Sean had expressed his reservations. "I'm not sure what I'm going to do when I finally meet this guy," he'd said, taking his eyes off the road to look at her for a moment. "I'm not sure if I'll want to punch his lights out or hug him."

"You'll want to hug him," Laura had said, reaching over from the passenger seat and rubbing his shoulder. "He's so guileless and sweet . . ."

When Joe stepped into the visitors' room, Laura and

Sean stood up. She noticed that he looked even skinnier than before. He had a bad buzz cut and wore an orange jumpsuit. His wounded arm was in a sling. He seemed a bit slow and fragile when he moved.

A part of her wanted to hug him, but Laura just shook his hand. It felt awkward somehow. If Sean hadn't been there, maybe she would have come around to the other side of the table and embraced him.

She introduced them, and watched Joe's face turn red. He shook hands with Sean, and murmured, "Pleased to meet you," but he couldn't look Sean in the eye. Then he sat down across from them.

"How are you, Joe?" she asked.

"I'm good," he said quietly. "I'm feeling better every day. And—and Dr. Halstead says that if I continue to do as well as I have been, then I'll be released from here in the spring." He glanced at Sean. "Dr. Halstead's my doctor, my shrink . . ."

Sean nodded and seemed to work up a smile.

Joe turned to her again. "I'm sort of like a trustee here, now. It's not bad at all."

"I'm glad to hear that." She reached into a shopping bag she'd brought along with her. "Listen, I come bearing gifts—a couple of things . . ."

She carefully took out another drawing James had created for him in his preschool art class. It was of Santa, and made from red felt, cotton balls, glue, and watercolors.

Joe got tears in his eyes looking at it. "Will you thank him for me, please?"

"Of course we will," Sean said.

Laura had also brought along a Christmas present. It was just a sketchpad and drawing pencils. But Joe made a big deal out of unwrapping them. Then he nervously went on about how much use he'd get out of them once his shoulder healed.

Then there was an awkward silence. Sean cleared his throat. "Joe?"

Joe finally looked Sean in the eye, but he still seemed so timid about it.

"Joe, I'm going to leave you and Laura alone for a few minutes," Sean said. "But before I go, I need to be honest with you. I really didn't want to meet you. I didn't even want my wife coming here. For a while, I wasn't at all happy with you, Joe. You put my family in grave danger. But you also saved their lives—so I guess that evens things out."

Sean stood up and put his hand out.

Joe got to his feet and shook his hand. "Thank you, sir. And pardon my left hand . . ."

"You can call me Sean," her husband said with a smile. "You said you might get out of here in the spring. That's a busy time for us at the vineyard. We might need an extra hand—if your shoulder is healed by then. Think about it."

Wide-eyed, Joe nodded and smiled. "I will. Thank you, sir—I mean, *Sean*."

"Happy Holidays, Joe," Sean said. He touched Laura's shoulder, and then went to wait outside with the guard.

"That's awfully nice of him," Joe said. "Did you ask him to offer me that job?"

"No, that was Sean's idea," Laura lied.

"You sure you or the kids wouldn't feel weird about

me working there? I mean, after everything that happened?"

"If we do, we'll get over it—and so will you, I hope."

He smiled nervously. "I have a Christmas present for you, too, something I've managed to hold on to . . ." He reached into his arm sling, then took out an envelope and a small package wrapped in paper with a holly design on it.

Laura laughed. "Well, you've got a great little hiding place there."

Joe blushed. "Open it."

Laura opened the envelope first, and saw on the back of the thin card that it was from a veterans' charity, one of those freebee greeting card sets people get in the mail along with a donation request. There was a Currier and Ives illustration on front. Inside, Joe had written:

> *Merry X-Mas to Mrs. Gretchell*
> *& All the Gretchells!*
> *—Joe*

"Thank you, Joe," she said. "That's very sweet." She unwrapped the present, which was about as big as the palm of her hand. She opened the box and saw the star she'd given Joe on his eighth birthday. His class picture was still on the front—though faded. On the back, he'd written: *TO MY FAVORITE TEACHER – MRS. G.*

"I saved it," he said.

Laura had tears in her eyes, but she was smiling. "I love it. Thank you, Joe."

"Thank you," he said. He reached over and touched her hand for a moment. Then he shyly pulled away again. "I guess I didn't get too many good breaks. But you were there for me, Mrs. Gretchell."

"I wish I could have done more," Laura said. "Maybe it would have made a difference in your life. Maybe you wouldn't have ended up here . . ."

"Like I told you, it's not so bad," he said. "Besides, I could have ended up being just like Vic—if you hadn't saved me. I'm a lot better off, Mrs. Gretchell. You made all the difference."

Laura reached over and took his hand in hers.

Joe nodded. "Sometimes, all it takes is one really good teacher."